TEXAS
NOON

Other books by Leonard Sanders:

Fort Worth
Sonoma
The Hamlet Ultimatum
The Hamlet Warning

TEXAS NOON

LEONARD SANDERS

Delacorte
Press

Published by
Delacorte Press
Bantam Doubleday Dell Publishing Group, Inc.
666 Fifth Avenue
New York, New York 10103

The trademark Delacorte Press® is registered in the U.S.
Patent and Trademark Office.

Library of Congress Cataloging in Publication Data

Sanders, Leonard.
    Texas noon / Leonard Sanders.
        p.   cm.
    ISBN 0-440-50095-8
    I. Title.
    PS3569.A5127T4   1989
    813'.54—dc19   88-17501
                                                                CIP

Manufactured in the United States of America

January 1989

10 9 8 7 6 5 4 3 2 1

WAK

For Florene

Author's Note

The standards and discipline imposed upon members of the Texas Boys Choir through the early years by founder-director George Bragg, and the results achieved, are now a matter of legend. As with the fictional choir member in this novel, the continuing effect on later lives also has been remarkable. Research for this book failed to find a single choir alumnus who did not express his love for George Bragg, and appreciation for the rigorous boyhood training. Many said that through Bragg's example they were inspired to accomplishments they otherwise might never have attempted. With greatest appreciation, I thank both Bragg and Dr. James R. Shadle, Jr., a former member of the choir, who were especially generous with their time. For story purposes, changes in the name of the choir through its first few years have been ignored.

BOOK
ONE

JOANNA

Chapter 1

Ahead, at the next intersection, a motorcycle policeman stood with arms upraised, booted feet spread, a silver whistle in his mouth. Cross-traffic came to an abrupt halt. Kelly glanced back. The funeral procession stretched all the way across the river bridge to the top of the bluff beyond. Motorists bound in the opposite direction had stopped in clusters along the curb. Everywhere Kelly looked, he saw strangers. How had all these people known his father?

He began counting the cars.

"Kelly!" his mother said.

Her face was partially hidden by a thick black veil. He could not see her expression. Her voice was low and different.

He obediently turned to the front as they entered the intersection close behind the hearse. The day was bright and sunny, but the north wind was cold. The warmth of the limousine was comforting. On the opposite jump seat, his brother, Weldon, studied the policeman's motorcycle as they passed. Only a little more than three months away from thirteen, Weldon was fascinated by anything mechanical.

Kelly's mother twisted a white handkerchief over a forefinger and reached beneath the black netting to wipe her eyes. Even her lush, normally auburn hair seemed darker under the hat. A vague concern that had been lurking in the back of Kelly's mind all day surfaced and assumed form: When the father of a close friend had died more than a year ago, the family had moved away overnight. Kelly had never seen his friend again.

"Mom, will we have to move?" he asked.

"Of course not!" His mother lifted a corner of the veil and looked at him. Her face was set in the slight frown she used when he forgot to comb his hair or his tie was crooked.

His grandmother patted his knee. "Kelly, please don't bother your mother right now. Everything will be all right."

Aunt Zetta, seated between Kelly's mother and grand-mother, stared straight ahead and ignored the exchange. She was terribly old and almost deaf. All three women were dressed in black and sat like crows on a fence, adding to the eeriness of the whole day.

The motorcycle policeman roared past, hurrying to the next intersection. Two old men walking along the sidewalk stopped and took off their hats. Following their gaze, Kelly studied the back of the hearse and once again tried to convince himself that his father truly was inside it, dead.

He had not yet cried, and he doubted that he would. He had never known his father—not in the way his friends knew theirs.

Now the possibility that he might, someday, was gone forever. He tried to shove that sickening thought out of his mind, but it persisted. He would not see his father from now on, and there was not much to remember.

For years his father had lived amid spooky quietness in the big bedroom at the head of the stairs. Only on warm days was he sometimes wheeled out onto the second-floor gallery, where he would sit for a while gazing into the distance, as if he were thinking of other times, other places. Kelly and Weldon constantly were warned not to make noise in their play about the house or yard. They could not bring friends home. Repeatedly they were told that their father must avoid any excitement whatsoever. Each evening they were taken into the bedroom to give him a good-night kiss. He had been a tall, thin man with deep wrinkles, a pallid face, and trembling hands. Each night he would smile at them with his blue lips and ask commonplace questions—how was school, what had they been doing all day? They would answer in monosyllables, uncertain how to respond. When he said good night, he sometimes clung to their arms for a moment, a hint of puzzlement in his eyes, as if he wanted to say something else but could not find the words. Then he would release them and sink back on the pillows, his white pajamas and pale skin almost lost among the bed linen. At the funeral home Kelly had overheard his mother and grandmother agreeing in whispers that the coffin should remain closed during the funeral services. They had said his father did not "look natural." Kelly had found no logic in that. He thought his father, dead, looked exactly the way he had always looked, living.

For years his father had been the center of constant, quiet activity that pervaded the entire house. Doctors and nurses came and went. Each weekday morning executives from the oil company arrived with their briefcases and stood outside the bedroom door, waiting to enter, one by one, so his father could tell them what to do.

In all that time, his father had never left the house.

So who were these hundreds of solemn strangers? How had they known his father?

At the church Kelly had sat amazed as the minister read a message from President Truman, saying the nation shared the family's grief, and that Broderick Barclay Spurlock had made great contributions to the final victory during the war.

Kelly wondered whether his father had been in the army, navy, or marines. Nothing had ever been said about it.

No one ever told him anything.

Ahead, the hearse entered the stone portal of the cemetery and moved with majestic slowness along a graveled drive through a sea of tombstones. At a curve it eased from the road onto thick grass and coasted to a stop. The limousine halted gently behind it.

Mr. Waldrop of the funeral home approached, opened the door, and spoke softly to Kelly's mother. "If you ladies will please wait here a moment, the family will proceed in a group."

Kelly's mother nodded agreement. Mr. Waldrop walked away. Cars from the procession moved on past. Two policemen stood in the road, waving their arms, directing drivers to park in neat rows along the graveled paths. Soon people were leaving the cars and walking across the grass toward a green canvas awning erected over an open grave.

Kelly could not take his eyes from the tombstones, nor his thoughts from the dead people beneath them.

Suddenly Aunt Zetta raised a long, bony finger and shouted, "There's where they put Papa!"

Gooseflesh rose at the back of Kelly's neck. Aunt Zetta was so deaf she lived in her own private world. She habitually ignored the conversation of others and made occasional, shouted announcements. She was pointing to a large granite tomb with an iron door. Kelly's own name, SPURLOCK, was carved into the stone. Smaller metal plates bore the full names of the dead people inside. All the names ended in SPURLOCK.

"See! Right there! Travis Spurlock! Your great-grandfather!" Aunt Zetta shouted, apparently to Kelly and Weldon. "They left an empty place right beside him. That's where they'll put me!"

Cold chills shot up Kelly's spine. Never before had he considered that a person might plan his own burial. He had always assumed that when a person died, the body became someone else's problem.

He wondered where they would put *him*.

Another worry added to the many.

"Your Grandfather Clay's grave is over yonder," Aunt Zetta said, again pointing. "Over there. See? Clayton Barrett Spurlock. He was killed in an oil well blowout. They really didn't find any of him to bury. We put his name up on a tombstone anyway. His brother Malvern's over there. We called him Vern. He died in the Great War, but he wasn't brought home till months later. Over yonder's your Uncle Loren. You may remember him. He made it back from the last war, but just barely."

Kelly's grandmother put a hand on Aunt Zetta's wrist, a device adults often used to stop the announcements.

The shouted information was more than Kelly could readily absorb. On the other side of the limousine, Weldon stared at the Spurlock tomb. His rare display of anxiety sent Kelly's own soaring.

He wondered about all the unknown, dead Spurlocks.

A flurry of activity commenced behind the hearse. The rear door was opened. Dark-suited men took positions on each side, reached for the handles of the rosewood coffin, and pulled it smoothly from the interior.

Walking slowly, they carried it up a slight rise toward the grave.

Kelly's grandmother was leaning forward, gazing toward the crowd gathering at the grave. "She's here," she whispered. "I just caught a glimpse of her."

No one ever used Aunt Crystelle's name. It was always "she" or "her." Kelly searched among the crowd. He did not see her.

Mr. Waldrop returned to the limousine and again opened the door. "If you ladies are ready . . ."

As they left the car, Kelly's grandmother took his hand. The cold wind quickly numbed his cheeks and ears. He walked with his grandmother across the close-cropped grass toward the awning, where folding metal chairs had been set up. Mr. Waldrop ushered them to the front row, almost within reach of the coffin, now resting on a metal frame. The same minister who had conducted the church services stood beside the grave, holding an open Bible, one hand flat against the pages to keep them from rustling in the wind.

Aunt Crystelle was seated at the end of the row. Kelly had never seen her before, but he recognized her instantly from pictures. For a long moment he could not take his eyes off her. He was certain she was the prettiest woman in the world. His own mother was beautiful. But Aunt Crystelle seemed to be from another world—like Lana Turner, Maureen O'Hara, or Gene Tierney.

Much to his surprise, his Aunt Crystelle rose from her chair and hugged and kissed his grandmother.

For as long as he could remember, he had heard they did not like each other, even though they were mother and daughter.

His grandmother seized his wrist and pulled him along the row of chairs. Her hand was now trembling. He looked up to see if she was angry because Aunt Crystelle had hugged her. He was not sure, but she was plainly upset, her mouth clamped in a firm line. He sat beside his mother. Weldon was already seated on the other side, next to Aunt Zetta.

The minister read from the Bible. Kelly could not concentrate on the words. He heard only the wind and the constant flap of the canvas overhead. He stared at the coffin, again trying to convince himself that his father truly was inside it, and would remain there for all time.

The minister ended his sermon. Other men came forward and gathered around the coffin. Over dark business suits they wore small white leather aprons—another oddity in this exceedingly strange day. A tall man with a deep, resonant voice spoke for several minutes, reciting passages that sounded poetic, like portions of the Bible, yet somehow different. Kelly did not understand all the words, but he gathered their meaning.

The man was saying that life was short and death was certain.

Kelly was not yet ten, but he already had figured that out for himself.

The minister offered a long prayer. Upon the "amen," Mr. Waldrop knelt, flicked a lever, and the coffin slowly descended into the grave. Weldon leaned forward and studied the mechanism.

A line of people formed and, one by one, men and women

hovered briefly over Kelly's mother and grandmother. They spoke in such low tones that he could not hear what they said. Most smiled down at him as they moved on. Mrs. Whitten from his third-grade homeroom kissed his cheek and told him he would have to be brave. He did not know how to reply so he said thank you.

Then it was over. His grandmother again took his hand and they walked back to the warmth of the limousine. His mother and Aunt Zetta lingered behind, talking with small groups of people, before coming on down the hill to enter the car. Mr. Waldrop closed the door and the driver started the engine.

As they drove away, Kelly glanced back. Already people were returning to their cars, leaving his father alone in this scary place. The open grave lay bleak and deserted under the green canvas awning.

"That was very nice!" Aunt Zetta shouted. "That Masonic rite was the one they said over Papa, all those years ago. A senator came all the way from Washington to give it. I forget his name."

Kelly's grandmother nodded and patted Aunt Zetta's wrist. His mother was not exactly crying, but from time to time she reached beneath the veil with the small white handkerchief. Ever since the day his father died she had talked little and always seemed to be thinking of something other than what was happening around her.

Kelly wondered if this would be one of the changes in his life—that from now on his mother would be even more distant, even more inattentive to him.

He had seen some indications that this might be so. Twice his mother and grandmother had broken off their conversation when he came near. From what he had overheard, he knew they were arguing over something that had to do with himself, Weldon, and the oil company.

Carefully he had added this information to the vast treasure trove of facts and suppositions he had assembled about his family, in the hope that some day it would all come together and click into place in a meaningful way.

His whole family seemed to be shrouded in a dark mystery that no one would talk about.

He glanced at his mother, grandmother, Aunt Zetta, Weldon, searching for any new clue.

All were silent, absorbed in their own thoughts.

Kelly sat quietly on the jump seat of the limousine, yearning for the time when he would be old enough to share in the family secrets.

Chapter 2

After dinner, Joanna sent the boys up to Weldon's room to play Chinese checkers, and suggested to Ann Leigh that they take their coffee into the living room. For two days she had postponed the inevitable. Now she wanted to get it behind her.

The sun had just disappeared in a burst of color over green pastures to the west. With growing darkness, lightning flickered in the distance. Joanna and Ann Leigh settled into chairs facing the fire and waited while Calla Lily cleared the dining table and retreated to the kitchen.

The moment they were alone, Ann Leigh wasted no time. "Joanna, I don't care what you promised Brod. The boys will need you now, more than ever. Brod couldn't possibly have expected you to go through with this."

Joanna checked an impulse for a quick reply. Too much was at stake. As chairman of the board, Ann Leigh had the power to stop her, even though the title had always been more or less honorary. With Brod's death, Ann Leigh held the majority of voting stock. The boys' shares would be placed in trust, to be held until they came of age. Joanna forced herself to speak calmly.

"Mother, I don't think you understand. Brod and I discussed in detail everything that was to be done after his death. It was his decision that this would be best, and I agreed."

"I wish he had talked to me about it. I would have changed his mind. The company can take care of itself. The *boys* should be your first consideration."

Brod had warned Joanna that she might have difficulty making his mother face facts. His grasp of the situation gave her confidence.

"But the boys *were* Brod's first consideration. He said that if we put the company in the hands of outsiders now, it would remain out of family control forever. He said that by the time the boys were grown, there would be nothing left. He only wanted me to preserve the company for them."

Ann Leigh's face was set in firm resolve. "Then he was asking the impossible. Those men down there will fight you tooth and nail. They won't tolerate a woman coming in to boss them. Brod should have known that."

Joanna now understood that she and Brod should have kept Ann Leigh better informed. "Mother, nothing will change as far as the people at the company are concerned. Brod kept a tight rein, right up to the final week. He always asked questions, and demanded answers. I'll simply take over where he left off."

"But it *will* be different. Their coming out to the house all those years wasn't the same as you being down there, contending with them day after day. They'll resent you, a woman in a man's world. It just isn't done, anywhere, let alone in Texas! Oh, I know women went into the factories and all, during the war. But surely you see how quickly everything has snapped right back into place, now that the men are back. Believe me, they'll gang up on you and exploit your every weakness."

Joanna spoke firmly to hide her doubts. "Ann Leigh, every decision Brod made concerning the company throughout the last five years, he discussed first with me. We went over every step, weighing the pros and cons. I'm familiar with every facet of the company."

"Even if you had the experience, it wouldn't be the same. Brod just didn't know what you'd be facing. No man could."

Joanna wished she had delayed the confrontation. She was emotionally drained from the demands of the last few days, and she could not reveal an overwhelming, stark truth, for it was too private: Her greatest concern at the moment was not with her two sons, nor with the oil company.

That empty bedroom at the top of the stairs pushed every other thought out of her head.

For the last five nights she had slept in the guest quarters in the west wing. She had not entered the bedroom since Brod's death.

She doubted Ann Leigh would understand. From all that Joanna had heard, in the years before he was killed in the oil well blowout, Ann Leigh's husband had preferred almost any bed to his own.

"The boys are at such a crucial age right now," Ann Leigh went on. "I'll grant Weldon's self-contained, self-sufficient, a lot like Brod. But Kelly's such a sensitive child. I'm sure he'll miss his daddy more than we'll ever know."

Joanna marveled that Ann Leigh could presume to offer advice on child-rearing. Her three children had grown up amid turmoil that had marred their lives. Now Crystelle was the only one still living, and she would scarcely speak to her mother.

Joanna kept her voice level, devoid of emotion. "Mother, the boys will be occupied with their schoolwork. I doubt they'll even miss me through the day. I'll be with them almost every evening. When they're a bit older . . ."

She abandoned the thought. It was too soon to make plans that far ahead.

"Then what?" Ann Leigh insisted.

Joanna could not hide her irritation. "I don't know. Good private schools, I suppose. Brod wanted each of them to have a first-class education."

Ann Leigh was silent for a moment. "When are you planning to start at the office?"

"Next Monday. I've already called a meeting of department heads."

Ann Leigh's cheeks turned pink. "Oh, Joanna! Brod's
hardly in his grave! Shouldn't you wait a decent interval?
What will people think? I hate to say it, but I do believe
you're upset, and acting irrationally."

Despite a quick flare of anger, Joanna did not answer
immediately. She merely sat and stared at Ann Leigh, unable to speak. It was a fault she knew and recognized: whenever she felt threatened, she often retreated into herself and
became noncommunicative. From childhood on, her parents had lectured her about this habit. "Don't you fish-eye
me!" her mother would always say.

Joanna was aware she was giving Ann Leigh the treatment. But the truth was that she did not know any way to
handle Ann Leigh's outrageous statement. Then, in the
midst of her quandary, Brod escaped from his coffin, as he
had so many times during the last few days, and spoke into
her ear, repeating phrases he had spoken many times:
"Emotional control is the key to handling people. Distance
yourself. Turn off your feelings. Let your opposition have
their say, then hammer at them with cool logic. It works
every time."

Joanna put Brod back into his grave and took his advice.
She spoke calmly. "Mother, I'm only following your son's last
wishes. You saw all the messages of condolence, from the
President on down. Brod's abilities were widely recognized.
He has drafted a comprehensive plan—a handwritten man-
ual—for me to use in taking his place in the company. On
the very first page he warns me that upon his death I must
act quickly, and put all doubt and confusion to rest. He said
that if this is not done, someone at the company might mistake the situation, and make the wrong move. He said the
first few days after his death are the time for 'quick action,
and no subtlety.' Those were his very words."

Tears came to Ann Leigh's eyes. She turned away and

watched the distant lightning through the west window. She sighed. "Brod was a lot like his daddy. He could overpower people, sell them a bill of goods. I just hope he hasn't talked you into something you may regret."

"I'll admit I'm not overjoyed at the prospect of taking over the company," Joanna said. "But I'm convinced Brod is right. It must be done. Someone from the family should be down there, and I'm the only one trained to do it."

Ann Leigh's tone softened. "Perhaps so. But I'm sure there'll be all kinds of difficulties he didn't foresee. I just wish he had talked to me about it."

"Mother, I don't think it occurred to him you *wanted* to be involved. He said you've never shown interest in the company."

Again Ann Leigh's eyes filled. "Oh, it was so easy to depend on Brod. When his daddy was killed he stepped right in, and within weeks had the company in the best shape ever. The bankers and investment people told me that. They were really impressed. And he was only a few months out of college at the time. All of us relied on him so. I suppose I just got into the habit. Now it's difficult to think of going on without him."

She hunted in her purse for a handkerchief and dried her eyes. Joanna waited.

"Joanna, I have my doubts about your going down there. But I won't stand in your way. Not right now. We'll see how it goes."

A warning flag went up in the recesses of Joanna's mind. She could not depend on stability in Ann Leigh, who possessed an unusual mixture of naiveté and shrewd common sense. One never knew what to expect from her.

Ann Leigh was still talking. "But if you're bound and determined to do this, why don't you talk with Beth Runnels? She could give you some good tips on how to deal with the situation down there."

At first the suggestion did not make sense. Beth Runnels was an institution, often referred to in print as the richest woman in America. With only a notable exception or two, she could buy and sell any man in Fort Worth or Dallas. She hired platoons of executives to do her bidding. What would she know of running a small, independent oil company?

Ann Leigh offered an explanation.

"Beth has had to fight every inch of the way since she was knee-high. Her daddy died when she was thirteen. He left her property in trusts, scattered all over. An uncle was named guardian. Beth's hands were tied until she came of legal age. At eighteen, she filed a whole string of lawsuits to get control of her own property. It took years. You may think Texas treats women as chattel today. Believe me, it was worse back then. And after she won in court, she had to go in and put everything back on its feet—the ranches, cattle, oil, railroads, everything. Those trusts had been robbing her blind. They'd let it all go to wrack and ruin. It took her ten years or more, but she cleaned house from top to bottom. Yes, sir! Beth probably knows every trick in the book when it comes to dealing with men in business situations."

Joanna's irritation with Ann Leigh vanished. It was a good suggestion. "Would she talk with me?"

"Of course! She may be a busy woman, but she has a heart as big as all outdoors. Besides, she was Brod's godmother. I saw her at the funeral. She sent the white lilies just to the left of the casket. I don't believe she went on to the cemetery. At least, I didn't see her there."

Ann Leigh gathered her purse and wrap, preparing to leave. She paused. "Did Brod ever mention the possibility of trouble from Crystelle?"

Brod had never talked much about his sister. He tended to be secretive in certain areas, and that was one of them. But he had been adamant on one point.

"Brod said there's no way she can hurt us. He said she's completely out of the company, without a dime's worth of stock."

Ann Leigh gripped her purse with both hands. "She's moving back here, you know."

Joanna did not know. She and Crystelle hardly traveled in the same circles.

"Last week she bought the old Curtis house in Rivercrest. You know the one, facing the golf course. I do confess I wish she'd find somewhere other than Fort Worth to live. She has absolutely no sense of shame. Never has."

Perhaps that was because her mother had enough for the whole family, Joanna thought.

"She hasn't been to the house, or even called," Ann Leigh went on. "When she came up to me at the cemetery, that was the first time I've seen her in three years. Three years! Wouldn't you think she would at least call in all that time?"

Joanna nodded vaguely, not wishing to risk comment. Spurlock family conflicts ran deep, and she was an in-law.

Ann Leigh made a ceremony of returning her handkerchief to her purse. "I must admit she looked wonderful. After all the stories I'd heard, I expected worse." She attempted to laugh. "Sometimes I think she must have a horrible picture in her closet. What was the name of that story, where the portrait ages, instead of the man living a degenerate life?"

"The Picture of Dorian Gray," Joanna said. "Oscar Wilde."

"Yes, that's it. If anything, she's prettier than ever. She should look like the wrath of God, the way she has been traipsing around. I've been told of at least six men she has lived with. I'm sure there are at least that many more. I don't know how many of them she married."

"Crystelle has the type of beauty that improves with maturity," Joanna said. "I thought she looked absolutely stunning."

"She still overdresses. I always tried to tell her. I thought that patterned suit most inappropriate to wear to her brother's funeral—or to any funeral, for that matter."

Joanna tactfully did not reveal that she agreed. The suit had been rather theatrical, with rounded shoulders, nipped waist, and long, flouncy skirt. Crystelle's accessories also had been striking—high heels, ankle straps, and a snood instead of veil. But Joanna felt she understood. After all the rumors and gossip, Crystelle probably had not wanted to appear the least bit dowdy or shopworn in seeing friends and acquaintances for the first time in years.

"She dresses dramatically," Joanna said. "But she does seem to have a flair for fashion."

"Always flashy. I used to tell her, over and over: 'Crystelle, simplicity never goes out of style.' But I've never seen her when I thought she looked truly elegant—not since she quit wearing the dresses I bought her." Again Ann Leigh gathered her purse and wrap. "I just wish I knew why she has come back to Fort Worth. I've never known her to do anything without a reason."

Joanna walked with her to the drive. Henry was waiting in Ann Leigh's car. The old fellow had been with the Spurlock family for many years as chauffeur and general factotum. Brod had worried about Henry's driving, but Ann Leigh refused to hurt Henry's feelings by hiring a younger man.

"Evening, Miss Joanna," Henry said, stepping out of the car and doffing his cap.

"Henry, I wish you'd come into the house, instead of waiting out here. Calla loves to cook. There's always something delicious in the kitchen."

"Thank you, Miss Joanna. But I went over to see my boy. We went to get us some good barbecue."

Henry's "boy" was past fifty. "Well, you're welcome here anytime," she told him.

Henry opened the door and helped Ann Leigh into the car. "I appreciate that, Miss Joanna. And I was awful sorry to hear about Mr. Brod. I was telling my boy tonight, Mr. Brod sure used the years the Lord gave him. He was a lot like his daddy in that. Seems to me Spurlock men always burn themselves out early."

The observation apparently did not set well with Ann Leigh. "Come on, Henry," she said from the backseat. "It's getting late."

Joanna waited in the drive until the lights of Ann Leigh's car vanished at the intersection up the street. She returned to the house, closed the front door and, on impulse, latched it.

Never in all the years she had lived in the house had the door been locked. She had never known a moment of insecurity, not even during the years Brod was away, working for the government.

Now, with him gone, she suddenly felt terribly alone and vulnerable.

It was as if her own life had been buried with him.

If it were not for the boys, she doubted that she could go on.

During the last five years Brod had given her instructions on many things—maintenance of the house, the management of insurance, stocks, trust funds, the company. His constant closeness to death had been mutually understood, never discussed. But on evenings when he was so weak he could hardly lift his head from the pillow, he seemed driven to prepare her. He used devious conversational ploys to tell her the location of heirlooms and important papers. Even while gasping for breath during his last days, he had lectured her on the necessity of a proper education for the boys. He had speculated on the postwar economy, describing specific steps she must take to protect the oil company in the face of competition, or to reduce costs during hard times.

But not once had he told her how she could possibly endure living without him.

Nor was she prepared for the anger she now felt toward him, and the strong sense of guilt it spawned.

She knew her anger was unreasonable. But he had diverted her from the life she had so carefully planned, and so badly wanted.

Now, only brief years later, he had left her a widow with two sons, an independent oil company to run, hopelessly embroiled in a Texas family not her own—a family relentlessly in the grip of a stormy, even scandalous, past.

It was a life she had never anticipated, would never have accepted under any circumstances.

Before she met Brod, music had been her world. She had fully expected to enjoy a successful career performing and teaching classical music. But on a dare from a classmate, at the end of her junior year she had auditioned for Billy Rose, who was assembling a production for the Texas Centennial celebration in Fort Worth. Much to her surprise, she soon found herself in Texas as a chorus girl. She had considered the role a lark, a fabulous, fun way to spend the summer. She fully intended to return home to upstate New York for her senior year.

But during that summer she met Brod. Her plans—and her life—changed forever.

Now she felt so cheated. Aside from a wonderful courtship, when she had danced away most of every night, circumstances had robbed her of happiness.

After Brod's father was killed in an oil well fire, Brod had taken over Spurlock Oil, devoting long hours to the office through the first years of their marriage. Joanna had not complained, assuming that someday they would have time for themselves. But then came the war. Soon Brod was away from home, working night and day, month after month, ruining his health, giving his life to his country just as certainly as any soldier on the battlefield.

President Truman had said as much in the telegram.

Now all bridges to her own past were burned. Her parents were gone, killed in an instant on a rain-slick highway while on vacation in Vermont. The family home in Ithaca had been sold. She had only cousins in the East, none close.

She still did not consider herself a Texan. Yet suddenly she was the head of a Texas family, saddled with awesome responsibilities—a situation she still regarded with amazement.

At times, thinking back over her years of preparation with Brod, she felt confident. But in weaker moments she was assailed by doubt. The oil game was incredibly complicated. Spurlock Oil owned a refinery in Houston, pipelines and pumping stations from the Panhandle to the Gulf. Thousands of acres across West Texas and New Mexico were under lease. Decisions would be required almost daily on where to drill new wells, whether to recondition the old. She would have to negotiate natural gas contracts with distributors, deal with retail outlets across the state.

She was filled with Brod's theories, but her practical experience was nonexistent. For instance, he had taught her basic geology, but in reality she could not differentiate chert from limestone.

And what did she know of rearing two boys on the verge of adolescence? She had been an only child, one who had kept boys at a distance until well into her teens.

Perhaps Ann Leigh was right; Brod might have expected too much of her.

She moved through the house, locking every outside door. After switching off the ground-floor lights, she walked up the stairs.

At the entrance to the master bedroom she stopped.

She could not imagine resuming her life there without Brod. But she was sure that the longer she delayed, the more difficult it would become.

Changing bedrooms was not the solution.

As long as the master bedroom remained empty of life, it would house Brod's ghost forever.

She stood at the door and fought another battle, and again her courage failed.

She walked on down the hall toward the guest quarters in the west wing.

But out of her failure came a firm resolve:

Tomorrow she would summon an interior decorator.

Repainted, refurbished, the room would not cease to hold memories. But perhaps the memories could be made more distant, less painful.

Somehow, she must go on.

Chapter 3

Mrs. Whitten clapped her hands and marched Kelly's class through the crowded lobby and into the big auditorium. Inside, most sections were already filled. Children were everywhere. Holding her mimeographed sheet at chest level, referring to it constantly, she led the class down the sloping aisle to within a few rows of the stage. There she stopped and, pointing, directed them into the proper seats.

Kelly cringed against the noise. Around him, children yelled, pounded on seats, and stomped the floor. As soon as Mrs. Whitten turned her back, many swapped seats, breaking alphabetical order so they could sit with friends. Kelly sat quietly. He was content with his place between Beanhead Spears and Marla Thompson.

For as long as he could remember, he had known that he was different. If he were Weldon, at least a half-dozen boys would be competing to sit beside him. Weldon exercised an awesome power over people that Kelly could not hope to emulate.

Kelly preferred to stand back, watch, and not participate. This was tacitly acknowledged by everyone. Teachers tended to worry about him, and labeled him "a loner."

Twice in recent weeks he had been sent to the school counselor. But the man had not known how to ask the right questions.

"Why don't you want to play with the other boys?" he had asked. "Are you afraid of something?"

Kelly had shaken his head no.

How could he explain that he was afraid of *everything*?

What would the man have done if Kelly had told him that his dead father was still hanging around the house, that Kelly felt his presence about a dozen times a day?

Would the man have believed him?

Probably not.

But it was true. Kelly's mother had told him he did not have to go to school today unless he wished, that no one would expect him in class only two days after his father's funeral. He had chosen to go because he wanted to get out of the house. It still reeked of death.

He glanced up. A huge balcony ran along the back of the auditorium. Although it was filled with students, it was not supported by posts. Kelly could not understand what held it up there. He sat studying it, awed by the potential for disaster. If that balcony fell, it would crush the hundreds of children below. He looked higher. Overhead, large steel girders soared to the plaster ceiling. They surely weighed tons and tons. He wondered how other people could sit under them and remain unaware of the danger.

Abruptly the auditorium hushed. Kelly turned to face the stage. The curtain parted. Onstage were three dozen boys, each wearing a maroon blazer, charcoal pants, and a huge bow stretching from shoulder to shoulder. They stood on risers, arranged in tiers. In front, a man raised a baton. He brought the baton down, and the Texas Boys Choir began to sing.

From the first notes Kelly was totally enraptured, lost in the clear, bell-like tones. The performers stood rigid, eyes locked on the director, blending their voices in marvelous harmony. Even the music itself was different. Kelly had never heard anything like it.

The entire forty-five-minute program passed as if he were in a dream.

When he again came to, he and the class were walking up the aisle, out of the auditorium. In the lobby a teacher was handing out leaflets. Kelly reached for one.

En route back to school most of the students folded the leaflets into paper airplanes and sailed them across the bus. Kelly sat and read his. He did not know some of the words, but he gathered that the Texas Boys Choir was seeking new members. He went over the leaflet several times, puzzling over the troublesome words. At last he put it in his pocket. His mother would know what the words meant.

Later that afternoon, as he walked home from school, he made tentative efforts to meld his own voice into the soaring grandeur of the music lingering in his head. Nothing he did sounded right. He remembered phrases, but he could not duplicate them.

Around him, the world went on with its affairs, heedless of the perils Kelly saw on every side. Automobiles dashed by, barely missing pedestrians, utility poles, and each other. A large airplane flew over. It was held aloft only by fragile wings, and was poised to plunge to earth at any moment, killing all aboard and scores of the unsuspecting, unconcerned idiots below. He passed houses where vicious dogs snarled and barked, held back only by flimsy fences. At a drugstore sat a pickup truck with two big guns perched on a rack behind the driver's seat. Kelly walked close and contemplated their cold, metallic deadliness.

Along a strip of business houses he closely examined the signs overhead. Most were attached by little eyelets or, at best, tiny chains. If one of those signs fell, it would be curtains for someone. Kelly gave them wide berth.

He could not understand how people could go through each day, oblivious to the dangers around them. It was a mystery to him how anyone lived to adulthood, let alone to old age. No one else seemed to notice that life was so terribly tenuous. Almost every time he turned on the radio, lightning and floods had killed more people. Disease killed others. A boy in his class at school had been fine one Friday; Kelly had seen him running on the playground. By Monday he was dead as a doornail.

Almost every day he found a new worry. And when he slept, nightmares came. Often he awoke in a cold sweat and could not get back to sleep.

Upon his arrival home he took his books up to his room, then set out in search of his mother. He found her in the library, talking with two men. Drawings and color charts were spread all over. She seemed irritated when he tried to show her the pamphlet and ask about it.

"Not right now, Kelly," she said. "Please find something to do. I'll be through here in a little while."

He went back to his room and began work on his arithmetic assignment. He was checking his solution to the final problem when he heard Weldon coming down the hall. The door burst open and Weldon entered without knocking. He stood over Kelly. "How much money you got, sport?"

Kelly did not want to answer. His money always went to Weldon as if drawn by a magnet. But he was sure Weldon would not rest until he got the answer. "Two dollars and forty-seven cents."

"What about your silver dollars?"

Kelly still had five Aunt Zetta had given him on his last birthday. They were in a sock stuffed into the toe of an old pair of tennis shoes in his closet. Kelly shook his head. "Mom said I shouldn't spend them."

Weldon made a face. "You can if you want. They're yours."

During the last year Weldon had grown thicker through the arms and chest. He habitually walked with a stiff-legged gait and kept his fists raised slightly, as if seeking something or someone to hit. He often was in trouble at school for fighting.

But he was not as tough as he acted. Not really. Sometimes Kelly awoke in the night and heard Weldon sobbing in his room. Kelly knew that deep down, Weldon was scared, too, and only hit people to keep them from hitting him first. He had never hit Kelly. Not hard.

Kelly shifted the point of argument. "What you want them for?"

Weldon walked over and eased the door shut. He reached into a hip pocket and pulled out several pink cards. "Football parlay," he whispered.

Kelly had heard of them. He shook his head emphatically. "No! I'm not going to gamble with my silver dollars."

"It's no gamble," Weldon whispered. "Look here."

He placed a card on the desk and pointed. "Oklahoma *always* beats the spread. They've got Bud Wilkinson for coach and they're getting better every week. Notre Dame *always* has trouble with Purdue, even when they're supposed to beat the piss out of them. With a fourteen-point spread, that's a lead-pipe cinch."

Kelly could not offer argument. Weldon was almost as avid about football as he was about things mechanical and the movies. He read every sports page and listened to every game carried on radio. If anyone could win, it would be Weldon. But Kelly was not confident enough to bet his silver dollars. Besides, gambling was against the law. "Where'd you get those cards?"

Weldon shrugged. "I know a guy." He arranged the cards in a row. "You see, most people go for the long shot. Ten-game parlays, that kind of stuff. That's stupid. Here's the way you do it. Say you have five or six games you're fairly sure about. You use them as your base. You play three-game parlays, mixing your base teams. If a third of your cards win, you break even. If more win, you make money. If all win, you clean up. You can't lose."

Again, Kelly could not dispute him. Weldon's money-making ability was legendary. He once had charged playmates a nickel each to see his sore toe.

"I got a plan," Weldon went on. "We'll get a bunch of guys together, and we'll each put up five dollars. Then we'll let the money ride, week after week. By the bowl games, we'll be rolling in dough."

Kelly was not surprised that the ante just happened to be exactly the amount he had hidden away in his closet. He was inclined to refuse. If Weldon lost the silver dollars, he did not know how he would explain their disappearance to his mother.

But Weldon had a knack with money. Kelly thought of how nice it would be if his stake turned into a small fortune.

Besides, he could not bring himself to say no. He and Weldon were not only brothers, they were also best friends. Through all the years when their mother had spent most of her time with their father behind the closed bedroom door, they had had only each other to depend upon. They shared everything, told each other their innermost secrets, like Batman and Robin or maybe the Lone Ranger and Tonto. Kelly benefited from the reputation of Weldon's fists. Although Kelly was the smallest boy in his class, no one picked on him. Everyone knew that if they did, they would have to answer to Weldon. He and Weldon looked out for each other, when no one else would. It had always been that way.

Now their father was dead.

But so far, nothing else had changed.

"Okay," Kelly said.

He walked into the closet and brought out the money.

He was not gambling on Oklahoma's gridiron prowess or Purdue's annual jinx on Notre Dame.

He was betting on Weldon.

Regarded in that light, it probably was a sure thing.

Joanna placed a swatch of fabric over the color chart and tried to envision the combination carried throughout the upstairs bedroom. Tomorrow the painters would arrive, and she had promised them a decision the first thing in the morning. She wished she had more time. For two days she had been thoroughly immersed in the project, enjoying it immensely. But Monday—and her debut at the office—was looming ever nearer.

She could not make up her mind. The beige was darker than she would prefer, but the next shade definitely was too light. Moving the cloth against the color chart, she sought to find precisely the color she wanted.

"Momma, what does this say?"

Kelly stood in the door, holding a sheet of paper. Joanna checked her irritation. She remembered that Kelly had tried to talk to her while she was conferring with the interior decorators, and she had sent him away. She took the sheet of paper from him and read the text.

"It says auditions for the Texas Boys Choir will be held during the next three weeks. Any boy with a B average or better and good recommendations may apply."

"What's 'audition'?"

"A tryout. It's like going out for basketball or football. They see how everyone performs, and pick the best."

"Can I audition?"

"*May* I." Joanna scanned down the leaflet. "They're auditioning several places in Fort Worth. But the choir's home is in Denton. That's much too far away for you to think about."

"How far?"

Joanna added distances. "From here, about forty miles. With the traffic, at least an hour's drive, each way."

Kelly's voice took on the whining tone that Joanna could not abide. "Every time I want to do something there's always some darn reason I can't."

Exasperated, yet concerned, Joanna studied her son. He had grown taller in recent months, but remained painfully thin and nervous. She once had asked one of Brod's doctors to examine him. The doctor had said his skinniness was "natural," and that he "would probably grow out of it." But sometimes she wondered.

He seemed more troubled by Brod's death than Weldon. She still had to talk to the boys, prepare them for the changes in their lives. But this was not the time. She wanted to talk to them together, put it in the context of family.

"Kelly, I'm sure you enjoyed the boy choir. But if you really want to sing, I think you'd be happier with a Fort Worth choir."

He shook his head. "No. There's nothing in Fort Worth like that. There's nothing like it anywhere."

Joanna understood. "Some boy choir music is hundreds of

years old. It was written for the church. It *is* different from anything you hear today."

"Can't I? Please?"

"Stop whining."

Joanna reexamined the leaflet. She had never heard of the Texas Boys Choir. But if the boys were singing traditional music, she could assume it was a superior organization.

Kelly's chances of acceptance were probably slight. Maybe the competition would be good for him. If he should win, the choir might help to keep him occupied while she worked. It seemed worth exploring.

"Well, I suppose you come by your interest naturally. Did you know I studied music in college?"

Kelly shook his head.

"Well, I did. And my mother—your grandmother—taught piano." She folded the leaflet. "Don't get your hopes up. But I'll call and find out more about it. I promise."

Kelly went back to his room, apparently satisfied. Joanna returned to her quandary. She tried several more combinations of colors, but none worked. After exhausting possibilities, she decided that surely the painters could adjust their mix to find the proper shade of beige. If not, she would go with her second choice, eggshell white.

She folded away the material and went upstairs to contend with her second pressing problem: clothing appropriate for day after day at the office.

In making way for the painters, she and the maids had taken everything out of the closets in the master bedroom. All of Brod's clothing had been sent to Goodwill. When her own wardrobe had been assembled on racks in a spare bedroom, she had been appalled at how little was still serviceable. Too many years had passed since she had thought much about new clothing. Throughout the war, not only was quality unavailable, but such luxuries as high fashion were deemed unpatriotic. After the war, with Brod at home an invalid, she seldom left the house. Consequently, most of her wardrobe was hopelessly out of style.

She had spent a day shopping, but it was late in the season

and the results were meager—a jumper, a few blouses, an elegant basic black dress, and a suit she felt too "churchy" for office wear. It seemed as if the manufacturers provided styles for every facet of female activity except that of entering a business as top executive. Joanna knew exactly what she wanted—suits and dresses not too masculine, yet not too frilly feminine. Nothing in the stores had seemed quite right.

Unfortunately, the fashion world was still in a period of rapid change. Several seasons ago Christian Dior had astounded everyone with the introduction of his "New Look" —rounded shoulders, pinched waists, and long, full skirts. Other designers had promptly jumped on the bandwagon with their own drastic departures. But even now, three years later, resistance to the new, outré styles pouring out of Paris remained strong. Only recently a fashion show in New York had been picketed by women who said they would not be dictated to by designers. Joanna wanted to create exactly the right impression. She would have to choose carefully, and use her ingenuity. But that would take time she did not have.

Locking the bedroom door, she methodically went through her wardrobe, searching for anything that might do. She tried on what only a few months before she had considered her best suits, and had to laugh. With the padded shoulders, and hemlines above the knee, she looked like something out of a Joan Crawford movie.

A gray tweed suit she had purchased earlier in the fall seemed too severe. Her full-skirted blue dress with the subdued floral pattern was much too feminine for a woman summoning men into serious discussion. One by one, she rejected each dress and suit. Somehow, she must avoid resembling an overdressed secretary, or projecting the aura of a grand dame ruling over her serfs. She must appear approachable, but not vulnerable. Nothing struck the right balance.

The totally impossible she piled in a corner to go to Goodwill. The possible she aligned on a single rack. Most of those needed alterations, new and different accessories. None seemed the obvious outfit to be worn into the office on fateful Monday.

As she tried to settle on a choice, her doubts flared anew.

How could she expect to run an oil company, and make multimillion-dollar decisions daily, when she could not even make up her mind on what dress to wear into the office?

Overcome by a wave of helplessness, she abandoned the project, at least for the moment.

After dinner she took the boys into the library, sat them down, and closed the door. They waited apprehensively while she searched for the right words.

"It's time we talked about the future," she said. "Now that we've lost your father, all of us will have to shoulder more responsibilities, to carry out all the things he wanted for us."

From their puzzled expressions she realized she was being too vague. She moved to specifics.

"Starting this week, I'll be taking over management of the oil company, as your father wished me to do."

Joanna paused. From their faces she could see that she was conveying her own insecurities. Kelly sat with eyes wide. Even Weldon had lost some of his cockiness.

Kelly's lips trembled. "Are we broke?"

The question was so unexpected that Joanna laughed. "Heavens, no! What gave you that idea?"

"If we're not, I don't see why you have to go to work."

"I'm trying to explain. I'm doing it for the two of you. Your father wanted me to keep the company going until you two are grown, and can run it for yourselves. I know that seems a long time away to you now, but it really isn't."

"Why can't those men run it?" Kelly asked.

"They need direction. With your father no longer here to supervise them, I'll have to go down every day and tell them what the family wants done. The company will be my responsibility. I'll be very busy, especially while I'm getting started. I won't have as much time to spend with you. So I'll be depending on you to take a very mature attitude for boys your age, and look after yourselves more. That is *your* responsibility. Do you understand?"

"Sure," Weldon said.

"It won't be as if you're on your own. Calla Lily, the household, will be here, so you'll never be alone. I'll expect to be home for dinner, most days. And I'll always be available if you need me. Any time you have a real problem, you can call me at the office. Is that understood?"

Both boys nodded.

"Whatever else, we must continue on as a family. That is what your father wanted. Maybe we won't be together as often, but perhaps we'll enjoy each other more when we are. Any questions about what I've said?"

Both boys shook their heads.

"All right. We understand what we have to do. We'll have these little talks from time to time. We can discuss any problems any of us may be having. Okay?"

The boys nodded. They trouped silently back upstairs.

Joanna was overcome with misgivings. She had hoped for a discussion, not a lecture. Somehow, she had failed to draw the boys out.

She was not sure she had accomplished anything at all.

How could she expect to manage a far-flung company filled with mature men, when she could not handle two preadolescent boys?

That evening, to restore her confidence, she plunged back into the notebook Brod had left her, reviewing all he had taught her during the last five years.

Chapter 4

Henry's well-intentioned but unfortunate remark continued to rankle Ann Leigh throughout the next several days,
for she recognized its truth: Spurlock men *did* seem to burn
themselves out early.

Belatedly, she was driven to consider whether she could
have prevented the destruction of her husband, or of her
two sons.

After pondering the past at length, she decided that in the
case of her husband, tragedy could not have been averted.
Clay had been a man possessed, determined to extract every
last morsel of riches from the earth, and to prove himself
better than any other man in every way. She long had
known of his other women. But she also had known that
confrontation would have brought complete turmoil to the
family. By keeping her silence, she at least had kept some
measure of tranquility in the house. She believed she had
done her best for the children.

Of her exact responsibility in the deaths of her sons, she
was less certain. She could envision scenarios wherein, if she
had spoken up, perhaps Loren, or Brod, or both, would still
be alive.

Once faced, that possibility did not rest lightly with her.

Now her own mistakes probably were being compounded by those of Joanna.

Woefully inexperienced, no doubt not wanted, Joanna seemed determined to take Brod's place within the company. Ann Leigh could see no way Joanna could do this without neglecting the boys right at the time when they needed attention the most.

She had told Joanna she would not interfere. But now she was plagued by second thoughts.

After agonizing over the situation at length, she took her worries across town to Aunt Zetta.

Years ago she and Zetta had been estranged. But now, in her old age, Zetta had perfected her direct way of looking at the world. Ann Leigh often found her invaluable for sorting out thoughts.

She found Zetta in the backyard, working in her garden. The setting was fortunate. In quiet surroundings, Zetta could converse almost normally when she chose to do so.

As was her habit, Zetta started talking the instant Ann Leigh came into view, jumping right into the middle of her chosen subject. "I thought that last cold snap got them," she said, pumping a cloud of dust on a rose bush. "Now I believe they'll keep right on blooming through Christmas if we don't have another hard freeze."

Freed from the dry summer heat, the rose bushes indeed had taken on new life, and were in profuse bloom. Ann Leigh raised her voice. "They're quite lovely, Zetta."

"They always die back on me in January, or at least by early February. I've never been able to protect them adequately. Maybe this year. Let's go into the house."

"Zetta, I don't want to take you from your work."

"Nonsense. It'll be here to do tomorrow. Maybe I'll be here to do it. If I'm not, no matter." She placed the can of rose dust in her basket. "Come on. It's time for my tea."

They walked through the house to the front parlor. With its dark furniture and heavy lace curtains, the room had not changed an iota in decades. Zetta rang the kitchen and waited impatiently. "I'll swear, that girl gets slower every day. I don't know why I bother to put up with her."

The "girl" was in her late sixties, and Zetta had been "putting up with her" for thirty years. Ann Leigh sat and listened to Zetta's pronouncements about flowers and the weather until the tea arrived and was poured.

At last a break came in Zetta's monologue. Ann Leigh seized the opportunity and again raised her voice. "Zetta, I talked with Joanna quite a while the other night. She's still determined to take Brod's place at the company."

"Might be the best thing," Zetta said.

Ann Leigh was left momentarily speechless. She had presumed that Zetta would be an ally.

"But Joanna has never done anything like this in her entire life!" she managed to say. "She's so ill-prepared!"

Zetta waved a hand, brushing aside argument. "The girl's intelligent. She's got spunk. I wish I had asserted myself more when I was her age. I sat back and allowed my father, my brothers to rule my life. If I had it to do over, I wouldn't put up with that for a minute."

Ann Leigh could not find the right words to define her unease about the situation. She tried again. "Sometimes Joanna has trouble dealing with people. The way she just sits and looks at you sometimes without answering. Not everyone knows quite how to take her. They misunderstand."

"You mean she sometimes comes across as a cold person," Zetta said. "That's true. She often holds people at arm's length. I'm not sure that would be a detriment in business. Maybe we should all do it more."

"But she's *not* a cold person."

"I never said she was."

"Still, people think she is."

"Well, if it gets the job done, it doesn't really matter, does it?"

Stymied, Ann Leigh changed the subject. "Mostly, I'm worried about the boys. Joanna the same as said she may send them away to school."

"Many children in this part of town are sent off to schools. Doesn't seem to hurt them."

"But Weldon and Kelly are so young! Maybe if they were older, it wouldn't seem so harsh. Weldon may be precocious, big for his age. But Kelly is so immature and high-strung. He needs attention."

"Without a father, they'll have to grow up fast. Who knows? Maybe they'll be the better for it. I always thought that the case with my father. He was orphaned early, you know."

Ann Leigh was determined not to be sidetracked by Zetta's reminiscences. "Crystelle's moving back here. She bought the old Curtis house. I think she may be up to something."

"I've never known her when she wasn't."

"I mean something to do with the oil company. She may try to cause trouble for Joanna."

Zetta did not answer for a moment, apparently considering possibilities. "I don't see how she could. But if she can, I'm sure she will."

"I've tried to reason with her. She won't listen to me."

Zetta leaned forward to pour more tea. "Crystelle always had a wild streak. You and Clay did precious little to corral her."

"I don't know why she resented me so. And the way she turned on Brod, when he was helpless and couldn't do anything about it. Sometimes I think she is just downright mean. She has no consideration for anyone."

Zetta added two lumps of sugar and stirred. "When she ran off with that boy that time, you should have let her go, find out for herself if she'd made a mistake. That's when she turned so hard against you. Brod had no business trying to be her father."

"But she was so young! Barely sixteen!"

"Good marriages have been made younger. It was her choice. She should have been made to live with it."

"The boy was only seventeen."

"But of good stock. I've known that family through three

generations. She could have done worse. And she has, several times, from what I hear."

Ann Leigh did not want to discuss Crystelle's marriages. She moved on to another worry. "I'm afraid Joanna may be faced with a situation she can't handle down at that company. She may have no idea of what she's walking into."

Zetta's hawkish eyes fixed on her. "What kind of situation?"

Ann Leigh was reluctant to put her darkest thoughts into plain words. She equivocated. "Maybe something from all that trouble right after Brod's first heart attack. When you come right down to it, we still don't know exactly what happened."

Zetta sat in silence, awaiting a fuller explanation.

It burst from Ann Leigh with a passion she no longer could contain. "Zetta, if I live to be a hundred, I'll never believe Loren committed suicide!"

"Ann Leigh, you don't have to beat around the bush with me. I know what's on your mind. If I were you, I wouldn't waste two minutes worrying about it. If anyone ever needed killing, it was Grover Sterling. If Brod had him killed, I say more power to him. But that's all water under the bridge. Brod's beyond reach. No one can hurt him now. So let's just forget it."

Ann Leigh felt unexpected, overwhelming relief that those long-festering possibilities at last had been voiced. Yet so many questions remained. She did not want to abandon the subject. "But how could Brod have had anything to do with it? He was lying flat on his back in bed when Grover Sterling was killed."

"There are ways. I'm sure Brod knew them."

Zetta remained silent, as if thinking back over the bewildering events of those terrible days. And for a time, Ann Leigh was also swept into the past, remembering the trip she had made to San Antonio with Brod and Joanna, just before Brod's first heart attack.

It was in the last days of the war. Long given up for dead, Loren had been found in a German POW camp in Poland.

He had been flown to the army hospital at old Fort Sam Houston in San Antonio, and they had received permission to visit him.

They had been escorted to Loren's quiet alcove in a corner of a big ward. There they had talked with him for hours. He described his capture in North Africa, after he had been badly wounded. He told of his trip to Italy, traveling in the bottom of an ammunition barge. He almost died in a hospital in Italy, where his right leg was amputated. He said he remained in Italy until after the Normandy invasion, when he was moved to Germany, and then to Poland.

"The Germans could have let me die in North Africa, and no one would have known the difference," Loren said. "A German doctor saved my life. The Italian doctors and nurses took care of me. Italian women came and prayed for me. After I was moved north, the Poles smuggled food into our POW camp when they had almost nothing themselves. Everywhere, everyone was so kind. They made tremendous sacrifices to save us. So I really don't understand this."

He gestured toward newspapers and magazines scattered about the ward. Earlier that week, the U.S. government had released the first news about the Nazi death camps. Newspapers and magazines were filled with horrible photographs of mass graves, crematorial ovens, piles of human hair, and of human skeletons still containing a spark of life. The nation, the world, had been stunned. The emotional impact was like that of Pearl Harbor or the death of Franklin D. Roosevelt all over again.

Around them, the San Antonio hospital was jammed with soldiers missing arms and legs, with faces burned and scarred. The horror of that weekend, of seeing all those maimed boys, had been enough to make Ann Leigh give up on the human race. But Loren had been so sweet through it all, talking about the kindness of the people he had met, the sacrifices they had made to keep him alive. He had been so optimistic. The doctors said he was in constant pain. Yet he never complained.

He had been so eager to get home, to get on with his life.

Ann Leigh also remembered every detail of the afternoon Loren died. She had heard him on the phone up in his room, his voice raised in anger. Grover Sterling had called with his ultimatum about refinancing the company. Grover and Crystelle were taking advantage of Brod's heart attack, and Loren's disability, to seize control of the company. Loren was furious. He came downstairs swinging his prothesis in the way he had perfected, carrying his crutches. He had stormed out the front door and driven off in his specially equipped car.

Four hours later he had been found dead in a city park, a pistol by his side.

The family had delayed telling Brod, fearing the news of his brother's death might kill him. But days later, when they told him with doctors in attendance, he had listened in cold silence.

And within a week Grover Sterling was dead, killed on a street in New York City. On the same evening, the Fort Worth department store belonging to Troy Spurlock, Brod's cousin, was destroyed by fire. Troy, who had been Grover's principal financial backer, disappeared.

Crystelle, defeated, had sold her stock to Brod and fled the country.

But now she was back, apparently to stay.

"We should have contested that coroner's verdict on Loren," Zetta said. "I thought so at the time."

"I'm sure Brod would have, if he'd been able."

"Ann Leigh, what reason do you have to think all that may come up again, after five years?"

"There's still speculation and talk. I'm told they call it the 'Spurlock War.'"

"Oh, people will talk, no matter what. Who cares?"

Ann Leigh refused to allow her greatest fear to be dismissed so lightly. "Zetta, I think something may yet come to light. Something that might reopen the investigation."

Again Zetta's hawkish eyes fixed on her. "With Brod dead, they won't reopen the investigation. They might not even if he were alive. I've long noticed that in Texas, murders at this level of society are seldom resolved legally. They just become legends, a part of the social fabric. It has always been so. The authorities are reluctant to indict, the juries to convict. Who wants to send a legend to jail? If any new evidence about Brod comes to light, it will just become a part of the family legend. I've learned to live with it. There's no reason you can't."

Chapter 5

Joanna entered Spurlock Oil on Monday morning as if walking in a dream. Although she had visited several times through the years on errands, the elevator, the long, carpeted corridors, the banks of offices, seemed oddly unfamiliar. As she walked through the building, she was acutely aware of covert glances from secretaries, bookkeepers, and other floor personnel.

She was early; the outer executive offices were empty as she passed them on her way to the presidential suite. The door to Brod's office was locked. She used her key, entered, and closed the door behind her.

The vast silence of the large office was overwhelming. Brod's desk sat in the center of the room, just as he had left it on his departure for government service. He had refused to relinquish the suite to Grover Sterling. That had been among the bitter issues between them.

Reluctantly, still feeling as if she were an intruder, she placed her briefcase on the desk, sat in Brod's big executive chair, and took stock of her surroundings.

The decor was heavily masculine—rich leather upholstery, dark wood paneling, crystal lighting fixtures.

She did not intend to change it, at least not soon. Every trace of Brod's presence would help her through the difficult days ahead.

She felt surprisingly confident, and that she looked her best. She had settled on the plain black wool. It was styled in a simplicity that was timeless. With small earrings and a single strand of pearls, she was sure she had achieved the right balance.

Opening her briefcase, she reviewed the list of department heads, and their profiles. Although she had met them, most were an unknown quality to her. On their visits to Brod they had always been subdued, all business. She could put faces with the names, but nothing more. Brod had not known much about their personalities, perhaps because he had been away all through the war, and had not taken part in the sweeping personnel changes. She was sure the executive offices were filled with cliques, alliances, and rivalries that not even Brod suspected.

In turn, she no doubt remained an unknown entity to them. During their brief weekday visits to the house, she had kept to the background, listening, seldom participating. They had known that she was taking part in Brod's decisions, but her role had never been defined. They possibly were intrigued that she was a former Billy Rose showgirl. Often she had seen curiosity in their eyes. But in their view, she was Brod's wife. They probably had never regarded her in any role beyond that.

No doubt consternation was widespread throughout the company now that she was taking over the presidency. And she was sure speculation still lingered over the Spurlock War.

Somehow she must deal with all this on a daily basis, and survive.

Brod had established ground rules for her. She was to remain congenial with everyone, but friendly with none. Whatever happened, she was to maintain her distance. She was to develop sources of information, but trust no one.

A soft knock sounded at the door. Bonnie Ledbetter entered hesitantly. "Mrs. Spurlock, I don't know if you remember me."

"Of course I do," Joanna said. Bonnie had been to the house several times with papers for Brod to sign. Years ago, while Brod was still in the hospital, Joanna had called upon her to baby-sit with Kelly and Weldon. Probably in her mid-thirties, she was short and comfortably overweight. On brief acquaintance, Joanna considered her both pleasant and efficient.

"Mr. Campbell thought that since you don't yet have a secretary, I might help today until you make a permanent arrangement."

Joanna felt Mr. Campbell was taking a great deal on himself. But she was careful not to show her annoyance. "That will be fine, Bonnie. We have a meeting of department heads scheduled at ten. Perhaps you can take notes."

"Yes, ma'am. Mr. Campbell suggested that I do so."

"Good. If you'll bring in your notepad, we might think of a few things that haven't yet occurred to Mr. Campbell."

While waiting, Joanna arranged her papers. Bonnie returned and perched on a facing chair. Reading from her notes, Joanna began dictating the long list of information Brod had recommended that she assemble during the first few days for orientation. She asked to see the personnel files of all department heads and key executives, production figures for the last three months, a detailed breakdown of exploration programs in progress, totals of sales made through each wholesale and retail outlet, a detailed dissection of refinery operations, a thorough report on the current disposition of hydrocarbon by-products, and a cost-and-profit analysis of each. She also asked for an inventory of all equipment in the field, along with an evaluation of mechanical condition.

As she dictated, Joanna thought she saw a marked change in Bonnie Ledbetter's attitude, shifting from apprehension to a measure of respect. "Mrs. Spurlock, this will take a while to get together. I'm not even sure it's all available."

"In that case, we may need to set up a small research unit," Joanna said.

She was still dictating when Arnold Campbell knocked perfunctorily and stuck his head in the door without invitation. "Good morning, Mrs. Spurlock. Good to see you! Sorry I wasn't here when you arrived. Frankly, we didn't expect you until about ten."

Joanna shook hands with him. "I'll be at my desk by eight-thirty every day," she told him. "At least for a while. I have a great deal of catching up to do."

"Of course. But I'm sure you'll manage in no time."

Joanna ignored the condescension.

As he stood smiling down at her, Joanna realized that she knew even less about this man than about the other department heads. He was tall and thin, with graying hair combed straight back and parted in the middle. She assumed he was in his late fifties. He now had been general manager of the company four years. Brod had said his background was in accounting and bookkeeping, and that he knew little about work in the field.

"Normally, we don't have meetings of department heads," Campbell said. "Everyone is too busy doing his job. But this will be a splendid opportunity to introduce you to everyone."

Again Joanna allowed his proprietary attitude to pass without comment. "Well, I'll see you at ten," she said. "If you'll excuse us, Bonnie and I have more work to do."

Obviously taken aback, Campbell stood awkwardly for a moment, then gave her an abrupt nod. He paused at the door. "I'll round up everyone, and have them in the conference room."

As the door closed, Bonnie giggled.

"We only have a few minutes to finish this," Joanna said. "Where were we?"

They worked steadily through the list. Joanna purposely waited until three minutes after ten before picking up her material and heading for the meeting, with Bonnie trailing in her wake.

As she entered the conference room, the five men rose.

"Mrs. Spurlock, I believe you know everyone," Campbell said.

Joanna spoke to each. Campbell came to hold her chair at the head of the table. She motioned for the men to be seated.

The department heads were an odd, disparate group. Campbell sat smiling at her from the far end of the table, as if suggesting that he would be there to comfort her, should she make a fool of herself.

On his right sat Mike Piersall, head of production. Brod had said Piersall was a former driller and toolpusher who had worked in the oil patch since his early teens. He seemed uncomfortable in a business suit. His skin was bronzed and weathered, and his dark eyes were wary. He wore his thick dark hair in a crew cut. Brod had warned her about him, saying Piersall probably retained a driller's contempt for the home office, even though he was now a part of it.

If he disdained white-collar executives, she easily could imagine his attitude toward a woman boss.

On her left sat Donald Parker, chief of exploration. With thick glasses, narrow shoulders, and a tall, question-mark frame, he appeared almost scholarly. He sat fiddling with a pencil, his face devoid of expression. Brod had said he was closemouthed, abrasive in attitude, and probably the best geologist in the oil game.

George Hollander, director of sales, sat on her right, just beyond Bonnie. He was a big man with a broad, open face. Of the five, he was the only one who seemed at ease. Brod had said Hollander's clownish demeanor hid a good mind, and that his opinions should not be dismissed lightly.

The fifth man was Walt Chambers, in charge of pipelines, storage, and refinery operations. Chambers had seldom visited the house, preferring instead to send lengthy memos. He was small, wiry, and bald. Joanna had never seen him without a cigar in his mouth, often unlit. Brod had said that Chambers knew his job, ran his department efficiently, and

—perhaps most importantly—had excellent contacts throughout the industry.

Campbell cleared his throat. "Mrs. Spurlock, I hope you'll allow me, on behalf of everyone, to welcome you to the company. We were all saddened by Mr. Spurlock's death. But we're looking forward to working with you, and we will help you in every way we can."

The executives gave Campbell's speech a polite round of applause.

"Thank you," Joanna said.

She allowed a moment of silence to pass, then began her prepared remarks, rehearsed so many times.

As she spoke, she met each of their gazes, one by one.

"We've all been through a very trying time. We owners are fully aware that all of you have carried on splendidly. We are most grateful. We will never forget your contribution in keeping Spurlock Oil on an even keel."

The department heads remained silent, their expressions guarded. She did not know if it was her imagination, or if she truly felt a growing wall of resistance. She struggled on, even though her carefully chosen words now seemed as hollow as Campbell's welcome.

"As most of you may know, my husband retained the presidency of this company throughout the war, and throughout his illness, in the hope that some day he would be able to return. That was his fondest wish. Deep down, I think he knew that was not likely to happen. Consequently, throughout the last three years, he asked me to participate in every decision affecting this company. It was my husband's wish that I assume his place here upon his death. He loved this company, and he made every provision to preserve it."

She paused for a moment, puzzled by a growing tension in the room. She spoke more firmly.

"In a sense, nothing has changed, except that I am assuming his title, and we no longer have the benefit of his knowledge and guidance."

Joanna saw it in their faces:

Hope had been mounting that she would reconsider, that some other arrangement had been made.

No doubt rumors to that effect had been flying.

She had just dashed all hope, brought them face-to-face with the reality that she was truly taking control of the company.

As she continued, she marveled over Brod's foresight in urging her to act quickly and to put all speculation to rest.

"We must meet a number of challenges in the months ahead. Most of our larger government contracts have been fulfilled and terminated. The majors are giving us increasing competition in the civilian market. They are pouring new capital into refineries, exploration, retailing. We owners have been aware of this. We also have known that for years all of you have been managing with inexperienced help, worn-out equipment, and reduced operating budgets. I can now promise some relief in those areas. More capital will be committed to operations. But all of us must be more cost-conscious. Although our gross revenues are up, net profits are down. During the next few months, we *will* correct these deficiencies."

Joanna pretended not to see the covert glances exchanged around the table.

She forced into her voice a tone of conviction she did not feel. "It was my husband's belief that, with the war and owner neglect, the company has become increasingly disorganized. Each of you has been running a department under difficult circumstances, without sufficient time to keep yourselves adequately informed on difficulties encountered in other departments. Sales have been made without knowledge of the limitations of delivery. Exploration has made commitments that production has not been able to meet. A lack of cohesion exists throughout the company. Consequently, our meeting today will become a permanent practice. Each Monday morning we will spend an hour here, discussing all phases of operations."

Chambers grunted, then whipped the dead cigar from his

mouth. "Mrs. Spurlock, my work takes me out of town a lot. I'm not always here on Monday."

"Very well. Your assistant can sit in."

"I don't have an assistant."

"Then get one," Joanna snapped, sharper than she intended. She took a deep breath and spoke more softly. "The object is to keep each of you better informed on the overall picture. It will make our jobs easier. You'll have more information on which to base every decision you make."

"Knowing other people's problems won't help me decide how to bring in a well," Piersall said.

"Perhaps not. But what Mr. Parker and his seismograph crews have discovered about certain formations may help you decide where to spud in next. And the production department should work hand in hand with whatever plans Mr. Chambers has made for gatherage and storage, and vice versa. It's simply a matter of keeping each other informed."

"Mrs. Spurlock, we *do* keep each other informed," Campbell said in gentle, fatherly tones. "We have done so for years."

"On a catch-as-catch-can basis, apparently. A number of costly lapses have occurred recently. It was not my intention to come here and complain. But if you want chapter and verse, I can provide them."

Campbell did not answer.

Joanna had expected some opposition, but not the unified front she now clearly faced. Campbell, Chambers, and Piersall were looking at her with eyes alive with resentment, if not outright anger. Parker assiduously avoided looking at anyone. He sat studying the wood grain on the tabletop. Hollander appeared to be mildly amused.

Joanna felt like crying. This was not at all what she had expected—not even in her worst moments. She was angry, confused, and a bit frightened that her first meeting had gone so badly. But she knew she must not show her emotions.

She allowed a cool tone to slip into her voice. "During the next few days I will meet separately with each of you, to discuss the operation of your department. You may wish to prepare notes beforehand. I shall expect you to be frank. I will want to know your departmental goals, your difficulties, your complaints. We will work together and fix whatever we can."

She checked the "first day" list Brod had given her. Only one item remained.

"And I shall need your help on another matter. I'm setting up a research team to reexamine our organizational structure. As you know, the company grew like Topsy throughout the war, often without rhyme or reason. Many jobs remain undefined. Areas of responsibility overlap. In some instances, there are situations where no one bears direct responsibility. This study will help us to become better acquainted with operations. Any questions?"

The scratch of Bonnie's pen was the only sound in the room.

"Then that's it." Joanna rose, gathered her papers, and left the room. Bonnie followed her back to the office.

As the door closed behind them, Bonnie turned her eyes upward, fanned her face with her notepad, and giggled.

For the first time, Joanna wondered if Bonnie would do. The last thing she needed was an us-women-against-them situation. "Bonnie, you understand that everything said in the conference room—or in this office—is confidential, not to be repeated, not at any time, anywhere."

Bonnie's mouth flew open in shocked surprise. "Mrs. Spurlock, I've been a private secretary more than ten years!"

"Then you understand that this is not a game for our amusement. Please type our lists. I may have additions later."

Chastened, Bonnie returned to the outer office and her typewriter.

Joanna sank into Brod's chair. She found that she was trembling. Lowering her face into her hands for a moment, she tried to summon Brod's presence, to ask him for guidance.

She did not succeed.

After several minutes she felt calmer, and began the re-arrangement of her desk.

She decided to leave all of Brod's paraphernalia in place—a framed photograph of Weldon, Kelly, and herself when the boys were hardly more than babies, the onyx-and-gold pen set she had given him one Christmas, and a flipboard telephone directory, no doubt now obsolete. The drawers of the desk were almost bare. Apparently Brod had cleared them upon his departure for government service.

Carefully, she placed the ring binder book of Brod's instructions in a bottom drawer and locked it.

The phone rang. Startled, Joanna answered.

"Mrs. Spurlock?" Campbell asked. "May I see you for a moment?"

"Of course," Joanna said.

He arrived solemn-faced and ill at ease. He took a seat across from her desk. "Mrs. Spurlock, in light of what you said this morning, I've been wondering exactly what my duties will be in the future."

Joanna thought she had made it clear. She could only repeat what she had said. "Mr. Campbell, nothing has changed, except that instead of reporting to Brod, you will report to me. The same holds true for all department heads."

He stared at the floor, then looked up at her. "Mrs. Spurlock, after Mr. Sterling's death, and with your husband's continued absence, I was considered to be the senior officer in this company."

"That remains the case," Joanna told him. "As vice-president and general manager, you are the company's second officer. You will continue to be in charge in my absence."

The news did not seem to make Campbell happy. "In that capacity, then, I think I should venture an opinion. I believe you are moving entirely too fast in altering our time-tested operating procedures."

Joanna opened her mouth to reply, but the impulse was interrupted. From beyond the grave Brod's voice came to her, as clearly as if he had spoken in her ear: *Never explain. Never let anyone know what you're thinking.*

She was certain that no one would ever have had the temerity to come into Brod's office and give him such a bald-faced, impertinent warning.

"That remains to be seen," she said.

Kelly lay sprawled across Weldon's bed, trying to follow what was happening. Weldon had three radios tuned to different football games, and moved constantly from one to the next, mumbling to himself. The din was deafening. Scores from the East Coast had been in for almost an hour, and Weldon had seemed satisfied with the results. But three crucial Southwest Conference games were still in progress. Judging from the noise made by the crowds, Kelly gathered that two were close, and could go either way.

In the final moments Weldon moved about frenetically. The uproar from fans drowned out the announcers. Kelly could not determine who was ahead, or who was about to score. Then the games ended in rapid sequence.

Weldon switched off the radios in disgust.

"We lose?" Kelly asked.

"One card. That moron Aggie dropped the ball in the end zone or we would've had a clean sweep."

That meant Weldon had almost tripled their money. "Can I get my five dollars back now?"

"No. We plow everything back. Those are the rules."

Weldon's rules. Kelly had heard no one else agree to them. "Just five dollars wouldn't hurt."

Weldon began folding the sports pages scattered about the room. He kept them arranged in weekly stacks. In making his bets, he often went back several weeks to determine who scored the most, or who completed more passes. "It wouldn't be fair to the other guys. Besides, I need all the money I can get. I may have to go away for a while."

Kelly thought he had heard wrong. He sat up and looked at his brother. "Go away? Where?"

"Hell, I don't know. Anywhere out of this hick burg."

Kelly was stunned. Batman never left Robin. The Lone Ranger never left Tonto.

"Why you going?"

Weldon was still dividing the newspapers. He did not look up. "I had another run-in with Old Man Gyger. It was a doozie. They may go to Mom about it this time."

Gyger was the assistant principal at Weldon's school. His reputation had penetrated even the lower grades. He kept a big paddle behind his desk and used it often.

Kelly eased to the side of the bed. "What happened?"

Weldon snorted. "He tried to whip me. I got hold of the paddle and wouldn't let go. He had to call in another teacher. It took both of them to whip me. But I still got in a couple of good licks."

Kelly remained silent. He could not imagine being in so much trouble.

"Gyger sent a note to Old Man Penfold. Gyger told him I'm incorrigible."

"You're what?"

"I looked it up in the dictionary. It means 'incapable of being corrected, improved, or reformed.' I'm going to get even with that son of a bitch. But when I do, I may have to clear out of town for a while."

Kelly could not envision life without Weldon. "Can I go with you?"

Weldon sat on the bed beside him and put an arm around him. "I'd like to take you with me, sport. But I don't think it'd work. You look too young. The cops would pick us up, sure as hell. What I'm thinking, maybe I can send for you later, after I get set up somewhere. How'd that be?"

The idea was so far out of Kelly's realm of experience that he could not begin to evaluate it.

"How'll you live?"

"I'm almost thirteen. I can get a job."

Kelly was doubtful. But if any thirteen-year-old could, it would be Weldon.

"We might as well leave home," Weldon added. "It's sure as hell not getting any better."

That was true. Their mother had not been home in time for dinner the last three nights. Kelly had hardly seen her. She had promised a week ago to find out about the boy choir. So far he had heard nothing.

"You get along with her a lot better than I do," Weldon went on. "She isn't as rough on you."

That also was true. Weldon and his mother argued a lot.

"Something sure as hell's going on," Weldon said. "I don't know what. She was crying when she came home yesterday."

"Maybe she was still crying about Daddy."

"She didn't cry much when he died. Why would she now? I think they're giving her a hard time down at the company. Calla Lily took a tray up to her room last night. Calla told me not to bother her right now, that she is upset about a lot of things. What else could it be but the company?"

Kelly did not know. He could not think beyond the bombshell Weldon had dropped. "When are you leaving?"

"I don't know. I'll hang around until Ol' Gyger gets his. That's for sure. I wouldn't miss that for the world."

That evening their mother again missed dinner. But when Kelly finished, she was in the hall waiting for him. She put a hand on the top of his head. "I want to talk to you. Let's go into the library for a minute."

She sat beside him on the leather couch. Her eyes were red-rimmed. Somehow she seemed older, tired. She did not smile, as she usually did while talking to him.

"Kelly, I looked into the Texas Boys Choir. I'm afraid it would be far too difficult for you."

Again Kelly felt the frustration of being blocked in everything he tried to do. "Why?"

"It isn't just a choir, like the one at church. The boys in the Texas Boys Choir undergo years of hard training. It isn't something you would do on a whim."

"I know that," Kelly said, close to tears. "I told you it was different."

She gave him her long blank look that could mean anything.

"Kelly, you'd be expected to stay with it at least four years. Did you know that?"

"No," he admitted.

"If you were accepted on audition, you would train two full years with the preparatory choir before you would be accepted into the performing choir. Did you know that?"

"No."

"You would have to attend practice all day every Saturday, and a half day every Sunday. You would have to keep your grades up or they would kick you out. There would be room for nothing else in your life but the choir and schoolwork. Do you think you could do that?"

Kelly remembered the magic of the music he had heard. Marvelous phrases still ran through his head at odd moments. He felt he could endure anything to be a part of it. Besides, with Weldon going away, and his mother gone all the time, he would need something to keep occupied.

"Yes," he said.

"If you *are* accepted, and you *can* survive two years of training, you would spend much time on the road, performing. Do you think you could be away for weeks at a time, and not get homesick?"

With Weldon gone, and his mother always at the office, he would not be missing much.

"Yes."

His mother sighed. "All right. I'll arrange for you to audition. But remember that dozens, maybe hundreds of boys will be competing. So don't be too disappointed if you don't make it."

"Okay," Kelly said.

"And I want you to think very hard about how difficult it will be. This isn't an obligation you can accept, and then quit when the going gets tough. Other people will be depending on you. It will be *your* commitment, no one else's. You'll have to see it through. Do you understand that?"

Kelly nodded.

But he suddenly felt alone, abandoned. Weldon was going

away. Now his mother was telling him that he was on his own.

He wanted to ask her what was going on at the company, and why she came home so late every night. He wanted to tell her that Weldon was in bad trouble, and thinking of leaving. But she sat looking at him as if from a vast distance. She seemed remote, unreachable.

As if in a dream he remembered times when she had spent hours with him every day. She had hugged him, kissed him, held him. Now sometimes she put a hand to his cheek, or on top of his head, but that was all.

He wondered if this new, devastating sense of loneliness was a part of growing up.

Chapter 6

By the end of her second week at Spurlock Oil, Joanna knew she was in serious trouble. Everywhere she turned, she met resistance, even outright defiance.

Without consulting her, Piersall initiated an entirely new phase of drilling. She did not learn of it until after three rigs were spudded in and making hole.

Furious, she called him into her office. He remained more puzzled than concerned while she vented her anger.

He even appeared a bit amused. "Mrs. Spurlock, I didn't think you would be interested. This is the way we've always done it. Those offsets had to be drilled sometime, and the rigs were available." He shrugged. "If you're like my wife, you don't want to be bothered with the mechanics."

Joanna could hardly contain her fury. "To begin with, I'm *not* your wife. Those offsets could have waited. We hold a monopoly on that play. We need those rigs to prove out our leases in the Green Pool. Texaco is already at work there. Now they'll be pumping oil out from under us and there's nothing we can do about it."

Piersall's cavalier attitude was a prime example of the kind of independent thinking she was trying to corral. And no one would cooperate. Even smiling, easygoing Hollander ignored her warnings and obligated the company to a large shipment of gasoline without the slightest consideration of other Spurlock commitments.

Joanna found the completed contract on her desk. When she revealed her anger, Hollander reacted with total surprise.

"Mrs. Spurlock, I've been doing business with those people for years. We understand each other. When they want a shipment in a hurry, they appreciate the fact that we can close the deal on the phone."

"It's a pity you can't deliver it by phone," Joanna told him. "We have a major order to fill on the docks at Baytown. Our lines, our refinery are overloaded. If we meet your contract, some of that gasoline will have to be trucked or shipped by rail. That's needless, expensive, and wasteful. We won't make a dime on it. This erratic handling must stop!"

Her first interview with a department head was a disaster. Brod had speculated that the insecticide labs at the refinery, set up at government instigation during the war, might be revived to produce civilian products. Joanna was willing to try.

But when she introduced the subject, Walt Chambers immediately became incensed.

"Those bug people were nothing but trouble. Everybody hated them. We run an oil refinery down there, not a bug laboratory."

Joanna tried to reason with him. "Our waste products must be disposed of in some way. We might as well turn them into a profit, if we can."

He shook his head. "All the government scientists are gone. There's nobody left down there who knows anything about it."

"We can hire our own scientists," Joanna pointed out. "Let's at least do a feasibility study on it."

But Chambers turned stubborn. The discussion on the bug lab consumed most of their allocated hour. She never got

around to Brod's plan for sweeping changes in refinery operations—the original purpose of the meeting.

But her most infuriating moment came with Campbell.
One afternoon he buzzed and asked if he could see her for a
moment.

He arrived so ill at ease that Joanna was immediately on
her guard. Taking a chair in front of her desk, he began
hesitantly, and would not meet her gaze. She even wondered if he was about to resign.

"Mrs. Spurlock, as you may know, the executive washroom is down at the end of the hall."

Joanna did not answer. She waited.

Campbell shifted uncomfortably in his chair. "We've been
aware that no similar facilities exist for you. We've talked it
over, and we thought it might be a good idea to partition off
a portion of the ladies' room for you, Bonnie, and perhaps
some of the executive secretaries."

Joanna could hardly believe that her executives had speculated upon, and discussed, her most private functions.

She indeed had been aware of the problem from the first
day. She had already taken steps to solve it. But she certainly
had not intended for it to become a matter of general concern.

Again Joanna did not answer. She only stared at him.

The tips of Campbell's ears grew pink. "We thought it
might provide you with better accommodations."

Joanna carefully kept her voice under control. "Thank
you, but that will not be necessary. I've already arranged for
a private bath to be attached to this office."

Campbell's gaze flicked around the office, as if trying to
find a suitable place.

"I planned to send you a memo," Joanna said. "But I'll tell
you now. Please have the storage space on the other side of
that wall cleared out. The contractors will begin work next
week."

Campbell hesitated. "Mrs. Spurlock, that's a long way
from the plumbing mains. It's liable to be expensive."

"Not as far from the mains as the executive washroom,"

Joanna said. "I'm not asking for your approval, Mr. Campbell. I'm only telling you to have your staff clear out that area."

Campbell paled. He rose to his feet. "Yes, ma'am. I'll have it done."

He walked to the door, paused, and turned to face her. "Mrs. Spurlock, I hope you haven't taken offense. We were only thinking of more comfort for you and the girls."

Joanna's face must have conveyed her rage. Campbell beat a hasty retreat out the door.

As Joanna's frustration mounted, day by day, the migraine headaches she had suffered in college returned. She made herself go to work despite blurred vision, nausea, and pounding pain.

She easily could imagine what the men would speculate upon if she called in sick.

On the Friday afternoon at the end of her second week, she caught up with correspondence and decided to clean and update files. The office safe and a row of locked cabinets still contained Brod's prewar and wartime material. She now needed room for her own files.

After ordering storage boxes sent up from the basement, she began sorting and weeding out old papers. She was deep into the work, determining what should be saved, and what should be thrown out, when Bonnie buzzed and announced that Beth Runnels Gaspar was on the line.

Joanna remembered that Ann Leigh had suggested she talk with Beth. She assumed the call had been initiated by Ann Leigh. But when she picked up the phone, Beth set off on a completely different tack.

"Honey, I know you're busy, so I'll only take a minute. Have you attended any of our local opera productions?"

The question seemed so nonsensical that Joanna was momentarily confused. "I've read about them. I've regretted I haven't been able to go."

"Of course you couldn't, you poor child, what with Brod and all. Let me explain why I'm calling. Eloise Snyder and Betty Spain got us started in opera four seasons back with an

absolutely superb production of *La Traviata.* They brought
Eugene Conley down from the Met, and Walter Herbert
came up from New Orleans to conduct. Eloise sang Violetta
and Mel Dacus was Germont. It was perfectly marvelous.
Anyway, now we're building a permanent opera company.
We want you on our board."

Joanna was flattered—and a bit embarrassed. Perhaps a
mistake had been made. Her musical education had ended
with her junior year. A summer of dancing for Billy Rose
could hardly be regarded as proper credentials for grand
opera.

"Mrs. Gaspar, I'd be happy to serve. But I feel I should
warn you. My operatic experience is limited to a course or
two in college."

"That's more than most of us have. Eloise is our expert. We
can hire singers and conductors. What we need is support."

"Then I accept."

"Good. I'm so glad. I'll send you some material. It will
outline what we have in mind. How is everything going with
you?"

Joanna almost voiced a thoughtless platitude before recognizing the opening. She answered honestly. "Not too
well."

Beth was not thrown off stride. "Honey, what's wrong?"

"I'm finding this company more of a challenge than I'd
expected."

"That surprises me. I thought Spurlock Oil was in good
shape. And I know you're no dum-dum."

"Maybe not. But I've found that ability has little to do with
it. So far, I've been a disaster."

"Surely it's not that serious. What seems to be the difficulty?"

"Men."

Beth offered a significant sigh. "Oh, I see. Well, you've
hardly had time to get your feet wet. It'll probably work
out."

"All the same, I would be grateful if you could talk with

me about it. You're the only person I know who has experience in this area."

Beth laughed. "That I have. In spades." She remained silent for a moment and Joanna heard the rustle of a desk calendar. "Honey, why don't you come over to the house about two tomorrow? Gyorgy will be playing golf. We'll have the place to ourselves. We can have a drink or two and talk about it."

"I feel better already," Joanna said.

She returned to her work. Carefully she packed away Brod's pictures of herself and the boys, his gold pen set, his little working model of an oil rig. Digging into the files, she emptied the contents of each drawer and examined old contracts, receipts, letters, memos, and geological reports. Only a few seemed important enough to save. Most she threw away.

In the back of the safe, hidden behind an assortment of ledgers, she found a locked metal box. Searching through desk drawers, she was unable to find a key. But the latch yielded easily to a letter opener.

Inside the box were bound bundles of correspondence bearing postmarks dated through the years of Brod's service with the government.

Much of his wartime work had been top secret—construction of the Big Inch pipeline, and later the distribution of fuel to the military throughout the world, in preparation for the invasions. She opened the letters and scanned the contents to determine if they should be saved.

Most dealt with delivery of materials. Aside from a few letters of praise and congratulations from officials with recognizable names, the bulk of the correspondence was mundane. She set aside memos from Harry Hopkins, Harold Ickes, and President Franklin D. Roosevelt. The rest she discarded.

At the back of the box lay a small bundle of letters that aroused her curiosity. All were written by an Al Schippoletti of Bayonne, New Jersey. Each brief note in the bundle was couched in innuendo: "Concerning the situation we discussed, I have taken the steps you suggested"; "I have arranged matters as per our agreement, and there should be no further difficulties at your end," and "the people who were causing the delay have now been persuaded. You can expect their full cooperation from now on."

The name and address triggered a vague recollection. On a whim, Joanna replaced the bundle behind the ledgers and locked the safe.

That evening after dinner she went into the west wing of the house and climbed the narrow stairway into the attic. Digging through stacked boxes, she located the cartons of letters and get-well cards Brod had received early in his illness. Eventually she found the one she sought. She had remembered the envelope because it was the only one that had not drawn some comment of appreciation from Brod.

Seated on the floor of the attic, she read yet another brief, cryptic note from Al Schippoletti:

Dear Brod,
    Received the package. Surely you know I did not expect it. If it causes complications, I will return it immediately. I mean that. Get well.

                                    Your good friend,
                                    Al

Joanna spent several minutes puzzling over the note.
Package?
How could Brod have sent a package without her help? At that time he was confined to his bed, forbidden by his doctors from making the slightest exertion.
What was "it"?
How could "it" cause complications?
She studied the date of the postmark and felt a chill run up her spine.
Carrying the note, she returned to her bedroom. As she reread Al Schippoletti's words, the implications continued to mount. The innuendos began to make sense.

She vividly remembered the night Brod had sent her and the boys out to a movie, leaving him alone.

And within hours, Grover Sterling was dead, ostensibly in a mugging on Forty-second Street in New York City.

She had never asked Brod what he did that night, or why he wanted to be alone.

At the time, she had not wished to know.

Now, under the burden of her new responsibilities, perhaps she should discover if her worst suspicions were valid.

She was fully aware of the danger.

The knowledge might make her an accessory after the fact.

To murder.

The ramifications were enormous. She might have to deal with the knowledge that for fourteen years she had been married to a murderer. Her discoveries could affect her sons throughout their lives—and their children, and their children's children.

She might find out far more than she wanted to know.

But she could see no other course. She must be prepared for any eventuality.

On Monday she would begin a quiet investigation, and try to determine exactly what Brod did that night.

Beth led the way down a hall toward the back of the house, chatting as she went. "Honey, everybody thinks it's just wonderful the way you took such good care of Brod all that time. And now you've moved right into the oil company without missing a lick. You're a brave little thing."

Short and amply built, Beth possessed relentless energy and indefatigable optimism. Trailing in her wake, fully a head taller, Joanna felt small and childlike.

Beth had that effect on people.

"I'm not a bit brave," Joanna protested. "In fact, I'm scared to death. So far, I've made a mess of it."

"Oh, surely not! It just takes anyone a little time to get settled in."

They entered Beth's fabled back room. Although Joanna

had been a guest in the house several times, she knew of Beth's exclusive retreat only by hearsay. It was huge. Cathedral beams soared three stories above her head. Joanna felt further diminished. Beth directed her to a white couch covered with rainbow-hued throws.

Beth hired internationally known architects and decorators, then blended their work with her own tastes, often to their lasting chagrin. Her huge house was not only imposing; it also was comfortable and eye-appealing. She had built and still kept similar houses in Palm Springs and Cuernavaca, and maintained apartments or town houses in New York, London, Paris, and Rome. But she called Fort Worth home.

"What'll you have, honey?" Beth asked. "José can mix about anything. I'm having sour mash and branch water."

Joanna said sour mash whiskey would be fine.

While Beth summoned the houseboy, Joanna sought to come to terms with her surroundings. The decor was stark white—furniture, walls, the distant ceiling. The plain background highlighted islands of color throughout the room. Chinese screens, brilliant throw rugs, potted plants, vases, chairs, and sofas were all arranged in an eye-pleasing chromatic symphony. Beth's exuberant personality warmly encompassed the gymnasium-sized room and its contents—including two walls totally devoted to priceless art.

In other portions of the house, each individual painting was showcased—a superb Renoir here, a Van Gogh there, a Matisse or Corot over a fireplace. But here in Beth's private room, two soaring walls were covered by paintings and drawings with hardly an inch of space to spare. The mix was eclectic, and probably would have given most art connoisseurs nightmares. Vermeers rested frame to frame with Gainsboroughs, Pissarros with Gauguins. American art—Grant Wood, Cassatt, Eakins—rested beside the European masters. Here and there a sketch by Watteau or Boucher or Picasso broke the sea of color. Joanna recognized works by Derain, Delacroix, Vlaminck, Cézanne. There were others she could not identify. The walls were multimillion-dollar jigsaw puzzles.

The effect was overwhelming, yet inspiring. And despite the erratic nature of the collection, there was a cohesiveness.

Beth loved every one. She could buy Rembrandts or Renoirs the way most women bought hats. So there they were.

Each piece of art was bright, full of life. There were no gloomy Daumiers or Goyas.

The drinks arrived. Beth settled herself into an overstuffed chair. "Now. Tell me all about what's bothering you."

As Joanna began describing the details of her day-to-day troubles and setbacks, her qualms grew.

Beth Runnels Gaspar controlled one of the largest ranch-and-oil empires in Texas. She sat on the boards of national and international corporations. She was a director of national arts organizations. Surely she would consider the troubles of Spurlock Oil trivial indeed.

But Beth listened attentively to the end, then raised her hands in mock consternation. "Oh, honey! It's plain what you've done. Oh, my goodness! You've tromped all over their poor little egos. No wonder they're all up in arms against you."

"I did exactly what Brod told me to do," Joanna said. "I followed his instructions to the letter."

"Of course you did! And they would have taken it from Brod, and thought nothing of it. But you've put them into a situation they're not equipped to handle." She paused. "I don't think any permanent harm has been done. Brod, bless his soul, just didn't understand how it'd be for you. You see, if Brod had done those things, everyone would have thought it perfectly wonderful. But a woman! Now, that's something different. My goodness, they have to go home at night and face wives who know they've been bossed around all day by another woman. It's demeaning for the wives, and it's hell for the men."

"What can I do about it?"

"You just go ahead and do the very same things, but in a different way. Lord, it took me long enough to learn. I made the mistake of marrying three Texans in a row. It didn't even occur to me I might have more money. They were all comfortably well off. And like Sid Richardson says, after the first hundred million, what the hell? But you know something? The fact that I had more money seemed to diminish them. Every time I was on the phone talking business, or left town for a board meeting, I'd see it in their eyes. And it did something to them in the sack! Honest!"

Joanna was a bit jolted.

She had heard frankness was a hazard one must accept with Beth.

"My fourth was a Californian," Beth went on. "An actor. Talk about irony: He married me for my money, then couldn't live with it. I was beginning to think I'd have to declare myself a pauper before I would find happiness with any man."

Joanna remembered reading about the actor. According to the Hollywood scandal sheets, it had been a stormy marriage.

"That's why Gyorgy is so precious. Gyorgy has been an impoverished aristocrat all his life. In his neck of the woods, aristocrats are a national treasure, to be pampered and taken care of. I know people say he married me for my money, but the truth is that money never once entered his sweet head. To his way of thinking, one of his poems is worth more than all the oil in Texas."

Joanna laughed. For the last five years Beth had been married to a Hungarian count, a war refugee who had cut a wide swath through Manhattan society before Beth snared him. Tall, distinguished, and charming, he immediately had become a favorite among Fort Worth hostesses.

The whole community had been amused when, in a listing of civic leaders in the Fort Worth *Star-Telegram*, Gyorgy had given his occupation as "poet."

Beth frowned, as if searching for the right words. "Honey, in every business situation you have to consider a man's self-esteem. Lord, the mistakes I made before I learned that! I would hand them a flat-assed ultimatum: You do this or I'll do that. To me it was just business. But to them it was pure ego. Some of them knuckled under. Some stalked out. And they all hated my guts. I couldn't understand it."

Joanna smiled in appreciation. Beth's analysis fit her own situation exactly.

"The trick is, don't *tell* your men to do things. *Ask* them if it wouldn't be better to do it this way, instead of that way. You don't have to be a clinging vine. Just give their precious egos room to operate. Appeal to their sense of chivalry. Every Texas male is born to it. Take them into your confidence—or let them think so—and say, 'Brod wanted me to do this. What would be the best way?' If the answer isn't the right one, you can suggest the proper alternative. Let the man make his own decision. I know all this is stupid. But it works."

"I see your point," Joanna said. "I can see why I've made a shambles of everything."

"Oh, honey, you've done nothing that can't be fixed. But it's an ongoing problem. You'll never be rid of the man-woman thing entirely. About the time you think you have it all squared away, it'll blow up again, right in your face."

"This is new to me," Joanna said. "I can't remember ever damaging Brod's ego."

Beth chortled. "You probably couldn't have dented Brod's ego with a stick of dynamite. Every Spurlock man seems to come equipped with a solid sense of his own worth. Brod was a chip off the old block. Did you know his daddy?"

Beth was known as an uninhibited gossip. Joanna had an uneasy premonition she was about to be told something she might not want to hear. "No," she answered cautiously. "He was killed the summer Brod and I met."

"Now there was a man! Handsome as could be! And he had a go-to-hell way about him that drove women crazy. He left bastard children all over the oil patch, you know. Just walked in and took whatever he wanted. Complete self-confidence. Take the way he died. When that oil well blew out, all the other men ran away from it. But Clay ran toward it. He actually thought he could cap it all by himself!"

Joanna had heard every detail. The blowout of gas from

deep within the earth had ignited like a giant torch, incinerating Clay, the rig, everything.

"And there's that priceless story about the way he married Ann Leigh. That was so typical. But I guess you know all about that."

Joanna knew only that for years Ann Leigh had been a virtual recluse. She had heard veiled references to some scandal in her past. But Brod had never talked about it.

"I've never heard the whole story," she said.

The answer seemed to bring Beth up short. She looked at Joanna for a moment, then seemed to make a decision. "Well, considering how long you've been a Spurlock, you're certainly entitled to hear it if anyone is. It isn't as if I were gossiping. Really, these are things you should know, if you are to live in this town. Old secrets have a long life here. And they're the warp and woof of what passes for society in Texas. If you don't know, you're apt to find yourself knee-deep in some awkward situation someday before you realize it."

She sipped her drink, frowning in search of memory. "To start with, I guess you know that Ann Leigh was first married to another man. He was from one of the packing plant families. It wasn't a happy marriage by any means. But Ann Leigh stayed with him through two or three years. Then at a New Year's Eve dance, with half the town watching, Clay beat her husband to a pulp and carried her off. Just like a caveman. Honest! I was there! It was my first grown-up dance. I saw the whole thing. The town could talk of nothing else for weeks."

She laughed. "Clay and Ann Leigh set up housekeeping in sin, right in front of God and everybody, and that was considered much more terrible in those days than it seems to be now. Clay spent a fortune for her divorce, and to keep the whole mess out of the courts."

Joanna had not even known that Ann Leigh had had a previous marriage. Brod had never mentioned it.

She wondered if *he* had known.

"Of course, it all turned out fine, as far as those things go.

Ann Leigh and Clay had three wonderful children. Well, two wonderful children, I guess. Crystelle was always a stinker. But I suppose you know all about that."

Joanna nodded. She was sure she did not know half the stories about Crystelle, but she knew enough.

Beth shrugged. "Ann Leigh was never able to live with the scandal. What she did was not her nature at all. But with Clay Spurlock chasing her, what was the poor girl to do? God, he was a devil!"

Joanna had seen photographs of him. The resemblance to Brod was uncanny.

"And speaking of handsome devils, I hear Gyorgy's car in the drive," Beth said.

A moment later he entered the room. He was decked out in natty gray plus fours and a cashmere pullover. When he saw Joanna, he swept off his tam-o'-shanter. "What is this? I spend the whole afternoon chasing a little white ball, and two beautiful women are having a party in my home without me."

His English was heavily accented, but pleasant to the ear. He leaned to kiss Joanna's hand.

"You wouldn't have been interested, honey," Beth said. "It was girl talk—about our difficulties with men."

Gyorgy's eyebrows soared in mock disbelief. "If I thought either of you ever had a moment's difficulty in making any man do your wishes, I would faint from the shock." He kissed Beth's hand and then stood holding it in both his own. "What are we drinking, love?"

"Jack Daniel's. Why don't you fetch us another and join us?" She beamed at Joanna, as if saying *See what I told you?*

"I really should be going," Joanna said.

"Stay for one drink," Gyorgy begged. "You must hear my new poem. I will give a special reading for a lovely lady."

Beth nodded meaningfully to Joanna, encouraging her.

"I would love to hear the poem," Joanna said.

Gyorgy went away to fetch the drinks.

"What are you doing at the office about lunch?" Beth asked.

That was a minor problem Joanna had not even intended to mention. She laughed. "Doing without, mostly."

"Oh, honey! At least send someone out to get you a sandwich. You're paying them good money. Or better yet, find a caterer. Lord, I remember starving while the men went off to their male preserves—the Men's Grill at the Fort Worth Club, Kiwanis, Rotary, Lions, or whatever. It was either that, brown-bag, mingle with the bridge ladies at the country clubs, dine alone at some restaurant, or battle the lines at a cafeteria. I may write a book on working with men."

"You should," Joanna said.

"Maybe someday there'll be mixed camaraderie in offices. But don't hold your breath."

Gyorgy returned with the drinks. Joanna became engrossed in his elaborate preparation for reading the poem. Notebook in hand, he painstakingly arranged two floor lamps so the light fell just so. He polished his reading glasses and rearranged them on his nose, making readjustments until he was satisfied. Only then did he begin to read with an arresting intensity.

The exact wording was lost amid his machine-gun *r*'s, the explosions of terminal consonants, and hopeless modifications of English vowels. But the essential meaning came through: One should remain true to one's inner voices, no matter how adverse the circumstances.

When he had finished, Joanna and Beth applauded.

"Thank you. Thank you." Gyorgy waved his notebook. "It is a pitiful effort. I do not yet have enough English words. Someday I will be able to say in English what I feel in my Hungarian heart. Then I shall write truly beautiful poems."

Joanna felt uncommon praise was required. "Your poem *is* beautiful. But I believe thoughts transcend the limitations of words in *any* language. It is the soul of the poem that contains the jewel."

Gyorgy leaped for her hand. "You are so right! So right! You see! I loved my country. But when terrible things began to happen, and disgusting ideas filled the air, I could not live there any longer! I could not breathe! I had to get away!"

"Europe's loss is our gain," Joanna said. "I heard someone say recently that you are already one hundred percent Texan."

The remark pleased Gyorgy immensely. He bubbled with delight. "There was a Hungarian at the Alamo. Did you know that?"

On the way home, Joanna thought back over Beth's advice. It seemed logical. She could not understand why she had not thought of it herself.

But the truth was, her experience with men was extremely limited. In her dating throughout high school and college, she had always managed to keep relationships on a superficial level. At the first hint of intimacy, she shied away, assuming that such closeness still lay far in the future. During the wonderful summer of the Texas Centennial celebration, she had run around with other dancers and musicians, but as a "gang."

There had been no one close. Not until Brod.

He had been her one experience with intimacy. But he had possessed depths he never revealed, not even to her. She had known that he kept a part of himself secret.

Now she knew it more than ever.

Perhaps, if there had been time, they might have grown closer. He might have shared those secrets with her.

Now she would never know.

Her visit with Beth and Gyorgy had left her deeply disturbed. The interplay between the couple had been so natural and intimate that she had felt an intruder.

Joanna was forced to consider the sudden emotional poverty of her own life, raising two sons alone, battling to preserve an oil company for them.

She found herself envying Beth, not for her wealth, but for her happiness with Gyorgy.

Joanna wondered if she would ever find such perfect rapport with anyone.

Chapter 7

Joanna went into the office early on Monday morning and made it downstairs to the bookkeeping department before anyone else arrived. After a search through old disbursement ledgers, she found an entry that would have escaped notice if she had not been looking for the telltale date:

$75,000 cash, Mr. Spurlock

The withdrawal had been initialed by Arnold Campbell.

She took the ledger back to her office and sat with it for some time, still debating how far she wanted to take her impromptu investigation.

Again she concluded that her own wishes were immaterial.

As president of Spurlock Oil, she *had* to know.

A few minutes after nine, she called Campbell and asked him to step into her office.

His usual morning cheerfulness vanished the moment he saw the ledger on her desk.

Keeping Beth's advice clearly in mind, Joanna softened her tone, and her words. "Mr. Campbell, I wonder if you could help me. This morning I came across an entry in this ledger. Seventy-five thousand is an unusual transaction in cash, isn't it?"

Campbell sank onto a chair. "Mrs. Spurlock, I have a voucher for that money, signed by your husband. It's in my safe, if you wish to see it."

"Please understand, Mr. Campbell, I'm certainly not questioning the withdrawal. I'm only trying to reconstruct how it came about. I wonder if you could help me by remembering the exact sequence of events that day, step by step."

Campbell bit his lower lip. "Yes, ma'am, I do remember. As you say, it was unusual." He paused, frowning. "As I recall, Mr. Spurlock phoned me just as I returned from lunch. A little after one o'clock, I believe. He asked me to draw seventy-five thousand dollars in nonsequential hundred-dollar notes from the bank, to place them in a sturdy box, and to bring it to your house that evening just after dark. Now that I think about it, I'm certain of the time, because I had to rush right over to the bank before it closed at two. I brought the money back here and kept it in my office through the afternoon. About seven, I took it to your house and gave it to Mr. Spurlock."

That was the same evening Brod had insisted that she take the children out to a movie. She wondered if Brod had brought anyone else in on his project.

"Was anyone else there? Did anyone see you come and go?"

"No. I remember I was surprised to find Mr. Spurlock alone, considering how ill he had been. He thanked me for my trouble, and gave me a receipt. I've retained it, in case there were ever any questions."

"Have there been?"

"Not at all. The withdrawal wouldn't attract notice among routine expenses, except for the fact that it was in cash."

"Did Mr. Spurlock offer any reason for wanting the money?"

"No, ma'am."

"Has there been any speculation?"

Campbell was sharp enough to know what she was asking. "Mrs. Spurlock, I think you'll find the people in bookkeeping very discreet. As for myself, I certainly saw no reason to question the right of the president of this company to draw cash. I don't recall, but I probably assumed that it was in connection with Mr. Loren's funeral expenses."

Joanna almost smiled. That was a good try. But Campbell's nervousness gave him away.

He had lived with the burden for five years. She was in his debt.

"Well, it's probably of no consequence," she said. "I was curious, because Mr. Spurlock usually kept me informed on everything concerning the company. He may have mentioned that transaction, and it slipped my mind."

"I would be happy to give you the receipt."

Their gazes met as they shared the same unspoken thought.

If Brod had lived, the receipt could have become essential evidence in a murder-for-hire trial.

And it still posed a hazard.

"No, you've kept it this long. My husband valued your confidence. So do I."

Campbell rose and walked toward the door. He stopped and turned back to face her. "Mrs. Spurlock, I worked closely with Mr. Loren when he first joined the company. I admired him, and considered him my friend. I was really looking forward to the time when he and your husband returned to resume management of this company. I've always regretted that didn't happen."

Joanna understood Campbell's implied message. He was informing her that his loyalties had always been with the family, never with Grover Sterling.

"I appreciate your saying that, Mr. Campbell. Those were terrible times. I'm glad they're behind us. And I thank you for your help."

Campbell gave her a brief nod. "I'm glad to have been of service."

Late that afternoon Joanna took legal papers involving

Brod's estate to Ann Leigh for her signature. As she left Ann Leigh's house, Henry was in the driveway polishing the car. Joanna seized the opportunity to speak with him in private.

"Henry, I want to ask you an important question. Do you remember mailing a package for Mr. Brod, not long after his first heart attack?"

Henry ducked his head, apparently pondering the violation of a confidence. He spoke hesitantly. "Yes, ma'am. I believe I do recollect something about that."

"Do you remember where it was sent?"

"Not exactly. It was to a man with a funny name. That's about all I recollect."

"Schippoletti?"

"Might have been that. It was something like that."

"How did Mr. Brod send it? Henry, anything at all you can remember about that day will help me a great deal."

The direct plea brought results. Henry wrinkled his brow in an effort to remember. "Well, I recollect that Mr. Brod sent word that he wanted me to telephone him. When I did, he said he had an errand for me, to come over to his house about eight o'clock. And when I got there, he had a package, about so big. He said I was to send it off as soon as the post office opened the next morning."

"How was it wrapped?"

"Just some ol' brown paper and cord. He inked in the place it was going. I didn't study on it. He gave me twenty dollars and told me to keep the change for my trouble. Next morning I took it to the post office and sent it right off." Henry paused for a moment. "That's about all I recollect."

"Henry, you've helped me a great deal," she told him. "I would appreciate it if you didn't mention this to anyone."

Henry solemnly shook his head. From his manner, Joanna suddenly understood that he had long harbored his own suspicions. "No, ma'am. I've never told *nobody*. Except you just now. I never will."

The next afternoon Joanna placed a person-to-person call to Mr. Al Schippoletti in New Jersey. On the open line she heard the operator ring a residence and receive an office

number. At the place of business, the operator encountered
a solid wall of resistance until she revealed that Mrs. Brod
Spurlock was calling.

The name apparently worked wonders. After a moment,
Joanna was put straight through.

Schippoletti's voice was deep and masculine. His speech
contained only a slight accent. "This is Al Schippoletti, Mrs.
Spurlock. What can I do for you?"

"Mr. Schippoletti, my husband died recently. In clearing
up his papers, I came across your name. Did you know him?"

The line was silent for such a long interval that Joanna
began to think Schippoletti might not answer. But when he
spoke, his voice had lost none of its strength. "Mrs. Spurlock,
your husband was one of my best friends. When I read in the
newspapers that he had died, I couldn't have felt worse if it
had been my own brother."

This mystified Joanna even more. "I'm hoping you can
give me some information. I recently found correspondence
indicating that Brod sent you a package several years ago. I
conceivably may have to account for its contents. Could you
possibly tell me the circumstances?"

Again the line was silent for a time. Schippoletti's voice
assumed a more pleasant tone. "Mrs. Spurlock, your husband and I worked closely together during the war. He did
many valuable favors for me. When the opportunity arose
for me to return his kindness with a small favor, I was happy
to do so. I tried to talk him out of sending that package. I
warned him it might complicate matters. But he insisted. If
it has caused an awkward situation for you, I'll be happy to
return it immediately."

"No, please don't. I'm sure Brod did the right thing. I'm
really not questioning that. I just feel I should be prepared
for any eventuality."

"A very wise precaution. I'm sure Brod didn't intend to
leave problems behind for you—or anyone—to worry about.
I'm sure you can go ahead and dispose of any old papers you
may have found."

Joanna understood he was telling her to destroy the notes.

"I'll do that. I thank you for your time and understanding. I'm sorry to have bothered you with this."

"No bother at all. In fact, if any questions should come up, don't hesitate to call. I remain deeply in Brod's debt."

After breaking the connection, Joanna sat for a time going back over the conversation, analyzing its significance.

Schippoletti had stopped just short of confirming her worst fears.

She was now almost certain that Brod had been involved, in some way, with Grover Sterling's death.

Uneasily, she concluded she could not live with the uncertainty of where she stood, legally.

She now knew too much—and suspected more.

If she tampered with the evidence, conceivably she could become an accessory after the fact.

Doubt no longer existed: she needed legal advice.

Retrieving Brod's black notebook from the bottom drawer of her desk, she turned to the back, where he had listed people to consult should she ever run into serious trouble.

She called and made an appointment.

Throughout the remainder of the afternoon she tried to put the matter out of her mind. She attempted to concentrate for a while on Piersall's proposed new exploration program. But when she reached the last page, much of it still failed to make sense. She had just started again at the beginning when Bonnie buzzed to inform her that the principal of Weldon's school was on the line.

Joanna panicked, imagining some horrible accident. Heart pounding, she picked up the phone. Her voice must have conveyed her alarm.

"Mrs. Spurlock? If I've frightened you, I apologize. This is Marvin Penfold. I'm only calling because we've had some new problems with Weldon. They're a bit more serious this time. I think we should talk about them."

Joanna had not yet recovered from her scare. She made an effort to speak calmly. "How serious?"

"Well, it's rather involved. But basically, it seems Weldon

has forced some of his fellow pupils to wager with professional gamblers."

"Forced?"

"As I understand it, a few may have participated voluntarily. But others claim they were threatened with a beating if they didn't fork over money for a gambling pool."

Joanna opened her mouth to say that neither of her children would do such a thing. But a more rational thought intruded.

Weldon might be capable of it.

"Naturally, my first concern is for Weldon's welfare, and for that of the other students," Penfold went on. "But now the police are involved, so my role is somewhat limited."

Joanna felt her heart skip a beat. "Police?"

"Yes, ma'am. Both detectives and juvenile officers have been here, questioning the students."

Joanna fought down a rush of anger. "Mr. Penfold, if Weldon *is* involved, why haven't the police contacted *me*? Have they been questioning my son, without informing me? Is that legal?"

"I don't know, Mrs. Spurlock. That's between you and the police. I thought they would've contacted you by now. I understand they're taking it very seriously. Weldon's winnings last weekend amounted to more than five hundred dollars."

"Did you say five hundred?"

"Yes, ma'am. But the gambling is a police matter. My concern is for discipline here at the school. If you could come by my office in the next day or two, I'd like to talk with you about Weldon."

Joanna thought ahead to the humiliation of entering the principal's office like a negligent parent. She felt she should not defer to the man, even if Weldon was in the wrong.

"Mr. Penfold, I don't think this should wait a single day. I realize the inconvenience, but if you could come to my home this evening, say about six, perhaps we could discuss this at length, with more privacy. I promise my complete cooperation."

"No inconvenience. Six would be most satisfactory."

After replacing the receiver, Joanna sat at her desk appalled.

Five hundred dollars!

She was sure most of the children carried little more than lunch money to school.

How could Weldon have compiled five hundred dollars?

How had he known where to place the bets?

And where had he gained the expertise to win—against professional gamblers?

She phoned the police station and was put through to the Juvenile Division and a Sergeant Coker. Joanna explained the reason for her call.

"Yes, ma'am, I can appreciate your concern. But the fact is, we're still investigating that matter, Mrs. Spurlock. We just haven't gotten around to calling you yet."

"Have you questioned my son without calling me? Is that your normal procedure?"

Coker hesitated. "Mrs. Spurlock, I can't say for sure, but I don't think formal charges will be filed against your son, since it's his first offense and all. Of course we'll be wanting to talk to you, to see if we can't get the boy straightened out. But right now we're much more interested in building a case against the adults involved."

"I can appreciate that," Joanna said. "And you can be assured that I want to talk to you."

She hung up the phone in anger. Briefly she considered calling the mayor, but decided against it.

Perhaps she should determine the full extent of Weldon's involvement before she became too vocal.

That evening she said nothing at dinner about Penfold's call. But as soon as the boys finished eating, she sent them up to their rooms.

When Penfold arrived, she led him into the library and closed the doors.

He seemed ill at ease. Joanna offered him a cup of coffee or a cold drink, but he declined. He sat on the edge of the couch, leaning forward, elbows braced against knees. He was a large man, with a florid face and athletic build gone pudgy. Joanna remembered that he was a former football coach.

"Mrs. Spurlock, we just *never* have this kind of trouble at the school," he said. "I hope you understand my position."

"I believe I do."

"The truth is, Weldon has been a growing problem throughout this school term. I've been very aware of his situation at home—your husband's illness, your recent loss. I've been reluctant to trouble you."

"I certainly appreciate your consideration."

"But during the last three or four months, hardly a week has gone by that at least one of Weldon's escapades hasn't been brought to my attention. I'm not talking about pranks, what one might expect from an active youngster. I'll give you some examples. When another boy refused to lend Weldon a ruler, the contents of the boy's desk later were found stuffed into the commodes. Weldon denied doing it, and no one saw him do it. There was no action I could take."

Joanna remained silent, but her resentment was building. Apparently there was no proof.

"That's always the way it is," Penfold continued. "One day a teacher reprimanded Weldon for talking in class. That very afternoon the teacher's purse disappeared. Vanished into thin air. Car keys, driver's license, a small amount of money. Just the other day, while I was away in Austin for a school conference, my assistant, Mr. Gyger, paddled Weldon for fighting. Weldon had shoved another boy down the front steps. The boy was only bruised, but it could have been more serious. Weldon resisted the paddling, and another teacher had to be called in to help subdue him. Both teachers were bruised in the scuffle. The next week, some shotgun shells— we don't know exactly how many—were shoved up the tail pipe of Mr. Gyger's car. Heat from the exhaust caused them to explode. Fortunately, neither Mr. Gyger nor his wife was injured. But the muffler of the car was blown apart, and some damage was done to the valves in the engine. The repairs will be expensive. Mrs. Spurlock, I must be blunt.

Everyone at school is afraid of Weldon, including the teachers."

Joanna felt her anger growing. A paddling without parents being informed?

Was that done?

And Penfold still had offered no direct evidence.

"Mr. Penfold, how do you know it was Weldon?"

"I don't. Not for certain. Nothing except the gambling.
But Weldon has a way of letting you know—a self-satisfied
smile—even while he's denying everything right to your
face."

Joanna did not respond. She had seen that same smile.
And she had noticed—even been amused by—the tough-
guy Jimmy Cagney stance Weldon had adopted. She had
assumed it to be a phase he would outgrow. Now she could
see she might be wrong.

Penfold rambled on. "Most of the teachers consider Weldon highly intelligent. His gambling operation was very
elaborate. The way it was explained to me, he had devised
his own system, using combinations to protect him against
serious loss. He manages passing grades without cracking a
book. It's a shame his abilities have not been directed toward
more constructive channels. I must confess that I consider
this my failure."

And perhaps mine, Joanna thought.

"Mrs. Spurlock, I'm not here to make a case for or against
Weldon. The juvenile officers haven't yet completed their
investigation. But it's now clear that Weldon forced at least
some of the other boys into it. He was charging them half of
the profits for his expertise. So he plainly was the ringleader.
That alone is enough for me to suspend him from school
until the matter is resolved. Certainly, I'll be required to
take *some* action. But as I said, my concern is for Weldon,
and for the other students. In telling you of the other inci-
dents, I'm only being frank. Every teacher has had trouble
with Weldon. The gambling only brought it all together. It
has created a situation we must deal with."

Joanna thought she understood where Penfold was

headed. She wanted to get on with it. "What do you plan to do?"

"At the moment, I don't know. I'm hoping I won't be forced into taking formal action. I'm hoping that maybe we can come to a mutually agreeable solution, privately. That's why I agreed to come here tonight. I would deeply regret following the normal procedure, which undoubtedly would result in suspension, or more probably expulsion. But unless we can find an alternative, that seems to be my only course."

Joanna fully understood that they were playing poker with Weldon's future. She felt she should make the issue plain. "Let me understand. What you are saying is, you want me to take him out of school so he won't be a blot on your school's record."

"Mrs. Spurlock, I'm also thinking of Weldon. Suspension or expulsion would seem rather harsh for a boy his age. It would remain on his record for all time. I'm reluctant to admit defeat. But I sincerely feel we've done our best with him. Obviously it hasn't been enough. He needs more attention—more discipline—than we can give him."

He waited. Joanna admired the man's tactics. From the moment he arrived, he had been gently pushing her into accepting the inevitable.

"I gather you're suggesting that I send him to a military school, or something of that nature."

"Of the alternatives, I believe that would be most feasible."

"Mr. Penfold, after our conversation this afternoon, I talked with the juvenile officers. They told me Weldon will be treated as a first offender, that no charges will be filed against him."

"I'm glad to hear that. But it doesn't remove my responsibilities. Fifteen boys were participating in Weldon's gambling ring. Weldon either led or forced every one of them into it. I must give the parents of those boys some answer. So I'm hoping you and I can come to a mutual solution."

"Are you insisting that I act immediately?"

Penfold hedged. "I believe we could delay the matter a few days. But not long. Not beyond the end of next week."

"At this point, I don't know what I'll do. I'll have to talk to Weldon, examine what options I have. I'll call you as soon as I make my decision."

Penfold seemed satisfied. He left, promising to help her in finding a suitable school.

Later that evening, as Joanna prepared for bed, she was struck by a vague memory. Pulling on a robe, she again went into the west wing and climbed the stairway to the attic.

Brod's guns were still secure in the glass-front case she had moved out of his den while the boys were toddlers. Just to be sure, she counted them—five shotguns of various gauges, and four rifles of different calibers. Then she noticed faint scratches on the wood at the bottom of the case.

Someone had tampered with the ammunition drawer.

Kneeling, she tugged experimentally on the handle. The drawer opened.

Inside, she found three boxes of twelve-gauge shotgun cartridges. Each carton was only partially filled. That in itself was not an indictment. The shotguns had last been used by Brod and Loren on a quail-hunting trip to the family ranch in Shackelford County before the war. The ammunition, now more than a decade old, was the remnant of that outing. She had no way of knowing how many cartridges had remained unused.

But the latch on the drawer had been broken. The perpetrator plainly had been after the ammunition, not the guns.

Joanna returned to her room and went to bed. She lay awake, thinking back over the years, wondering how she could have gained more rapport with her sons.

She did not need to consult a psychiatrist to understand Weldon's acts of rebellion. He had been denied attention through his most crucial years. She could even imagine a psychiatrist's condescension in explaining the simple facts: Weldon had been old enough to remember the thrill of his father's company, the warmth of his mother's undivided devotion when he was younger.

And that devotion *had* existed. She remembered the intense pleasure of nursing him, her feelings of intimacy and sublime love in tending to him as a baby.

Then, with the war, Weldon's comfortable world had fallen apart. While still a toddler, he had been told that someday his father would return, that all would be set right again.

But that day never came. His father had returned an invalid.

Moreover, his father's illness also had taken away the soothing presence of his mother.

Joanna recognized her own failure.

Somewhere along the way something had slipped, and she had lost the knack of mothering. She had dealt superbly with her sons as babies. But as they had grown older, and acquired personalities, she had been forced to turn her attention elsewhere, and she had lost touch with them.

Yet she could not see how she could have spent more time with them, with Brod constantly at death's door. For the most part, he had rejected professional care and depended upon her for his every need.

Now there was a limit to what she could accomplish alone.

Perhaps Ann Leigh was right. Maybe Brod had expected more of her than she could deliver, raising two sons, running an oil company.

Somewhere in his notebook, Brod had advised that when she became overloaded with burdens, she should narrow the field, and concentrate on the most important.

Perhaps it was time for her to establish priorities.

Brod's first consideration had been for the boys' inheritance, the oil company.

He had believed that his own virtually fatherless boyhood had tended to make him tougher, more independent. He had assumed the effect would be the same for his sons.

"Don't coddle them," he had warned her many times. "Too much mothering is worse than too little."

Against her every instinct, she had accepted that philosophy.

Now she had to consider the possibility that Brod had been wrong.

She remained awake most of the night, trying to find some way to spend more time with the boys, and still fulfill all that was expected of her at the oil company.

Toward morning, she came face-to-face with a chilling thought:

If Weldon were committing such acts at twelve, what might he be doing in another five or ten years?

She whispered into the darkness. "Brod, tell me what to do. I can't handle this alone."

She heard no response in the silence of the bedroom.

Chapter 8

The audition had been not at all what Kelly expected. He was asked a few questions, sang "America" and "Danny Boy," and that was that. A week later he received a callback. He again sang, and was asked to imitate piano phrases with his voice. It was easy to do. The man conducting the audition thanked him, and said they would let him know.

Thus far he had heard nothing more.

On the day after the gambling raid, Kelly again ran all the way home, hoping the postman had brought something from the Boys Choir. But he searched through the stack of mail on the table in the foyer and found nothing.

Immediately his hope shifted to the possibility that the choir directors had called his mother at the office.

He hurried on upstairs to talk to Weldon. Some of the kids at school said that Weldon might have to go to jail. Kelly did not believe them.

However, he fully understood that the situation was serious. All day he had found himself the center of unaccustomed notoriety. Even the teachers were looking at him strangely.

The Fort Worth *Star-Telegram* said on page one that four

adults had been arrested, and that sixteen pupils were involved. None of the students was named, but everybody at school knew the gambling had been Weldon's idea.

Old Man Penfold had been quoted in the newspaper as saying that appropriate disciplinary action would be taken.

Kelly found Weldon lying across his bed, fully dressed, staring at the ceiling. Weldon did not bother to turn his head. "Mom home yet?"

Kelly sank into a chair facing the bed. "No."

"Well, you can get ready for another lecture. The shit has hit the fan for sure. Old Man Penfold was out here last night."

Kelly found that news even more incredible than what had happened at school. "Penfold here? How do you know?"

"Hell, I saw him drive up and come into the house. Mom took him into the library. I sneaked down and listened. But I didn't hear much."

"Does she know I was in on it?"

"If she does, she didn't get it from me. I'm no squealer. The cops grilled me for two hours. I didn't tell them a damned thing."

Sometimes Weldon cast himself in movie roles. Kelly was never certain how much his stories were exaggerated for effect.

"What about the money?"

"The cops got it. That's what." Weldon rubbed his eyes. "I ought to light a shuck out of this hick town. But I can't. Now I'm flat broke."

"I still have a dollar and thirty-six cents."

Weldon snorted. "That wouldn't get me to the edge of town." He hit the bed with a fist. "Shit! Next weekend our stake would have gone to a thousand or more. And half of it would've been mine!"

Kelly felt that Weldon was right. Somehow, it did not seem fair that the cops should keep the money, especially after Weldon worked so hard for it.

"Will you have to go to jail?"

"Nah, I don't think so. But Old Man Penfold told Mom he's

expelling me from school. She's going to send me off to a military school someplace."

That was the worst news yet. "Where?"

"How in hell would I know. Nobody tells me anything. Somewhere in China, probably."

Again Kelly tried to envision life without Weldon. The house would be an even lonelier place.

"Maybe we can write to each other," he said.

"Maybe. If I'm not too busy marching with rifles and all that shit. We'll see."

They heard their mother's car in the drive. As Weldon had predicted, she was early. Kelly scooted back to his room.

Nothing was said at dinner. If it had not been for Calla Lily looking at them, shaking her head and making her clucking noises of disapproval, all would have seemed normal.

But after dinner their mother again summoned them into the library.

The corners of her mouth were compressed and her eyes were red-rimmed. She sat and looked at them for a time in silence. When she spoke, her voice was low and hoarse.

"Boys, do you remember that when your father died, I told you it meant you would have to assume more responsibility?"

Kelly and Weldon nodded.

"I told you the company would demand a lot of my attention, and that you would have to look after yourselves more. Do you remember that?"

Again they nodded.

Kelly had never seen her so solemn. He glanced at Weldon.

For once Weldon also seemed subdued.

"I'm so disappointed in both of you. I've spent most of the last two days talking with Mr. Penfold, the police, and your teachers. I think I have the full story. But before I say anything, I want to hear it from you."

Kelly again glanced at Weldon, who was staring at the floor.

"Kelly, I was shocked to find your name on the list of

gamblers. According to the police, you bet forty-five dollars last weekend. Where did you get it? Have you been stealing from my purse?"

Kelly was shocked almost speechless. "No!" he managed to say.

"Then where?"

After the accusation, the truth came surprisingly easy. "The silver dollars Aunt Zetta gave me."

"That was only four or five dollars."

"He won the rest," Weldon said.

"I see. Well, I hope you learned something, Kelly. What you were doing was wrong. You've squandered your keepsakes. Now you have nothing. You've also gained a reputation at school. People probably will remember this escapade as being committed by the Spurlock brothers. How do you feel about that?"

Kelly did not answer. In truth, he was not as chastened by the thought as he knew he should be.

"Aw, Mom, it was only a football parlay," Weldon said. "Everybody does it."

"Not everybody. Certainly not schoolchildren."

"You gamble at the company. I've heard Dad say every oil well is a big gamble."

"That's not the same."

"Why not?"

"Because it's not. The money we put into an oil well is an investment. We find oil that people need. Gambling is not only illegal, it's also nonproductive."

"It is too," Weldon said. "I was making money. If they'd left us alone, we would've cleaned up."

Weldon and his mother locked gazes for a long moment. Kelly wished he were elsewhere.

"Weldon, don't be impertinent. You're old enough to know the difference. I really don't know what I'm going to do with you. I was horrified by what Mr. Penfold told me about your conduct at school. How could you possibly do such things?"

Weldon shrugged. "Everything that happens, they blame on me."

"Are you saying you didn't organize the gambling ring? Force other boys into it?"

Weldon put on his Jimmy Cagney face. "Mom, I just set up a deal so they could make money. I only charged them half of what we made. What was wrong with that?"

"I'll ask you again. Did you force them? Threaten them?"

Again Weldon shrugged. "Most of them wanted in on it. I only had to talk one or two into it."

"What about your little brother? Did you force him into it?"

"No," Kelly said.

His mother studied him for a moment.

She turned back to Weldon. "You're the oldest. You know better. Yet you led your younger brother into it."

"Mom, I gave him the silver dollars," Kelly said.

She ignored him. "I was sickened by something else Mr. Penfold said. Weldon, look at me."

Weldon again met her gaze.

"Now, don't lie to me. Did you put those shotgun shells into the tail pipe of Mr. Gyger's car?"

Kelly looked at his brother in surprise. He had heard about Gyger's car blowing up. But he had not connected the mystery with Weldon's pledge to "fix" Gyger.

Something in their mother's tone put Weldon on guard. "Not exactly."

The answer threw her off stride. "Then you *do* know something. What?"

Weldon again looked at the carpet. "Maybe I know who did it."

"Who?"

Again he shrugged. "I said maybe."

"Weldon, if you know anything, we should tell the police."

"I can't tell them anything. I'm just guessing."

She spoke so quietly that Kelly almost could not hear her. "Weldon, I know where those shotgun shells came from. I know you broke into your father's gun case."

Weldon looked up at her. "Did you tell the cops?"

As his mother glanced away, Kelly understood that at least for the moment Weldon had gained the upper hand. She had not told the police.

Weldon was looking at her with a self-satisfied smile. His mother wiped away a tear.

"Weldon, why did you do it?"

Weldon traced the pattern of the carpet with his toe. "It didn't hurt him. Ol' Gyger just needed to be woke up a little."

"You might have killed him. Or his wife."

Weldon shook his head. "Without a gun barrel around it to direct the charge, a shotgun shell just explodes like a firecracker. It's mostly noise."

"No wonder your teachers have given up on you. No wonder Mr. Penfold is threatening to expel you."

"I don't care if he does," Weldon said. "I'm not learning anything there anyway. All those teachers are stupid."

Again they looked at each other for a long moment.

"Weldon, you have quite a way to go before you'll be half as smart as you think you are. And don't think you can quit school. One of the last things your father said was that he wanted me to place the education of his sons above every other consideration. He was talking about college and post-graduate work. Not grade school."

She had regained control. Weldon's face had grown taut with worry.

"The company is taking far more of my time than I thought it would," she said. "I have to face the fact that I've failed with both of you."

Kelly felt terrible. She again turned to him.

"Kelly, do you realize what you've done? How could you hope to get into the Boys Choir, pulling stunts like that? You need the recommendation of your teachers. Who would give you a recommendation after an escapade involving the police?"

Kelly felt even sicker. He had not thought about that. "Have they called you? Did they say that?"

"No. But when you were called back, I knew they were seriously considering you. Now, I don't know."

She again turned to Weldon. "Do you understand that if the police had been less sympathetic, you would now have a police record before your thirteenth birthday?"

Weldon did not answer.

"Do you understand that if Mr. Penfold didn't have your best interest at heart, he would have expelled you without giving us any other way out? A black mark would have been placed against your name for all time."

Again Weldon remained silent.

She wiped away another tear. "I really don't know what I'm going to do. Weldon, you've worn out your welcome in the public schools. I'll have to find a private school for you."

"Where?"

"I don't know. In the middle of the school year, it'll be difficult to find one with a vacancy. But I'm trying. Do you think you'd like to go to a military school?"

Weldon shrugged. "Maybe."

"You can think about it. And while I'm deciding what to do, I want both of you to stay out of trouble. Do you think you can manage that?"

Kelly and Weldon nodded.

They went back to their rooms. Later, Weldon came across the hall and sat on Kelly's bed.

"Well, it looks like military school for sure," he said. "That might not be so bad. At least it'd get me away from here."

Kelly was still crestfallen over the possibility that he had lost out on the Boys Choir. "You think maybe she'll send me too?"

"No. You're her precious little angel. She's not going to send you anywhere."

Weldon said it so matter-of-factly that Kelly did not take offense. "I wish I knew what's going to happen," he said.

"Whatever happens, you and me got to stick together. Right?"

Kelly nodded, thinking again of how lonely the house would be without Weldon.

"You remember that movie, *Beau Geste?*"

Kelly shook his head. He remembered the fort in the desert with everybody in it dead, but not much else. Weldon remembered everything about every movie he liked.

"Well, there were these three brothers, see. They grew up in an old house and went through a whole bunch of shit, just like you and me. But they always looked out for each other because they were brothers. They joined the Foreign Legion and had a lot of trouble, but they fought for each other and stuck together always. That's the way it'll be with you and me. You look out for me, and I'll look out for you. Okay?"

Kelly nodded.

"Promise?"

"I promise," Kelly said.

"I promise too. Cross my heart and hope to die. Now don't forget."

"I won't," Kelly said.

Weldon tiptoed back to his room.

Kelly lay awake, trying to imagine life without Weldon.

Chapter 9

Walter Trammel's office more resembled a comfortable apartment than the private sanctum of a nationally known corporate attorney. Subdued lighting, overstuffed chairs, and oriental rugs provided an appealing, relaxed atmosphere. A small rolltop desk in one corner seemed almost an afterthought, as if it had occurred to him at the last moment that he might need a place to sign documents.

Joanna sank into a well-cushioned chair. "Mr. Trammel, I'm not even sure I should be here. I may be imagining things. After you hear me, you may think I'm crazy."

Trammel smiled as if to suggest he was accustomed to anxious and uncertain clients. "Try me."

Joanna hardly knew where to begin her story. The fact that Walter Trammel had been Brod's close friend helped in some ways, but inhibited her in others. Trammel and his wife lived in an English Tudor only three doors away from Joanna, yet he was almost a stranger. She had met him only once, years ago. That brief encounter had hardly prepared her for his sheer physical attraction. A tall man, he was calm, self-assured, and handsome in a dark, brooding way. He was impeccably tailored in a navy blue pinstripe, club tie, and English oxfords.

Joanna took a deep breath and plunged. "Mr. Trammel, I have reason to suspect that Brod may have—and I stress *may have*—instigated a crime several years before his death. Obviously, he is beyond prosecution. But others may be involved. My concern is the possibility that I now could be in the position of withholding evidence, or something like that, if the others are ever prosecuted. I'm here to determine what my situation is, and what I should do about it, if anything."

Trammel appeared not to have heard. He sat with his chin resting against the knuckles of his right hand. Joanna waited.

At last he stirred. "I've been trying to imagine Brod involved in a crime. He was always so damned honest and direct. But I remember a time or two when he was pushed to the wall. Yes, he could be tough. Maybe what you've said isn't as inconceivable as it first sounds. What is your evidence? What is the crime? Start at the beginning. Tell me everything that brought you here."

"I warn you, it's quite involved. Some of my worries sound stupid even to me."

"We have plenty of time."

Joanna described in detail the days following Brod's first heart attack—Grover Sterling's move to gain control of the company, Loren's attempt to stop him, and Loren's subsequent so-called suicide.

"No one in the family believed at the time that Loren killed himself. No one believes it now. But Brod had just come home from the hospital—against the advice of his doctors. For several days, we kept Loren's death from him. When the doctors felt we could, we told him."

Overwhelmed by the memory, she stopped for a moment. Trammel waited.

"I had never seen Brod the way he was that day," she went on. "We had two doctors standing beside his bed, and I think they were puzzled and concerned by his lack of reaction. He showed no emotion whatsoever. Instead, he seemed to be filled with cold fury. He stayed that way throughout the day. Twice, when I dashed downstairs for something, I thought I heard him on the telephone. Then that night, he asked—demanded, rather—that I take the boys out to a movie. I didn't want to leave him alone, but it reached the point where I became even more concerned over arguing with him."

Joanna hesitated, searching for a way to describe her feelings that night. "It was a perfectly miserable evening. My sons knew I was upset. They were irritable. Kelly was whining about something. I was tempted to leave the movie and go back home—to reassure myself about Brod, if nothing else—but I kept seeing his face, that cold, impersonal stare. I knew he'd be furious with me if I returned early, and the doctors had warned us to keep him as calm as possible. So I sat and watched a movie screen for two hours."

"Did he give you a definite time to return?"

"Not exactly. I think that was why he suggested a movie. He knew it would keep us out of the house at least that long."

"Did you suspect what he might be doing?"

Joanna carefully considered her answer. She knew his reason for asking: if she were ever brought to court, it would be a key question.

"I assumed at the time that it had something to do with the fight for control at the company—something he didn't want me to know. His sister, Crystelle, was involved. She had pledged her support to Grover Sterling. I thought it might have been that. I also thought it might be connected with Loren's death. I just didn't know. I was beside myself with worry. But when I returned home, his mood had changed completely. He laughed and joked, and asked the boys about the movie. He teased me about my night out—as if it were a special treat he had planned."

"He never mentioned the real reason for asking you to leave the house?"

"Never."

"You didn't ask?"

Again Joanna hesitated. "I suppose I hoped that eventually he would tell me."

Trammel regarded her in silence. Joanna sensed he knew her answer was not entirely candid.

"Deep down, I probably didn't want to know," she added.

He gave her a hint of a smile. "You didn't worry about it at the time. Tell me why it concerns you now."

She described the recent sequence of events—finding the Schippoletti correspondence in the files, the ledger entry, the mysterious note from Schippoletti among the get-well cards. She told of her talks with Arnold Campbell and Henry, and described her strange telephone conversation with Schippoletti.

"Obviously, some kind of collusion existed between Brod and Schippoletti," she concluded. "There was dialogue—an exchange—between them just before Grover Sterling was killed. If you remember, another of Grover's financial backers, Brod's cousin Troy, was ruined financially by arson that same night. I don't know much about the law. But it occurs to me I might be an accessory after the fact. I have in hand evidence that conceivably could be of use in solving a crime —assuming that one occurred. Brod told me to come to you if I ever needed legal advice, and here I am."

Trammel picked up a small Lalique figurine of a unicorn from a side table and turned it slowly in his hands, studying it intently. Although slightly nettled by his silence, Joanna also was intrigued.

He was an unusual man. He appeared to shun the trappings of his own profession. Nowhere in sight were the lawbooks, notepads, briefcases. To the casual observer, he might be an art connoisseur contemplating a purchase.

At last he put the figurine down and looked at her.

"I believe your concern is valid. I doubt it's something we should spend a great deal of time worrying about. But we probably should be aware of the hazards, and take precautions."

He brooded for a time before continuing.

"Understand, I'm not a criminal lawyer. I did serve as an

assistant district attorney for a while, years ago, so I know the procedure. The New York police probably never closed the file on Sterling's death. The case would be inactive—they're no longer working on it—but it is open to receive any new information that comes along. With the possibility that several persons are involved, new clues might come to light at any time, and reactivate the investigation. Do you know anything at all about Schippoletti?"

"Nothing."

"He sounds like a big-caliber hood. During the war I was in intelligence. I met a few of them. It isn't generally known, but the underworld helped us a great deal with labor, with guarding the docks along the East Coast, and later with planning the invasions in the Mediterranean. Schippoletti could be our greatest hazard, simply because he himself is vulnerable. When small-time criminals are caught, their only bargaining chip may be evidence on a really big fish. Schippoletti could be a very big fish."

"Then what should I do?"

"At this point, I wouldn't destroy the letters, any of the evidence. That could be deemed active participation, and possibly implicate you, whereas at the moment, you are merely a knowledgeable but uninvolved bystander. We'll just sit back and let matters take their course."

"I feel as if it's a ticking time bomb. I don't know if I can live with it."

Again Trammel gave her the trace of a smile. "It may be a bona fide bomb. But let's think of it as a dud. It probably is. I'll make some discreet inquiries about Schippoletti. Don't contact him again. Someone could be listening in on his conversations. And if worse comes to worst, your telephone toll charges could be subpoenaed."

"What if he calls me?"

"Talk pleasantly, as if he were a good but distant friend of your husband's, one you've never met. Don't commit yourself. If you receive any correspondence from him, bring it to me, and we'll decide what to do about it."

"I feel as if I'm halfway to Huntsville."

Trammel laughed. "Goree," he said. "The women's prison is at Goree."

Amused, he seemed a different person. His eyes took on new life and his voice conveyed unexpected warmth. The change from his habitual sadness was abrupt. But his humor vanished quickly.

"Now that I've frightened you sufficiently, let me add that I doubt you are in danger of prosecution. I can't imagine any jury convicting an innocent widow for defending her husband's memory."

"I feel better already."

"Good. Don't worry. When I have some information on Schippoletti, I'll call you."

Joanna rose and prepared to leave. "It has been good to see you again, Mr. Trammel. Brod often talked about you. He felt especially bad that he wasn't able to see even his best friends during his final years. Perhaps in a small way I can make amends for him. Could you and your wife come over for dinner some evening soon?"

Trammel was opening the door for her. He paused with the door half open. "Thank you. But my wife is now an invalid. We don't go out."

Joanna was momentarily confused. His wife was a pretty, vivacious woman. Occasionally Joanna saw her in the drive and waved. She now realized that it had been many months since she had seen her. "I'm so sorry. How dumb of me! I feel terrible I didn't know."

"No reason you should. Peggy was struck by polio last summer. She demanded that it be kept quiet. I think she thought she would recover with no one the wiser. But the paralysis hasn't improved. It's almost total."

"How awful. For her. And for you."

"She's slightly better. She's spending more time out of the lung now. We're optimistic."

Emotions swept through Joanna too fast to assimilate. Looking up at Trammel, she saw the same sadness, the same self-denial she had known throughout the five years of Brod's illness.

For a moment she hardly trusted herself to speak.

"Peggy shouldn't keep her illness to herself," she said. "I intend to do something for her, if it's only a gesture."

Trammel smiled. "She would appreciate that."

Joanna said no more. She fled from the office, resisting possibilities already beginning to tug at her imagination.

Through the remainder of the week Joanna called military academies and other private schools throughout the country. None among the first rank had an opening. She was just starting to canvass the less desirable ones when the director of the New Mexico Military Institute phoned her back to report that due to illness, a cadet would not be returning to school after the holidays.

He said the vacancy was available, if Weldon met the requirements.

Joanna accepted immediately. But to remove all doubt that she was doing the right thing, she telephoned leading educators to check on the military school's qualifications.

She received glowing recommendations from all quarters.

And in subsequent conversation with the director, she was further impressed.

She contacted Penfold. He said he would forward Weldon's records.

Although she had known that Kelly was being seriously considered by the boy choir, the phone call confirming his selection still came as a surprise.

In her confusion, she hesitated in accepting, saying she would have to see whether she could arrange transportation.

But the truth was that she was having second thoughts.

Kelly was such a thin, sensitive boy. She was not at all sure he could endure the strain of such a work load.

She knew how badly he wanted to be a member of the choir. Every day he met her at the front door on her arrival home, asking if she had heard. Now that he had been selected, she felt she should investigate further before making a commitment.

That evening she managed to slip into the house while the boys were at dinner, and hurried up to her room.

She remembered a musician she had known while dancing for Billy Rose. After the Centennial, he had gone on with his education. She had seen his name, Tom Anderson, in the newspapers occasionally. He was now a professor of music at North Texas State University in Denton. She searched by phone and found him at home.

She briefly explained the reason for her call.

"From what I hear, I'm afraid the choir may be too difficult for Kelly," she summed up. "But his heart is set on it, and I don't want to see him disappointed. I'm trying my best to make an intelligent decision about it."

"That indeed would be a hard one to make," Anderson said.

"Tom, what would you do, if you were me?"

Anderson did not answer for a moment. "I'm not sure. I can tell you this, though. The boy you get back from that choir won't be the same boy you put into it."

"In what way?"

"Let me give you some background. The choir was founded by George Bragg about five years ago. I'm convinced he's a genius, not only in music, but also in training boys. George is a perfectionist. He drives everyone around him to accomplish feats no one would dream of attempting on his own. He is the most thoroughly organized person I know. He expects total effort out of those boys, and he gets it. That's quite a burden to place on a boy that young, week in, week out."

"Are you saying Kelly might break under the strain?"

"No. I really doubt that'd happen. George screens his boys very carefully. More often, it'll be the family that can't keep pace. What I'm saying is, the discipline brings changes in the boy. He reaches a certain kind of maturity much quicker than he normally would."

"Yes, I can see that."

"I'm told the Marine Corps claims that once a young man goes through boot camp, the training stays with him the rest of his life, that he's always a marine. But a marine drill instructor has a recruit in his custody only twelve to fourteen weeks. George has control of those boys for four years."

"You make it sound tough."

"It is. I've seen boys get rapped rather sharply on the head when their attention strays."

Joanna was appalled. "Really?"

"The boys seem to take it in stride. It's the mothers who come apart at the seams."

Joanna laughed.

"Joanna, there are pros and cons. The training is beyond price. The choir performs with symphony orchestras, full-scale opera productions, with professionals who have spent their entire lives in music. Those kids don't do it by rote. George turns them into pint-sized professionals. He teaches them the lives of the composers, how every piece came to be written. He drills them on how to stand, how to walk, how to talk with adults. Even table manners. They practice bowing to applause for two years before they ever face an audience. He teaches them how to memorize. He has a system. By the time they go to the performing choir, they have an amazing repertoire in their heads. It isn't generally known yet, but they're probably as good as any choir in the world. I believe that in another season or two, they'll be as good as the Vienna Boys Choir."

"I suppose I should feel honored that Kelly was selected."

"You certainly should. But there are cons. The choir will rob him of what most people consider a normal boyhood. He might resent that, later."

"I don't know what I'll do," Joanna said. "But I thank you. I now feel I can make a much-better-informed decision."

"I suppose it boils down to what you want your boy to be," Anderson concluded. "Four years in the choir will turn him into a perfectionist. He'll be highly disciplined, maybe a bit of a martinet. He'll have exceptional poise and confidence. He'll be well organized and artistic. And I'm certain of this: Whatever you decide, it will affect your boy throughout his entire life."

In the wake of the call, a migraine that had been threatening all day came to full flower. Joanna lay on the daybed, a cold cloth across her eyes, and worried over whether she was making the right decisions about the boys.

She kept returning to Brod's oft-repeated warning: "Whatever you do, don't coddle them."

Military school, a martinet choir. She certainly could not be accused of pampering them.

Penfold and other teachers had stressed Weldon's need for discipline. The director of the military institute had said his staff was accustomed to handling troubled boys.

She thought of Kelly's whining ways, his shy, timid nature. Anderson clearly believed the choir would put some backbone into him.

The more she thought back over the events of the last few days, the clearer it became that all of her decisions had been made for her.

Despite his unimposing manner, Kelly had been chosen over scores of competitors.

The vacancy at the military academy had been a fluke. It almost seemed preordained.

With that comforting thought, Joanna drifted into a familiar migraine stupor that slowly yielded to deep sleep.

Chapter 10

On a gray Sunday afternoon Kelly took his book into a quiet corner of the living room to read. It was his favorite spot. Sprawled on the floor behind a sofa, next to a window, he had plenty of light yet he was well away from traffic through the house. Not even Weldon knew about his private hideaway.

Kelly had not yet regained his equilibrium from the ecstasy of learning that he had been accepted by the Texas Boys Choir. For days he had thought of little else. Not even Weldon's imminent departure dampened his exhilaration.

He had known that *Beau Geste* was not only a movie but also a book. He had located it at the library and was already past the point where the famous jewel is stolen and the three brothers run away to join the French Foreign Legion.

Lost in the drama, he was only vaguely aware when his mother, his grandmother, and Aunt Zetta returned to the house from their trip to the cemetery. At first the drone of their talk failed to penetrate his consciousness. But his attention shifted as they entered the living room.

"Joanna, I believe you're making a big mistake," his grandmother said as she came right to the sofa where Kelly was hidden. "Why can't the boys stay with me, at least through the weekdays while you're working? If Weldon's having trouble with his grades, we could hire a private tutor. Henry could take Kelly wherever he needs to go for that choir. Can't you see? It would be ideal. Then they could come back here and be with you on weekends."

Kelly's grandmother lowered her weight onto the sofa. She was so close that he could have reached up and touched the back of her neck. With a thrill of anticipation, he understood they had no inkling he was home. He had intended to go to a movie with Weldon, but at the last minute decided to stay home and read.

Weldon would watch any movie. Kelly drew the line at Charlie Chan.

As the women took their places before the fire, he could easily imagine how they were seated—Aunt Zetta ramrod-straight in the big wing chair, his mother on the smaller chair by the fireplace, and his grandmother on the sofa, with either her purse or a handkerchief clasped firmly in her hands.

"It's more than Weldon's grades," his mother said. "There have been a few problems with discipline. Nothing serious. But I have to face the fact that he's getting too big for me to handle. He needs a firmer hand."

Kelly could hardly believe his ears. Clearly his mother was keeping Weldon's threatened expulsion a secret.

"But why New Mexico? It's so far! Couldn't we find a place just as suitable, closer to home?"

"Mother, it's a fine school, with a marvelous record. They're accustomed to handling boys with disciplinary problems. The director explained the system to me at length. They use rewards to motivate the cadets into studying. I've been told that Weldon tests well in intelligence. But he has never applied himself. I'm hoping the school will make him use that intelligence. The director even said that boys who enter with disciplinary problems often become their best cadets."

"But he's so young!"

"He'll be with boys his own age. He can come home often. He'll have close attention twenty-four hours a day. I don't see how I can do better by him."

"Won't Kelly miss him terribly?"

"I'm sure we all will. But Kelly's school counselor suggested it might be a good idea to separate the boys for a while. Some of Kelly's teachers agreed. Weldon tends to dominate Kelly so. And of course Kelly has his new passion— the choir. Right now I'm concerned that it may be too big a burden for him. But if it should work out, he'll be too busy to miss Weldon much."

Springs creaked softly close to Kelly's ear as his grandmother shifted her position on the sofa. "Joanna, there's something I've never discussed with you. But with all that's happened, and with Brod gone now, perhaps I should. There seems to be a genetic strain in Spurlock men that gives them a propensity for trouble. Zetta knows what I'm talking about."

Aunt Zetta did not respond. Kelly's grandmother raised her voice. "Zetta? I was telling Joanna there's a genetic strain in Spurlock men that makes them prone to trouble. Don't you agree?"

"What do you mean?" Aunt Zetta shouted back.

"I'm not saying anything derogatory, Zetta. And it's not so unusual. In Shackelford County I knew a family who could trace their lineage back to Austin's Old Three Hundred. Fine people. But over the generations, the family was beset with suicides and insanity. Melancholia, I think they said it was. Some of that family refused to marry. They said they didn't want to pass the strain on to innocent children."

"Watch your mouth," Aunt Zetta shouted. "There's no insanity in the Spurlock family!"

"I didn't say there was. But Zetta, you can't deny there's a willfulness, a certain ruthlessness, in some of the men. From all I've heard, your father rode roughshod over people all his life. Clay was just like him. Clay never cared about the feelings of others. You know that's true."

"Ann Leigh, shut your mouth right now! I'll not have you talking against Clay."

"Zetta, you can just get mad. I don't care. I'm the one who had to live with the shambles he left behind—his oil patch women, his bastard children. I'm not saying anything new. Everyone in town knows the whole story."

"Clay was a good man," Aunt Zetta shouted. "You never appreciated him. I'll not sit here and listen to you running him down. And you can keep your tongue off my father. You don't know anything about him."

"Are you denying he built his fortune out of saloons and bordellos, and left his family to face the music?"

An awful silence fell. Kelly could hear the big clock ticking in the hall.

"I don't want to talk about it," Aunt Zetta said in a quieter voice. "And I don't want to talk about why I don't want to talk about it."

Kelly almost stopped breathing, afraid they would discover him. After another long silence, his mother spoke in a loud but conciliatory tone. "Aunt Zetta, please don't be angry. What Ann Leigh is saying is that Spurlock men seem to have an adventurous nature, a high-spirited, competitive approach to life. Ambition. I've always considered it to be an asset, not a flaw. It was what first attracted me to Brod."

"My father, Travis Spurlock, came to this town as a penniless orphan," Aunt Zetta said. "He was barely fifteen years old. But he had seen terrible things in the war. The Civil War, that was. There was no town here then, only a village. He helped to build it into a city. He helped to bring in the railroads. He made his money in railroads and real estate. All the other, what you're talking about, he did as his civic duty to entertain the cowboys on the trail drives, and the railroaders, so they wouldn't go elsewhere. I know they say bad things about him now. But they aren't true. He came from good English stock. I've looked into our ancestry."

"Joanna, whatever face you want to put on it, I think you should consider this Spurlock trait very seriously," Kelly's grandmother said. "I sometimes see profound evidence of it in Weldon."

"Papa was a United States senator, a close confidant of President Roosevelt," Kelly's Aunt Zetta went on. "The first one, Theodore. Papa was a friend of the king of England and of the Comanche Indian chief Quanah Parker. Everyone knew he was a great man. Now all they can say about him is that he owned whorehouses and saloons."

"Weldon may seem only high-spirited to you now," Kelly's grandmother said. "But I see Spurlock written all over him."

"My brother Clay was never content to be mediocre," Zetta said. "If that's insanity, I'm all for it."

"Brod was never rebellious as a child," Kelly's grandmother said. "He was sweet as he could be. But when he was crossed, he could turn to icy fury in an instant. I used to worry about it. Maybe on occasion you saw that in him."

Kelly's mother did not answer.

"It's the Texan thing to do," Aunt Zetta went on, as if talking to herself. "Texans build, create. And Spurlock men have always been more Texan than most. Papa once made a beautiful speech to a woman who criticized him for some of the things he had done. He told her that he and men like him had made Texas what it is today. He told her, 'Madam, we did whatever we had to do.' "

Kelly's grandmother raised her voice. "Zetta, what we're talking about isn't the same at all. I've heard that story. Your father was defending himself over his friendship with outlaws and fallen women."

"It *is* the same," Zetta shouted. "Times change. Human nature doesn't. Weldon and Kelly will have to grow up and make their way in the world. They have good blood. I'll not sit by idly while you run the family down."

"Zetta, for the last time, I'm *not* speaking against the Spurlocks. I'm only stating a situation we both know exists— the tendency Spurlock men have for trouble. Maybe some of the women, too. Look at Crystelle. She's never given us a moment's peace. Weldon and Kelly are Spurlocks. Joanna should take that into consideration. She should be watchful, and take proper measures if need be."

"There's not a thing wrong with those boys!"

"Weldon is rebellious. Kelly is high-strung and nervous. I worry about both of them."

"Kelly'll be the strong one someday," Zetta said. "You'll see. He's got more bottom to him."

"Please, both of you," Kelly's mother said. "If I hadn't thought we could discuss the boys' situation calmly, I wouldn't have brought it up."

"I don't feel well," Aunt Zetta said. "I want to go home."

Kelly hugged the carpet as his mother and grandmother jumped to their feet and moved about, fussing over his Aunt Zetta. They made several trips to the kitchen for water, aspirin, and cold cloths.

Zetta dismissed their attentions. She again said she wanted to go home.

After some delay, Aunt Zetta was helped out the front door. Kelly waited until he heard his mother's car leave the drive. He then ran upstairs.

Late that night he slipped into Weldon's room. They turned on the desk lamp and sat on the floor.

Whispering, Kelly told Weldon what he had overheard that afternoon—or all he could remember of it.

Weldon listened in silence until Kelly had finished. "Skeeter Burcham once said our great-grandfather made his money in whorehouses. I thought he was lying to hear his head rattle. I beat the shit out of him. What did Grandmother say about the bad blood? Did she say what kind?"

"I don't think so. Aunt Zetta kept shouting, saying it wasn't insanity. Grandmother said it always got Spurlock men into trouble."

"Well, maybe she's right about that. I'm sure ass-deep in it. Did Mom say why those shitheads at school want us separated?"

"No."

He had not understood all of that.

"I don't see where it's any of their damned business," Weldon said.

Kelly remembered something else. "Grandmother said Grandfather had oil patch women and bastard children. She was awfully mad at him. Aunt Zetta said Grandmother just didn't appreciate him. She didn't say it wasn't so."

"I've heard he was a real piss-cutter. You remember the guy at the company that got killed? Grover Sterling? Somebody at school told me he was Dad's bastard half brother. I didn't know whether to believe it or not."

Kelly thought back over all he had heard that afternoon. He had mentioned everything except Aunt Zetta's opinion that someday he would become the strong one.

He doubted Weldon would like that, so he did not mention it. "I wish there was some way we could find out about all that bad-blood stuff," he said.

"What I want to know is why they want us separated. They must think we're turning queer or something."

"I don't know," Kelly said.

"Whatever they're trying to do, it won't work." Weldon punched him on the shoulder. "If they keep us apart a hundred years, we'll still be brothers. Right?"

"Right," Kelly said, finding a measure of security in Weldon's intensity.

He returned to his own room and went over and over the conversation he had overheard, committing it to memory.

At the moment much of it did not make sense.

But he hoped that eventually, combined with other revelations he might acquire, it would.

A week later Kelly and his mother drove Weldon to the airport to catch the plane for Amarillo and Roswell. They arrived early. The plane was not yet ready.

"Let's sit here for a few minutes," their mother said. "I want to talk to both of you."

The day was cold and blustery. Puffs of wind occasionally shook the car. Weldon sat by the passenger door, and their mother was behind the wheel. Kelly was in the middle.

Frowning slightly, she turned to face them. "When I said you boys failed to uphold the responsibilities your father expected of you, I should have added something else. I failed him too. Somehow I should have been able to keep you two out of trouble."

She paused, and her lower lip trembled. Kelly hoped she would not begin to cry.

"We've been given a second chance," she went on. "It'll be harder on all three of us. But we must measure up. You understand?"

Both Kelly and Weldon nodded.

"Weldon, it'll be especially difficult for you. At least until you get adjusted to being away from home. Keep in mind that the first few weeks will be the worst. If you get home-sick, call home anytime. Understand?"

"I'll be okay," Weldon said.

"Kelly won't be seeing much of me either. During the next few months, I'll have to spend even more time with the company. Your father wanted me to make a lot of changes. I'll be traveling, putting his ideas into practice."

She put her hand on Kelly's knee. "So, Kelly, it won't be easy for you either. I've arranged to place you in a car pool with four other boys. The group will meet at a drugstore in North Fort Worth for the drive to Denton. On some days I'll be able to take you there. On other days, Bonnie at the office can drive you. Your grandmother has volunteered Henry's services. I may hire Henry's son. One way or another, we'll get you there. If no one is available, you can take a taxi. But it'll be up to you to be certain you have transportation when you need it. Do you understand?"

"Yes," Kelly said.

"You'll be responsible for keeping your grades up. I'll have too many things to worry about to wonder every day whether you've done your homework. We'll never talk about it. It'll be your responsibility. Do you understand that?"

Again Kelly nodded.

"Our separation won't be forever. There'll be holidays,

breaks, summers. We'll be together again quite often. And Weldon, I really think you'll enjoy it. If I didn't think so, I couldn't bear to send you away."

Weldon did not respond.

"So we'll all be heavily involved in different things. Kelly with his choir and schoolwork. Weldon with the military school. Me with the oil company. We'll be apart most of the time. But I want you always to remember that we are a family. What time we will have together we will enjoy all the more. Do you both understand?"

Again Kelly and Weldon nodded.

As they left the car to walk Weldon to the plane, Kelly did not voice his doubts.

They had not been a family while they had been together. How could they become a family while they were apart?

Chapter 11

Joanna gripped the edges of her seat as the old Spurlock DC-3 lumbered down the airstrip through driving rain. Slowly it became airborne, engines thundering. As it climbed she felt wind gusts tugging at the wings. Sheets of water constantly turned to writhing rivulets across the windows. Outside she soon could see only clouds and rain.

The plane rattled and shuddered with each new gust. It had seen two decades of hard use and she knew it was not in the best of shape.

From behind her came a ripple of laughter conveying general relief. A whiff of whiskey informed her the men were passing the silver flask again. She wondered if they would offer her a drink or continue to hide it. Beth's tips seemed to be working and Joanna was finding her way into a new relationship with the men. Often she did not know what to expect.

They had planned to fly the four hundred miles to Fort Worth late Friday, but storms and heavy rains had delayed their departure overnight. Now at last they were on their way.

Casually, she glanced back over her shoulder. Piersall and

Hollander were playing a two-handed game of cards on an empty seat with a bravado she was sure they did not feel. Hollander held the open flask in his hand. He grinned mischievously and raised the flask, offering her a drink by sign in deference to the deafening noise around them. She declined with a shake of her head, but smiled to convey her tacit approval. The men had been working hard for three days. In all fairness, they should be home for the weekend with their wives and families instead of bouncing across West Texas in the rain.

For a time she attempted to read, but with the jostling of the plane it was impossible. She put her head back and was dozing when she heard the pilot talking over the radio. He was flying with one hand and cupping his right earpiece with the other. He turned in his seat and shouted to her. "Bad storms building between here and Sweetwater. They're advising us to set down wherever we can."

As if to confirm his words, the plane was buffeted so severely for a moment that he had to focus his full attention on the controls. When the wind abated, he again turned to her and completed his message. "They now report solid precip with embedded thunderstorms all the way to Fort Worth. We can probably dodge the storms. Want to chance it?"

His name was John McDermott, but everyone called him Smiling Jack, after the comic strip hero. He had flown dive-bombers off carriers in the Pacific until receiving a medical discharge for injuries late in the war. He now had been chief pilot at Spurlock Oil for five years.

"Don't take any unnecessary risks," Joanna called back. Beth's warning sprang to mind; the directive perhaps had sounded too authoritative. She softened it. "I'm inclined to take their advice," she shouted. "What do you think?"

Smiling Jack frowned, as if giving the matter serious thought. "We probably could make it. But there's a good chance Meacham would be socked in when we got there."

"Then I'm all for finding terra firma," Joanna said. "What seems best?"

"Pick a wet spot," Hollander shouted. "I remember three days we once spent in Lamesa. Seemed like a year."

At first Joanna thought "wet" referred to the weather. Then she remembered that Texas had local option. Prohibition was still in force across much of West Texas.

"It looks like Andrews," said Smiling Jack.

Hollander groaned. "Dry as a bone. Not even beer."

The plane banked as Smiling Jack turned onto a new course. Within minutes the buffeting grew more severe. Lightning flashed close to the plane.

"It's only thirty-four miles from Andrews to Odessa," Mike Piersall shouted over the noise. "Maybe we can find rooms there and wait it out."

Joanna understood his logic. Odessa was on the main highway across the barren stretches of West Texas. Recently a number of new tourist courts and motels had been built along it to accommodate travelers.

"I just hope the telephone lines aren't down," Hollander said. "My wife worries."

Joanna was sure that Hollander, McDermott, and Piersall were making an effort to keep the conversation normal to put her at ease. But she was also certain they shared her concern.

To her left, Arnold Campbell sat erect in his seat, staring out the window, his spidery hands grasping his knees. He had not spoken in an hour. Behind him, Donald Parker pretended to be engrossed in his charts and maps, but he glanced out frequently at the storm. Piersall sat with both feet braced, as if prepared for a crash. Only Hollander and McDermott came close to success with their pretense.

"Stay clear of barbed-wire fences," Hollander shouted to the pilot. He explained to Joanna. "About two years ago we landed at Brownfield in a storm. At night. Jack caught a glimpse of the highway and thought it was the end of the runway. He landed a little short. We taxied up to the hangar trailing about a hundred yards of barbed wire."

"He's exaggerating," McDermott called back. "It was only about fifty feet of wire."

Joanna laughed to show she appreciated the gallows humor. But as Smiling Jack reduced speed and began the descent, her anxiety mounted. She could see only clouds and lightning flashes outside the plane.

"How can he see where we are?" she asked Hollander, keeping her voice too low for Smiling Jack to hear.

"He probably can't. But don't worry. He's the best."

The blind descent seemed to take forever. Joanna sat mesmerized, certain they would smash into the ground any second. At last a hole cleared beneath the plane, and through it she saw brush and land startlingly near. Almost immediately a blacktop road shot beneath the plane, so close, she could see rain-filled potholes. The plane continued to sink. A blur of shrubbery raced by. Just as Joanna thought Smiling Jack was landing in open country, the runway appeared and the wheels thumped on firm asphalt.

"Missed the fence," Hollander yelled up to McDermott. "That'll go against your record."

McDermott did not answer. He was occupied with bringing the plane to a stop on the short runway. Braking hard, he turned the plane onto a sidestrip and taxied up to a tin-topped hangar. He cut the engines and the propellers twirled to a halt. The puffs of wind rocking the old DC-3 were even more alarming, now that they were no longer airborne.

McDermott left his seat and donned a yellow rain slicker. "If y'all will sit here for a little bit, I'll check in, and see if I can arrange us some transportation."

"Isn't the wind apt to turn the plane over?" Joanna asked.

McDermott smiled. "We'll tie it down. But it'd take a lot of wind to flip this old bucket of bolts."

He jumped from the plane and trotted across the concrete to the corner of the big hangar, where signs proclaimed a small office. Three men came out in the rain and hooked cables to the wings. The plane no longer rocked so violently. After several minutes, Smiling Jack returned.

"Looks like we're stuck here twenty-four hours at least," he said. "What we've got is a tropical storm from the Gulf,

TEXAS NOON 117

mixing with a Canadian cold front. Solid rain from Wichita
Falls to the Big Bend, and from Hobbs to Texarkana. Some
places have received fifteen inches since yesterday. It's a
mess."

"That's just great," Hollander said. "Is there a decent hotel in this town?"

"They say everything's full. But I managed to rent wheels.
We should be able to find something along Highway
Eighty."

He went back into the hangar. A short time later, he drove
a car out on the ramp, close to the plane. One by one, they
made the dash from the plane to the car. It was an old
prewar Cadillac, but the interior was clean and neat. Joanna
sat in the front seat between Smiling Jack, who took the
wheel, and Hollander. The other three executives rode in
the backseat.

They drove south through blinding sheets of rain, sometimes slowing to a crawl when visibility dropped to almost
zero. Several times they crept through places where water
was running over the roadway. The thirty-four miles
seemed endless.

When they at last arrived in Odessa, they drove to the
east-west highway and began searching. They soon learned
that high water had closed the highway near Big Spring to
the east, and the other side of Monahans to the west. Traffic
was being turned back from each direction. Every motel
was full.

For a time the situation seemed hopeless. Then Hollander
spent several minutes talking with some men in the lobby of
a new motel. He returned triumphant.

"I gave two salesmen our hard-luck story and talked them
into doubling up. So I got a room for Mrs. Spurlock. The rest
of us can sleep in the lobby."

"You'll do no such thing," Joanna said. "We'll manage
somehow. We should get out of this cold and rain before we
all catch pneumonia."

But once the six of them were crowded into the small

room, she soon wondered *how* they would manage. The room did not even have enough places for everyone to sit.

Hollander again donned his raincoat. "Surely they'll have folding chairs we can borrow."

Piersall went with him. A few minutes later they returned in a jubilant mood, carrying the chairs and a folding card table. Hollander waved a fifth of bourbon. "How about an internal overcoat to ward off the chill?"

The men quickly organized, setting up the card table, hunting glasses, ice, and soda, and mixing and serving the drinks. Joanna sat on the edge of the bed and accepted the proffered highball. Soon the warmth of the bourbon was spreading through her body, and the only hindrance to total comfort was her damp woolen suit.

"I think I'll change out of these wet clothes," she announced as she finished the drink. "If you men wish to do the same, I'll give you twenty minutes."

She carried her suitcase into the bathroom. As she peeled off her suit, she found that even her underclothing was wet. Feeling a bit daring with the men so near, she changed from the skin out. Through the small bathroom window came the sounds of the continuing downpour. From the other side of the door she heard the men laughing and joking. She smiled to herself, easily imagining the scene as the five changed clothes in the crowded room. Taking her time, she fluffed and dried her hair and tended to her makeup. A few minutes later Hollander signaled the "all clear." When she reentered the room, the men were gathered around a small radio, listening solemnly to a news broadcast. Hollander handed her another drink.

It was the first time she had seen any of them in casual clothing. All appeared surprisingly different. She had assumed that they had worn business suits on the trip into the field in deference to her presence. Now they seemed to have shed all formality. In shirt sleeves and open collar, Campbell no longer wore his imposing facade. He had turned into a gentle, approachable old man who reminded her vaguely of her father. In khaki trousers and shirt, Piersall seemed fully at ease. Hollander, in a rumpled gray sweatshirt, was down-right collegiate. Donald Parker for once had put away his maps and charts, and sat in a loose-knit sweater, sipping his drink.

The news ended with a singing commercial for Pep-sodent. Hollander switched off the radio. "Can you imagine? We're on an island right in the middle of West Texas."

"Maybe the Permian Basin is turning back into a sea," said Donald Parker.

It was the first droll remark Joanna had ever heard him make, and it struck her as unusually funny. The Permian Sea had evaporated more than 280 million years ago.

"When they do get rain out here, they usually get a four- or five-year supply all at once," Piersall said.

"I can see the Fort Worth *Star-Telegram* headlines now," Hollander said. " 'Scores Drowned as Beneficial Rains Soak West Texas.' " He produced a pack of cards. "Who's for poker?"

"I really should call home first," Joanna said. Both Bonnie and Calla Lily were staying at the house to look after Kelly, but they had expected her back last night.

"I already tried," Hollander said. "The line is out this side of Sweetwater."

"Can't they reroute?"

"Apparently not. I wasn't able to get through."

The men arranged the chairs, making a place for her at the card table. She had not played poker since college. For a brief time it had been a fad among the sororities.

They agreed on five-card stud, table stakes, pot limit. The men played with great seriousness. Through the first few hands Joanna lost steadily. But as she began to remember more about the game, her luck changed.

Soon she was winning consistently.

After several hours of play, Hollander went out for an-other bottle. On his return, he reported that the rain had slackened only slightly. A short time later Campbell, Parker, and Piersall tossed in their cards, moved into more comfortable chairs, and dozed. Hollander, Smiling Jack, and Joanna played until light peeked through the windows.

Joanna and Smiling Jack were the big winners, almost fifty dollars each.

With daylight, rainfall dwindled to a light sprinkle. Hollander went out for coffee and doughnuts. When he returned, he said several truckers were leaving in an effort to drive on westward to El Paso. He had reserved their rooms.

Not waiting for the rooms to be cleaned, the men moved out, leaving Joanna to herself. Exhausted, she managed only a single cup of coffee before collapsing on the bed, clothes and all.

She awoke at four-thirty in the afternoon, famished. She called Hollander. The men agreed to meet her at five-thirty. Hollander said he would attempt to locate a decent restaurant.

Dinner became an impromptu interdepartmental meeting as they discussed the discoveries they had made on their trip, and what to do about them.

Smiling Jack left the table to phone nearby airports. He returned full of information.

"I think we should give it another twelve hours, at least," he said. "The weather is clearing some here, but it looks like another rough night from Abilene on eastward. There were tornadoes and hail north of Ranger this afternoon. The way this front's moving, it should clear out tomorrow."

"I know you all want to get home," Joanna said. "But I think your wives would agree that there's no need to take risks."

Somewhat reluctantly, the men concurred.

Joanna was not disappointed over the delay. The forced idleness brought her first moments of true leisure since Brod's death.

She returned to her room and left the men to their own pursuits. With the radio tuned to soft music, she lounged on the bed and thought back over the past few hectic months.

She was amazed to realize that she had now been a widow

a full half year. It did not seem possible. So much had happened in that short time.

On reflection, she could find nothing she would have done differently. She felt that Brod would have approved.

The company was in good shape. Of this she was now certain. The tour had given her a much better perspective, replacing so many of her theories with firsthand facts. Brod's instructions had been made even more valuable by her tour, and by actually seeing oil wells and drilling rigs in operation.

She now felt she was holding her own in discussions with her executives. On this trip, made at her insistence, they had cleared away several bottlenecks. They had found that additional storage facilities in the field were essential. Production at some points was being curtailed, simply because there was no place to put the oil. Although storage tanks were still in short supply, they had located some old tanks for sale, dating from the twenties and thirties. The tanks could be moved, cleaned, and reconditioned. Campbell had argued that they should wait for new equipment. But after examining the situation in the field, the other executives had sided with Joanna. They had decided to buy the old tanks.

Most of Brod's most immediate goals were being met. Production was up, and exploration looked promising. True, refinery profits were down, but she was sure new markets would be found.

She had even turned the adversities of the present trip into an advantage. During the storm she had become far better acquainted with the company executives than she would ordinarily have through years of work at the office.

She was even more proud of her accomplishments with the boys. From the military academy she had received encouraging reports recently about Weldon. The director said that after a few initial disciplinary problems, he seemed to be finding his niche. His grades had improved. His superior officers now termed him "a natural leader."

Her qualms over sending him off to school had not vanished, but she now felt she had made the right decision.

Kelly's absorption with the boy choir seemed total. At

times she worried over the work load he had taken upon himself. But she could not question the results. He was now earning straight A's. Every teacher had commented upon his improvement.

Her quandary over rearing two fatherless sons seemed to be resolving itself.

Slowly, lulled by the now gentle rain on the roof, Joanna drifted off to sleep, with no inkling of harsh facts as others would see them, and as they eventually would be spread throughout Fort Worth society:

She had spent the night in a motel room with five men.

Chapter 12

The department heads filed in and took their seats. Joanna nodded to them, but dispensed with the usual Monday morning pleasantries. In the weeks since the West Texas trip her relationship with them had improved. But as Beth had warned, one never seemed to get rid of the man-woman thing.

This morning Joanna intended to be all business. She began without preliminaries.

"We haven't talked about this before. But long range, we simply must find new production. I've gone back over the figures for the last five years. The totals go steadily downward."

Mike Piersall spoke defensively. "Mrs. Spurlock, a lot of our wells are old. They're playing out. That's to be expected."

"I know. That's why we should be looking to the future. For the last two or three years, most of our new production has been no more than developing proven areas. We need to find new activity."

Again she felt the wall of resistance building. Perhaps a bit belatedly, she remembered Beth's advice. Again she put it into practice.

"Brod always felt there was great possibility in our New Mexico leases. Don, what do you think?"

Despite his brilliance, Donald Parker was forever reluctant to commit himself. He spoke hesitantly. "We're into unknown geology out there. Hard to say."

"Brod acquired those leases years ago and held on to them, sometimes against the advice of others. He was convinced there's a significant buried fracture zone through that section. Have you seen any indication of it?"

Parker slowly shook his head. "Nothing positive. If there's a fracture, it's well hidden. But as far as I know, no one has drilled within fifty miles of there."

"Humble has had shot trucks in there during the last few months," Piersall said. "I haven't heard any rumors about what they found."

"Seismograph might not show much for sure," Parker said. "There's a lot of unconformity. The deeper returns might be too jumbled to read, even for Humble's labs."

"What about a deep test well?" Joanna asked. "Wouldn't that give us a good indication of the possibilities for the whole bloc?"

The men exchanged glances.

Arnold Campbell cleared his throat. "Mrs. Spurlock, that would be very expensive. Even if production were found, it might be years before we'd see any returns."

Walt Chambers whipped the dead cigar from his mouth and placed it carefully on an ashtray. "You're at least fifty, sixty miles from any other production out there. Gathering lines would cost a mint."

Joanna persisted. "But a deep test well *would* tell us a lot, wouldn't it? Don, don't you think it would give us some valuable information?"

Parker nodded. "Sure. We know the Permian shore line retreated westward. So the chances are fairly good. But deep geology that far west is still guesswork."

Joanna unfolded her most recent research, spread it on

the table, and pointed. "I've updated the lease map. Humble has placed thousands of acres under lease during the last three years. Humble and Spurlock now hold a virtual monopoly from here to here. Almost fifty-fifty. Do you think Humble might go in with us on a joint venture for a deep test?"

Again the men exchanged glances.

Campbell gave her a condescending smile. "Mrs. Spurlock, I seriously doubt Humble would consider it. They wouldn't want to share the information. They'd consider the findings more valuable than the well."

"We could at least ask them, couldn't we?"

Chambers reached for his cigar. "They'd laugh at us."

"Why?"

No one seemed to want to answer. An awkward silence fell.

It was broken by Campbell. "Mrs. Spurlock, as a small independent, Spurlock Oil is hardly in Humble's league. They can absorb a deadweight expense like that. But it'd put a significant dent in our cash flow."

"We're already paying out considerable money each year for those leases," Joanna pointed out. "They add up. Wouldn't it make sense to spend a little more, and learn what the leases are worth? A deep test, with all the gadgetry, would cost what? A million? Two million?"

"Somewhere in that ballpark," Piersall said. "It'd depend on how much road we would have to build, access to water, other intangibles. Two million for a really deep test, down to fifteen or twenty thousand feet."

"Surely Humble isn't so free with their money that they wouldn't entertain the possibility of saving a million dollars. George, you know some of the top people at Humble, don't you?"

Hollander raised his eyebrows. "Just to speak to, Mrs. Spurlock. I'm not on close terms with them."

"Anyone else acquainted with the top people down there?"

"I know Mead, head of production," Piersall said. "Not

well. But I've dealt with him. I've talked with some of the others from time to time."

"During the war Calvin Spears was head of production," Campbell said. "We attended government meetings together. He's now president of the company."

"Does anyone see any objection to just floating the idea of a joint venture?" Joanna asked. "We wouldn't be going to them hat in hand. Just a simple business deal to save us both some money. You can say it's something that has occurred to us. I don't think they'd laugh. Especially if we imply we're preparing to go ahead with a deep test on our own."

Campbell shifted uncomfortably in his chair. "Mrs. Spurlock, it could be five, maybe ten years before we'd see any significant return on the money, if then."

"That's true," Joanna said. "But I hope you'll all think about this, and give me the benefit of your experience. It seems to me that if we go on as we have been, drilling offsets, proving out existing pools, watching our production slowly dwindle, we won't be in good position for rapid expansion if the opportunity ever arises. This way, we might have oil in reserve, available when we need it. Does anyone, at the moment, see any other alternative to our slowly dwindling production?"

The men remained silent.

"Well, we'll talk more about it later," Joanna said. "But I believe it's a problem we should all be thinking about."

She went on to other items on her agenda, feeling she had made progress, that she was moving the company out of the doldrums it had fallen into since the war. She could see a definite change in attitudes, not only toward her, but also toward the company. Everyone's demeanor had changed. There was a quicker pace in the halls, a new intensity to discussions about company business.

Joanna was sure that this new excitement about the company was trickling downward from her Monday morning meeting of department heads, where innovative ideas were constantly being hatched.

She closed the meeting within the allotted hour and returned to her office.

The finishing touches had just been completed on her private bathroom. She had concealed the doorway with a bookcase divider, now almost filled with the volumes she had been absorbing on the petroleum industry during the last few months. One title had led to another. She had now plowed her way through more than a hundred books.

She had removed Brod's huge desk and replaced it with one more to her taste. The crystal chandeliers, leather chairs, and sofa she retained. But she had lightened the overall decor with less bulky tables and more colorful drapes.

She felt she had made the office her own.

The day passed smoothly. Late in the afternoon, as she finished a lengthy memo to Piersall on some of his proposals, Bonnie buzzed.

"Crystelle Spurlock is on the line."

Joanna steeled herself. For years she had heard of Crystelle's knack for making trouble.

"Put her through," she said.

Crystelle's voice came over the phone stronger and more forceful than Joanna remembered.

"Joanna, I want to set up a meeting. With you, Mother, the Spurlock board, your lawyers, and mine."

Joanna answered carefully. "For what purpose?"

"I will make a formal offer to buy back my stock in Spurlock Oil."

Joanna fought back an impulse to laugh. "Crystelle, that's out of the question."

"Joanna, I'm not going to argue about it on the phone. But you better listen and listen good. My lawyer tells me I could force this meeting in front of a judge. So get off your high horse and set it up."

"Crystelle, our board meets infrequently," Joanna said. "Every three or four months at most."

"I want this meeting set up within a week. If it isn't, the next thing you hear from me will be a subpoena."

Joanna felt her pulse quicken. Crystelle must have found a lawyer who had convinced her she could win a big settlement by filing a nuisance suit.

Joanna remembered advice from Brod's notebook: From the first sign of anything that smells like litigation, let your lawyers do the talking.

"Crystelle, this is unexpected," she said. "It'll take time. I'll have to mesh schedules. I'll call you back."

"Make it soon," Crystelle said, hanging up abruptly.

Joanna immediately called Walter, even though she now felt an awkwardness in talking with him.

Despite her promises, she still had not made any gesture toward his wife. For reasons she did not fully understand, she had been putting it off.

Walter's secretary said he was in conference. Joanna insisted, and after a few minutes he came on the line. She described Crystelle's call.

"Did she name her attorney?"

"No."

"I wish I knew who it is. There's something odd about this. If she's really into litigation, the call would have come from her attorney."

"What should we do?"

The line was silent a moment. "I believe at this point we should appear to cooperate, and listen to whatever she has to say. We wouldn't be placing ourselves under any obligation. And conceivably it could go against us later that we refused to listen." Joanna heard the rustle of papers. "I'll be in court through tomorrow morning. But I'll be free by two. Would that be feasible?"

"I don't know if I can round up the board that quickly."

Walter hesitated. "I'm not sure we should summon the whole board, especially since we don't know exactly what's involved. How about just you, Ann Leigh, and Campbell? That'd be a quorum, so we'd be complying with her request. If any board action needs to be taken, it could be done later."

Joanna agreed. "I'll set it up, and call you back to confirm."

"Try to find out who's representing her. That may tell us something."

Joanna next phoned Ann Leigh and told her about the call.

"Oh, Lord! I knew she was up to something. You remember, I told you that, when she first moved back here. She can't *make* us sell her the stock, can she?"

"I doubt it. But I don't know. We'll just have to hear what she has to say."

"I'm surprised she has the money to make an offer. I know the lady who lives right beside her, and another who lives on the next street over. The maids talk back and forth, and they say Crystelle's been spending money like it was water. She's been to Europe three or four times, sending things back to decorate the house. She went to Japan once and bought a bunch of hand-painted screens. They say she has bought clothes until all the closets are full. And I'm sure that house didn't come cheap. As far as I know, she hasn't had any income to speak of for years. So she must be spending principal from the sale of her stock."

Joanna did not respond. As an in-law, she did not feel comfortable discussing Crystelle with Ann Leigh.

"Joanna, if there's a way into the company, she'll find it," Ann Leigh went on. "I hate to say it about my own daughter, but sometimes I think she's just plain mean. She won't give up. She'll keep trying, until she gets her own way."

"Mother, I'll conduct the meeting as if we were the full board. But in case she does have some legal maneuver up her sleeve, I think we should allow Walter Trammel to guide us through the talking. I'll take my cues from him."

"I just wish Brod were alive. He wouldn't let her get away with anything."

When Joanna called Crystelle to propose the time of the meeting, she had no trouble learning the name of the lawyer.

"Tate Middleton," Crystelle said.

Walter's reaction to the name was immediate.

"Tate Middleton isn't one of my favorite people. But to give the devil his due, he is a responsible attorney. He wouldn't take a frivolous case. There's the possibility he may think Ann Leigh wouldn't want to air dirty laundry—such as the questions you came to me about."

Joanna felt her pulse quicken. "What should I do about that material I have?"

"For the moment, nothing. I doubt they'll arrive with a search warrant." He hesitated. "But still, there's something strange about this. Ordinarily, Middleton wouldn't allow her to carry the ball like this. Maybe tomorrow we'll find out more."

Crystelle and her lawyer arrived five minutes late. Joanna, Walter, Campbell, Ann Leigh, and Bonnie were already seated, waiting.

Sweeping into the room ahead of the men, Crystelle came straight to Joanna and held out her hand.

"Joanna! You look perfectly marvelous! I think it's wonderful you've managed to keep your weight down so well, with your big bones and all."

Joanna did not reply. She had no intention of getting into a cat fight with Crystelle.

"And Mother! That suit does become you." She crossed the room and straightened Ann Leigh's blouse. "But it needs something. I'll lend you a scarf and belt to give it a bit more color."

Ann Leigh did not speak. Crystelle gave her a fleeting hug, turned, and introduced the men.

She then glanced at the group around the table as if noticing the missing board members for the first time. "Joanna, where *is* everyone? I asked for the whole board to be here!"

"Crystelle, we have a quorum," Joanna said. "That's sufficient."

Crystelle turned to Middleton as if asking a silent question. He only gave her a noncommittal look. She seemed to take that as a signal and did not make an issue of the missing board members.

She was wearing a stunning Dior original. Her blond hair was swept back into a ballerina ponytail, and her skin was taut and flawless over high cheekbones and a smooth, delicate chinline. Joanna thought of Ann Leigh's comment about Oscar Wilde's *Picture of Dorian Gray.*

Middleton was tall and imposing in a blue pinstriped suit. His iron-gray hair was neatly crew-cut. He and Walter nodded to each other, but did not shake hands.

Joanna assumed her place at the head of the conference table and gestured for everyone to be seated. Walter sat to her right, with Ann Leigh and Campbell next to him. Crystelle ignored the chair immediately to Joanna's left and took the second. Middleton sat beyond her, quarter-turned to the table, as if he were a mere spectator.

"Now, I think we deserve an explanation, Crystelle," Joanna said. "What is this all about?"

"I told you. I'm here to buy back my stock in Spurlock Oil."

"And I told you it's not for sale."

Crystelle slapped the table with her bare palm. "Joanna, you'd better listen to my offer!"

Middleton spoke in a low, soothing voice. "Mrs. Spurlock, I assure you it would be in your best interest to listen to what Mrs. Calcart has to say."

Joanna was momentarily confused until she remembered that Calcart was Crystelle's married name. She offered Crystelle a neutral expression and waited.

"I hear that Spurlock Oil is in a terribly run-down condition," Crystelle said. "And since I've not had access to the books for years, I have no idea what the stock is worth. But I'm prepared to buy it back at exactly the price Brod paid me for it five years ago. I think anyone would agree that's a very fair offer."

"And immaterial," Joanna said. "The stock is not for sale. Your offer is rejected."

"I'm making the offer to the board, not to you."

"The board has little to do with it," Joanna said. "Since Brod's death, there has been a considerable redistribution of stock. But since you raise the issue, may I point out that the three board members who own stock are present in this room. Our two outside directors, who do not hold stock, are not. However, the three here today constitute a majority of the board. In declining your offer, I believe I speak for the other board members present."

Ann Leigh and Campbell gave abrupt, concurring nods.

"All right. This is my final offer. I'll give you a five percent override on what Brod paid me."

"The stock is not for sale at any price," Joanna said.

Again Ann Leigh and Campbell nodded their concurrence.

Crystelle spoke directly to Ann Leigh. "Momma, I want what's mine. That's my name down there over the front door. I want my inheritance. I've been shit on by my family since the day I was born. I'm sick of it. You've always been afraid of scandal. Maybe you haven't seen anything yet."

Middleton stirred. "Mrs. Calcart, I don't believe there's any need to pursue this discussion further. You've made a very fair offer, and it has been rejected."

Crystelle turned on Joanna. "And you have no business running this company. It ought to be me. My father founded Spurlock Oil."

"Mrs. Calcart," Middleton said gently.

Crystelle rose. "All right. I'll go. But you can bet your boots I'll be back. Momma, there's going to be a day of reckoning for you. Next time you'll be damned glad to take my offer."

Walter spoke for the first time since the meeting began. "Mrs. Calcart, when you surrendered your stock for suitable compensation five years ago, you signed severance papers. I remind you that those papers are still retained by the company, and that they are still legally binding."

"Not if they were signed under duress."

Walter paused, his eyebrows raised slightly. "That's a serious allegation, Mrs. Calcart. If your brother were alive, it might be actionable."

Middleton stepped in front of Crystelle. "Mr. Trammel, we're not making allegations at this point. We've done what we came here to do. We've made you a fair offer for Mrs. Calcart's stock, and it has been rejected. Good day."

He ushered Crystelle out of the room.

The door slowly closed behind them. Joanna waited until she heard their footsteps fade down the hall.

"Walter, what in the world was that all about?"

He was still frowning in thought. "It's plain they were laying groundwork so that later they can say, 'We tried to be reasonable. We went to them with a fair offer. But they wouldn't cooperate.' I believe I should warn the board I doubt we've heard the last of this."

"I'm sure we haven't," Ann Leigh said. "Believe me, I know my daughter. I know the kind of mischief she can cause. I assure you I'm going to keep a close eye on her and see if I can find out what she's up to. She said she'll be back. She will."

"Middleton has the worst kind of client a lawyer can have, one he can't control," Walter said. "You remember she said, 'not if it's signed under duress.' That's not a phrase most people would use in ordinary conversation. That's legal terminology she picked up, from Middleton or some other lawyer."

Ann Leigh agreed. "I didn't notice it at the time, but you're right. She probably would have said, 'Brod made me sign it,' or something like that."

Walter was still frowning.

"Middleton is crafty. He knows police matters. He's adept at that level. But he has his limitations. He's a small-town lawyer, with no significant connections. Crystelle strikes me as being smart enough to know that. If she really intends to make a campaign of this, she'll need to find someone far more intelligent, with much better connections. I wonder who it will be."

BOOK TWO

CRYSTELLE

Chapter 13

Crystelle was secretly amused by the stir she created as she crossed the bank lobby. Both men and women turned to stare. Two businessmen almost collided.

On the way up to Moon's floor, the elevator boy kept sneaking glances at her. After she emerged, she did not hear the cage close behind her until she was well down the corridor.

Moon's name was printed in gold across the entrance to his suite. Crystelle pushed open the glass door and swept through to the receptionist.

"I'm Mrs. Hampton Calcart, Jr.," she announced. "I have an eleven o'clock appointment with Mr. Belford."

The receptionist looked up, blinked, and examined Crystelle with undisguised curiosity. Slowly, hostility rose from her like a fog. She flipped through an appointment calendar and spoke with undisguised satisfaction. "I'm afraid I don't have a record of an appointment. What did it concern?"

"That I will discuss with Mr. Belford. The appointment was made Monday morning by telephone."

"Well, I certainly don't have it listed. If you'll be seated, I'll see if Mr. Belford has a moment."

Crystelle knew the woman was lying. But she did not want to give her any satisfaction by hinting at her annoyance. She examined the waiting area. Two mismatched chairs, a nondescript sofa, and a wooden coffee table piled with magazines constituted the furnishings. Three prints—faded reproductions of Currier & Ives'—decorated the walls. Crystelle chose a chair and made it her own. She tossed her fur over the back, arranged her skirt, lit a cigarette, and calmly studied the receptionist with an unwavering gaze.

To the left of the receptionist, down a narrow hallway, three shirt-sleeved young men labored over calculators and typewriters in small glass-enclosed cubicles. Crystelle assumed that was where Moon's now famous investments newsletter was assembled and produced. To the right of the receptionist was a door marked PRIVATE.

Taking her time, the woman picked up a stenographer's pad and disappeared through the door marked PRIVATE.

Traffic increased in the corridor. One by one, three distinguished-looking executives walked past and glanced, oh so casually, through the glass door. Again Crystelle was amused. Clearly word had reached the far corners of the building: That little Spurlock bitch is back in town, all grown up and loaded for bear. She has to be seen to be believed. Looks like a movie star.

The receptionist returned. "Mr. Belford will see you now."

Crystelle kept the woman waiting while she tamped her cigarette, smoothed her hair, and gathered her fur and purse. She smiled at the woman and followed her into Moon's office.

Moon rose from his desk with the beginning of an apology. "Mrs. Calcart, I'm sorry. Apparently there was a mixup—"

He stopped in midsentence.

His face paled.

"Hello, Moon," Crystelle said. "It's good to see you again."

He had always been quick on his feet. That was one of the things she had always liked about him. He was *smooth. Graceful.* He had been strikingly good-looking as a teen-

ager. She always had known that some day he would make a
hell of a handsome man. The results exceeded her expectations. At thirty-one, he still retained an abundance of chest-
nut hair, with thick locks tumbling over his forehead. His
eyes were as she remembered—brown, devilish, and knowing. They were now further enhanced by a crinkling at the
corners that added even more character. His eyelashes were
still thick, lending his habitual intensity a dreamy, moody
quality. As he came around his desk, she saw that he remained lean and athletic.

He was the most handsome—and manly—man she had
ever known.

He took her hand. "Crystelle! This *is* a surprise."

He always had a way of using his large, strong hands that
gave her goose bumps.

The receptionist stood gawking in the doorway, gathering
every crumb. Moon glanced at her.

"That will be all for now, thank you."

The woman went out, closing the door behind her. Moon
motioned Crystelle toward a chair and held it for her. He
returned to his seat behind his desk and looked at her with
the wide, roguish grin she remembered so well. "Mrs. Calcart! That was what threw me."

"It's my legal name. Hamp was my fifth—counting you.
We're in the process of divorce. But it isn't final."

"You look terrific! I like that dress."

"Thank you. You don't look so bad yourself."

Moon deflected the compliment with a shrug. "Lord, it's
been a long time."

"Fourteen years, seven months, and four days. You made a
big mistake that day, Moon. I would've died for you. In fact, I
almost did."

She pushed back her bracelets and bared her wrists.

He winced, and in that moment Crystelle knew she was
not wasting her time.

He still cared.

They sat in silence, gazing at each other. Crystelle assumed he also was remembering the abrupt knock on the

door of their hotel room in San Antonio—a rude awakening that ended their elopement, their honeymoon, and their marriage. Brod and Moon's father had tracked them down. Moon was taken away by his father. Afterward, Crystelle had sent Brod downstairs so she could dress. She then had slashed her wrists with Moon's abandoned razor.

"We were just a couple of kids," Moon said softly. "What the hell did we know?"

"No regrets?"

Moon hesitated, and looked away. "For years I wished I had stood up to Dad that morning. Maybe we *were* underage. But they had no right to treat us that way." He paused. "Odd the way things work out, though. Now I'm happily married. With three precious daughters."

He turned a gold-framed triptych on his desk so she could see the photographs. Crystelle leaned forward to examine them. The woman was pretty, in a bovine blond sort of way. Crystelle could detect no intelligence in her eyes or individuality in her face. The children were ordinary. Not one seemed the least bit appealing.

Crystelle could not connect Moon with the mundane faces.

"Nice family," she said.

Moon smiled and readjusted the triptych. "What about you? Any regrets?"

"Only that we never got over to see the Alamo."

Moon laughed and, to her surprise, blushed.

The Alamo had been just across the street from their hotel. They had talked of joining the lines of tourists. But for the two days and nights of their honeymoon, they had ordered all food sent up, and did not leave the room a single time.

He clasped his hands. "Well, time marches on. What can I do for you?"

"Moon, I want you to make me rich."

He studied her, apparently wondering if she was serious. "From what I've heard, I wouldn't have thought you're hurting."

"I mean really rich. Richer than Beth Runnels. Richer than Sid Richardson, H. L. Hunt, anybody."

Moon laughed, a deep, resonant chuckle that had always tugged at her heartstrings. "That's a tall order."

"You can do it."

Again Moon hesitated. "Why me?"

"I just told you. I know you can do it."

He frowned. "Ordinarily, I'd be happy to take you as a private client. But under the circumstances, maybe it'd be better if you found someone else."

Crystelle shook her head. "I want you. No one else. I'll speak plain English. I find I'm seldom misunderstood when I do. Moon, I consider you an unmitigated son of a bitch for the way you treated me. I wanted to kill you then, and when I think about it, I want to kill you now. I may yet. But I also know you're a smart son of a bitch. Right now I need a smart son of a bitch."

Moon winced. "That's a recommendation?"

"Ever since I came back from Europe, I've heard nothing but praise about you. I see you mentioned regularly in the national business magazines. Every time I turn around you're off to some five-hundred-dollar-a-plate investment seminar. I'm told you're consultant to the boards of any number of international corporations. I'm told you've already built a reputation as one of the best investment counselors in the country."

Moon spread his hands and allowed the compliments to pass without comment.

"Naturally, I'm also impressed that the business magazines usually list your newsletter as tops for accuracy in its predictions. But there's something even more important. I need someone I can trust. You have your faults, God knows. But you were always honest."

Moon looked up at the ceiling. Slowly he shook his head. "Crystelle, it wouldn't work. Everyone would be wondering about our relationship."

"Who's everyone? Your wife?"

"It *would* place a burden on her. One she doesn't deserve."

"Worried?"

"Not at all. Josie knows about our elopement. She understands. It's just that she'd be the innocent victim of any loose talk."

Crystelle met his gaze for a long, significant moment. "Moon, you owe me. My troubles with Brod started that morning in San Antonio. He tossed me out of the company like an old shoe. Now I'm the only Spurlock sibling still alive —or at least the only one with any legal claim to the name. But that long-legged, snooty bitch Brod married is in the saddle, right where I ought to be. Moon, I want to get back what's mine—my part of Spurlock Oil."

"Crystelle, if you're legally out, with the company privately owned, I see no way—"

"Maybe I'll find a way," Crystelle interrupted. "Brod wasn't as lily-white as everyone seems to think. When the time comes, I'll be ready. I'll pull the rug right out from under Dear Mother and Dear Sister-in-Law."

Moon grinned. "Sounds as if you and your mother are still great buddies."

Crystelle could not contain herself. "Momma has never done anything but criticize me my whole life. And to hear her tell it, her precious Brod never did any wrong. Well, I'll show *her.* But I may need a lot of money to do it. I want to put what I have to work, make it earn a lot more. I've spent more than I intended the last few years. It costs so damned much to live these days."

Moon chortled into his fist. "Oh, boy! Things are tough all over!"

"Well, anyway, I blew too much of what I had. Now I want you to take what I have left and double it, triple it."

"That might take a while."

"I know. I've moved back here now. I have plenty of time. Why don't we work it this way. I'll put two million into an account for starters. You'll have carte blanche, within reason. If it works out, we'll keep upping the ante."

She was sure a two-million-dollar portfolio was not un-usual among his clientele. But he would know she was good for much, much more.

"Crystelle, anytime you invest money, there are risks."

"Moon, don't give me that simple shit. You're talking to the daughter of a wildcat oilman."

"I'm only saying this could be the worst time for high-risk investment."

"Why?"

"Most analysts are worried because England, Europe, are still shot. Entire sections of cities still in ruins. Factories destroyed. Food shortages, the works. Here at home, we're feeling the strain of keeping armies of occupation in Europe, Japan, a dozen other places. We've had fourteen million men reenter the job market in the last five years. Others made use of the GI Bill, training programs, and the fifty-two–twenty club. Now they're also reentering the work force. Some experts say we've probably reached the satura-tion point, that the postwar boom is over. They say we may be facing another worldwide depression. It happened after World War One. It could happen again."

"Some parts of Europe are a mess," Crystelle agreed. "And with England's austerity program, I could believe an-other depression. But that's what *they* say. What do *you* say?"

Moon took a deep breath. "I say we're only beginning an economic upswing that'll last at least another ten years. Look around you. A lot of people are still driving prewar cars. It'll take Detroit another two or three years to catch up with demand. People want clothing, appliances, furniture— quality merchandise that hasn't been available since we en-tered the war. Through the war years, most people made more money than they've ever made in their lives, and there was nothing in the stores to buy. With nowhere to spend it, most people socked it away. War bonds. So far, most money has resisted the shoddy stuff rushed out since the war. Only now are quality goods coming onto the market. People are beginning to spend. This is a time of renewal.

Half the people in the whole damned country are thinking of a new home, a new car, new clothes. There'll be jobs galore, and that'll create *more* money to spend."

"I like what you say better."

"Ordinarily, that analysis in a private consultation such as this would cost you a thousand bucks. But I'm the first to admit I could be wrong. The doomsayers could be right."

"I'm willing to bet on you. Is it a deal?"

Moon's hesitation was brief. "It's a deal." He reached across the desk for a handshake.

She held on to his hand. "I have only one codicil. I'll want to know all there is to know about every investment we make. I'll want to know about other possibilities you considered, and why you rejected them. Moon, I want to *learn*. By the time we're finished, I want to be as smart about business as Brod ever was."

Moon eased his hand free. He shrugged. "I keep all my private clients informed. That's a big part of what I do."

"Then we're agreed. I'll set up the account in the next few days and we can get started."

He came around the desk, helped her with the fur, and escorted her to the door. There Crystelle paused.

"Moon, you really should do something about your reception area. It's horrible. Early Hooverville."

Moon gave her a startled glance. "Is it that bad? I hadn't really thought about it. When I moved in, I just used what the bank had available."

"Well, it isn't what a nationally known investments counselor should have representing him before the public."

Moon grinned. "Maybe I've been so busy I've never taken a good look at it. I don't spend much time here. I'm out of town a lot."

"You deserve better. Call in a decorator. Tell him the Depression is over and you want new furniture, the works. Get rid of those awful prints. You need something whimsical —Lautrec, Vuillard, or Picasso maybe. I can lend you something. Have your man call me."

Moon frowned. For an instant, Crystelle feared she had

moved too fast. Then his gaze went from her face to her feet and back up again. She saw the old, familiar hunger in his eyes, so she pushed even further.

"And the next time I come for an appointment, I want to see that woman out there gone. Not only is she incompetent, she looks totally ridiculous."

She did not wait for his reaction. She opened the door herself and walked out past the receptionist.

"Good day, Mrs. Calcart," the woman said.

"Thank you," Crystelle said. "But it already has been a very lovely day."

Chapter 14

Joanna sat in the corner of the church hall and listened as Kelly and the preparatory choir practiced. The Director was drilling them in the first portion of the *Lord Nelson Mass,* apparently new to their repertoire.

It was the first time she had heard Kelly's group and she was tremendously impressed. Considering that this was only the preparatory choir, still more than a year away from performance, the level of musicianship was astounding. Around her sat mothers, fathers, and families of members of the choir.

After a heavy week at the company, the drive to Denton with Kelly's car pool had been a pleasant diversion. Kelly and the other boys had sung all the way, clowning around with the four-part harmony, showing off for her. The boys had arrived in such high spirits that she had worried about whether they would settle down enough for practice. But rigid discipline seemed firmly ingrained. The boys stood ramrod-straight as they sang, their eyes firmly fixed on the Director.

The first portion of the mass was repeated several times. The Director then described the phrasing of the next segment. As he talked, Joanna noticed that Kelly's eyes kept cutting in her direction, apparently to gauge her reaction to the performance.

Joanna knew she should not participate. She kept her expression neutral.

The Director raised a hand, cuing the start of the next segment. All eyes in the choir were locked on him—all except Kelly's. At the last moment, his gaze flicked in her direction. The Director's hand remained poised for a moment. Then the Director's hand came down.

From the opening notes Joanna saw that Kelly was in trouble. He was hesitant, uncertain.

On a crucial phrase his voice soared a full beat before the others in his section.

Immediately the Director stopped the choir and again explained the timing. Again he raised a hand, and the choir restarted the piece from the beginning.

Twice more Kelly glanced in her direction. His face grew taut, and she knew he could not regain his concentration. At the crucial point, he voice again soared prematurely. This time, he also led the boy beside him into the wrong notes.

The Director stopped the choir and strode straight toward Kelly, reexplaining the beat as he went. For emphasis, he rapped Kelly over the head with his knuckles.

The boy beside Kelly also received a solid lick.

Furiously Joanna rose from her chair, fully intending to march down to the choir and yank Kelly from the ranks.

But in that moment there was such a transformation in Kelly and the choir that she hesitated.

Tears were coursing down his cheeks. The boy beside him also was crying. But both were singing with total concentration.

Joanna sank back into her chair as the choir went all the way through the piece with marvelous perfection.

Her anger was not diminished, but she no longer was certain of what she should do. She remembered that her professor friend had warned that the boys sometimes got rapped on the head.

She also remembered that the professor had said the boys invariably rose to the challenge, and that it was the mothers who could not keep pace with the demand for perfection.

Around her, the incident had not gone unnoticed. But no one appeared unduly excited. From the reaction of the audience, Joanna gathered that while such discipline was not routine, it was not exceptional.

When practice ended, Kelly came toward her with the Fort Worth group. He had wiped the tears from his face and was subdued, but not cowed and whining as she would have expected only a few weeks ago.

"Go on to the car," she told him.

The boys filed out, looking back, recognizing her anger, wondering what she would do.

Joanna walked down the aisle toward the Director. He was talking with a group of parents, resolving a conflict in schedules. The conversation was relaxed, pleasant.

Joanna stopped. She knew she was too angry to handle the situation rationally. And she did not intend to wade into the group and make a spectacle of herself.

She turned and walked out the door to the car. The boys were waiting.

"Get in," she told them.

She drove without speaking until they were on the outskirts of Denton. There she pulled onto the shoulder of the highway and stopped.

"He actually struck you," she said to Kelly. "Has he ever done that before?"

"No," Kelly said.

A huge truck roared by, rocking the car.

"What about you other boys? Has he ever hit you?"

She looked at them, one by one, demanding a reply.

"Once," Tommy said.

"Twice," Bobby admitted.

Pete and Archie shook their heads negatively.

"It was just a tap," Kelly said. "It didn't hurt. Not really."

Joanna felt it useless to challenge such an obvious lie.

"Well, it won't happen again," she said. "I'm taking you out of that choir."

"No!" Kelly said. "Mom, I can't quit. They depend on me."

The other boys were sitting in silence. Joanna recognized that there was more to the situation than was evident on the surface.

"What about you other boys? Do your parents know this is going on?"

They were reluctant to answer.

"No," Bobby said.

Tommy nodded, indicating his parents knew.

"What did they say about it?"

Tommy gave a slight shrug. "Mom got mad. Daddy laughed."

"But they didn't do anything?"

Tommy shook his head.

There was nothing she could do at the moment. The parents of the other boys would soon be arriving at the rendez-vous in Fort Worth. If she was late, they would worry. She waited until a string of cars passed, then pulled back onto the highway.

She drove the rest of the way to Fort Worth in silence, delivered the other boys to the rendezvous, and took Kelly straight home. She followed him up to his room and sat him down on his bed.

"Kelly, I want you to tell me all about this—exactly what happened, how long it has been going on. Why were you disciplined? Tell me everything."

Even as he began, the thought came to Joanna that only a few weeks ago Kelly probably would have been crying, and speaking in a whine.

He sat up straight and was dry-eyed.

"I goofed. Twice. And you're supposed to keep your mind on the music."

"But you were doing your best. He shouldn't have hit you."

Kelly spoke with a conviction Joanna had never seen in him before. "Mom, I'm not any different from the other guys. Everybody's got to do it exactly right, or it doesn't work."

Joanna was disconcerted by his attitude. She attempted to explore his reasoning. "If I understand what you're saying, all must be done to perfection for this man."

Kelly nodded. "That's the way music is."

"Well, let me tell *you* something. I studied piano twelve years. And three years of music in college. I had some very demanding teachers. But I managed it without getting hit in the head."

"This is the Texas Boys Choir."

Kelly said it as if that explained everything.

"Oh, I see. It's better than other choirs."

Kelly nodded.

"Do the other boys talk about being hit in the head?"

"Some. It's just a part of it."

"In other words, you've got to be tough to be a member of the Texas Boys Choir—tough enough to get knocked around a little. Is that it?"

Kelly hesitated, and again nodded.

"Is this something the boys actually take pride in—a sort of trial by torture they've survived?"

Kelly shook his head. "Nobody wants to be the guy who goofs."

Joanna felt she was beginning to understand. "I see. You don't mind being hit in the head. You just don't want to be singled out as the one who disappointed the Director, the one who fell short of Texas Boys Choir standards. Is that it?"

Kelly nodded emphatically.

"Well, I can understand that. But I still think it's too severe a discipline to be imposed on a group of young boys."

Kelly's reaction was immediate. "Mom, we're not just a bunch of boys. We're singing music few adults can sing— music that goes way back to the Middle Ages, to a long time before Jesus, even. To the Egyptians. We have to do it exactly right, or not at all."

Joanna assumed he was borrowing phrases from the Director.

Her anger had not faded. But she now felt that perhaps she should move cautiously in challenging success. The changes in Kelly during a few short months had been nothing short of phenomenal. She had not had to remind him one time about his schoolwork. His grades had improved until they were almost scary. He was leading his class, while devoting at least fifteen hours a week to the choir.

She had hoped that the choir would transform him.

Perhaps she should not object that it was doing more than she asked.

"All right, Kelly. I'll say no more about it. If you want to go around with lumps on your head, that's your business. But promise me one thing. If the choir ever becomes too much for you, or you develop negative feelings about it, I want you to come to me and tell me. Promise?"

Kelly promised.

As she left the room, he already was returning to his homework, as if there were not a moment to lose.

Peggy Trammel lay propped in a sitting position in a large wing chair, her wasted body almost lost in a loose, flowing red hostess gown. Only a pale reflection of her exquisite beauty lingered in her clear blue eyes and long blond hair, and in her flawless skin.

"We're not used to visitors," she said, her cadence timed to exhalation. "Please excuse us if we seem rusty with our manners."

"Oh, come on, now! We're hardly that bad," Walter said.

"I certainly don't wish to intrude," Joanna said. "But I know how devastating a long illness can be, and I wanted to see if I could help."

She had put off the visit for months. Even now she was not sure she should have come. We're all trying too hard, she thought. Walter was stiff in his chair, watching his wife, alert to every nuance. A nurse hovered just beyond the doorway, attempting to be unobtrusive, but failing.

"It *is* wearing," Peggy said. "All the therapy and baths. I don't seem to have time for anything else. But I make myself remember that Franklin Roosevelt endured all this, and still went on to become President."

The paralysis apparently had not affected her face, and she seemed to have some use of her neck muscles. But her arms rested motionless on the chair. Her hands lay lifeless.

"The medical routine has tended to turn us into recluses," Walter said. "Maybe too much so."

"I know the hazard," Joanna said. "But I think it's understandable. You have to trim obligations to the point that you can cope with them."

Peggy rolled her eyes in an eloquent gesture. "During the first year I tried to answer, personally, every card and note I received. But it was impossible. I had two secretaries, and they kept getting in the way of the medical people. I had to give it up and send form letters."

The drinks arrived. After serving Joanna, the houseboy placed drinks for the Trammels on a small table near Peggy's chair. In a movement so effortless that it was clearly habitual, Walter slid to an ottoman beside his wife. He raised their drinks in toast, then held Peggy's glass for her to sip from a bent straw. Joanna and Walter were drinking Scotch and water, but Joanna was sure that Peggy's drink was an artfully disguised Shirley Temple.

"I've neglected all my friends unforgivably," Peggy said. "Walter rigged a phone I could use while in the lung. But it was so tedious for anyone trying to talk with me. I felt such a burden. I'm sure most people couldn't stand the sound of the lung. Finally I quit trying."

"People mean well," Joanna said. "But I learned that few friends can continue a relationship through long illness. They don't seem to stop and think that you no longer can do all the things you once did with them. I suspect they even feel a bit guilty that it happened to you, and not to them. Some even seem relieved when they feel they've fulfilled their obligations and can go on with their own lives."

She stopped abruptly. She had said far more than she had intended. She seldom ever spoke on such a personal level, and she was appalled that she had.

"I'm speaking from experience," she added.

"You can't blame people," Walter said. "It's only human nature."

"I feel so fortunate to be home now," Peggy said. "I don't think I could have kept my sanity much longer in the hospital." She paused. "How are your sons? Are they recovering from their loss?"

Joanna recognized the change of topic as an effort to get away from the subject of illness—surely a weary one in this household.

She offered a sanitized version of Weldon's rebellion, and told of the glowing reports she had received recently from the military school.

"Now his goal is to make the polo team. I'm afraid he'll be hurt. But it's the school's philosophy to motivate the cadets with tangible rewards. So I'll probably give my permission."

She described Kelly's infatuation with the choir, and told of today's incident.

"I was absolutely furious. But I remembered that a friend warned me it was usually the family who couldn't adjust to the choir's demands, and not the boy. That brought me up short."

She told of her talk with Kelly, and of learning that he was taking the head knock in stride.

"So I'm letting him sink or swim," she concluded. "Maybe I *was* being too protective."

"I don't think so," Peggy said. "That sounds too drastic a discipline for a boy, just over a moment of inattention."

Walter laughed. "He'll probably be grateful for it later. I imagine most men wish they'd had someone to make them toe the mark more during their formative years. It seems like wonderful training for him."

Joanna recognized the remark as one that Brod might have made, and for the first time realized that Brod would have heartily approved of the head-knocking.

"The discipline of the choir does seem to be having a good effect," she conceded. "Six months ago he would have been in tears. But he handled the whole incident like a little man. I already see a new maturity in him."

"I'm sure you have nothing to worry about," Walter said.

Joanna thought she saw signs of fatigue around Peggy's eyes. "I should be getting back to the house. Kelly will be wondering what has happened to me."

Walter's lack of protest confirmed her impression. "We're glad you came. We hope you'll come again soon."

Joanna rose and looked down at Peggy. "Listen, I've had experience with your situation. I know there are a thousand and one things that never get done. I'm practically next door. So I hope you'll let me help."

"That's very thoughtful of you. But I really have everything I need."

"Peggy, I'm not just being polite. But I'll come over only on the condition that you won't feel obligated to entertain me, or to interrupt your routine."

Peggy smiled. "On that basis, I accept. Come over anytime."

"I'll walk you to your car," Walter said.

In the drive, he held the door for her. "I really appreciate this. She was in better spirits tonight than I've seen her in months."

As Joanna drove the half block home, she regretted that she had put off the visit so long.

Ever since that first day in Walter's office, she had been tormented by visions of a poor woman lying helpless only three doors away.

She had wanted to help. But she was deeply troubled and confused by her motives.

She recognized the attraction Walter held for her.

And the danger.

Chapter 15

Crystelle had been waiting for the phone call all day. When it came she was fully prepared.

"I have the papers ready for you to sign," Moon said. "If you'll drop by Monday, we can go over them. I want to explain exactly how I've set it up, what I'm doing."

Crystelle gave him a practiced sigh of exasperation. "Oh, shit, Moon! I'm leaving in the morning for New York. I won't be back till the end of the week."

The line remained silent while Moon considered alternatives. "We really should get this done. I'd like to put your money to work as soon as possible. It's almost five. If you can come downtown now, I'll stay late."

Crystelle paused, as if assessing complications of her own. "Moon, I'm right in the middle of packing. I have a better idea. Why don't you just drop by here in about an hour?"

She almost could hear the wheels turning in his head; she knew him better than he knew himself. He spoke slowly.

"Crystelle, I'm not sure that'd be wise."

"What's the matter? Afraid of me?"

He was. But he would never admit it.

"I'm only being practical. If someone saw me or my car at

your house, it'd get around fast. When it comes to gossip, Fort Worth is the biggest small town in the world."

Crystelle did not have to pretend her anger. "Moon, I'm damned tired of being told I should do something or not do something because of what other people might think. To hell with them!"

Again the wheels turned. "All right. I'll be there. It won't take long. I'll see you in about an hour."

Crystelle showered and artfully arranged three half-packed suitcases about her bedroom. She went down to the kitchen, made a pitcher of martinis, and set it beside two glasses in the refrigerator. After checking the lights in the living room—not too dim, not too bright—she returned to the bedroom and changed into a red silk hostess gown she had found in Mexico the summer before. She left her hair loose and slightly damp. Moon once said wet hair was sexy. He had been only a teenager at the time, but leopards seldom changed their spots. Not too much makeup. Moon always said it got in the way. Just a hint of fragrance. Moon claimed nothing a woman could put on smelled better than the woman herself. Crystelle had always allowed him that conceit.

She examined herself one last time in the full-length mirror and was satisfied.

When Moon arrived, she met him at the door.

"Please excuse the confusion," she said. "Since I'm leaving in the morning, I've already given the maids the weekend off."

She led him into the living room and served the martinis herself.

Moon opened his briefcase and arranged the legal papers on the coffee table.

"It's a bit complicated," he said. "I want to go over each one carefully, and explain exactly what it means."

For a time they worked side by side on the sofa, their heads and shoulders almost touching, but not quite. Moon talked at length about the various investments accounts, the reasons for each, and what documents he needed to act in her behalf.

Crystelle hardly listened. She concentrated on shifting her position occasionally, while pretending to follow all the legalese. She was well aware that her gown clung exactly where it should—and of the effect on Moon.

Twice she poured fresh martinis.

As they finished the third drink, she felt the charade had gone on long enough. She signed the papers.

Returning them, she allowed her hand to brush lightly against his thigh.

Moon put the papers back into his briefcase and buckled the straps. He smiled. "Well, that's it. I'd best be going."

Crystelle stood between Moon and the door and did not move out of his way. "You really don't have to go, do you?" she asked softly.

He looked into her eyes for a long moment.

When he reached for her, it was like going over the top on a big roller coaster. The rest was inevitable. At the proper moment, Crystelle led him upstairs to her bedroom.

Moon proved even better as a lover than she remembered. Experience had made him more considerate and adept. Yet the unforgettable wildness was still there.

Their lovemaking was as frantic as their first delicious coupling in a thirties tourist court before the ink was hardly dry on their marriage certificate.

Time ceased to exist. Nothing else mattered. Crystelle gave him no relief. She used every trick she knew and Moon responded, taking her over hurdle after hurdle, higher and higher, until at last all came crashing down in a glorious final climax.

They lay cuddled while their pulses stopped racing. Gradually they drifted into the twilight of mutual contentment.

Exhausted, Moon slept.

She remained awake, watching him, cataloguing the changes.

After an hour, she awakened him with kisses. "It's almost eleven," she said. "I don't want you to get into trouble."

It was too early in the game to put his marriage to the test. Moon was unconcerned. "I told Josie not to wait up."

"Where are you supposed to be?"

"Out to dinner with a client."

Crystelle laughed. He had known all along what would happen.

He smiled in acknowledgment that she had seen through his thinking.

"I suppose this was inevitable," he said. "But it mustn't happen again."

"Why not? We're not hurting anybody."

"We could. Josie. The girls. I wouldn't hurt them for the world."

He was silent for a time. "You may not believe me, but I've never cheated on Josie before."

"I believe it."

"There were a couple of times I came close. But I never did." He paused, tracing the line of her shoulder. "It probably wouldn't have happened this time, except that you were always special with me." Again he smiled. "I used to think about you a lot, in college, all through the war. I'd wonder what you were doing, if you'd found someone else. I used to fantasize that maybe we'd get back together someday."

"We should never have been separated in the first place," Crystelle said.

"I remember the day when I heard you had married again. Someone wrote me. I was in North Africa, a hellhole of a place. I paid a hundred dollars for a fifth of cheap bourbon and got as drunk that night as I've ever been."

"I went kind of crazy for a while," Crystelle said. "I really didn't have good sense. Most of those marriages didn't mean anything. They were just something to do to keep from going completely crazy."

He pulled her to him and held her for a long moment. She felt him growing firm against her.

He laughed and moved away. "You've always had that effect on me, like no one else. For a long time I would remember you, the things we'd done, and I'd get a tremendous hard-on just thinking about it." He paused, thinking back. "One of my biggest surprises, when we got married, was finding out you wanted it almost as much as I did. But you always fought like a tiger. How'd you manage to hold out so long?"

Crystelle remembered those steamy, frustrating nights in Moon's old Ford. "It wasn't easy," she said.

"But why? We went steady what? Almost two years? I'd begun to think you were frigid or something, and was just talking a good game to lead me on."

Crystelle thought about it. She now had difficulty understanding herself as a teenager.

"That's the way it was in those days," she said. "I'd had it drilled into me since I was knee-high that good girls didn't do it. Only bad girls did it. That was some of Momma's propaganda, and I bought it. If you let a boy do it, two things could happen. You could get pregnant, and your life was ruined, or word would get around and no decent boy would have anything to do with you. Back then, I believed it."

"Maybe it *was* true, back then," Moon conceded. "Boys did talk a lot. We had some nutty ideas."

Crystelle raised her hands to show her wrists. "That's part of the reason I did this. I knew everybody in town would hear what happened. I thought I was ruined for life."

Moon held her hands, traced the scars. "And I did it."

"You did it. And I helped. But Brod was the one who took something beautiful and turned it into trash. I never forgave him for that. I hated his guts right up until the day he died."

Again Moon was silent for a time. "Well, it happened, and there's nothing we can do about it now," he said. "It'd be a mistake to try to revive it, after all these years. It was probably a mistake for me to accept you as a client. Maybe we should make it a point to stay away from each other."

Crystelle understood that she would have to maneuver carefully.

"Moon, I'm a different person now. And you're different, with your career, all your responsibilities. You're right. We shouldn't even try to revive the way we were as teenagers.

But damn it, we've been robbed of a lot of happiness together. A whole lifetime. I don't see anything wrong with taking back a little of what was stolen from us."

Moon studied her face. He shook his head. "We'd be risking too much. I'm not only thinking of Josie and the kids. I'm also thinking about you, and me. It would be a dead end, and no future in it for you. I'd feel much better if you could go on with your life, find someone who appreciates you half as much as I do."

"Moon, I'm not about to make any demands on you. And if we see each other occasionally, I won't feel any obligations toward you, either. If someone else comes along, fine. But in the meantime, I'll take whatever happiness I can get."

Moon rolled onto his back and looked at the ceiling. "Crystelle, it wouldn't work. This is too small a town. Someone would see us together, somewhere, no matter what precautions we took."

"It doesn't have to be here. You travel a lot. I travel a lot. No one would notice if we were in the same city at the same time, and just happened to stay at the same hotel."

"Mostly, I attend investment seminars, board meetings. There are always people around who know me."

Crystelle passed a hand lightly over the hair on his chest. "Surely they don't follow you through hotel corridors in the dead of night. Who'd ever know?"

Moon raised his hands to his face and rubbed his eyes. "It wouldn't work," he said again. "We'd be playing with too many people's lives." He turned onto his side and cupped her face in his big hands. "Understand, I'm not saying I regret this happened. I'm very glad it did. I think we both can look on it as a precious reprise of a very good time in our lives. But it'd be wrong to try to extend it into something more."

"I guess I can live with that," Crystelle said. She pushed herself out of bed. "If you're supposed to be having dinner with a client, we mustn't make you into a liar. Would you settle for a quick omelet?"

While he showered she went down to the kitchen, put

together a Denver omelet, and made toast and coffee. In a few minutes Moon came downstairs fully dressed.

He ate with enthusiasm. When he had finished, he took her hands in his.

"Crystelle, I'll never forget this. I'll always treasure the memory."

He lifted first one of her hands, then the other, and kissed the palms.

Then solemnly, gazing steadily into her eyes, he gently kissed the scars on her wrists.

Crystelle did not try to stop quick tears. It was one of the most moving moments she had ever known.

Moon went back into the front of the house and gathered his papers. They stood for a time embraced. Then Moon kissed her and was gone.

Crystelle remained leaning against the door, savoring her night of accomplishment.

The hook was set.

After a few days, it would begin to fester. Moon would miss her more than he dreamed possible. Absence truly made the heart grow fonder, especially if accompanied by a strong genital itch.

She could safely forget Moon for a while, and go to New York to meet with the people who might be able to help her.

Chapter 16

The idea for a deep test well was planted with Humble, but weeks passed before it sprouted. Joanna already was considering other ploys when Piersall came into her office one afternoon to report he had just talked with Harry Mead, head of production at Humble.

"He asked, offhand, if we're still interested," Piersall said. "I told him we were preparing to go ahead with something, but I wasn't sure what. I said I'd ask you."

Joanna felt a wave of relief, tinged with apprehension. Campbell and Chambers were strongly opposed to the deadweight outlay. She had not yet brought her plan before the Spurlock board, but she knew Ann Leigh would be heavily influenced by Campbell and Chambers. In turn, the two outside board members would tend to go along with Ann Leigh, the majority stockholder.

Joanna knew she would have to handle the situation delicately.

"Did Mead indicate he was ready to discuss it?"

Piersall nodded. "He suggested I might come down next week, and tell them what we have in mind."

That was a tiny wedge—one she must use.

"Why don't you tell him we're prepared to make a formal proposal. Ask him to set up a meeting with Calvin Spears, anyone else they want to sit in on it. Tell him you'll bring me, and Don Parker."

Piersall hesitated. "Mrs. Spurlock, I'm not sure he'd go along with that. I think he's planning to put together a package to take to Spears."

One of Brod's oft-repeated warnings came to mind: Always talk with the top people, not the hired help.

As president and CEO of Humble, Calvin Spears was the top.

"No. We've got to get Spears in on it from the beginning," she said. "Maybe we can even convince him it was his idea."

"What about attorneys?"

"I can't see any reason for them to be brought into it at this point. Can you? Why not tell Mead we can just rough out the deal? That we can put the lawyers on the details later."

Piersall set up the meeting for the following Monday. Through the remainder of the week Joanna spent all her spare time in preparation. She pulled every joint-venture contract from the files and studied the terms. She went back through her texts on the oil industry, rereading each item pertaining to cooperative efforts.

When Monday came, she felt she was ready.

By daybreak they were airborne in the Cessna, flying steadily southward with the sun rising on their left wing. There was little conversation. Don Parker was preoccupied with his charts. Piersall put his head back and dozed. Smiling Jack was kept busy by the heavy air traffic in the Fort Worth–Dallas, Austin, and Houston corridor.

Joanna had brought along some overdue correspondence. She spent the flight leisurely making notes, occasionally glancing out the window to watch the landscape turn from rolling plains to the rugged hills of central Texas, gradually giving way to the coastal plains.

When they arrived on the outskirts of Houston, their clearance to land was delayed. Smiling Jack circled out over the Gulf.

Joanna was irritated by the loss of time. They were on a
tight schedule. Unable to continue her work, she watched as
they flew over lower Galveston Island and outbound shrimp
boats.

As they returned to the Houston suburbs, she was amazed
by the city's postwar growth. New construction was in progress everywhere below. She felt as if she were watching a
huge amoeba expanding under a microscope.

When they landed, a car and driver were waiting, cour-
tesy of Humble. Joanna, Piersall, and Parker were whisked
through traffic to the Humble Building in downtown Houston.

As they stepped out of the car in front of the new Humble
headquarters, Joanna began to have serious qualms. She had
not quite known what to expect, but the effect was overwhelming. There was no comparison with the six-story Spurlock Building in Fort Worth.

And she was here to deal one-on-one with this major oil
company, proposing a fifty-fifty split.

No wonder Chambers had said they would laugh.

She steeled herself with the thought that Brod probably
would not have seen the incongruity.

He had dealt with men far more powerful than anyone at
Humble.

The elevators were swift, as if no one in Houston had a
moment to spare. As they emerged on the proper floor they
were met by a receptionist, who escorted them toward the
executive suites.

Joanna found herself surrounded by men. The few women
in evidence were young, clearly office menials.

They were ushered into a large, dark-paneled conference
room. Three executives rose at the far end of a big mahog-
any table. One stepped forward.

"Mrs. Spurlock? I'm Harry Mead. This is Marty Sutter, and
Calvin Spears. Good to see you."

Joanna introduced Piersall and Parker. Mead gestured toward the table, and the two groups sat facing each other.

She knew the men only by title and reputation. Mead was

tall and heavyset, with the stamp of outdoor work still evident in his complexion. Sutter, chief of exploration, was a
smaller man, dark-featured, of a studious demeanor. Spears
was bald, sleek, and surprisingly trim in build.

As the hosts asked politely about their flight down, Spears
watched Joanna intently, as if taking her measure. He remained quiet. Apparently he intended for Mead to conduct
the meeting.

"We expected a larger delegation," Mead said.

Joanna smiled. "We're it."

"I've dealt with Arnold Campbell a time or two," Spears
said. "He won't be involved?"

Joanna met his gaze. "Mr. Campbell is our general manager. I'm the president and chief executive officer."

Spears glanced at Mead, his expression plainly saying,
What the hell is this? What have you gotten me into?

Mead's hearty manner vanished. "Well, I suppose we
should get down to brass tacks. Mrs. Spurlock, what exactly
are you proposing?"

Joanna knew that the purpose of the meeting had been
made plain to Mead. She assumed he now wanted her to
state it for Spears' benefit.

"In moving forward with development of some of our
leases in New Mexico, it occurred to us that Spurlock and
Humble have a virtual monopoly on potentially valuable
play. Our holdings in that region are almost identical. We're
proposing a joint venture for a deep test to define the geology to fifteen, maybe twenty thousand feet. I believe the
effort would be of great benefit to both companies."

Mead raised his eyebrows. "Mrs. Spurlock, a deep test in
that remote area would be expensive. And even if production were found in quantity, it might be years before any
return would be realized."

Joanna ignored the condescension and gave him a blank
stare. "Mr. Mead, you have just stated why I'm proposing a
joint venture. Splitting the expense would make it easier on
both our companies."

"I see your point. But an agreement of this type would be

extremely detailed and technical. There are many aspects to consider."

Again Joanna spoke coolly. "That's why we're here, Mr. Mead. We're prepared to discuss them."

"All right. What specifically are your terms?"

Joanna clipped her words. "Standard contract. Independent driller. Extremely tight hole. Total access for both Spurlock and Humble exploration and production people. Complete sharing of information. All expenses split down the middle. Our only exceptional requirement would be that the test must be drilled into the fault zone."

Mead's eyebrows again raised slightly. "What fault zone?"

Joanna glanced at Sutter, Spears.

Their faces showed nothing.

She was hit by another moment of uncertainty.

Could Brod's theory about the submerged fault have been wrong?

She remembered the many hours he had spent with maps, charts, and aerial photographs.

Surely he had been right.

Carefully keeping her own face devoid of expression, she held out a hand to Parker. He passed the lease map to her. She spread it in front of Mead and Spears.

"The submerged fault that runs from about here, to about there." She glanced at Mead. "You've had seismograph crews working in that area for months. Surely you've defined it by now."

Spears looked at Mead, and back to Joanna. His face reddened. "Mrs. Spurlock, what do you know of our seismograph crews? Am I to understand you've come here to bargain with illegally obtained information? That just isn't done."

Joanna did not bother to hide her anger. "Mr. Spears, my husband discovered that fracture years before your company ever optioned a single acre in that region. That's why he invested in those leases and held on to them through the years. With the slope of the formations, there's a good chance of a new pool along that fault, if not a new field."

"What slope?" Mead said. "Most of that country is so pre-
dictable you could set your depth gauge by the formations."

"Not here," Joanna said, pointing to the map. "You're
edging into range and valley folding."

Spears spoke without inflection. "Where did you learn
your geology, Mrs. Spurlock?"

"From my husband. If what I've heard here today is any
example, I think I can assume I attended a very good
school."

Spears laughed and glanced at Mead, who blushed.

"Well, we all have our little secrets, Mrs. Spurlock," Spears
said. "As you may know by now, we sometimes have to play
it very close to the chest in the oil game." He paused. "What
if the test should find production? What about profits?"

"Fifty-fifty. Just like expenses."

Spears toyed with a pen for a moment. "You've made us a
very interesting offer. How soon would you be prepared to
go ahead with it?"

"Immediately."

"What if we decide we wish to go it alone? What will you
do?"

Joanna was tempted to tell him it was none of his business.
But she understood his implication that as a small company,
Spurlock Oil might not have the resources to undertake
such a project on its own.

"Mr. Spears, I'm sure I can assume your company isn't
holding on to those leases on mere idle speculation. Neither
are we. You've done considerable surface exploration. So did
my husband. I see every indication you're moving ahead to
determine the worth of your leases. So are we. In answer to
your question, I assume that if you reject our proposal, you
will drill your deep test, and we will drill ours. I also assume
we will obtain essentially the same information, at double
the expense."

Spears smiled. "Mrs. Spurlock, we're competitors. With
adjoining leases, almost checkerboarded in some areas, we
conceivably could be placed in a race to pump oil out from
under each other, if indeed oil is there. Frankly, before I

would enter into such an agreement, I would have to have an ironclad contract."

Joanna did not smile back. "So would I."

Spears glanced at Mead, Sutter. "Well, this is an interesting idea. I'm perfectly willing to explore it further. Suppose we put our legal beagles onto it, on the terms you've proposed, and see what they can work out."

"Fine," Joanna said.

She rose and shook hands with Spears.

Joanna and her executives did not discuss the results of the meeting in the elevator, or in the car on the way back to the airport. But once they were aboard the plane, she asked the men what they thought.

"Spears is only leaving himself an out," Piersall said. "They've spent a lot of money on surface exploration. They'll be reluctant to share it. But to take advantage of the other, I think they'll let us in on it. I believe it's a done deal."

Parker agreed.

As they became airborne, enroute back to Fort Worth, Parker offered another thought.

"I'll tell you something else," he said in his droll way. "I don't think *those* three fellows will ever play poker with you."

His opinion was confirmed the following week when George Hollander told an anecdote at the regular Monday morning meeting of department heads.

"I was with a group at the Petroleum Club in Houston," he told Joanna. "Calvin Spears came over to our table. He was very complimentary about you."

Joanna was curious. "What exactly did he say?"

"He said you were smart as a whip, and a very tough young lady."

Joanna's executives laughed, apparently appreciating Spears' acknowledgment that perhaps she had gotten the best of Humble in the deal.

But Joanna did not respond.

She was not at all sure Spears had intended it as a compliment.

* * *

On her second visit with Peggy, Joanna quickly saw what an effort the Trammels had made on that first evening. In the iron lung Peggy seemed even more fragile. The noisy contraption hummed and hissed constantly. Only her head was free, with the rest of her body held captive beneath the rubber collar around her neck.

Joanna could not look at the machine without battling claustrophobia. But Peggy smiled into the large, curved mirror above her head.

"Now you see me . . . in my natural habitat," she said, timing her words to the pump of the bellows.

Perched on a stool, chatting about her day, Joanna stayed longer than she had intended. But as she prepared to leave, Peggy locked gazes with her in the mirror.

"Please stop by . . . any time . . . I do need to hear . . . about the outside world."

In the weeks that followed, Joanna's frequent visits to Peggy became a habit. She soon discovered that Peggy was an unusually intelligent person. Gradually they explored their mutual views on current events, local politics, art, music, fashions. They found they had much in common.

One evening Peggy remarked that she had been unable to find cosmetics to match her altered skin tone. The shadings she had used before now seemed garish against her paleness.

Joanna shopped and they experimented until they found a combination more suitable. Afterward, Joanna made other personal selections for her—nightgowns, bed jackets, housedresses.

As they became friends Peggy began to share her fears.

"Sometimes I think I'm making progress. But then I'll have a setback, and I never seem to regain the ground I've lost. I don't want to believe it, but I know I'm fighting a losing battle."

Joanna demurred and tried to sound optimistic. She pointed out the improvements she had seen.

Yet, to herself, she could not deny her own impression that Peggy indeed was slipping away, day by day, week by week.

In early fall, Peggy made an odd request. They had been

talking about music, dance. Joanna had been bragging a bit about Kelly, who already was substituting occasionally for the performing choir.

"I'm worried about Walter," Peggy said. "He has been a prisoner of my illness as much as I. And he's such a social man. He loves all of the arts. We used to attend every opera, ballet, and symphony performance in Fort Worth and Dallas. We made special trips to Santa Fe, San Francisco, New York. Now he has hardly been out of the house at night since my illness began. I'm afraid that eventually he'll begin to hate me for it, at least subconsciously. I know I'm an albatross around his neck."

"Peggy, that isn't the way it works," Joanna told her. "Don't forget I've been through all this. What he truly feels is a helplessness that he can't share your pain. He's frustrated because he can take so little of the burden from you."

Peggy lay quiet for a time in the lung, waiting for it to rebuild her strength. "All the same, he deserves better. I want you to help me get him out of the house occasionally. We can make up something. Maybe you can tell him you're saddled with extra tickets you bought at company expense. I'll pay for them. I assure you. If you're not dating, you couldn't ask for a better escort."

Joanna was deeply disturbed. "Peggy! Good Lord, I couldn't do that! People would misunderstand."

"Nonsense. You're my best friend. Everyone knows my situation, and Walter's love of the arts. Maybe you could take Kelly along, as a sort of chaperone. You'd just be three near neighbors, going out to a performance."

"But I'm sure there would be talk."

Even as she said the words, Joanna knew she sounded exactly like Ann Leigh.

"Let people talk. We'll know the truth. That's all that matters."

Joanna kept insisting she could not possibly do it. But Peggy persisted.

At last Joanna relented.

But as the first concert approached, her qualms returned.

She and Walter had worked closely for weeks in hammering out the agreement with Humble. Sometimes they met in his office, sometimes in hers. She kept remembering how her pulse always quickened at his mere touch, how she was always so keenly aware of his presence.

Again she began questioning the compulsion that drove her to form a friendship with Peggy.

Had she intended it as a protective device against her natural attraction to Walter?

Or had she unconsciously created this situation to betray a friend, and to have Walter for herself?

Through the first few months after Weldon left, Kelly did not think he could endure the loneliness. His mother spent more and more time at the office, and often she went out of town for days at a stretch, leaving him alone in the house with Calla Lily, the maids, and, occasionally, Bonnie Ledbetter. And when his mother came home from the office, it was usually after dark. She invariably went straight to her room. Sometimes late at night he would slip into the hall and stand near her door, merely to hear her voice as she talked on the phone.

On his way home from school one afternoon, he stopped in a store and found a postcard bearing the picture of a bull and the printed sentiment: *We Miss You and That's No Bull.* He mailed the card to Weldon. For several weeks he did not receive a reply. In an issue of *National Geographic* he discovered a map of New Mexico and kept it on his desk where he could see it. Through long intervals he sat studying the dot marking Roswell, convincing himself that Weldon was truly there. Sometimes at night he went into Weldon's room to feel his presence.

At last came the first letter from Weldon. It was brief and scribbled on rough tablet paper, but Kelly easily could imagine its cost in effort. Several false starts had been marked out and erased. Weldon was not in the habit of putting his words on paper:

Dear Brother,

I did not write you before because I have been busy marching off demerruts on the grinder. Now I have about got them all walked off so I am ready for some more. Ha! This place is OK I guess. The teachers are not as dumb as you know where. They got a polo team here and they say that if I make good grades and keep my nose clean I can go out for it. Maybe I will. Well I got to close now because I got to pollish my boots.

Your brother,
Weldon

After the initial effort, the letters began arriving every week or ten days. Kelly quickly surmised that even surrounded by hundreds of cadets, Weldon was lonely too. Kelly answered each letter, describing what he was doing, what was happening around him.

As the months went by he fell into a routine that filled his every waking moment. The choir, once a gentle passion, became an obsession.

"Music is the most eloquent expression of man," the Director told them often.

Kelly came to believe it. In the shower, eating, walking home from school, he listened to the grandest music ever written, constantly coming from inside his own head.

Chapter 17

"We've been extremely lucky," Moon said. "The market won't always be this good. Those Idaho mining stocks were a fluke. They were more of a risk than I feel comfortable with. I've been thinking we should start playing it a little more conservatively."

Crystelle struck his knee with her open palm. "No! Not on your life! Moon, I need the money!"

They were drinking a white Bordeaux of Moon's choosing before a crackling fire in Crystelle's suite at the Ritz-Carlton. Moon was sprawled in a wing chair, with Crystelle on the carpet at his feet, her head resting against his thigh. Moon had completed a two-day conference at Harvard, and they had finished dinner in the room. Tomorrow they would fly back to Fort Worth.

On different planes.

Moon seemed amused. "If you really need the money, you could always cut down on expenses. You buy enough clothes for ten women, not to mention every piece of jewelry you see. You don't need that big old house, the staff it takes to keep it running."

She turned to face him. "Moon, I'm serious. I may need

quite a bit of money through the next few months. I have a lot of expenses you don't know about."

He looked down at her, posing a question with his silence.

During the last few days Crystelle had decided the time had come to bring him into her project.

"Moon, you remember I told you once that Brod wasn't as lily-white as everyone thinks? Well, that was an understatement. If you want to know the truth, murder wasn't the half of what he did."

Moon did not answer. Crystelle was certain he had heard rumors about the Spurlock War.

"Yes, I'm talking about Grover Sterling. Brod had him killed. I'm certain of it. All I've got to do is prove it."

Moon spoke cautiously. "But why now? After all this time?"

"Because I want my part of the company back. Brod made me sell it to him. He said if I didn't, I'd get a taste of what Grover Sterling got."

Moon's eyes widened. "Brod said that? To you?"

"You better believe it. There's no way I can prove it. But you see, if I can prove he killed Grover, and burned Troy out of business, I can show that I was in fear for my own life when I was coerced into selling Brod the stock. That's what my lawyer says."

"You've hired a lawyer? Who?"

"Tate Middleton."

Moon grimaced. "Surely you could have done better than that!"

"Oh, I know he has a bad reputation. But Moon, you don't want a boy scout when you go into something like this. Middleton's sneaky mean. He's exactly what I need. You should hear him describe how we're going to do it."

"Crystelle, I think you should talk to other lawyers, make sure of what you're doing before you start work with Middleton."

"We've already started. First we went before the Spurlock board. I offered an override. We knew we'd be turned down.

We just did it so later we can prove we tried to be fair about it and they wouldn't listen."

"I wouldn't let Tate Middleton mow my lawn. What's next on his list?"

"We're pressuring the New York police to reopen the investigation into Grover's death. Middleton knows some people at police headquarters. I must have greased half the palms in the police force by now."

Moon remained silent for a time. Crystelle knew he was reluctant to talk about her project. He did not want to get involved. But his curiosity was stronger. "Any luck?"

"Some. We found out that they had a suspect, back at the time. They just didn't have enough evidence. This same guy's now in prison on another charge. We also know there was a woman who helped set Grover up. I'm trying to find her." Crystelle waited a moment. "But you see, we're dealing with the wrong end of the stick. We should be rattling cages in Albany, so we can talk with this guy. And Middleton doesn't know anyone at the state Capitol. Moon, do you have any connections in the New York State government? I need help."

Moon did not answer immediately. He spoke slowly. "Crystelle, I can't get into something like this."

She refrained from pointing out that he already *was* involved. He was discussing it with her; Middleton had said she could use that in court, if necessary.

Moreover, she and Moon had now slept together in six cities. That would be a hot item with any jury.

"Moon, I really need to get to this guy. Maybe he'd talk if I offered him enough money, and helped him get out of prison."

"While he talks his way right back in on a murder charge? Come on! That'd never happen."

"He was just the middleman," Crystelle explained. "Somebody hired him. It wasn't Brod, because this was just days after Brod went home from the hospital. We figure Brod called someone who set it up. Middleton says this guy in prison might name names, turn state's evidence, make a deal, if he's offered immunity. But he won't talk to anybody. I can't get to him. The people in Albany won't help. Moon, if you know someone . . ."

She let the question hang. Moon was unusually solemn, thinking the problem through.

"I know the state attorney general. He might at least listen to you. I'm fairly well acquainted with a former New York City police commissioner. He could advise you on how to go about putting pressure on the police department, the prison system."

Crystelle rolled her head in his lap and looked up at him. "Moon, that's exactly what I need! Power! People who can get things done. Can you set it up for me?"

"Crystelle, I won't work with Middleton. Good Lord! He's a complete asshole. I don't trust him."

"We don't have to tell Middleton anything about what we're doing. I've known all along he's too small for the big leagues. I just used him to get started. I knew eventually I'd have to bring some hotshot New York lawyers into it. All the legal stuff will have to be filed there. Maybe they can work with Middleton, tell him what they've done after they've done it."

"I'm not sure that's cricket. Certainly, Middleton won't like it."

"Listen, he'll be happy to get what he can. I know his type. He'd double-cross me in a minute for a buck. What's wrong with me double-crossing him first?"

Moon laughed and refilled the wineglasses. Crystelle touched her glass to his and sipped.

"You know any hotshot New York lawyers?"

Again he answered reluctantly. "A few."

"Could you set it up? Moon, I really need you to run interference for me with this attorney general, the police commissioner, the lawyers. You can do it. You're awfully good at that sort of thing."

He remained silent, thinking. Crystelle knew he never moved into a new situation until he explored all the possibilities.

She gave him all the time he needed.

"I'll do it on one condition," he said. "I'll tell them I have a client who has been done out of family money, and who needs their help. They must never know about our true relationship, or even guess."

"Of course not," Crystelle said.

"And Middleton must never know I had anything to do with it. Let him think you hired the lawyers, and they set everything else up."

"There's no reason for Middleton to know."

"Give me a few days. I'll tell you when all is ready, then you can make your own appointment with the lawyers."

"What about the attorney general? The police commissioner? Should I offer them money?"

"Absolutely not. Just tell them your story, and say your lawyers may call them. Let the lawyers do the bribing, if any is needed."

"You can bet it'll be needed," Crystelle said. "That's one thing I've learned in this old world. Everybody's out for everything he can get."

Moon went to the phone and called down for another bottle of wine. When the busboy brought it, he wheeled away the dinner cart. Crystelle turned the lights off and opened the drapes. She sat in Moon's lap while they drank the wine, savoring the view of Back Bay, with the lights of Cambridge and Harvard in the distance across the Charles.

Crystelle laid her head on Moon's shoulder. "This is absolutely perfect. Let's stay over another day."

"I'm sorry. But I can't. I have to get back. My oldest daughter is in a school play. I promised I'd be there."

Crystelle did not respond. She made it a point to seem never to interfere in his family life.

"When I'm with you, it's like nothing else ever existed," Moon said. "I feel like I'm living in two different worlds."

Crystelle hugged him closer.

The admission confirmed a decision she had made during the last few weeks:

The time was approaching when she could bring him over into her world on a permanent basis.

"I really don't know what to make of all this," Graham Elkins said. "Maybe you can find some sense in it."

Ann Leigh took him into the parlor. He was a nondescript man, bald, with a receding chin. But he was surprisingly well dressed for his profession, she thought, although her experience with private investigators was limited to a few movies.

"Would you care for coffee? Or maybe tea?" she asked.

"No, thank you, ma'am. If there's just some place I could put all this, I'll explain it the best I can, and leave it with you."

Ann Leigh took the knickknacks off the coffee table and put them on the mantel. Elkins spread his stack of papers.

"To sum it all up, she has been to seven different cities in the last two months, staying two or three days each place. New York, San Francisco, Denver, Chicago, Miami, Los Angeles, and Boston. Only on the New York trip did I see much of her. But more about that later. On all the other trips, she stayed in her room mostly. At first I couldn't figure that out. Then I had a bit of luck. Do you know a Moon Belford?"

Ann Leigh prepared herself for the worst. "I know of him."

"Well, in Los Angeles she was at the Beverly Wilshire. You know how it's arranged? A court, really a sort of driveway, in the middle, the new building on one side, the old on the other?"

"Yes," Ann Leigh said, although she really did not. She wanted him to go on with his story.

"It's difficult to keep an eye on the comings and goings there without making yourself conspicuous. I was in the bookshop there off the entrance, trying to keep an eye on the lobby, when Moon Belford walked through. I recognized him because he had been to her house. I had checked him out earlier. He handles her investments. I thought it a bit chancy that two people from Fort Worth who knew each other that well would be staying in the same hotel at the same time. So, on a hunch, I checked every hotel she stayed at in all the other cities. In every instance except New York, Moon Belford was registered at the same time."

At first Ann Leigh did not understand.

And then she did.

She felt heat rise to her face.

"They were married to each other once," she said inanely. "A long time ago."

"Well, he's certainly married now, and to someone else. Wife and three daughters. Apparently his father-in-law is a real wheel about town."

"Yes," Ann Leigh said. "That's right."

She suddenly felt dizzy, trying to absorb what the man had just told her. When what Crystelle and Moon were doing became common knowledge, the whole town would be set on its ear. The Moon Belfords were considered one of the most stable couples in Fort Worth. They were pillars in their church.

"Like I said, the only difference was in the pattern of this New York trip, way back early. She stayed at the Plaza. Do you know it?"

"Yes," Ann Leigh said, again only in order to get him to go on.

"It's much easier there to monitor comings and goings. There's a lot of lobby, and of course the Palm Court. She was there five days, and she gave me a merry chase. She met with a man several times, in restaurants, at museums. I checked him out. He's a homicide detective with the New York Police Department. It's all here in my report."

Ann Leigh felt her nausea growing. Her first suspicions of what Crystelle was doing had now been confirmed.

Elkins apparently did not notice her discomfort. "The fellow passed papers to her each time they met, and they talked twenty, maybe thirty minutes at a stretch. Mrs. Spurlock, I didn't know how far you wanted me to take it. But those hotel rooms are duck soup for anyone who knows what he's doing. One afternoon, when she obviously was out on a shopping spree, I went into her room and copied all the papers with my Minox."

He spread out the forms. Ann Leigh did not have the heart to look at them.

"The copies are not too clear, but I think you can read them. They're from the police files of the investigation into the murder of Grover Sterling, on Forty-second street, back in 1945. He was general manager at Spurlock Oil. Am I right?"

"Yes," Ann Leigh said.

"The files don't reveal much. Apparently there was a suspect, back at the time, but not much to hang on him. I gather the investigation fizzled out rather early."

Ann Leigh felt she should learn as much as possible about what Crystelle had discovered.

"This suspect. Do the files indicate where he is now?"

"In Sing Sing, serving thirty to life on another murder charge. From the reports, I gather that about all they had on him for the Sterling murder was that it fit his M.O., his way of setting up the victim, using a knife, and so forth."

"Has she done any more than talk to this policeman about it?"

"Not that I can find. Frankly, the New York visit seemed more a shopping trip. She spent most of her time in the stores."

"What is your opinion, Mr. Elkins? Has she succeeded in reopening the investigation, or anything like that?"

"Not so far. She would have to do a lot more work on it. The way the police look at it, their only suspect is behind bars, and will be there for some time to come. I can't believe they'd be interested, unless something new turned up, or some pressure was applied from higher up."

"So you believe she may have explored, and encountered a dead end?"

"That's the way it looks to me. Since then, she has been to all these other cities, and done no more in that direction that I can see."

"Well, I thank you, Mr. Elkins. I'm sure all of this material will be most helpful for my purpose."

Elkins started to rise, but hesitated. "There's really not much there. Mrs. Spurlock, I know this is expensive, and I'm not sure you're finding enough to make it worthwhile. If you want to terminate the case at this point, I can understand why."

"No, let's go on with it," Ann Leigh said. "Frankly, this is about what I expected to find. It's worth the time and effort to me."

After Elkins left, Ann Leigh took the material into her bedroom and spent several hours going through it. Most consisted of Elkins's detailed account of where he had gone, what he had observed. His expenses were carefully recorded, even to taxi tips. The rest of the material came from the New York police files. The reports were couched in police jargon, and not everything made sense to her.

By the time Ann Leigh finished reading, she was deep into the throes of a sick headache.

She did not know what to do with the information, now that she had it. She thought of calling Joanna and seeking her advice. But Joanna already had so many responsibilities, so much to worry about. Ann Leigh did not wish to burden her further with something that might be no more than her own unfounded fears. Also, she found herself reluctant to admit to her daughter-in-law that she even suspected her dead son might be guilty of murder. Moreover, she herself felt cheapened that she had to resort to someone like Mr. Elkins and his methods.

She would rather that Joanna not know.

She consoled herself with the thought that, thus far, no danger seemed to exist. Mr. Elkins did not believe Crystelle had discovered anything of importance. Certainly there was little in the files beyond what had been in the newspapers back at the time.

Ann Leigh decided to do nothing at the moment, but merely to wait and see.

She did not want to keep the material in the house, where

anyone might find and read it. Yet she felt it too important to discard. Conceivably she might need it later.

After considering the problem, she asked Henry to drive her downtown, and she put the papers into a special safe-deposit box at the bank.

Chapter 18

Joanna worried for months over Crystelle's threat. But as time passed and nothing happened, immediate concerns gradually pushed the incident from her mind.

Not only was the company demanding her full attention, she also felt she was emerging from the cocoon that had enveloped her for years. For the first time since Brod's death, she was appearing in public, meeting new people, enjoying life in the community around her.

She purchased three sets of season tickets for the opera, ballet, and symphony. She told Kelly that with his new interest in music, he might enjoy the performances. In what she hoped was an offhand manner, she added that their neighbor and attorney, Mr. Trammel, might go with them sometimes. She explained that Mr. Trammel's wife was an invalid, and that he might like to have company.

Kelly apparently accepted the situation without question.

But when she phoned Walter with her invitation, he balked.

"Joanna, I know this was Peggy's idea. I appreciate your thoughtfulness. But I don't think I should do this. Surely you of all people will understand. I feel I ought to be with Peggy as much as possible."

For a fleeting moment Joanna felt relief.

Then she remembered her promise to Peggy.

"Walter, you put me in an awkward position. Naturally I understand your feelings. But I also see Peggy's side of it. She feels guilty, taking you away from pleasures you once enjoyed. Besides, *she's* bored. Don't forget that. She wants to give you two something to talk about besides her illness. To her mind, it would restore a degree of normalcy if you would go out occasionally."

"No. There would be people who would tend to misunderstand."

Since it was precisely the same argument Joanna had used with Peggy, she was ready for it.

"Let them. We'll have Kelly with us. They'd have to work hard to read anything into that. I've told a number of my friends about Peggy—how courageous she is, how she's always so cheerful. It's widely known that she's my friend. I hardly see how anyone could say anything."

Still Walter hesitated. "Maybe I'm old-fashioned. Let me talk with Peggy. I want to make absolutely sure she feels right about it."

The next day he phoned and accepted.

On the evening of the first performance, Joanna and Kelly stopped by the Trammel house to pick up Walter, in keeping with the plan she had worked out with Peggy.

As she took Kelly in to meet Peggy, Joanna was apprehensive. Peggy was so emaciated that her appearance might be startling for the uninitiated. But Kelly handled the situation with total aplomb. Joanna was immensely proud of him.

From the moment they left the Trammel house, Joanna kept Kelly sandwiched firmly between her and Walter.

If Walter noticed, he gave no indication.

The first evening was a complete success. Walter had wide acquaintance with music and composers, and Joanna was amazed by the extensive background Kelly had acquired.

Walter and Kelly conversed expertly through the evening, commenting on the program, the performance.

Afterward, Joanna invited Walter in for a nightcap. He countered with a suggestion that they have ice cream with Peggy.

Joanna's lingering qualms over the evening were quickly erased by Peggy's obvious enjoyment of their descriptions of the performance, especially Kelly's vivid account.

That first evening set the pattern for the entire fall season. Before each performance, Joanna and Kelly would go over to the Trammel house and visit with Peggy for a few minutes. Walter would kiss Peggy and ask if she was sure she would be all right. Peggy would scold him with mock seriousness, warning he would make them late for the curtain.

After each performance, they returned to the Trammel house and shared the evening experience with Peggy.

By the time the fall season drew to a close, Joanna was gradually becoming comfortable with the situation.

But when the opera ball came along in late November, her concern with propriety was revived.

The black-tie affair would offer dancing, drinking, and Las Vegas–style gambling. She could not take Kelly along. Moreover, the ball clearly was a social event, not a seated performance.

That placed it in a totally different category.

She could not possibly consider attending the ball with a married man as her escort.

Yet, as a member of the opera board, and chairman of the budget committee, she felt she at least should make a brief appearance.

She did not mention the ball to Walter, nor did he broach the subject.

So when she encountered him in the crowd only a few minutes after she arrived, she was both surprised and disturbed.

He gave her a rueful smile. "Peggy insisted. She wants to know who's here, what they're wearing, all that. You can help me with it. May I get you a drink?"

They walked downstairs into the casino. Most of the furniture at the country club had been removed for the evening to make room for roulette wheels and gambling tables. With the tacit approval of the district attorney, players were allowed to gamble with chips, later to be redeemed for prizes ranging from a Cadillac and full-length mink to autographed best-selling books—all donated by Fort Worth and Dallas merchants.

As Joanna entered the casino, she was acutely aware of Walter at her side. She was alert for knowing glances. She saw none.

The crowd was a curious mix. Most prominent were the old guard, the first families, attending from a sense of duty and plainly in charge. It was one of the few evenings of the year that gave social climbers the opportunity to rub elbows with the owners of vast corporations.

Joanna walked to a blackjack table and began to play. Walter brought her drink, then vanished into the milling throng.

She became immersed in the game, the people around the table. At first she lost more often than she won. But she soon found a rhythm of play and began winning consistently.

Eventually she grew tired of the concentration the game demanded. She was preparing to leave the table, and the ball, when Gyorgy Gaspar came bounding out of the crowd.

"Here you are!" he said, raising his voice over the noise of the casino. "I've been hunting for you all over. What are you doing here playing cards while there is music? Ever since I came to Fort Worth I have heard that you danced for Billy Rose. Marvelous! To dance with you will be the pinnacle of my career!"

His enthusiasm would not be denied. Reluctantly, Joanna allowed him to escort her upstairs to the ballroom.

She had not danced in years, and with her high heels she towered over Gyorgy. But he did not seem fazed in the slightest. He guided her onto the dance floor with authority.

He was an excellent dancer, light on his feet, accom-

plished in an assortment of fillips designed to show his partner to best advantage.

In her peripheral vision, Joanna saw other couples turn to
watch as Gyorgy maneuvered her across the ballroom.

At the close of the third number, Walter came to her
rescue. Gyorgy surrendered her with promises to return
later.

Walter led her back onto the floor. "When I saw you dancing with Gyorgy, I probably turned green. I used to enjoy
dancing so much."

Joanna did not comment. She was savoring a time warp to
the years when ballroom dancing had played a large part in
her life—all through high school, college, and later, when
she first came to Texas, during that magic summer of the
Texas Centennial.

Even after an arduous show, she and Brod often danced
until dawn at the Lake Worth Casino.

Walter was a good dancer, graceful and confident. She was
aware of the envious glances from other women.

They danced much longer than Joanna would have
deemed wise. At last she risked looking at her watch.

"Walter, it's after eleven. I really should be getting home."

"What about your chips? Didn't you win quite a few?"

The chips could not be exchanged for cash. Only merchandise. She was willing to forget about them. "I doubt I
won enough to buy anything I would want."

"Let's go see."

They walked back downstairs. The casino was still
jammed. Walter gently pushed their way into the side room
where the prizes were displayed. Each was tagged with its
value in chips.

Joanna found nothing she really wanted. "I wish I had
enough for that jacket," she said.

It was muskrat—a "fun" fur—tastefully made and cleverly
designed. She had seen and admired it in Neiman's.

Walter gestured toward the tables. "Why don't you try
your luck at craps? Play all your chips, double or nothing."

They made their way back into the casino. Hesitant to

place all her money on one roll of the dice, Joanna wagered half on the shooter and won. She continued that ploy, sometimes losing, but more often winning. Then the dice passed to her.

She made three straight passes. Each time she made her point, the crowd at the table applauded. More people came to see the cause of the cheering.

Joanna counted her pile of chips. She had almost enough for the coat.

"One more roll," she said.

She tossed a nine—a six and a three.

On the next roll she made her point with a five and a four. The spectators broke into noisy applause.

Somewhat disconcerted by the attention, Joanna passed the dice, picked up her winnings, and turned away from the table.

"Congratulations," said a familiar voice to her left. George Hollander was standing with an arm around his wife, Deena. She was a small brunette, more cute than pretty, with rather startling large, innocent eyes. Joanna had met her several times, but only in passing. She felt she should make a gesture to acknowledge their attendance, their support of the opera.

"Thank you," she said, moving closer to them in the jam of people. "It's been my night, it seems."

"Hasn't it?" said Deena. "But I thought strip poker was your game."

Joanna assumed she had misheard. "I beg your pardon?"

Hollander almost yanked Deena off her feet. "Deena!" he said.

Deena smiled at Joanna. "I heard about that all-night poker game in Odessa."

Joanna now understood that Deena was drunk. Hollander again attempted to pull his wife away. She tossed her shoulders and evaded his grip.

Joanna kept her expression as dispassionate as she could manage. "Be very careful what you say, Mrs. Hollander. I've never played strip poker in my life."

Deena leaned forward from the waist to aid in giving her

voice volume. "Like you never spent the whole night boozing with five men in a motel room?"

Conversation around them ceased.

"I'm on to you, Mrs. Spurlock," Deena shouted. "Just for the record. Isn't that good-looking date of yours married?"

Hollander gave Joanna a beseeching glance, put an arm around his wife, and dragged her away bodily. They disappeared into the crowd.

After an awkward moment, activity resumed at the crap table. Walter stood unperturbed at Joanna's side, as if he had not heard a thing.

Joanna suddenly felt nauseated. She searched for an exit, trying to remember where the rest rooms were located on the lower level. "Please excuse me," she said.

Walter looked at her with concern. "Give me your chips. I'll get the fur. Then we'll go."

"I don't want it. It's ruined. The whole evening's ruined."

"Don't be foolish. It's a lovely coat."

Joanna fled, fearing that at any moment she would be sick.

Only two women were in the lower lounge and they were in the process of leaving. Joanna dampened a towel and applied its cool texture to her forehead, neck, and wrists.

Gradually her giddiness and nausea faded.

She was finishing with her makeup when three women came in, talking. Joanna rose, nodded to them, and left the lounge.

Walter was waiting, holding the coat in a garment bag. "I'll drive you home. I'll leave my car here. I can send for it in the morning."

Joanna knew it was not the right thing to do. But at the moment she did not care. She did not feel like driving even the short distance home. She did not protest as Walter escorted her out of the club. They skirted the line at valet parking and walked through the tunnel to her car in the members' parking area.

Once they were in the car and moving, Joanna could not hold back tears.

"That horrible, horrible woman!"

"Oh, try not to take it too seriously. She plainly has a screw loose. No one paid any attention to her."

Joanna could not stop sobbing. "Why did she say such things? She made it sound so awful. It wasn't like that at all."

They were approaching the entrance to Westover Hills, the turnoff to their street.

"You need time to pull yourself together. Want to ride around a few minutes?"

Joanna nodded.

Walter drove on past the entrance.

Joanna felt she had to make him understand. "We were grounded by weather. There was high wind, rain coming down in sheets, reports of tornadoes and hail. All the roads were under water. The phone lines were out. All the hotels were full. We were lucky to find a room at all."

She described the entire weekend. By the time she finished, they were approaching downtown.

Walter turned into the park beside the river and stopped under the trees.

"Did I handle it wrong?" Joanna asked. "Should I have taken the room, let the men sleep in the lobby?"

"No. I don't think so."

"I suppose I could have refused the drinks, declined to play poker, sat in the lobby myself all night. But that would have been false. I'm sure the men would have resented it if I'd tried to be Miss Goody Two-Shoes."

"They would have," Walter agreed.

"Then how did Deena get this terribly twisted story? Did she make it up? Did George tell her that was what happened?"

Walter frowned, his hands resting on the wheel. "Judging from his reaction, the way he looked back at you, I doubt it. If he'd lied to his wife, he would have been embarrassed for himself, unable to look you in the eye. As it was, he seemed embarrassed for his wife. He acted as if you and he had a mutual problem. This is a lawyer's instinct talking."

"Then how could such a story get started?"

"I don't know. But let's try a scenario. Those men were

stranded with their boss lady in a motel room, overnight, in a storm. She's a very good-looking, desirable woman. She bent enough to enjoy a few drinks with them. Then she beat them at stud poker, a man's game. That's a good story. They probably told it straight, allowing an exaggeration here and there for dramatic license. But in the retelling, by people who don't even know you, the stud poker may have become strip poker, your drinking embroidered. Deena may have heard it that way."

"What can I do about it? If Hollander's innocent, I don't want to fire him."

"If he's half the man he appears, he'll take the initiative. I'd just wait and see what he has to say."

"He's so happy-go-lucky, so much fun. I can't imagine him married to that vicious woman." Joanna lowered her head into her hands. Again she could not fight back tears. "I feel so awful. I'd give anything if it hadn't happened."

She felt Walter's arm encircle her with comforting firmness. As she yielded to his embrace, the moment seemed inevitable. Walter covered her face and neck with kisses.

Desperately, hungrily, Joanna responded with her own.

Without releasing her, Walter started the engine. Driving with one hand, he reentered the deserted streets. Joanna knew they were headed toward downtown, but she did not allow herself to wonder why. With her face buried in Walter's shoulder, all her hardships and loneliness vanished. She surrendered completely to his presence, savoring the moment, her mind a perfect blank.

At last the car stopped. Joanna looked up. They were beside the building that housed Walter's law offices. Wordlessly he helped her from the car. Hardly aware of her surroundings, she heard his key in the lock, the pneumatic hiss of the front door.

In the elevator they kissed all the way to the sixth floor. He led her through the receptionist's area and down the hall to his private office. After bolting the door behind them, he switched on a small lamp at his desk in the corner.

Then they were on the couch and they could not seem to remove the barrier of clothing fast enough.

They made love with fierce passion. Joanna felt herself swept upward to half-forgotten heights of ecstasy.

For a delicious interval she abandoned herself to the sensations sweeping through her.

Then, at a crucial moment, under the subtle interplay of dim light and shadow, Walter became Brod. Not Brod as he was in later years, but Brod when he was young, hard, lean, and so relentlessly demanding.

Consciously Joanna sought and held the illusion, riding it to a lengthy, consuming fulfillment.

Entwined, still joined, they lay in silence, recovering.

Brod was gone. Walter loomed over her, kissing her.

"I've dreamed of this ever since that first day you came here," he said softly.

Joanna did not answer. She was paralyzed by an overwhelming sense of guilt. She did not know whom she had betrayed most—Walter, for her fantasy at the crucial moment; Brod, for the final dissolution of their marriage; or Peggy, for an unforgivable violation of trust.

"It's after midnight," she said. "Peggy will be frantic."

They dressed hurriedly. On the way to the car Walter seemed distracted. But on the drive home he held her hand.

"I have no regrets," he said. "I hope you have none."

"Walter, let's not talk about it now. I don't know how I'll feel."

He looked at her for a moment but did not press further.

After parking the car in her drive, he came to hold her door. Belatedly Joanna thought of his car, by now no doubt acutely obvious on the expanse of the country club parking lot.

"You could tell Peggy you had car trouble," she suggested.

"No, I won't lie to her. I'll tell her about the incident with the Hollander woman, that you were upset, and that we talked about it afterward."

"She'll know."

"She may suspect. But she'll never know. We'll keep her

mind occupied with the half-truth. That's a highly effective, time-tested defense, as old as lawyering."

Abruptly he kissed her on the cheek and walked away. Joanna went into the house and up to her room, filled with emotions too fleeting and diverse to define.

Chapter 19

Moon reached for a cigarette and lit it. "I'm beginning to think Josie may know something."

That *was* news. Crystelle rolled to face him. "What makes you think so?"

"The way she looks at me every once in a while, like she can't quite make a connection. She knows something's different. But she can't put it all together."

Crystelle found herself more irritated than encouraged. Early in the game she had concluded that Josie was hopelessly dense. And despite his brilliance, Moon had dumb spots. He was still pretending to himself that he was a loyal husband and father.

During the last few days Crystelle had come to the conclusion that both Moon and Josie needed a good jolt.

She was prepared to give it to them.

She rolled away, gathered the sheet around her, and sat up. They were in Moon's fishing cabin on Possum Kingdom Lake, more than an hour's drive from Fort Worth. It sat on a bluff near the water, offering a magnificent view of the lake. From the bed, looking through the bedroom door and the front room, Crystelle saw two boats in the distance, far out on the water.

The cabin itself was Spartan but tasteful, with bearskins on the floor and Moon's hunting trophies on the walls.

"Moon, if you think Josie's on to us, maybe we should cool it for a while," Crystelle said to test his response.

He stared at her. "Are you serious? Is something wrong?"

"Oh, no! Everything's great! You're knocking yourself out, living two lives. You spend half your time plotting and scheming so we can be together. I'm half crazy, waiting all day for the phone to ring. I have you, yet I don't have you."

Moon caught her hand and put it to his lips. "Crystelle, you have me. Don't ever doubt that. When we're together like this, it's like my marriage to Josie is something that happened to someone else. It's like you and I have never been apart."

"I don't like this sneaking around worth a damn. It's killing both of us."

Moon rubbed his eyes with the heels of his palms. "Lord, I don't know what to do. It's an impossible situation. I can't give you up. That's out of the question. But Josie and the kids don't deserve to be hurt."

Crystelle remained silent.

"It'd really be a mess if my marriage went sour. I can't even imagine all that'd happen. Her daddy could get on the phone and cut me off from half the town in a single afternoon."

It was the first time he had even hinted the possibility of divorce.

Crystelle recognized it as another step.

"Moon, you don't need him. You never have. Your friends are just as influential as his. You're building your own sand-pile. And you've never needed his damned money."

"Oh, I'm not saying I wouldn't survive. But still, it'd be pure hell."

"It's hell any way you slice it. What do you have mapped out for our next rendezvous? Hong Kong?"

He laughed. "How about New Orleans?"

"When?"

"Week from Friday. I'm to give a lecture at Tulane, meet with some of the faculty. But mostly, it's research. I have good sources on some start-up companies down along the Gulf. I need something hot for the newsletter, and that might be it. I thought we might go by train, adjoining compartments. That'd give us five days and nights together."

"That's a long time away from home. Won't Josie wonder about it?"

"No reason she should. I mentioned the lecture to her several months back, asked her if she wanted to go. New Orleans is one of her favorite places. So she knows it's been on my calendar for months."

Crystelle hesitated. "Moon, I really should meet with those lawyers in New York, and get that deal started."

"You've waited more than five years. Another few days won't matter."

The first hint of a plan came into her mind.

She thought it through, and found no holes in it.

"All right," she said. "I'll go."

"Good. I'll set it up, phone you the details."

He reached for her. Once again they made love while an elk, a tiger, and a Dall sheep stared at them from the bedroom wall.

Moon was in a rare mood, playful, and especially ardent, taking her to new heights of passion. Eventually they became tangled in the sheets, rolled off the bed laughing, and finished on the bearskin rug.

Afterward, Moon lay for a time without moving. At last he sat up, reached for his wristwatch, and stared at it as if unable to believe his eyes.

"Oh, Lord! I have to go!"

"Where you supposed to be?"

"Playing tennis. If I'm late getting home, Josie may call the club."

He began struggling into his clothes.

Crystelle lay on the floor, watching him. It was the first time in years that she had seen him in casual clothes. Today he was more boyish, lively, adventurous. His whole attitude had changed.

Normally he would never have risked a rendezvous at the cabin.

She wondered if he was subconsciously tempting fate.

"Moon, when you tell a lie, play it loose," she said. "Always leave yourself an out. I may be here, I may be there, or I may be someplace else. Throw up a smoke screen."

He sat in a chair and pulled on his socks. "You sound as if you know how it's done."

"Believe me, growing up in my family, it was the only way to survive."

He struggled into his boots. "My lies always sound far-fetched, even to me."

The time had arrived to give him the first good jolt.

"Moon, Josie's going to catch on before long, sure as shooting. You better decide beforehand exactly what you'll do about it."

His face lost some of its color. But he did not turn away. Crystelle took that as a good sign.

"I *have* thought about it. Crystelle, I don't know what I'll do. I only know I can't stand the thought of losing you again."

He knelt beside her for a long, lingering kiss, then gently slapped her backside.

"Get your clothes on! I've got to go!"

Crystelle dressed hurriedly. They left as they had arrived, in separate cars. Moon took the lead and set a fast pace. On straight, level stretches through the ranch country, the needle on Crystelle's speedometer often crept to ninety. Moon kept sticking a hand out the window, playfully waving for her to come on.

She had never seen him act so idiotic. Who would believe it of solemn, straitlaced Moon Belford?

As they approached Fort Worth from the west, Crystelle drove close enough to Moon's car to blow him a kiss with the horn. Then she braked and turned off on a back road. Moon continued on down the main highway. They entered town from different directions.

As traffic thickened on the edge of town, Crystelle hardly slowed.

With luck, she could beat him home by several minutes.

She passed cars on hills and curves. Twice she raced through stoplights seconds after they turned red, an instant before cross-traffic began to move.

Other drivers blew their horns at her. They were not sending kisses.

Tires screeching, she whipped through the residential streets of Monticello and entered Rivercrest. She wheeled into her drive, leaped from the car, and dashed into the house. Wadding a handkerchief over the mouthpiece, she dialed Moon's home.

A female voice answered. "Belford residence."

Crystelle was not sure if she had Josie on the line, or the maid. She lowered her voice. "Mrs. Belford?"

"Yes?"

"This is a good friend. I hate to be the one to tell you, but your husband's playing around on you."

Crystelle heard a gasp, a sputtering sound. "What? What? I can hardly hear you."

Crystelle removed the handkerchief. "I said your husband is playing around on you, Josie."

"Who is this?"

"A good friend who sees what's happening, even if you don't. Just ask your husband where he's been all afternoon."

Crystelle slammed down the receiver.

The first seed had been planted with Josie.

Laughing, charged with adrenaline, Crystelle ran upstairs to her bedroom, tossed her purse aside, kicked off her shoes, and rolled on the bed in glee.

Tonight, the inquisition.

Then the fireworks.

She lay for more than an hour, evaluating the consequences of what she had done.

The possibility existed that she was moving too soon.

Moon's sense of respectability held an exaggerated importance for him. Forced to choose, he might make the wrong decision.

But risk was the name of the game.

All that weekend Crystelle half expected Moon to call with a report that all hell had broken loose. But she did not hear a peep out of him. And when he phoned on Tuesday with the details of train schedules and tickets, she detected nothing different in his voice.

Slowly it began to dawn on her that Josie might be a more formidable adversary than she had assumed.

So she put the second part of her plan to work.

Late Wednesday, she phoned the Santa Fe Railway.

"This is Mr. Moon Belford's private secretary," she said. "He has booked adjoining compartments, southbound, Friday evening. He's very concerned about the arrangement of the compartments. Just so there's no slipup, would you please telephone confirmation to his residence sometime Thursday afternoon?"

She provided the number.

The reservations clerk, who sounded efficient, promised that the call would be made.

Again Crystelle spent considerable time analyzing what she had done, and considering the possibilities.

No matter if Josie was smart, dumb, or indifferent, no doubt could possibly remain in her mind that Moon was playing around.

The only question was what she would do about it.

With another evening to kill before the trip to New Orleans, Crystelle opened a bottle of Chablis and spent an hour in a sudsy bath. In a way, she welcomed the respite. She had spent most of the afternoon in conference with Middleton and his investigators, who had flown in from the East to give a report on their progress.

They claimed to be close on the trail of the woman who had been with Grover Sterling on the night he was killed.

Unless they were shooting her a line of bull, it could be a big breakthrough.

When she raised the possibility that they might be leading her on, taking her money for nothing, Middleton quickly replied that he trusted them.

The problem was, Crystelle did not trust Middleton.

But during the morning she had succeeded in obtaining an appointment with the lawyers Moon recommended. As soon as she returned from New Orleans, she would go to New York and meet with them.

By using both the top echelons of the law, and the lowest, maybe she at last could get something accomplished.

She was stepping out of the bath when the phone rang. Hurriedly she pulled on a wrap and rushed into the bedroom.

But it was not Moon, as she had hoped. The voice was familiar, yet elusive.

"Well, hello again, Crystelle. How in the world are you?"

She never appreciated being placed at such a disadvantage.

"Who is this?"

The man laughed. "You have so many old lovers you don't remember them all? That doesn't surprise me. But you sure ought to remember me. We spent more than three months together, sweetheart. They were the best and worst three months of my life."

Crystelle could not put a face with the voice.

"So?"

"So I'm in town and I thought I'd give you a call. I'd like to see you again. Talk over old times, if nothing else."

Crystelle still did not have a clue. "If you don't tell me who you are, I'm hanging up."

"I'm real hurt you don't remember. This is Bern. Bern Arnheiter."

Crystelle remembered. The merchant marine.

From the depths of her mind came vivid images of a huge body, a wide, grinning face.

"I have plenty of reasons to remember you," he went on.

"I lost my mate's papers over you. Our little whing-ding put me on the beach for good."

They had partied up and down the West Coast for more than a month. Bern had missed ship movement for the second or third time.

With the war at its peak, he had landed in considerable trouble.

"I remember, Bern. What the hell are you doing in Fort Worth?"

"Well, after I lost my papers, thanks to you, I shipped out as an ordinary, one step ahead of the draft. But the fix was in. I could see there was no way I'd ever make mate again. I screwed up but good. Now, with all the cutbacks, I can't even find a berth. So I thought maybe I'd get on at the Convair plant here. You know the one I'm talking about?"

Crystelle remembered something else: Conversation with Bern was often painfully simple.

"Yes. They make airplanes. Those things that fly."

"They're giving me a song and dance, claiming they're not hiring right now."

Crystelle was appalled at the thought of Bern's living in the same town. He was a bull in bed, but a clod of a man. She thought she had covered her tracks.

"How did you ever find me?"

"Funny part is, I really wasn't looking for you. Not at first. But the minute I hit Texas I started seeing those Spurlock Oil signs all over. I told myself no, that can't be. But I went down to the newspaper and checked the files. I found the stories about when your brother died. And right there among the survivors was Crystelle Spurlock Calcart. I said to myself, that's got to be her. Crystelle spelled the same way. You always had money, but I never knew you had *that* kind of money. I called your mother, but she wouldn't give me shit. Then I started checking around. One day I drove by your house and there you were, turning out of the drive in that big green Packard. You took off like a turpentined cat. I followed you all the way downtown."

Crystelle felt a chill up her spine. She could not imagine

being caught so unawares. She put some Spurlock steel in her voice. "Bern, what do you want?"

"Like I said, I just thought we'd talk over old times. Remember that party we had in Dago? When I passed out and woke up to find out you'd pulled a train with practically the whole starboard watch of the SS *Gordon Hall*? Remember?"

Crystelle did not answer. That escapade had occurred during the time of craziness after losing Moon. Bern and his friends had been an exciting diversion. All were veterans of the North Atlantic convoys. They talked of the Murmansk run, of torpedoed ships, of tankers vanishing in an instant ball of fire, of life rafts and floating bodies. When she met them, they were bound for the western Pacific and the war out there. A little sex had seemed the least she could do for them.

It had been a different time, a different world.

"We were a real close bunch on the old *Gordon Hall*," Bern continued. "We still keep in touch. The boys still ask about you. Wait till I tell them you were a Texas oil heiress all along!"

"Bern, I have nothing to do with the company. I don't have a penny's worth of stock in it."

"I know that. As a matter of fact, I know the whole story. It's common gossip around town. I haven't had much to do during the last few weeks while I waited to get on out at Convair. So I've been nosing around. I've even found out you're up to your old tricks. I checked out the guy you went to see that day. And you know what? He's married and got a houseful of kids."

"You're probably talking about my investments counselor."

Bern snickered. "Sure he is. I've heard that story, too, about how you two ran off together in high school. You see, Crystelle, I know an awful lot about you. And here I am, out of a job, damned near broke, lonesome, just dying to tell all I know. And there you are rich, with all your dirty little secrets. I wonder what your boyfriend would say if he knew what I know about you."

Crystelle's heart skipped a beat. It would not do for Moon to hear about her life during the war. The details would be too much for him to handle. His strong streak of puritanism would overrule his reason. She might lose him.

"Bern, what do you have in mind?" she asked quietly.

"Well, I thought we might meet and come to a sort of mutual understanding. I think we both would feel better about things."

Crystelle needed time to think. And for once, she could tell the truth.

"Bern, I'm leaving town tomorrow. I have another trip scheduled right after that. But I'll call you as soon as I get back. Three weeks from tomorrow."

"You won't forget, will you? I really want to see you. I'll be awfully disappointed if I don't. No telling what I might do."

"I'll call you. I promise."

He gave her the number.

She hung up, appalled that she had given in to his demands.

But what the hell else could she have done under the circumstances?

Her knees grew weak. She sat down on a hassock and put her head in her hands.

Why did this have to happen now, just when everything was going so great?

Before long, she should have Moon all to herself. She was making money, big money, through his expertise. Her project to get back into Spurlock Oil was moving forward rapidly. Once she had the goods on Brod, her mother would fold, agree to anything to keep it quiet. She could oust Joanna, and take over the company.

Everything she had come back to Fort Worth to get was almost in her grasp.

Now this!

Bern was the only person around who could bring it all tumbling down.

She would not tolerate it!

Somehow, she must get rid of him.

She went to bed and lay awake, thinking of various ways.

Chapter 20

Kelly awoke one morning with nothing to do all day. School had been dismissed for a state teachers' meeting. At breakfast, he mentioned that fact to his mother.

"Are you sure you don't have homework?"

"No." He had just completed a six-week tour of the northeastern states with the choir. On his return he had discovered that his tutor had taken him a week ahead of his class in homework. He already had completed all assignments for the unexpected holiday.

"Then why don't you spend the day with me at the office? You can get a taste of your future. I'll treat you to lunch."

Kelly was intrigued. "Okay."

"Then run change your clothes. Why don't you wear those gray slacks—the new ones that fit so well—and that good-looking blue blazer?"

Kelly wondered why he had to dress up. But from the moment they entered the building he understood: he was on display. Although his mother attempted to be oh so casual, she gave herself away by keeping her hand on him. Dozens of employees beamed smiles at him as if he were visiting royalty. Kelly was embarrassed, yet oddly proud and pleased. He walked solemnly, responding to the smiles with polite nods.

From the time he was a toddler, Spurlock Oil had assumed the aura of a complete abstraction for him—a mysterious place that housed the dark-suited men who came to stand outside his father's bedroom door each weekday morning and, later, the place where his mother went each day, expending her energy so that she came home exhausted each night.

Somehow, Spurlock Oil had never seemed real.

As he walked along the wide, lengthy corridors, he was impressed by the high ceilings, the rich wood paneling, and the platoons of employees. He was surprised by his mother's bearing as she guided him through the maze. He was awed by the size of her huge office and the ornate desk where she placed her briefcase. Not even the principal at school had anything half so grand.

"Make yourself at home," she said, gesturing to encompass the office. "Look it over. This may be yours some day. Or Weldon's."

The remark disturbed him. He had known that she was "preserving the company" for him and Weldon. But that also had become an abstraction.

He had never consciously considered that he might spend much of his life in this place.

His mother settled effortlessly into the large chair behind her desk and punched a button on the intercom.

"Bonnie, I'm ready for the mail. Please get me Senator Johnson in Washington. After I talk with him, please get me Commissioner Albritton in Austin. Then Mr. Spears at Humble in Houston."

Kelly sank into a chair and watched, not knowing what else to do.

"I'll be through in a minute," his mother said. "I want to get these phone calls behind me."

As soon as the first call went through, Bonnie came in with the mail. Kelly knew her well. In years past she had come to the house often. She winked at him, put the mail on his mother's desk, and quickly withdrew.

He wandered over to the window and looked into the street below, eavesdropping on his mother's end of the conversation with the senator. She was telling him she had just read a bill that was now before the Congress, and was disturbed over its possible effect on the oil industry. Her argument was filled with technical terms unfamiliar to Kelly.

Restlessly, he walked back to a couch and picked up a magazine. The senator and his mother talked more than twenty minutes.

"The other two calls won't take as long," she promised him.

She discussed proration with the man in Austin. She was protesting some point, and apparently she won.

The call to Houston was to reach agreement over the final details of a contract. The man in Houston did most of the talking. His mother listened, commenting only occasionally.

She seemed pleased with the results. When the call ended, she held down the button on the phone for a moment, then dialed a three-digit number.

"Don, if you have a moment, could you bring up that Humble material? I think we're ready to move on it."

She rose from her desk and motioned to Kelly. "Come here. It's high time you learned what this place is all about."

She led him to a large panel on the wall and opened it with a key. The doors swung back to reveal a map of Texas and part of New Mexico. She pointed.

"All those dots are Spurlock wells. Black for oil, green for gas. Blue for mixed. Some were drilled by your grandfather twenty, even thirty years ago. Some are still producing, making money for us. Others were drilled by your father before he went off to work with the government during the war. The red dots are dry holes. That one there was where your grandfather Clay was killed. It was never redrilled. The yellow dots are projected drilling sites—places where we have reason to suspect we may find oil. That's why this map is kept under lock and key. You're seeing our biggest secrets. But I guess you're entitled."

Kelly had not dreamed there were so many Spurlock wells. While he stood studying the map his mother returned to her desk. Parker arrived with the material she had requested. He came across the office and shook hands with Kelly.

"You've sure sprung up in the last few months," he said. "I wouldn't have recognized you."

Kelly did not know how to answer.

"He takes after his father mostly," his mother said. "But my family also tends to be tall."

"Well, your father had an inch or two on me," Parker said. "It looks like you will, too, before long."

Kelly was relieved when Parker and his mother turned their attention to the charts and maps on her desk. He stood at the map case, listening to their discussion.

Parker was a solemn, dignified-looking man. Kelly was surprised by the deference he gave his mother's opinions, and by her thorough knowledge of the technical details they were discussing. Their talk was relaxed, with free give-and-take. They argued at times, but apparently reached agreement.

After Parker left, Kelly's mother motioned for him to come over to her desk.

"You might as well know what we were talking about. We're entering a joint venture with Humble Oil to drill a test well right here." She pointed a long, slim finger at the center of a chart. "You see these crosshatched areas? They show our leases. The vertical lines are Humble leases. Between the two of us, we hold most of the play in that area. So it's to our mutual interests to discover if oil or gas exists there in productive quantities. So we're sharing the cost and information. Actually, it's a bit to Spurlock advantage. Humble has done extensive seismographic surveys. They have a far better idea of the geology, and they're sharing *that* information with us, too."

Kelly looked at the map and asked his first question.

"How did you learn all this stuff?"

She laughed. "Most of it your daddy taught me. But I've learned a lot since I started here. And I've read books."

She walked to a bookcase, ran a finger across the spines, and pulled out two large volumes. "If you're really interested, these will give you a start. This one offers an overview of the oil industry—from exploration through drilling to refining. The other contains an introduction to basic geology."

Kelly took the books over to a chair by the window and began to read.

Throughout the remainder of the morning a stream of executives came into the office. He knew most of them. They were the men who used to come to see his father—Campbell, Piersall, Hollander, Chambers. Each shook hands with him and commented on how much he had grown.

Pretending to read, he sat and marveled as his mother discussed an amazing number of subjects with them—all having to do with the operation of Spurlock Oil. Most of the time she seemed to be deferring to them, asking questions, soliciting suggestions.

But Kelly noticed that in the end she made all of the decisions.

At noon Bonnie brought in barbecued beef sandwiches, potato salad, and coffee. Kelly and his mother dined at a small table in the corner of the office.

"I do this every day," she said. "It's my only quiet moment. I used to go out to restaurants, but it was so taxing, and it took too much time."

Kelly had never tried to envision his mother at the office. But the reality was more impressive than anything he could have imagined.

"You think you'd like to do this someday?" she asked.

Kelly shrugged. "I don't know."

He had never thought about it. A long time ago, when he was small, he had wanted to become a forest ranger, working with trees and animals and the outdoors. Later, he had thought he might become an explorer. But he had known, deep down, that those ambitions were a form of fantasy, never to be fulfilled.

More recently he had thought he might become a musician. But that goal also was impractical; he could not play a single instrument.

In truth, he did not know what he wanted to do as an adult. Any career had always seemed far in the future.

But now, surrounded by the activities of Spurlock Oil, that future suddenly loomed much closer.

"This office is the center of the company," his mother said. "Every major decision is made at that desk. In your Grandfather Clay's day, the most exciting place to be was in the field. The big decisions back then were made at the wellhead, as they drilled through each formation. He made his decisions from the cuttings, the cores they brought up from the bottom of the hole. The oil industry was all new then. No one could anticipate what they might find. He had to be in the field to tell the crews what to do. Now we're in contact with every well by radio and telephone, and we make most of the decisions here at the office. Only rarely does Mr. Parker or Mr. Piersall go out to a drilling site."

She sat toying with her coffee cup. Outside, Kelly could hear people walking in the halls. The sounds were faint and remote.

"In your grandfather's day, most of the money was made in the field. When he found oil, he made money. When it was a dry hole, he lost all the money it took to drill it, all the work he had put into it. Now most of our money is made on paper, taking advantage of every benefit in the tax codes, watching expenses, making deals to share risks, gathering mountains of information so the right decision is always made. Your father saw all this coming. He was one of the first. He pioneered the running of an oil company from behind a desk."

She rose and walked to the far wall, motioning for him to follow. "Look at these. In cleaning out your father's things, I found them and had them framed. Here's a letter from President Franklin D. Roosevelt to your father, thanking him for the work he did during the war. Here's another, dated two years later."

"What did Daddy do?"

She looked at him in surprise. "I thought you knew. He helped to build the Big Inch."

"The what?"

"A big pipeline. Before the war, German submarines were sinking tankers all along our East Coast. The government knew that if war came, we would have no way of transporting oil to the industries in the East and Midwest. So the government asked your father and some other men to build a pipeline from Texas and Louisiana all the way to New Jersey. It was a huge job—across rivers, over mountain ranges. But they did it within one year. The President was so pleased with your father's work that he asked him to help plan the fuel supply lines for the invasions and military campaigns that came later. It was a tremendous responsibility. That's the way he worked himself into his early grave. It was all secret. I didn't learn what he was doing until late in the war. I suppose we got into the habit of never talking about it. But I thought you knew."

Kelly was slightly disappointed. He had built up a fantasy that his father had been a secret agent.

"Anyway, he wanted the company preserved for you and Weldon. He expected you to take the reins someday. That's why I brought you here today. You should start thinking of the future."

Through the following days Kelly spent every spare moment reading the books. As he gathered a smattering of knowledge he began to imagine himself behind a huge desk at Spurlock Oil. Using the tricks he had learned in the choir, he memorized the names of the different parts of a drilling rig, the intricate arrangement of a refinery, the geological-time tables.

But even as he daydreamed about running Spurlock Oil, he realized that Weldon, three years older, would be out of college two years ahead of him.

The job was probably Weldon's, if he wanted it.

But the thought did not blunt Kelly's fantasies.

Once again it would be the Spurlock brothers against the world, this time directing a far-flung empire.

Already Kelly found himself so much more mature than his classmates at school. He no longer had much interest in their games, their talk. The choir had introduced him to an outside world that few kids had any opportunity to see. Much had been demanded of him, and he had proven himself capable. On tour, every choir member was assigned tasks from morning to night, loading and unloading costumes and sets, making certain the right sheet music was available. Every choir member had responsibilities he could not evade; if he did not do his assigned tasks, they were not done, and the performance would be jeopardized.

Kelly did not expect to travel with the choir for the rest of his life. But he now knew how organizations worked. He was sure that when the time came, he could move on to something else and assume responsibilities even more sweeping.

The oil company became an immediate, irresistible lure. Each schoolday afternoon he rushed to catch the bus on Camp Bowie Boulevard and rode downtown to the Spurlock Building. There he spent an hour or more before riding home with his mother.

Don Parker's office and lab on the fifth floor held special enchantment for Kelly. On shelves along one entire wall rested core samples from wells all across West Texas. Coached by Parker, Kelly soon learned to identify the different formations and the approximate geological time period of each.

He loved the smells of raw crude, brought to the lab for testing, and of the pungent chemicals Parker used to determine acidity, specific gravity, paraffin content, and dozens of other things. Sometimes Parker gave Kelly a rubber apron and put him to washing and preparing well samples for micropaleontological determination.

Although Parker had four assistants, he preferred to do the determinations himself. He did not seem to mind when Kelly stood at his elbow, monitoring the results. To the contrary, he talked to Kelly as he worked, lecturing on the different rock samples. Sometimes he placed various shales, sands, and limestones under low power in the microscope and drilled Kelly on how to identify each.

Under Parker's tutelage, Kelly learned of worlds that existed millions of years before his own. The knowledge was stunning. Parker brought to life eras populated by dinosaurs, large flying mammals, huge fishes, and primordial turtles. In his own hands Kelly held their teeth, bits of their bones, and —to his amazement—their fossilized turds. In stone he saw impressions of leaves that fell from trees hundreds of millions of years ago, snails that lived on the floors of oceans long since vanished, and tracks of animals extinct eons before man walked the earth.

Quietly, patiently, Parker told Kelly the secrets of the earth's past.

"Did you have to go to college a long time to learn all this stuff?" Kelly asked him one afternoon.

"You better believe it," Parker said. "Six years. But that's only the start. Too many people think you can go to college, get your head crammed with facts, and you're set for life. It isn't that way. If you want to amount to anything as a geologist, you have to keep studying throughout life."

Kelly was aghast. "Is there *that* much to learn?"

"Sure. There'll always be new theories, new discoveries, new techniques. When you go to college, don't let the profs con you. They'll act like they're preaching the gospel. But half of what they tell you will be outdated within a few years. Colleges should give you the basics, and teach you to think. They don't always do that."

While Parker worked, Kelly spent a few minutes digesting the observation. "What didn't they teach you?"

"Oh, a lot of things," Parker said as he lit a Bunsen burner. "If anyone had seriously proposed the theory of continental drift while I was in college, he'd have been laughed right out of the classroom. But now the theory is beginning to make sense. Remember my telling you about faults and uplifts hundreds, maybe even thousands, of miles long?"

Kelly nodded and waited. Parker paused while arranging his equipment. He was attempting to identify a thin vein of crystal embedded in a sample of feldspar.

"There's now strong evidence that entire continents may be moving, bumping into each other, causing these upheavals. It sounds crazy, but it's slowly becoming accepted as the best explanation. All the theories I was taught may go out the window. You believe in evolution?"

"Sure." Kelly had learned about it in fifth-grade science.

"That's a perfect example of what I mean. You were probably taught evolution as a fact. But it's only a theory—the best explanation we have at the moment for a whole range of phenomena. Those learned teachers don't tell you there are some troublesome facets to it. No one has ever evolved a new species, or found proof one specie ever evolved into another. No one has ever found the links to tie man and apes to a common ancestor. It *looks* like that's what happened. But no one really knows. Keep an open mind, Kelly. Hang loose. Take whatever they tell you with a grain of salt. Only people with small brains are ever positive about anything. When you come right down to it, we don't even know for certain where oil comes from. We have theories. But no facts."

He jotted notes on a pad. "Hardness seven, gravity two point three. Loses luster on heating, regains it on cooling. What does that tell you?"

"Quartz?" Kelly guessed.

"You're learning. Some form of quartz. Basically silicon dioxide, with a few impurities. Tridymite. Or cristobalite, maybe. But it's a rare bird. New in my experience."

Kelly was still thinking about drifting continents. "How could continents float?"

"There the theory gets complicated," Parker said. "I have a couple of magazine articles on it, if you're really interested."

Kelly followed him into his office. He rummaged through a treasure trove of material and handed Kelly two magazines.

"Just read for the meaning and don't bother with the math. It's only approximate, anyway. Get out of here, now. I have some reports to write."

Kelly took the two magazines up to his mother's office. He was not surprised that she was out. She often went down the hall to confer with other people. He walked across the office to his favorite place—a high-backed wing chair facing the street—and soon lost himself in the magazines. He sank down into the cushions and braced his feet against the windowsill.

The first article was indeed fascinating. He learned that the theory of continental drift dated from the last century, when two guys had suggested it. Other scientists had laughed at them. But soon other scientists began to notice that geological formations on some continents matched exactly those on others, across oceans and seas. The man who wrote the article insisted that all over the world, continents were in motion, pushed by magma forced up through the ocean floor.

Engrossed in trying to fathom how this could be, Kelly was only vaguely aware that his mother had returned to the office. He heard her using the phone, the intercom, the scratch of her pen as she signed papers.

A while later Mr. Trammel came into the office. Kelly heard his mother talking with him, but paid no attention.

He was alerted by an unnatural silence. Curious, he peeked around the edge of his chair.

His mother and Mr. Trammel were standing by her desk, embracing. Even as he watched, his mother put her hands on Mr. Trammel's chest and pushed away.

Kelly jerked his head back.

"No, Walter, this is wrong," his mother said.

Kelly sat in a dilemma. It was far too late to reveal his presence. But the longer he waited, the worse it would be if he were discovered.

Before he could decide what to do, Mr. Trammel spoke in a low voice.

"Joanna, you can't keep avoiding me. Eventually, Peggy will notice. We must talk about this."

"There's nothing to talk about. We made a terrible mistake. It must never happen again."

"We can't ignore our feelings, and who we are," Mr. Trammel said.

"Walter, I thought I had made myself plain. For Peggy's sake, if nothing else, we should see to it that we're never alone with each other, ever again. I wish you hadn't dropped by. I don't feel right, even about this."

"I have a legitimate reason for being here. I've done some research, and found that the Humble agreement fails to cover several contingencies. They should be mentioned."

Kelly heard his mother sigh. "Does this mean the whole contract will have to be rewritten?"

"No. A simple addendum should take care of it. I've written a proposed draft. Nothing unusual. I'm sure they'll accept it."

Kelly heard the rustle of paper.

"Joanna, you can't go on avoiding me," Trammel said again. "It's becoming too obvious."

"Walter, please! I said I don't want to discuss it!"

The room was silent for a time. Kelly sat motionless, clutching his magazine.

"I'm sure Peggy knows," his mother said, her voice low and husky. "I can see it in her eyes every time she looks at me."

"That's just your imagination working overtime."

"No, it isn't. She's a very smart woman."

"Even assuming you're right, it only means we must go on, normally. Peggy knows I love her, and have all these years. Maybe you and I made a mistake. But it happened. I won't walk away from it. You're a fine, wonderful person, and I love you. Whatever you want me to do, I'll do it, as long as we don't hurt Peggy."

"There's nothing we *can* do. That's what's so terrible. The damage is done. I'll just go on, acting as normally as I can around her. There's no other way. But I mean it, Walter. We must never be alone together again. I'm trusting you to see to it."

Again the room was silent.

"Joanna . . ."

"No, don't touch me. I think you should go now. I'll walk you to the elevator."

Kelly heard the door open, their voices in the outer offices.

After waiting only a cautious moment, he grabbed his magazines and fled back downstairs to Parker's laboratory.

Chapter 21

The attorneys Moon recommended were located in Rocke-
feller Center. Crystelle was ushered past black marble, lush
carpeting, and heavy furniture, into the sanctum sanctorum
of one of the senior partners.

He was a small man, with a well-combed, heavy head of
black hair and a pencil-line moustache. He introduced himself as Stephen Waxler. His name was high among those in
the company title. He ushered Crystelle to a comfortable
chair and took his place behind a large desk.

"Mr. Belford wasn't very specific on the details of your
case, Mrs. Calcart. If you'll describe your plight to me, perhaps we will have a better understanding of whether we
may be able to help you."

He kept his dark, impassionate eyes firmly on her, as if
studying every gesture and mannerism. Yet Crystelle felt at
ease with him. He seemed fully in command of himself, the
situation. Crystelle sensed she at last had found a lawyer who
might get the job done.

But she also knew his competence probably cut both
ways. No doubt he had made a preliminary inquiry into her
background, her status, her reputation.

If he had talked to people in Fort Worth, no telling what he had heard, or what kind of an opinion he had formed.

She felt she should make every effort to get her version of her life on record.

"I grew up as one of three siblings, and the only daughter, of a Texas oilman," she began. "When my father was killed, half of the company went to my mother. The other half was divided equally among myself, my brother Brod, and my brother Loren."

Waxler gave an abrupt nod. He was not taking notes. Crystelle assumed he had switched on a tape recorder.

"During the war my brother Brod, who was president of the company, went off to work for the government. Loren was in the army throughout the war. He was badly injured, and spent time as a POW. For five years the company was run by my illegitimate half brother, Grover Sterling. Although my mother was chairman of the board, she took absolutely no interest in company affairs. And Brod wouldn't give Grover enough control to do anything. The company went downhill all through the war."

Again Waxler nodded encouragement.

"At the end of the war, Brod had a massive heart attack. He became a hopeless invalid. But he still wouldn't give up control of the company. For a while, Loren was in and out of an army hospital in San Antonio, undergoing treatment. The company was still going downhill."

Crystelle paused, wondering how much Waxler believed, how much he questioned. His face remained expressionless.

"I was living in Florida at the time. Sterling came to me with a plan to refinance the company, realign the board, and squeeze Brod and Loren out. I gave him my support. So did my cousin Troy. You understand, I was concerned with the value of my stock. It seemed the only way to bring the company out of the doldrums."

Waxler waited without comment, his eyes still studying her.

"Then all hell broke loose. Loren was found shot dead in a city park. It was ruled a suicide. About the same time,

Grover came to New York to raise money for the restructuring. He was killed on his way back to his hotel from the theater district. His death was called a mugging. But on the same night, Troy's department store was burned to the ground. Also on the same night, I received a phone call from my brother, saying if I didn't sell my stock to him, I could expect something bad to happen to me."

Waxler's eyes widened slightly.

"I know. I have no proof. But I *was* threatened. And why wouldn't I be scared, after I heard the news the next day? I knew my brother, and what he could do. You may hear he was lily-white, but believe me, he was a ruthless son of a bitch. I knew that. At the time, I didn't have much money, aside from my stock. I couldn't fight him. So I agreed to sell my stock. He also got most of Loren's share, so he wound up owning almost half. Now he's dead, and his wife is running the company."

Waxler asked his first question. "And all this was what, eight or nine years ago?"

"Right. I didn't think I could do anything while Brod was alive. But when he died three years ago, I went back to Fort Worth to see what I could do about regaining my inheritance. I'm still working on it."

"And how do you think we might be able to help you?"

"I've hired a lawyer in Fort Worth. I know. I shouldn't be talking to you when I've already got a lawyer. But I want you to work together on this. He's not exactly blue-chip. But he knows jails, the way police work, the people that live in that world. I figured he was a good place to start."

"Have you told your Fort Worth attorney you've approached us to represent you?"

"Not yet. I will."

Waxler frowned, but did not comment.

"We've found the police had a suspect in Sterling's death, a man named Jerry Atchley. He was known to do murder-for-hire. But they didn't have enough on him. He's now in Sing Sing on another murder charge. I know as well as I know anything that Brod hired him, some way, to kill

Grover Sterling. You see, Brod thought Sterling killed Loren."

"What do *you* think?"

Crystelle was certain now that Waxler had looked into the case before making the appointment. She decided to be honest, for once.

"I really don't know. I wasn't there. I suppose Sterling was capable of it."

"What evidence do you have that Brod hired the murderer of Grover Sterling?"

"So far, not much. But Atchley knows what happened. And there was a woman with Grover that night. We're tracking her down. We tried to trace Troy. But that was a dead end. We just learned he drowned three years ago, swimming off one of those Greek islands."

Waxler remained silent for a time, frowning. "Mrs. Calcart, this isn't normally our type of case. Exactly what is it you think we might be able to do for you?"

"I want to offer Atchley a deal. He's doing thirty to life, so he doesn't have a hell of a lot to lose. Moon Belford said your firm has solid contacts in New York City government and in Albany. I want to put the pressure on, make it worthwhile for Atchley to tell what he knows."

"I see. And what will you do with that information?"

Crystelle hesitated. Middleton had warned her the wrong phraseology could be interpreted as blackmail.

"I'll use it to convince my mother that Brod wasn't the angel she thought. With her support, I can get my inheritance back, and have a voice in the company again."

Waxler made a slight movement behind his desk. Crystelle assumed he had turned off the tape recorder.

"Let me look into it," he said. "Of course, we'll have to contact your Fort Worth attorney, coordinate with him. If you can give me four or five days, I'll call you."

"I have some shopping to do. I'll be at the Plaza. You can leave a message for me there."

"Perhaps I should warn you. An extended investigation like this, dealing with high officials, could be expensive."

"I know," Crystelle said. "But I'll pay the price, as long as I get what I want."

Crystelle was awakened by the ringing phone. She glanced at her watch on the nightstand. Almost 2:00 A.M. She picked up the receiver.

"Did I wake you?" Moon said.

"You don't get two guesses."

"I'm sorry. But I thought I ought to warn you what to expect when you come home. Josie has filed for divorce."

Crystelle sat up in bed, gripping the phone.

This was the best news yet.

"What happened? A blowup?"

"No. That's the weird part. She didn't say a word to me. She just packed up and moved out while I was at the office. Took the kids and went to her parents. She won't even talk to me."

"Where are you now?"

"At the club. I sent word for her to move the kids back into the house, that we should act as normal around them as possible."

"You have any clue on what set it off?"

"Oh, hell, yes. The divorce action lists just about every place you and I have been together. A constable served the papers on me this afternoon. She demands full custody of the kids, claiming I'm not a fit father." He paused a moment. "You're named as corespondent."

"You want me to fly back tomorrow?"

"No need. In fact, the way things are, it might be better if we didn't see each other for a while."

Crystelle sensed that Moon needed room to maneuver. She was sure he felt boxed in.

She knew the feeling.

"Moon, I'll go along with however you want to play it," she said. "But don't think for a minute you have to protect me in all this. I don't give a damn what people think. You can move in with me at the house anytime you want. You know that."

"They'd use it against me. They already have the kids thinking I'm the worst villain since Simon Legree. Josie's daddy came into the office right behind the constable and shouted at me for half an hour. He said he'll see to it that Josie gets every cent I've got, and then he's going to run me out of Fort Worth. We had a good cuss-fight, right in my office, with everybody on the floor listening. I almost hit the old bastard."

"I'm sorry she's putting you through this," Crystelle said. "I wish there was more I could do."

"The old man said I've dug my own grave. He told me that if it takes every cent he has, he'll keep me from seeing my daughters again, ever."

"He can't do that."

"He might, if he finds a way to get it before the right court and the right judge."

"Maybe *we* can get it before the right judge."

"Well, anyway, the next two or three weeks will be sheer hell. I'm right in the middle of a client newsletter. And I'll be busy with lawyers and meetings. I plan to file a cross-action, do whatever it takes to win visitation rights. I'll be living in a goldfish bowl. I may not be able to call you very often."

"That's okay. I understand."

"How did it go up there?"

"So far, so good."

She told him about the interview, Waxler's promise to look into it.

"He's one of the smartest men I know," Moon said. "He has a lot of clout. If anyone can do it, he can."

"You sure you don't want me to come home, just to be with you?" Crystelle asked again.

Moon did not answer for a moment. "Crystelle, things have been happening so fast that I've lost my perspective. I really need some time alone, to think. I'm hoping you can understand that."

Crystelle felt a twinge of apprehension.

Her most formidable opposition might not be Josie, but the kids. She attempted to keep her voice untroubled.

"Of course I understand. Just remember that whenever you need me, I'm always here. Okay?"

"Okay," Moon said.

After they said good night and broke the connection, Crystelle became so agitated that she got up and paced the room, half tempted to fly back to Fort Worth the next morning.

Already Moon was weighing his two lives, about to make a choice.

And Bern was in the same town, with all that he knew about her.

It was an intolerable situation.

She worried over the quandary through the long weekend.

On Tuesday, Waxler's secretary called and arranged for an appointment that afternoon.

Again Waxler received her in his private office. This time he was more friendly.

"We may be in luck," he said. "We found that many people are interested in Jerry Atchley. If we work it right, we may be able to bring pressure on him from the state, the city, the Justice Department, and maybe even a congressional racketeering committee. The information you want is only a small part of the big picture. Atchley apparently knows the inside workings of considerable mob activity in the East. If he talks, you'll get what you want."

"Why bring these other people into it? Why can't we make our own deal?"

"Because if he talks at all, he'll need plenty of protection. This will involve cooperation between state, city, and federal governments. Protection, plea-bargaining on various levels. All this will take time."

"I've already put years into this. How much longer will it take?"

"We should be able to bring everyone concerned together within a few months. All of these groups have been looking at Atchley, thinking about making the effort. We'll just coordinate the effort. I imagine the first step will be to move him to a secure location for interrogation, to see how much he knows. I'm sure I can get our questions high on the list to be asked."

Months. Crystelle did not know how she could stand waiting that long.

"Can't we speed things up?"

Waxler smiled. "We'll try. Certainly, we'll get right on it. I'll keep you informed of our progress."

"Mr. Waxler, do you think this'll work?"

He hesitated, rubbing his pencil-line moustache with a forefinger. "Mrs. Calcart, there's no guarantee. But let's look at it from Atchley's standpoint. He has a lot of information. No doubt some powerful individuals would like to see him dead, just to remove him as an ever-present threat. If he has any brains, he'll understand that. He's serving a long prison term. Any possible parole is still years away. But if he makes a deal, serves as a witness against certain crime figures, he'll receive protection, special attention, and might even get the slate wiped clean. I believe he'll go for it."

"But you don't think he'd talk to us alone?"

"No. We wouldn't be able to offer him the guarantees he would need."

"In the meantime, what if we find the woman?"

"That would be a good lever, and help convince Atchley to talk. But again, we can't act alone. If we ask for the cooperation of the governmental agencies, we'll have to work with them all the way."

Crystelle easily could imagine the whole effort bogging down in red tape.

But she also could see that Waxler was probably right: it was the only way to get to Atchley, obtain his testimony.

"All right," she said. "I'll go back to Fort Worth and wait. Speed it up as much as you can."

That evening, back at the hotel, she also arrived at a decision about Bern.

Even if she paid him whatever blackmail he demanded, he would not go away. He would see her as a golden opportunity, the font of continuing money.

There was only one way to get rid of him.

She thought back over the mess Brod had left behind by hiring others to do his dirty work.

Now, years later, witnesses were still around.

If Brod were still alive, he would not be able to rest easily. He would be at the mercy of everyone who knew.

The job on Bern would have to be done right, leaving no such lingering mess.

That meant she would have to do it alone.

Chapter 22

As the independent contractor spudded in on the deep test well in New Mexico and began making hole, Spurlock Oil entered its most exciting period in decades. Hardly a day went by without at least one significant revelation. Each morning Joanna could hardly wait to enter the office to learn what had been discovered during the night. Samples from the bottom of the hole arrived daily. Each morning Joanna and most of the executives gathered in Don Parker's lab to inspect new cores and assorted specimens.

By the time the driller reached two thousand feet it became evident they were into new geology, pioneering the way for others. Day after day, almost every turn of the bit promised further surprises.

With so much riding on the outcome, Joanna soon had trouble sleeping. She could think of little else but the huge investment, the thousands of acres of Spurlock leases awaiting the results.

The first good show of oil came just below forty-five hundred feet in a thick bed of limestone. At forty-seven fifty, the driller halted operations and ran a choke test. Under ordinary circumstances the results would have been cause for rejoicing. But due to the remoteness of the region, profitability of the well still remained in doubt.

However, hopes were raised that even better production lay deeper.

Joanna was encouraged enough to broach a plan that had been growing in her mind for weeks. She did not want the partnership with Humble to end the moment the contractor stopped drilling.

She telephoned Spears in Houston.

"I suppose you've heard the good news."

"Well, we haven't tossed a big party yet, but that choke test was encouraging," Spears said. "Maybe we'll be able to recover some of the cost. I'm assuming you agree we should ignore this possible production for now, run casing, and go on down to China."

"Of course," Joanna said.

If no additional oil was found deeper, they could plug back, perforate the casing into the oil-bearing limestone, and complete a producing well.

"The big question around here is where we are in relation to the fault," Spears said. "Parker have any thoughts on that?"

"He says we're still on the up side."

"He's probably right. That'd be my guess."

"Cal, I have another proposition for you. I want to see what you think. Why don't we go into partnership on a pipeline company for those leases? We could split the cost of moving the oil out, just as we've done on the test well."

The line was silent as Spears considered the idea.

"I think maybe it's a bit premature, little lady. Sure, we've found oil. But we don't know how much. We may have hit a small pocket that'd dry up in a month. There's no indication yet there's enough oil to begin to pay for laying forty miles of pipe."

"Cal, I know that. But I think we ought to discuss it now, before we become competitors again."

Spears burst out laughing. "You have a point."

"I think we're both fairly certain we're into a good pool, if not a new field. Why don't we go ahead, do a preliminary route survey, block out the plan in rough, and put it on hold? When we both begin drilling our stepouts, and prove the size of the strike, we'll probably need gathering lines in a hurry. When that day comes, our plan for a partnership pipeline will be ready and waiting."

Again Spears laughed. "You present a convincing case." He paused, thinking. "I'll have to take it up with my staff."

"So will I. But I thought we should put it into motion."

His hesitation was brief. "I'll float the possibility. There'd be a lot of details to work out. I agree with your thinking, though. We should be looking ahead."

But when Joanna introduced her plan to her executives two days later, she met strong opposition.

"If this turns out to be a big strike, Humble will be drilling two or three wells to our one," Piersall said. "They'd monopolize the line, squeeze us out."

Joanna felt he missed the point. "The money we'd save could be put into drilling more wells, quicker," she pointed out. "There's no reason we can't keep pace with Humble. Besides, it'd be understood from the start that use of the pipeline would be fifty-fifty, just like the cost."

"They'd find ways around it," Chamber argued. "This is a cutthroat business. They know all the tricks."

"They've cooperated on the test well. Does anyone have any complaints about the way they've shared information?"

"That's different," Chambers said. "If we find oil in quantity out there, it'll be a mad scramble."

"I doubt Humble will go along with it anyway," Piersall said. "They'll want total control of their production."

"Right now it's us—Spurlock and Humble—doing joint exploration," Joanna pointed out. "The psychology could be the same in moving the oil out. But unless we come to an agreement with them now, it'll be us and them again when the drill bit stops turning on that test well. And we'd be facing total expense for a pipeline. I don't want that to happen."

"We've used their lines along the Gulf," Hollander said. "They've been helpful in the past."

"Look, we have three alternatives," Joanna said. "We can let Humble build a pipeline, and sign a contract with them for use. We all know that'd probably be on an availability basis. Second, we can go into partnership with them fifty-fifty. Third, we can build our own line."

"That'd be terribly expensive," Campbell agreed.

"I hope you'll all think about this," Joanna said. "Spears seemed interested. If he indicates it's a possibility, I want to be in a position to move fast. I need your advice. I hope you'll weigh the alternatives, give me the benefit of your experience."

The matter became even more pressing through the following days as two more pay zones were discovered. The first, just above ten thousand feet, was impressive, but not spectacular. The second, at twelve thousand two-twenty, proved beyond anyone's doubt that a massive amount of oil awaited development.

Spears called from Houston. "Looks like we've got our strike, little lady. Shall we shut her down now, or go deeper?"

"Deeper. Don says we're into some interesting formations. I think we both might benefit from knowing more about them."

"That's what I'm hearing around here. But unless we run into something even better, I think we should stick to our original plan and close her out at about fifteen thousand."

"I agree," Joanna said.

But later, thinking back on the call, it seemed to her that Spears was growing impatient to close out the test well, and she was certain she knew the reason.

She called her department heads into a special meeting.

"I think Humble is already moving on development of their leases. We can't let them get ahead of us at this point. Don, can you put your people onto this? We should be ready to move as soon as the test well is completed."

Parker offered one of his rare smiles. "For once, I'm ahead

of you. We've been correlating information from the well with what we know of Humble's seismograph survey. I think we can predict the fault zone through our leases with a fair degree of accuracy."

Joanna had been pondering a question for weeks. She now asked it, hoping to supplement her own limited knowledge.

"Which should we do? Should we stick with the fault zone, or branch out with a few experimental wells to define the extent of the strike?"

"The fault zone," Piersall said. "Every foot away from it raises the odds of drilling a duster."

"I'd like to see the pool defined," Campbell said. "If we should need temporary financing to meet all these expenses, it'd be nice to have known reserves on the books."

"We should drill at least six or eight wells right along the fault as quick as we can," Chambers said. "Gathering and storage would be simplified. If production turns out to be limited to the zone, and the strike turns out not to be a major pool, we'd still be getting our share."

Joanna felt the views of Chambers made the most sense.

But so much depended on what they did not yet know.

"Don?" she asked.

Always reluctant to commit himself, Parker hesitated. "Mrs. Spurlock, I'm almost certain we're into a good-sized pool. Everything points to it. But there's no guarantee. In a sense, an offset any distance from the zone would be another test well. On the other hand, from the slope of the formations, I'm fairly certain some of our leases will prove better than the test we did with Humble."

"Have you decided where we should concentrate?"

"Roughly." He spread a lease map. "I think our best bet would be along here. The geology looks ideal."

"Geology is one thing," Piersall said. "But that's rough country. The best places to drill may be impossible to reach. We'll need water, roads passable in any kind of weather for tons of equipment. We can't go off half-cocked."

Joanna had been thinking along the same line. "Mike, I think you're right. If you, Don, and Walt can arrange it, I'd like the three of us to spend the better part of a week on our leases. We can look over the land, decide exactly where we'll start our drilling, and plan our step-by-step development."

Chambers whipped the dead cigar from his mouth. "Mrs. Spurlock, have you seen that country?"

"Only from the air."

"I can tell you, it's hardly a picnic ground."

"I'm well aware of that. We can take tents, and use the test well as our headquarters. It'll be hard work. But after a few days, we should have a good idea of how to proceed."

The following week they flew to Hobbs in the Cessna and drove out to the test well in Jeeps.

Joanna was prepared for the ruggedness of the landscape. But she had not expected the vast transformation the search for oil had already brought to the region.

A few miles out from Hobbs, they left the highway for a new dirt road, built by the contractors as the route for equipment and supplies to the test well. All along the way to the rig they met returning service trucks. The traffic raised clouds of alkali dust that could be seen for miles. The road traversed rock-strewn gullies, and hills covered with yucca and soapweed. In the distance the higher elevation of a sawtooth ridge formed the backdrop.

The test well itself had grown into a small city. Because of its remoteness, the contractor had brought in mobile houses to serve as dormitories for the crews. A water well had been drilled, and the same engines that ran the rig also supplied electricity.

As Joanna and her Spurlock group arrived, the crew was in the midst of making "a trip" to replace a worn bit. Drill pipe almost filled the derrick. The roughnecks were busily performing their dangerous ballet, lifting the lengths of drill pipe one by one, attaching them to the drill stem, and lowering the two and a half miles of pipe back into the hole. Drilling mud showered the workers, turning them into brown-flecked clowns. The noise and clatter were awesome.

"No need to set up camp," the contractor insisted. "Mrs. Spurlock can use my trailer. You men can bunk with us."

Joanna agreed to the arrangement. With that problem solved, they could drive out to their leases the following morning and start to work. But first, she wanted to give Don Parker time to examine the most recent findings at the test well.

She went with him into the toolhouse, and for several hours they studied the drilling logs, along with the most recent cuttings brought up from the well.

Later the tour crew completed the trip and the rotary table resumed its work, turning the bit deep within the earth. Since the tremendous weight of the entire drill stem was suspended from the derrick, the drilling floor and surrounding ground vibrated with each turn of the stem. Joanna felt the persistent rhythm throughout her body. Soon it seemed as if she were a part of the well itself.

"Let's go look at the new cuttings," the contractor said.

He led Joanna and the Spurlock group onto the drilling floor. The crew were leaving the rig in a jovial mood, heading for showers and beer, content that they would not be required to make another trip on their tour. Joanna's field outfit of boots and jodhpurs received considerable attention, ranging from covert glances to uninhibited stares of admiration.

Near the drilling floor, the mechanical shakers were sifting through the drilling mud, separating the rock cuttings brought up from more than fourteen thousand feet below the surface of the earth. Don Parker reached past Joanna and expertly plucked a specimen from the mud. He held it up for her inspection.

"Woodford chert. We're edging out of the pay formations."

Joanna understood his implicit message: The test well had served its purpose. Soon Spears would want to stop drilling and complete the well.

"We're getting a lot of pressure from the bottom," the contractor said. "Sometimes it's all the mud can do to hold it."

Joanna thought of the weight of a column of heavy drilling

mud more than two miles deep, and the amount of gas pressure that would be required to lift it.

She raised her voice to speak over the noise of the rig. "Judging from your experience, how big a strike do you think we have?" she asked the contractor.

He laughed. "Mr. Spears asked me the same thing. I'll tell you what I told him. I think this may be my biggest. You get a feel for the other end of that drill stem. The fault may have helped. But I really think that fault zone is only an anomaly in at least a fair-sized pool."

Joanna and Parker exchanged glances.

Parker had said the same thing in different words.

That evening they dined with the crew, eating barbecue and beans from paper plates. After dinner most of the off-duty men went to bed. Only a few piled into trucks and drove in the direction of town.

"It's rough work," the contractor explained to Joanna as he escorted her to his trailer. "Most of them are pooped at the end of their tour."

He removed his bedroll. Joanna spread her sleeping bag on his cot and lay down in her clothes. Walt Chambers had warned her the conditions would be primitive. She did not intend to complain. With darkness the rig became a tower of light, visible for miles. The steady turn of the rotary table dominated the countryside. Lulled by its rhythm, Joanna quickly dropped off to sleep.

She awoke at dawn and washed her face at the spigot that served all. Her executives were already up and ready for the field. After breakfast, they piled into the Jeeps and set out to find the Spurlock leases.

Using the odometers, they located benchmarks. With a measuring chain, they defined and marked boundaries.

It was hot, exhausting work. Joanna quickly gained a new appreciation of her executives. Don Parker possessed an unerring eye for detail. Using the charts he had brought along, he soon delineated the path of the fault through the Spurlock leases, and oriented it to the landscape. Mike Piersall pointed out unseen hazards of certain drilling sites, the obscure advantages of others. He laid out possible roads through gullies and washes, and over hilly terrain. Walt Chambers clambered ceaselessly over the rough ground, drafting possible routes for future gathering lines. Each evening they returned to the test well. Joanna fell into bed each night physically depleted, yet exhilarated that so much was being accomplished.

By the afternoon of the third day they had chosen fourteen potential drilling sites. After the selection, they conferred on the crest of a high hill, planning the most logical progression of development. As they agreed on their findings, Don Parker carefully conveyed all the information to a key map.

That night they drove back to Hobbs for their rendezvous with Smiling Jack. He had just hauled a load of emergency equipment to Midland, and was flying the old DC-3. It was slower and a rougher ride, but Joanna was too tired to care. She unrolled her sleeping bag at the back of the plane and slept most of the way to Fort Worth.

On landing, she found herself in a twilight state between sleepiness and wakefulness. She was sunburned, covered with insect bites, and badly in need of a bath. Her skin was parched, her hair an impossible mess hidden under a bandana and battered Stetson. But she was still riding the high of her accomplishments during the last few days. Although it was after midnight, she drove by the office on her way home.

A stack of messages waited on her desk. She leafed through them. The refinery in Houston had experienced another serious breakdown. Parts had been ordered, and repairs were expected by tomorrow. A Spurlock well being drilled near Odessa had lost mud circulation at midafternoon. The driller had managed to prevent a blowout, but the well remained unstable. Acting in her behalf, Campbell had called in mud experts from Houston. Spears had called, wanting to discuss the pipeline partnership; he asked that she return his call as soon as possible. An old Spurlock well near Breckenridge had plugged itself with an accumulation of paraffin. The pumper wanted to know whether he should

shut her down, or expect an acidizing crew. And Walter
Trammel had called. Peggy was back in the hospital. Walter
asked that Joanna call as soon as she returned, no matter
what the hour.

She picked up the phone and dialed the Trammel house.
After a moment, Walter answered.

"Walter, I'm so sorry," she said. "How serious is it?"

She could imagine him shifting position, sitting up in bed.
"She's listed as critical. There's a buildup of fluid they can't
seem to control."

"Is she conscious?"

"Off and on. She drifts in and out. She has asked for you
several times."

"Can she have visitors?"

"Normally, no. But I've arranged for you to go in briefly."

From the depths of her own experience, Joanna remembered how these situations were; the greatest burden did
not necessarily fall on the ill.

"How are *you* holding up, Walter?"

He did not answer immediately. "It's wearing on both of
us. For a while there'll be improvement. Then comes a disappointment like this. Over and over. Somehow, it seems I
should be able to do more for her."

"I know. But Walter, you're providing her with every
medical benefit, all attention possible. She knows and appreciates that."

"Still, it isn't enough."

Joanna spoke from the heart. "Walter, that's part of loving.
We always fall short of our own idealized expectations."

He was silent for a moment. Joanna sensed he knew she
was thinking of more than Peggy's illness.

"Maybe you're right," he said.

Afterward, as she wrote quick memos and took care of
some of the most immediate problems on her desk, she was
troubled by her observation. She sat for a time in the darkened office and thought of how she had failed everyone she
loved.

Through her moment of weakness, her friendship with Peggy and Walter was irretrievably flawed.

Kelly was away on a long tour across Canada. Surrounded by other boys, he was trapped in his own loneliness. Despite her efforts, she had never been able to establish the rapport with him she wished.

Weldon seemed completely absorbed in his own world, but she knew he was filled with resentments. His brief letters made no mention of home or family. He had remained at the school through holidays and vacations, making excuses, passing up opportunities to come home.

Now it seemed absurd that she once had assumed that the operation of the oil company would be the most difficult part of her new life.

By comparison, it had proved relatively easy. With hard work, concentration, and persistence, she thus far had taken care of every crisis.

It was the intricate dilemmas involving human emotions that had been most difficult.

They were far, far more complicated, and consistently defied solution.

Chapter 23

Cutlery was in the corner, hidden behind glassware, china, all the pots and pans. The two clerks in the department were occupied with other customers. Crystelle was able to devote full attention to the merchandise.

It was a wondrous array. She would never have imagined that knives came in such infinite variety: huge butcher blades, as heavy as machetes. Paring knives, small, sturdy, and viciously sharp. Carving knives, long and slim. Steak knives. Bread knives with plain, scalloped, and serrated edges. Barbecue knives. And big cleavers for chopping.

Crystelle carefully considered each. The smaller were hopelessly inadequate. The big butcher blades and cleavers were ungainly. She had envisioned several scenarios. Anything used for hacking would not do.

It must be something for stabbing.

After carefully examining all, she chose a medium-sized boning knife. It had a thick blade, adequately long, with a cutting edge gently curved for effortless slicing. Yet its thickness lent it strength.

As a customer departed, Crystelle caught the eye of a

saleswoman. She waved the boning knife in the air. "I think this is what I want. But how will I ever carry it home?"

The saleswoman seemed amused. "It comes in a sturdy box, madam. It will carry quite safely."

Crystelle paid cash for the knife and a cute little salt-and-pepper set that caught her eye.

She did not worry about the purchase being traced. Surely the woman sold dozens of knives every day.

At home, she held the knife and experimented with it, plunging the blade through the air in ways she imagined would be necessary. She found a cardboard box in the pantry, arranged it on her bed, and drove the knife into it several times, searching for the best angle. She discovered that by using one hand to hold and guide the knife, she could use the heel of her other to drive the blade with more strength. She practiced until she could do the maneuver perfectly every time.

Next she needed to find a way to carry the weapon. Bern was a hugger, a kisser, a pawer. She would not be able to hide it on her person.

She pulled her largest purses out of the closet. Wrapped in a hand towel, the knife fitted neatly into her tooled leather handbag.

Once that problem was solved, she was ready to call Bern and let him know she was home.

He answered on the first ring. "I'd about given up on you," he said.

"I told you it'd be three weeks. It's three weeks to the day."

"Have a good trip?"

"So-so. Bern, I don't have much time. What do you want?"

"You know what I want. But I'm sure as hell not going to discuss it over the phone."

"Okay. Where can we talk?"

"Why don't I come by there?"

That would not do.

"No," she said. "I have servants, nosy neighbors. They'd

wonder about you. I don't want to have to explain you to anyone. I could come to your place."

He chuckled. "I was hoping you'd say that. In fact, I've been dreaming about it."

He gave her the address. She agreed to be there by eight.

During the afternoon a spring thunderstorm moved through Fort Worth with heavy rain, wind, and small hail. For a time Crystelle was concerned that her plans might be jeopardized. But by sundown the sky cleared.

The address he had given her was in a section of prefabricated housing, typical of those thrown up throughout the country a decade ago for defense workers and still in use now that so many people uprooted by the war refused to go back to wherever they came from. Crystelle drove slowly along the drab streets, hunting the number, dodging tree limbs and branches left on the pavement by the storm. The cheap, uniformly gray houses were jammed cheek to jowl, leaving no room for driveways. Battered, ancient automobiles filled every available space along the curb. Television antennae had sprouted on every roof. These people could not afford decent housing, but they could find the money for an expensive new diversion. The windows flickered with the telltale white light. Warnings had been issued not to watch the sets in the dark, that it was bad for eyesight, but no one seemed to listen.

She located the number painted on the curb at the very end of a narrow cul-de-sac. After circling twice, she found a place to park a half block away. She locked the car and, clutching her big leather handbag, made her way up the walk to Bern's front door.

He answered her knock immediately, stood for a time grinning at her, then opened the sagging screen door for her to enter. His voice still sounded like a diesel engine.

"Sweetheart, I couldn't wait for you to get here. Damn but it's good to see you. You're looking great!"

He enveloped her in a bear hug that hurt and kissed her, forcing his tongue deep into her mouth. She did not resist. He still smelled of rum, sweat, and rose hair oil.

They walked on into the tiny house. The ceiling light fixture had no shade. The naked bulbs were blinding.

"My little mink," he said, patting her on the behind. He had always said she fucked like a mink, which was strange. She had no idea of how a mink fucked.

"How about a rum and Coke?" he asked. "You see? I remember that was your favorite."

It was not her favorite. But rum had been the only liquor available at certain times and places during the war. Perhaps she drank mostly rum when she was with him. She did not remember.

Bern lumbered away to mix the drinks, offering her first good look at him.

He had gained weight, at least twenty pounds, and lost much of his hair. He and his friends had caught her attention with their exuberant boyishness and their lean, hard bodies. Now Bern was flabby, with a paunch. His large forehead, once partially hidden by dangling curls, now stretched across the top of his skull. His face was tracked with creases and folds.

The last ten years had not treated him well.

She sank onto the soiled sofa, hoping her white linen suit would not pick up stains. The room was claustrophobic, hardly larger than the walk-in closet in her bedroom.

Bern returned from the shoebox kitchen with the drinks and leaned to kiss her again. "You look terrific. I've never seen you dressed up like this."

That was probably true. During the time she had known him she had taken little interest in clothes, or anything else. Two or three simple dresses, a skirt and blouse or two, and a pair of shorts were all she had needed. Everyone had lived out of suitcases in those days.

Now she could hardly relate herself to the woman she had been.

She pushed him away. "Bern, this isn't a social call. I told you, I don't have much time. What's on your mind?"

He placed his drink on a small table beside the couch and

looked at her. "Don't you try to high-hat me! I won't stand for it. Don't forget. I knew you when."

"That was then. This is now. If you've anything to say to me, say it."

Bern kept her under his steady stare. "We had us some good times, Crystelle. We could have some more."

"Those days are gone forever. I'm home now. You have no place in my life here."

He reached for his drink. "Well, by damn I'll just *make* a place for me. I told you on the phone. I can upset your little applecart but good. You know it. I know it."

Crystelle waited a moment before responding. Bern had a mean streak. She had seen him pitch temper tantrums when crossed.

"All right. What would make you go away?"

"Fifty thousand dollars."

"Ridiculous. I don't have that kind of money."

"Crystelle, don't give me that bullshit. Everyone in town says you're worth millions. I've driven by your mother's house. I've seen where you're living now. I've been in that building with your family's name on it. I've seen the gas stations everywhere. It's common knowledge your brother bought you out for cash. Fifty thousand is pocket money for you."

"All my money is tied up. I can't get to it."

"Crystelle, just how goddamn dumb do you think I am?"

She hesitated. True, Bern was not dumb. She shifted her tactics. "If I gave you the money—and I said if—how would I know you won't be back for more."

He spread his hands. "Look, I'll level with you. I'm flat broke. I don't think I'm going to get on at Convair. After I knew you, I got into a little trouble. Frank and I—you remember Frank—well, we knocked over a gas station one night for a few dollars. We got caught. I did six months in correction. With this Cold War, Convair is checking backgrounds. I think they found out I've done time. Crystelle, all I need is a stake. Fifty thousand and you'll never see me again."

She did not believe him. But she had to pretend.

"Bern, I could let you have a little money, if you'll really leave town."

"How much?"

"Maybe twenty-five thousand."

"No. If you never want to see me again, it's fifty."

She shrugged. It really did not matter. "All right," she said. "Fifty. But that's not pocket money. It'll take me a day or two to get it together."

Bern's face split into a big smile. "Now, that's my girl! Let's drink to it."

He took the tumblers and went back into the kitchen. Through the doorway she saw him sneaking rum straight from the bottle, controlling the flow with the tip of his tongue. Bern had always been a heavy drinker. Apparently his habit had progressed.

Carefully, she tucked her handbag behind a cushion at the corner of the sofa.

He brought the drinks back and sat down beside her. Immediately he began to fondle her shoulder. "Crystelle, I've thought about you thousands of times. You always drove me wild. You still do. I've had a lot of women, but nothing like you."

She allowed her hand to fall on his knee. He began kissing her, and for several minutes they wallowed on the couch. Then he lifted her and carried her into the bedroom.

He put her on a faded blue chenille bedspread entangled with grimy, wrinkled sheets, and began to undress her, fumbling with the buttons. Crystelle helped him, hoping to prevent damage to her dress.

She had planned to allow him to use her, and to remain aloof. But as he went to work she felt herself responding. Bern was not in Moon's league, and never would be, but she could not ignore his animal-like ferocity. Soon she was swept up in his physical demands.

That was the start. It seemed to go on forever. The entire evening was filled with an unbroken chain of sex, cigarettes, and rum.

Crystelle endured, and waited.

At last Bern was satiated. And drunk. He rolled onto his back and closed his eyes, smiling in contentment.

Crystelle lay quiet, hardly daring to breathe, while he sank into a stupor.

Soon he was snoring steadily.

Slowly, moving only a few inches at a time with her heart pounding, Crystelle eased out of bed.

In the soft light from the bathroom, Bern lay naked on the soiled, tangled sheet, his mouth open, his arms and legs spread.

Barefoot and nude, Crystelle walked into the front room and latched the front door. Opening her purse, she removed the boning knife and unwrapped it.

She returned to the bedroom. Bern had not moved. He was still snoring. Circling to his side of the bed, she stood over him, the knife blade cool against her thigh. Her mouth was dry and her hands were trembling.

Somewhere she had read that the heart is not really on the left, as most everyone believed, but more toward the middle.

She raised the knife and poised the tip over Bern's chest, slightly left of center.

Then, with all her weight and strength, she plunged, using both hands, just as she had practiced.

For a sickening instant, Bern's chest seemed solid and unyielding. Then the blade scraped past bone and sank to the hilt.

Abruptly Bern jerked as if hit by a bolt of lightning. His eyes flew open. He stared up at her and his mouth opened as if to shout. But no sound came. His hands rose and seized her biceps in a crushing grip. She struggled, but she could not pull free. Again his mouth tried to form a word. He managed only choking sounds.

The moment seemed to stretch into eternity.

Then Bern's hands fell away and the body sank back onto the bed.

His eyes remained open, unblinking, unseeing.

Crystelle stepped back. She was relieved to see only a small amount of blood, a tiny puddle around the hilt, running into the hollow above Bern's stomach, and down his rib cage, onto the sheet.

In the light from the bathroom she examined her own body. No blood had splattered.

She pulled the bedspread over Bern and used it to wipe her fingerprints off the handle of the knife. She dressed, taking her time, making sure she left nothing behind in the bedroom.

In the minuscule bathroom she repaired her makeup and checked to see if she had sustained bruises or scratches, either in lovemaking or in Bern's final struggle. She found none.

She rounded up the tumblers and placed them in the kitchen sink. After opening the faucets, she poured soap flakes until the tumblers were covered with suds. She folded the hand towel and returned it to her purse.

For a full minute she stood at the front door, thinking back over each step to be certain she had left no clues.

She then slipped out the front door, pulling it closed behind her.

The street was deserted. Most of the houses were dark. Crossing the muddy lawns, she stumbled over a toy. Thinking it safer, she stepped into the street and hurried along the string of automobiles parked at the curb.

She was passing an old Ford when the door on the driver's side suddenly shot open, striking her on the hip. Knocked off balance, she almost fell.

A man staggered out of the car. "Goddamighty, lady! Where'd you come from?"

He seemed drunk. Crystelle backed away.

"You hurt?"

"I'm all right," she said. "It was my fault. I didn't see you."

The glow from a distant streetlight was so dim, she could not see his features plainly. Nor, she reasoned, could he see hers.

"Excuse me, I'm late," she said, walking on. "Good night."

The man said something unintelligible behind her. She hurried the half block to her car before looking back.

His shadowy form was moving across the lawn toward the house next door to Bern's. She waited until he entered the front door before stepping into her car and starting the engine.

She drove straight home and, after a thorough shower, went to bed. But she could not sleep. She kept thinking back over the evening, hunting any mistake she might have made.

The knife was all she had left behind, and it was as common as pig tracks. Surely it could not be traced. In fact, the investigators probably would assume it came from Bern's own kitchen.

Throughout the evening she had taken care not to leave fingerprints, even though hers were not on file anywhere. She doubted anyone had noticed her car. The people in those cheap housing developments came and went at all hours. They were as gregarious as sheep. A strange car would not attract attention.

True, the drunk from next door had seen her, but in poor light. He would not be able to identify her.

She concluded that the evening had been worth the risk.

Now nothing stood between her and Moon.

Chapter 24

"Kelly, I'm telling you this in confidence," the Director said. "Next fall, the choir is going to Europe. We'll be staying in Vienna, as guests of the Vienna Boys Choir. I'd love to have you along with us."

Kelly was left speechless. He had assumed that he had been summoned to the Director's office for a farewell talk. With the traditional Homecoming Concert, his two years with the performing choir had just ended.

"It won't be easy for you," the Director continued. "Your voice change is probably only months away. But I believe you can delay it long enough for the European tour if you remain quiet this summer, don't run, never get heated, take cold baths, stay indoors and read under the air conditioner. I know what I'm asking. The decision is yours."

"Sir, I'm enrolled at Choate for next fall," Kelly said.

"I know. But if you want to go with us, I'm sure arrangements can be made. There's no hurry. All I'm asking is that you think about it."

Kelly left in a quandary.

Until he entered the Director's office a few minutes ago, his life through the next few years had seemed simple. He would enter Choate in the fall. On the basis of his grades, he had been accepted for an accelerated program. By the time he entered Harvard two years from now, he would have many of the freshman requisites out of the way.

But Vienna!

The city was every musician's dream. He would meet and sing with the Vienna Boys Choir. He and the Texas choir would perform for European audiences and world-renowned music critics.

For the first time since its founding, the Texas Boys Choir would be compared with the best, by those most qualified to judge.

It was an opportunity they had sought and talked about for years. He badly wanted to be a part of it.

Through the next several days Kelly thought he would say yes.

He even started the cold baths.

But second thoughts came unbidden.

The tour through the Northeast and Canada, just completed, had been the longest he had made with the choir. He was still reeling from the moving kaleidoscope of auditoriums and audiences, from life on the bus, from the work and heavy responsibilities.

He found himself tired of the demands the choir had made on him during the last four years. He was weary of the constant cheek-to-jowl life with other boys, of seeing girls only fleetingly and from a distance. Girls still remained a mystery to him—one he wanted to explore.

Years ago, his celebrity status as a member of the choir had been exhilarating.

Now he was tired of being different. He yearned for a measure of normalcy.

Already Weldon was entering Texas A&M. He had written that he would be home only briefly, that he and friends had enrolled in orientation and other courses through the summer months.

If Kelly loafed through the summer, and went to Vienna in the fall, Weldon would move even further ahead of him.

Kelly called Choate. He was told by a faculty advisor that since his transcripts had been forwarded, he would experience no difficulty in enrolling for the summer term. After examining the pros and cons, Kelly decided it was no contest.

The time had arrived to grow up, to get on with his life.

He returned to the Director's office and thanked him, but declined the invitation to accompany the choir to Vienna.

Afterward, he ran all the way home from the bus stop in the warm spring sun.

He arrived home sweating, thoroughly heated.

"Kelly and I have been having quite a row the last few days," Joanna confided to Peggy. "He wants to go to summer school. But he's been working his heart out for the last four years, doing more than any boy should be expected to do. He's so thin! I'd like to see him rest for a while, at least through the summer."

After five weeks of steady improvement, Peggy had been brought home from the hospital. Again Joanna had developed the habit of dropping by every few days. Now Walter was in Austin for the week, pleading a case before the Texas Supreme Court. Joanna had promised him she would make special effort to keep Peggy company.

"I thought you two never had any difficulty," Peggy said.

"We seldom do. That's why this has been so upsetting. I'd like to see him just loaf for a while. But he can't seem to sit still a minute. He's got to be up and doing. I think the choir made him that way."

They were seated in Peggy's "sickroom," where she endured her therapy, her long periods in the lung. She was propped in a sitting position in a comfortable chair. A nurse hovered only a few steps away, cleaning the equipment they had been using.

"Kelly's a remarkable boy," Peggy said. "One night not long ago Walter remarked right out of the blue that if he had a son, he'd want him to be exactly like Kelly."

Joanna was surprised, not that Walter felt that way, but

that he would reveal the thought to Peggy. She knew they had wanted children.

Peggy apparently was following the train of Joanna's thoughts.

"We decided early we wanted to enjoy each other before having children," she said. "That has been one of the tragedies of my illness. Walter very much wanted a family."

Uncomfortable with the direction of the conversation, Joanna sought to inject a lighter note.

"Brod and I made the same decision. Obviously it didn't work out that way. Weldon was born just over a year after we were married." She paused, thinking back. "It doesn't seem any time since he was just a baby. I can't adjust to the fact that he's now going off to college."

Peggy smiled in the way she often did to soften remarks. "Maybe that's why you're opposing Kelly. Could it be that you're just not ready for him to leave the nest?"

Joanna was brought up short by the question.

Peggy could be most perceptive. On reflection, Joanna could see she *had* realized, if only vaguely, that this indeed could be Kelly's final departure from home.

After two years of prep school would come college, and he might be gone from home forever.

"Maybe that enters into it," she conceded. "But there's more to it. Kelly and Weldon are still close. They exchange notes quite often, talk on the phone. Yet there's a competitiveness between them I don't understand. I've always been aware that a big part of Kelly's academic drive has been an effort to catch up with Weldon. Now Kelly just can't stand the thought of Weldon earning summer credits, while he sits idle. He feels Weldon is getting further ahead of him."

"I can sympathize with that," Peggy said. "And if Weldon can go to summer school, why not Kelly?"

"In Weldon's case, summer school makes sense," Joanna explained. "He's mainly enrolling for a course in campus orientation. But Kelly wants to load himself down with work. He has found he can move onto the college level quicker by sheer drudgery through the summers. I know it's nothing but this competitiveness."

Again Peggy smiled. "Most parents would be beside themselves with pride in such an industrious son. I've wondered. Could you be subconsciously worried about his health, that he may be taking after his father?"

Joanna had considered that possibility.

"There *are* parallels. Kelly has Brod's build, the same temperament. Yes, I've worried about it."

"Walter says Kelly's secret is that he's so well organized. He explained it all to Walter, how he devotes certain segments of time to each task throughout the day. Walter was really impressed."

"It's almost frightening, all that he accomplishes," Joanna admitted. "He started visiting the office a while back and made friends with Don Parker, our head geologist. Don says Kelly has memorized the geological-time tables, and can identify most rocks. I didn't even know he was doing it. He just seems to soak up information, wherever he is." She paused. "I'll probably let him go to summer school, once I become more accustomed to the idea. Maybe you're right; I'm just not ready for him to leave the nest. But also, I suppose there's the lingering guilt that I should have been more of a mother. The company has robbed me of so much of the time I would have spent with them."

"Nonsense," Peggy said. "You've made such a great contribution to them, keeping the company going. I'm sure they'll understand that eventually, if not now."

"It *has* been a battle," Joanna admitted.

Peggy liked to hear of Joanna's daily routine at the company. Shifting the subject away from her sons, Joanna brought Peggy up-to-date on recent events, her current worries.

The first two wells she had drilled in the new pool were spectacular producers—fifteen-hundred-barrel-a-day giants. She was now drilling four more into the same formations, and signs were good. While the wells could not be expected to produce forever, her most immediate problem of revenue had been solved. The Houston refinery was still proving costly, and income from retail sales was down. But the new pool had hardly been tapped. Already it was more than making up the difference.

"Walter admires you so much," Peggy said.

The remark, coming without a hint of preamble, caught Joanna completely off guard. She felt her face grow warm, and wondered if Peggy noticed.

She spoke carefully. "Walter has been a comfort to me through all of this. He's always there with the right advice, the proper measure of confidence."

Peggy seemed firmly locked in her own thoughts. "By all rights, I should be dead by now."

Joanna struggled to hide her shock. "Peggy, I won't listen to that kind of talk. You're much stronger now than when you went to the hospital."

"Saved by another wonder drug. So far, I owe my life to them. The Salk vaccine came along too late for me, but most of the wonder drugs haven't been a minute too soon. Any one of a dozen secondary infections would have carried me off long ago. I know, though, that the antibiotics are gradually losing their effectiveness, and I can't expect the doctors to keep coming up with new ones. My life is limited and I know it."

Joanna opened her mouth to protest but found she could not speak. To her absolute dismay, tears came unbidden and coursed down her cheeks.

"Joanna, I have a purpose for telling you this," Peggy went on. "I'm worried about what will happen to Walter after I'm gone. He seems so competent, on the surface, but he isn't. Not really. He becomes so concerned about others that he forgets to look after himself. And he's such a moral man, full of old-fashioned ideas. Joanna, I hope you'll help me. After I'm gone, I don't want Walter to suffer because of any archaic loyalties to me. I want you to help him go on to a new life, one he deserves."

Joanna could not stop crying. But at last she found her voice.

"Peggy, I can't make a promise like that!"

"You can. And you will. I think God brought you to me, to Walter. We've both benefited immeasurably from your experience, your strength, your compassion. You've been our best friend, and you'll go on being our best friend, because that's the way you are. Now, I want you to promise me you'll help Walter after I'm gone."

At first Joanna did not believe it possible she could make such a promise, not after all that had happened.

Then she slowly came to understand there was no way she could refuse.

"I promise," she said.

Peggy made a feeble forward motion with her neck, one of her gestures more eloquent than words.

Comprehending, Joanna folded Peggy in her arms.

Embracing, they both surrendered to tears.

From the corner of her eye Joanna saw the nurse approach, start to intervene, and apparently decide against it. She retreated, leaving Joanna and Peggy alone in their private moment.

Afterward, Joanna remained badly shaken by the experience. She had not felt so close to anyone in years, not even Brod.

She recognized that Peggy's evaluation of her chances was probably accurate. Despite the new antibiotics, Peggy's general condition had been going slowly downhill.

She knew that Peggy's death, when it came, would have a profound effect on her own life.

But she had no inkling of what Walter would do.

Or, if he eventually asked her to marry him, what she would do.

She remembered how, in the depths of her passion, Walter had become Brod for a crucial moment. She thought of her heartrending embrace with Peggy, and instinctively knew that for the remainder of her life she would never be entirely free of it.

Inevitably, Brod and Peggy would forever be a part of her relationship with Walter.

With two ghosts in the matrimonial bed, could a marriage possibly survive?

Chapter 25

The lawyers in New York promised everything and delivered nothing. Each time Crystelle called, they offered only excuses. After months passed with no results, she returned to New York for another talk with Waxler.

He was friendly enough in greeting her, but strongly implied he saw no reason for her impatience.

"Mrs. Calcart, I told you this would take considerable time," he said. "We're progressing as well as can be expected."

His dapper manner, his pencil-line moustache, were beginning to grate on Crystelle's nerves. He sat behind his desk smiling, as if all was right with the world.

"What exactly *have* you done? I haven't heard of anything yet."

He reached for a folder and leafed through it slowly, as if refreshing his mind on details. He closed it before replying.

"This is a delicate matter you have brought to us. We must feel our way into it carefully. As I explained on your earlier visit, basically we are coordinating the efforts of various state and governmental agencies, bringing them together for our mutual benefit. Naturally, problems arise. The state doesn't agree with the city on how to proceed. A federal agency is reluctant to share its information with the congressional racketeering committee. We've found we must bring other groups, such as the city crime commission, into it. I assure you we have four excellent men working on it full-time. We're doing all we can."

"Apparently it's not enough," Crystelle said. "Why do we need to bring all these people into it? Why not just work with one group?"

"Because Atchley needs these assurances from *everyone.* We must be able to guarantee he won't incriminate himself at any level. Since this involves potentially pending cases, we also have to enlist a number of prosecutors and judges."

"Can't they be bought?"

Waxler assumed a pained expression. "In some instances, perhaps. But even when that's possible, it takes time, and must be handled with care."

Crystelle was beginning to lose her temper. Plainly she had made the trip for nothing. Waxler was still giving her the same line.

"What if we found the woman involved in Grover's death?"

"As I said before, it might be a lever. But we'd still need to attend to these other matters. They must be done."

"Meantime, we're growing old," Crystelle said. "When can I expect some action?"

"I would say sometime after the next election. Frankly, some of our principal players must consider what's expedient in an election year. We may even lose some of them. If so, we'll have to bring the newly elected officials up to speed. But I believe that'll be when it'll all come together. If you'll just go back to Texas and wait, I feel confident we'll have good news to report."

Crystelle returned to Fort Worth in a foul mood. She called Middleton and gave him an account of her meeting with Waxler.

Middleton listened without comment until she finished. "Waxler has explained to me at length what he's doing. But

I'm still not convinced that's the best way to get the job done."

From the beginning Middleton had said they should concentrate on finding the woman, build a case against Atchley using her testimony, and then pressure him to cop a plea by naming the person who hired him.

"What more can we do to find her?" Crystelle asked. "I'm about to give up on those people of yours."

"We might put someone on the street, full-time, masquerading as a petty criminal. Our man might be able to work his way into the life enough to ask questions and get some answers. It'd be a twenty-four-hour-a-day job, and expensive."

"Do it," Crystelle said. "It can't be more expensive than Waxler's outfit."

That evening she took up to her bedroom all the Fort Worth newspapers that had arrived during her absence. She went through them carefully, page by page, item by item. Bern's murder had not been mentioned in print for months, but she still monitored the Fort Worth *Star-Telegram* and the Fort Worth *Press* in case some new development brought it back into the news.

At the time of the murder the story had made the front pages. A police spokesman had told reporters that detectives were looking for "a woman in white" who had visited Bern Arnheiter on the evening he was slain. He quoted their sole witness as saying that the woman was "really beautiful," and "looked like an angel." The tabloid *Press* had considerable fun with that, labeling the suspect the "Angel of Death."

After a few days, the story had vanished from the news.

Now Crystelle no longer thought of Bern except on rare occasions when the sight of a knife, a spot of blood, or a huge, potbellied man brought him briefly to mind.

She had painstakingly thought through every conceivable possibility and concluded there was no way anyone in Fort Worth could ever connect her with Bern.

Gradually she had quit worrying about it.

Almost.

"How was the trip?" Moon asked.

"Lousy," Crystelle said, dropping into a chair across the desk from him. "I think Waxler's giving me a snow job."

Moon laughed. "I doubt that. He runs the best legal firm in the country. He doesn't have to con his clients. He has plenty of legitimate work to keep him busy."

She did not like to come to Moon's office, but belatedly he had become painstakingly circumspect. He now insisted that all her business be conducted in his office. On his trips out of town he traveled alone. Although he had leased a house, Crystelle had not been invited to see it, much less use it. Apparently he kept the house solely for the brief visits of his daughters allowed by the court. Crystelle assumed that to his mind she in some way would contaminate that precious house.

Slowly Crystelle was beginning to understand that she was losing Moon, not to Josie, but to those vapid daughters.

She could not allow that to happen.

She listened idly while Moon explained her most recent investments, what he had done, and why he did it. Watching him as he went through each step, she assessed the changes in him during the last few months. He was tense, more tautly controlled. Loose flesh had softened his features, and the flecks of gray were spreading in his hair. She waited until he had exhausted his explanations.

She spoke softly, in almost a whisper. "How's your love life these days, Moon? You getting any?"

His face froze. "Crystelle, please. Don't start that."

She gave him a long, searching look. "Once I said I had you but I didn't have you. And you said I had you, that I should never forget that. What's happening to us, Moon?"

He glanced at the door, as if maybe his secretary could hear. "Crystelle, I've told you. We've got to be patient. My lawyers tell me I have to be very careful."

"I've been patient. Where has it gotten me?"

"Just a little while longer. I promise."

"Moon, I'm losing my mind. Why don't you park your car somewhere tonight and sneak across the golf course? Nobody would see you."

"Someone would see my car, and wonder about it. Your neighbors have eyes. Word could get around."

"Then let's meet in another town. We could do that again. No one would notice. I could register under an assumed name."

He shook his head. "I'm sure Josie's lawyers are keeping a close watch on me."

"Why now? They've got all they need. Legally separated, divorce pending, you're a free man. You can do anything you want."

"Crystelle, my behavior could affect the court's decision about the girls. Please understand. This has been a long, bitter battle. Josie's father is making it as tough as he can. I need every edge I can get. Whether we like it or not, you're the 'other woman' in the case. I must show the court I'm acting with cool, reasonable judgment, that I haven't been carried away by passion."

"God forbid."

"All I'm asking is a little more time. Then it will be all over and we won't have to sneak around anymore. We can be together right out in the open, the way it should have been from the beginning."

Crystelle could see she was not making a dent in his new-found respectability. She abandoned the effort.

"I just hope that when that day comes, we're not too old to enjoy it."

Yet she left Moon's office feeling much better about the situation than she would have thought. At times she also hungered for respectability, the life she should have been allowed to live. If she could win back her rightful place at Spurlock Oil, and move into a normal relationship with Moon, she could have that life. No longer would she be the 'other woman.'

She would be the president, perhaps board chairman, of a prestigious oil company.

The months dragged on. Josie's father succeeded in further continuances, delaying Moon's court settlement. Waxler kept offering only excuses and explanations. The elections came and went and, a year later, still nothing had been done.

Then came the telephone call Crystelle had long expected.

"Mrs. Calcart, we've had a breakthrough," Waxler said. "Atchley's talking. We're receiving copies of the transcripts. If you and Mr. Middleton can come up, we can go over them, and determine precisely what you need."

Crystelle and Middleton flew to New York the next day.

Waxler had the transcripts waiting on a table in a small conference room down the hall from his office. After Crystelle and Middleton were seated, he began leafing through and separating the stacks of papers.

"We've succeeded in having Atchley transferred to a safe facility. He's been talking for five days now. These are the transcripts of all the questions and answers. From them, we'll go back later and obtain our depositions, going much deeper into his testimony. So in a way this is still exploratory material. His questioners are determining what's available."

He shoved a stack of papers aside. "Most of this concerns other crimes. You'll notice the questions keep moving abruptly from subject to subject. That's a common technique in this type of interrogation. But a pattern has surfaced in the murder of Grover Sterling. Atchley claims he was hired by a man named Al Schippoletti, who is believed to be connected with the Mafia. Does the name mean anything to either of you?"

It did not. Crystelle was momentarily confused.

How had Brod come to know a Mafia gangster?

For the first time, she wondered if Grover could have been killed for other reasons, unconnected with Brod.

But her doubt was quickly eased. Waxler handed her a portion of the transcript.

"We were able to have several questions asked. These pages pertain to Atchley's recollection concerning the Sterling murder."

Crystelle read through the segment, passing each page to Middleton as she finished it:

Q. Mr. Atchley, do you remember a stabbing on Forty-second street, a man named Grover Sterling, back about nineteen forty-five?

A. That big tall Texan? Yeah. I remember. That was another little job I did for Al Schippoletti.

Q. Could you tell us about it? Whatever you happen to remember.

A. Well, let's see. I got a note Al wanted me to come over to his office at his construction company in New Jersey. So I went. He took me out into the yard, away from everybody, and told me he had a rush job for me, that there was a Texan on a visit to New York who needed to be dead.

Q. Those were his words?

A. Yeah. He talked that way.

Q. What were his instructions? Did he tell you how he wanted it done?

A. No. He said he didn't care how I did it. Just so it was done. But he said it had to be done the night before this guy left town.

Q. How did he convey this information to you? Did he write anything down?

A. No. He just told me the guy's name, and the hotel where he was staying. I was to do the rest.

Q. How did you arrange it?

A. Well, I hired a woman I'd used before on jobs like this. A really good-looking broad. Let's see, Phyllis. That was her name. Phyllis Lattimer. She shook her ass a little at this guy in a bar and he fell for it. They were together most of two days. They'd had dinner, and she talked him into walking back to his hotel from the theater district. I stuck him right on the sidewalk and took his billfold and papers, so the cops would think it was robbery.

Q. Did Schippoletti say why this guy needed to be dead?
A. No.

Q. He gave you no reason at all?
A. Oh, he did say something about an oil deal out in Texas that went sour. He said we were doing it for a friend of his.

Q. For a friend of Schippoletti's?
A. Yeah. That's what he said.

Abruptly the questioning shifted to another crime.

Crystelle was disappointed. She assumed that the "Texas oil deal" and "a friend" would constitute strong evidence.

But it still was not good enough.

"Phyllis Lattimer," Middleton said, finishing the last page. "We had the Phyllis. But we couldn't get a make on the full name."

"We checked with the NYPD," Waxler said. "She has been booked several times for prostitution, but not recently. No other record. We haven't been able to locate her by that name."

"I'll put my people on it," Middleton said.

Crystelle and Middleton remained in New York three more days, reading the transcripts as they came in. Although the Sterling murder was mentioned several more times, no new information surfaced.

"We'll be able to go deeper into it when we get permission to take depositions," Waxler said. "Meanwhile, we've been handed plenty of leads to develop."

On her return to Texas, Crystelle called Moon and told him of the new situation.

"You might move me into a more liquid position," she said. "I think we're close."

"I also have news," Moon said. "Josie's newest appeal for continuance has been denied. We're set for a hearing week after next."

Crystelle had not felt so optimistic in years. Suddenly all was falling neatly into place.

"Moon, when I go before the Spurlock board, I want you with me. You're my financial adviser. You should be there."

Moon barely hesitated. "Of course I'll be there. I wouldn't think of missing it."

But the best news of all came the following day.

"We've located Phyllis," Middleton said. "If we can obtain immunity for her—and I'm sure we can—she'll testify to what she knows."

That would help. But for Crystelle, Middleton's next bit of news was the real stunner.

"Also, I obtained a court order and subpoenaed your brother's long-distance toll charges for the month in question. And guess what? Just before the murder, a twenty-seven-minute phone call was made from the Brod Spurlock residence to Mr. Al Schippoletti in New Jersey. Person-to-person."

Crystelle could hardly contain her elation.

That was the final link in the chain.

It connected Brod to Schippoletti to Atchley in the right time frame.

No jury in the world could ignore that evidence.

At long last, she was ready.

Chapter 26

"Joanna, this is the same song, second verse," Crystelle said. "I want to meet with your board, your legal advisers. And this time you're going to dance to my tune."

Joanna had long steeled herself to the day Crystelle would come back on the scene. The worry had lain at the back of her mind for years. She intended to handle the situation with all the intelligence she possessed. She spoke carefully.

"What does this concern?"

"You know damned well what it concerns. Joanna, I have all the ammunition I need. So you better set it up."

Joanna remembered the information Walter wanted last time. "Who will you be bringing with you?"

"Middleton. Moon Belford. And I want the full Spurlock board there."

Joanna felt she should show a bit of resistance, demonstrate that she was not taking orders.

"No, Crystelle. I gather you're making another attempt to buy the stock you sold. I think the stockholders on the board will be sufficient."

"Suit yourself. But if you don't cooperate with me, you may find yourself explaining to your outside board members how you wound up in litigation without their knowing a damned thing about it."

"I'll see what I can do," Joanna said.

A strong sense of déjà vu persisted as she phoned Walter and told him of Crystelle's call. This time, he took it even more seriously.

"I think I'd better come right over," he said. "We need to talk."

He arrived within minutes. Patiently, he led Joanna back over her conversation with Crystelle, word for word.

"One aspect of this worries me," he said. "Since she has mentioned litigation, conceivably they could arrive any time with a search warrant. We should be aware of any physical evidence that might be damaging. As an officer of the court, I'm not telling you to destroy evidence. I'm leaving it to your common sense."

Joanna thought of the notes and letters from Schippoletti, the ledger in her safe. She could burn everything, except for one item.

"There's the receipt in Campbell's safe," she said. "I don't have access to it. But maybe it isn't important. If he were subpoenaed, he could be forced to testify that he took the money out to the house and gave it to Brod."

"Generally speaking, physical evidence—a receipt, a signature—carries more weight than verbal testimony. A signed receipt speaks for itself. It's difficult, if not impossible, to refute."

Joanna nodded her understanding.

Somehow, she must obtain and destroy the receipt in Campbell's safe.

"What about the outside board members?"

"At this point, I doubt you'd be jeopardizing yourself by not bringing them into it. We still don't know what Crystelle's 'ammunition' is. We can guess, but we don't know. If it involves company business, the other board members can be brought in later."

Joanna found herself close to panic. "Walter, what can I

do? I'm not going to let that woman into the company. Do you have any idea what she may have found?"

"No. But I long ago learned not to try a case before it gets into court. Let's keep an open mind, and listen. Then we can take care of it. For now, do what you have to do, and try not to worry. Go ahead and set up the meeting."

After Walter left, Joanna called Ann Leigh, who took the news more calmly than Joanna had expected. Again, Joanna repeated her conversation with Crystelle.

"Did she give any indication what her litigation might involve?" Ann Leigh asked.

"No. Only that she has all the ammunition she needs."

"Joanna, I don't believe we should have the whole board there. She'll be making all kinds of wild accusations. I wouldn't want just anyone to hear."

"Walter felt the stockholders on the board would be sufficient."

"She'll probably repeat all those rumors that have been around for years. Joanna, I hope you won't pay any attention to them."

Joanna did not answer. She had not told Ann Leigh of the evidence she had found, indicating the rumors might be true.

She scheduled the meeting for two o'clock the following Friday.

She gathered all the damaging evidence from her safe and stuffed it into a large manila envelope. That evening she took the material home and considered alternatives.

The furnace was supplied by natural gas, and contained no facilities for burning waste. The fireplaces were awkward, and would leave messy debris. The long-unused barbecue pit in the backyard seemed best.

She waited until Calla Lily had left for the evening, then found a flashlight and matches in the pantry. In the garage she located a can of gasoline the gardener kept for lawn equipment. She carried the evidence to the barbecue pit, arranged it over long-dead coals, and saturated it with gasoline. Standing well away, she tossed matches toward the grate.

The third one caught.

The resulting pillar of fire startled her. Its light illuminated the trees on neighboring lots. But the night remained silent, except for the gentle murmur of the blaze.

After the initial flareup, the flames died back to a small bonfire. Joanna stood watching for almost an hour. At last only coals remained. She examined the debris by flashlight. A few charred pieces of the ledger lay among the embers, but no one would be able to identify them.

Early the next morning she walked down to Campbell's office.

"You once mentioned a receipt you have in your safe," she said. "You offered it to me, and I declined. If you now offered it to me, I wouldn't decline."

Campbell did not say a word. He rose from his desk, went to his safe, rummaged in it, and handed her the receipt bearing Brod's signature.

Taking it back to her office, Joanna tore it to bits and flushed it down the commode.

The week crept by. Despite Walter's comforting words, Joanna could not keep from worrying. When at last Friday arrived, she was so distraught, she skipped lunch.

At two, she walked down the hall to join Ann Leigh, Walter, and Campbell in the conference room.

Again Crystelle and her group were late.

From the first Middleton made it plain he was in charge of the delegation.

Crystelle seemed unnaturally subdued. Joanna assumed that Middleton had lectured her on how she was to behave. She nodded and spoke to her mother, and to Joanna, but ignored Campbell and Walter.

Middleton introduced Moon Belford, and arranged the seating for his group, with himself closest to Joanna, Crystelle next, and Belford beyond her. The atmosphere was tense.

Crystelle plainly could not contain herself.

"Momma, you remember I told you there'd be a day of reckoning. Well, this is it."

Ann Leigh did not reply. Her lips compressed into a straight line, the only sign she had heard.

Middleton was arranging legal papers in front of him. Crystelle took advantage of the lull to smile at Joanna.

"I'm just curious. What happened to my stock after Brod died? Did you get it? Or did it go to the boys?"

Joanna saw no reason to be friendly. She gave Crystelle a blank stare. "I really don't think that's any of your business."

Crystelle did not seem the least bit fazed. "I'll bet it went to the boys, or into trust for them when they become adults. That's probably the way Brod would've done it. I've lost count. They must be almost grown now, aren't they?"

Middleton was hunting in his briefcase. Joanna answered to fill the silence.

"Weldon's at A&M. Kelly's preparing for his first year at Harvard."

"How nice for you, that they're out from underfoot."

She cut her eyes at Walter in a knowing way, making it plain she had heard something.

Joanna was furious with herself for having fallen into the trap. Middleton apparently found what he was hunting. Joanna quickly called the meeting to order.

"All right," she said to Middleton. "The Spurlock board is prepared to hear what you have to say."

Middleton opened a folder. "First, let me say that Mrs. Calcart is represented not only by my firm, but also by Garrity, Waxler, Karnow, and Barron in New York. Also, I wish to make plain that our purpose in visiting with you this afternoon is to offer you a final chance to avert serious litigation."

"Of what nature?" Walter asked.

Middleton glanced at the papers before him. "Mr. Trammel, we're now prepared to prove that Mrs. Calcart sold her inheritance under duress, in fear for her life. We can demonstrate that Mrs. Calcart came here once before and offered to buy back her inheritance at a fair price, and that the offer was rejected. We now make the same offer. If it is rejected this time, we will have no alternative but to go ahead with our suit."

Walter smiled. "Your phrasing is adroit, Mr. Middleton. But that statement appears to be kissing kin to blackmail."

Middleton's cheeks turned pink. "Mr. Trammel, I won't tolerate such aspersions. If it were left to me, I would just as soon try the suit. The papers are prepared. We're ready to file before the courthouse closes at five o'clock this afternoon. But due to the sensational nature of the evidence we're allowing you this one last opportunity."

Joanna glanced at Ann Leigh. Her face was pale, and frozen in an expressionless mask.

"Naturally, we can't make a judgment without hearing the specific allegations," Walter said.

"They're rather detailed. But basically, we'll prove beyond a doubt that Brod Spurlock arranged the murder of his illegitimate half brother, Grover Sterling. We'll show that Brod's cousin, Troy Spurlock, who supported Grover Sterling in a futile attempt to reorganize Spurlock Oil, lost his department store to arson on the same night."

"Mr. Middleton, those rumors have been around for years," Ann Leigh said. "No one has ever put any truth to them."

"Momma, you'd better listen!" Crystelle said.

"Believe me, Mrs. Spurlock. We'll put the truth to them," Middleton said. "We've located the man Brod hired. This man has now turned state's evidence in exchange for immunity. He names an Al Schippoletti as the go-between. We can prove communication between the Spurlock residence and Mr. Schippoletti's home in the proper time frame before the murder."

Joanna hoped her face showed nothing at the mention of Schippoletti. Ann Leigh's expression remained frozen. Walter smiled as if the allegations were preposterous.

"We also have located the woman involved in Sterling's death," Middleton went on. "She will testify. The fire marshal who investigated the arson here will testify. Mrs. Calcart will testify as to the telephone conversation between herself and Brod, and the direct threats on her life which led to her sale of her stock. I assure you, Mr. Trammel, we have an ironclad case."

Ann Leigh was looking at her daughter. "Crystelle, you'd better think twice before you do this."

"Momma, *you're* the one who better think about it. And damned quick. We mean it. We'll file suit before the courthouse closes this afternoon. You can be sure it will hit the front page of every newspaper in the country."

"I'm afraid she's right, Mrs. Spurlock," Middleton said. "Newspaper editors will love it. They'll see it as pure Texas gothic. Beautiful young lady robbed of her inheritance by her own brother. A family battle for millions in oil money, involving murder and arson."

"Momma, you've always been afraid of scandal. Well, I warn you. By the time I'm through, everybody in the country will know what Brod did."

Middleton help up a cautionary hand to Crystelle. He spoke directly to Ann Leigh.

"Mrs. Spurlock, it isn't our purpose to destroy the reputation of your son. But under the circumstances, there'll be certain facts we can't suppress. And I must tell you in all honesty, we have an excellent case."

Joanna felt overwhelmed. If they truly had tied Brod to Schippoletti, and Schippoletti to the killer, then the damage would be done, no matter whether Crystelle won her case.

She thought of the effects such a sensational trial would have on Weldon and Kelly, perhaps even on their children and children's children, years into the future.

But she also thought ahead to having Crystelle inside the company, further using her blackmail to dominate Ann Leigh.

Already Crystelle had said that by rights she should be president of the company. Joanna knew she would make every effort to bring that about.

Joanna looked at Walter, hoping he would get her message.

He did.

"Mr. Middleton, I'd like to confer with my clients. Why don't we take a ten-minute break?"

"Of course," Middleton said.

"If you'll excuse us," Walter said.

Joanna led her group down the hall to Campbell's office, which was closest to the conference room. Ann Leigh, Campbell, and Joanna sank into chairs around Campbell's desk. Walter crossed the room to the windows and stood looking out for a time before turning to face them. His tone was grave.

"As you've all probably gathered, this does indeed sound as if Crystelle may have a case. At this point there's no way I can determine the merit of their evidence. Clearly, they don't intend to show us the specifics of their suit until it's filed. At this point I don't know how much is bluster. But Crystelle is right on one point. She'll cause headlines."

Joanna could not contain her fury. "Walter, if you think we have any chance at all, maybe we should fight. I can't see just turning the company over to her. And that's what we'd be doing."

"Mr. Trammel, Joanna's right," Ann Leigh said. "She wouldn't rest until she was running things."

Walter studied Joanna's face. "If they have the evidence they claim, they may have an excellent case. The only way we'd know for sure is to allow it to be filed."

Joanna was still thinking ahead. "Walter, if we give in to her now, there'll be no end to it. She'll keep using those stories about Brod from now on. We'll have to live with them until we die. So will Weldon and Kelly. I want to try to put them to rest, once and for all. I don't care what it costs."

Walter looked at Ann Leigh. "Mrs. Spurlock?"

"Mr. Trammel, ever since Brod died, I've felt the company really belongs to his sons. I feel we all hold it in trust for them. Joanna's right. If we give in, she'll never let it rest. I see terrible trouble for us either way. I don't know what to do. I'll support whatever you and Joanna decide."

"Mr. Campbell?"

"Mr. Trammel, I'm a minority stockholder. I really don't think it's my place to say."

"If the suit is filed, you almost certainly will be called upon to testify. That could be difficult."

Campbell did not answer.

"We have a few advantages," Walter went on, as if thinking aloud. "They are baldly bargaining with evidence in a criminal case, promising to withhold that evidence for certain considerations. I don't know how they could resolve that with the court, if it came under scrutiny. Also, Middleton still has a highly emotional client who speaks her own mind without thought of the consequences. We might be able to use that tendency to her detriment."

"No one could ever control Crystelle," Ann Leigh said. "She was hopelessly headstrong from the day she was born."

Joanna's confidence was returning. She could not see giving up without a fight. "Walter, I'm ready to take it to trial," she said. "They may have strong evidence. But we have Brod's excellent reputation, all he accomplished. We can make what they say sound absurd. I have letters to him from President Roosevelt, high-up government officials. We could show he had acquaintances at all levels of life in this country. Even if they do connect him with Schippoletti, we can explain that away by the fact that they worked together for the good of the nation during the war."

"We could try to negotiate," Walter said. "Maybe they don't have all they claim. This meeting could have been nothing but a maneuver to force a settlement. They might accept less than they're asking."

"I won't settle at any price," Joanna said.

"I agree," Ann Leigh said. "And I don't think that'd be a solution, Mr. Trammel. Crystelle would never settle for half a loaf."

"There's another aspect to consider," Walter said. "The New York firm Middleton mentioned is top-drawer. I can't imagine those attorneys working with Middleton. There's something here that doesn't add up. Middleton obviously considers himself the trial lawyer. But that New York firm has clerks who could make mincemeat of Middleton. I wish we had time to learn what the role of this firm is, and how they got into it."

"Moon Belford was probably Crystelle's connection with them," Ann Leigh said, as if thinking aloud.

"It may be that the New York attorneys have already placed themselves at arm's length," Walter said. "Maybe they just helped to obtain the evidence, and want nothing to do with the trial. That's the only explanation I can see."

"If it's that distasteful, then maybe it also would be to a judge or jury," Joanna said.

"I wish we could find out more about what she has," Ann Leigh said.

"I think we can assume that's the reason for this ultimatum. They are allowing us no time to investigate their allegations. But I believe their suit has some substance, or Middleton wouldn't be filing."

"I think we at least should see the full extent of their case before giving in to her," Joanna said. "Let's tell them to go ahead and file."

Again Walter looked at her for a moment before answering. "Joanna, the instant they file, most of the damage will be done. At that point it will become a public matter, open to the newspapers. We can file an answer. But what we say in reply probably won't receive nearly as much attention."

"Walter, are you advising us to settle?" Joanna asked.

"No. That's for you to decide. But I wouldn't be doing my job if I didn't point out the hazards. You also should consider that Crystelle conceivably could win a court settlement far greater than what she's now asking."

"I'm willing to risk that," Joanna said.

"Then that's your decision?"

Joanna thought again of the boys, the long-term effects of having Crystelle in the company. By the time the boys returned from college in a few years, control easily could have passed to Crystelle. They might never receive their inheritance as their father intended.

"I'm for rejecting the offer, facing them in court," she said.

Ann Leigh nodded agreement.

Campbell did not respond.

"Then let's go on record from the first that it's total war," Walter said. "When we go back in there, don't bother to be polite. If you can nettle Crystelle, do so. An angry opponent is an irrational opponent."

They returned to the conference room and resumed their places.

Joanna waited until everyone was again seated.

"Crystelle, I can well understand your desire to purchase respectability, a good name . . ."

"Mrs. Spurlock, that was uncalled for," Moon said.

Joanna ignored him. ". . . but the stock is not for sale. Your offer is hereby rejected."

Crystelle jabbed a finger at the clock on the wall of the boardroom. "Then I'll file the suit within the hour. Newspapers, radio stations, the wire services, will receive copies of it, with all the juicy details. We'll see who's respectable!"

She rose, pushed back her chair, and looked down at Ann Leigh. "Momma, you're making a big mistake. I'll drag the family's name through the mud until it becomes a household word for murder, double-dealing, and corruption. That's exactly what I'll do."

She turned and started furiously for the door.

Ann Leigh spoke so softly that Joanna almost did not hear her. But her words stopped Crystelle in her tracks.

"No, you won't!"

Some quality in Ann Leigh's voice held Crystelle. For a long moment, mother and daughter stared at each other.

Almost in a whisper, Ann Leigh said, "You see, I know how Bern Arnheiter died."

Crystelle's hands flew to her throat. Her face lost color. She slowly sank back into her chair.

"Momma, what are you talking about? How could you know anything? You're bluffing!"

"I'm not bluffing, Crystelle. If you take one step to file that suit to destroy your brother's name, to destroy this company, I'll go straight to the police."

"You wouldn't dare!"

"Oh, yes, I would. Ever since you were a little girl I've let you have your own way. Well, no more. I'll not see you wreck everything your father, your brother, and your sister-in-law have worked so hard to preserve."

"You're only guessing! You have no proof!"

"The police have a witness who can identify you. I also have a witness, one the police know nothing about. He was there the whole time. He can tell what he saw and heard."

The room remained deathly quiet as mother and daughter stared at each other.

Joanna was mystified. Everyone in the room seemed bewildered except Ann Leigh and Crystelle.

Crystelle broke the silence. "This is the same as it has always been, isn't it? You'd sacrifice me to protect Brod."

"It isn't Brod. He's dead, beyond hurt. I'm protecting the company, the future, my grandchildren. I would gladly sacrifice the both of us to preserve that."

"You've never cared about me! You never have! Not in my whole life!"

Crystelle put her hands to her face for a moment. Then she rose abruptly and fled the room.

Moon stood, hesitated, and hurried after her.

Another long, awkward moment passed.

Middleton rose and glanced around the table, as if seeking an answer from someone. Not finding it, he gathered his material, turned, and quietly walked out the door.

Joanna, Walter, and Campbell waited, expecting Ann Leigh to offer some explanation, now that the opposition had gone.

But she remained silent. Slowly, she picked up her purse. Her face was deathly pale and her hands were trembling.

"Mother, are you all right?" Joanna asked.

"I'm fine," she said. "Henry's waiting for me. He'll see me home."

"I'll walk you to your car," Walter said.

Joanna waited until Ann Leigh and Walter were gone, leaving her and Campbell alone in the conference room.

"Well, I suppose we can assume the meeting is over," she said.

She walked back to her office. A few minutes later Walter returned.

"I didn't push, and she didn't explain a thing," he said. "Did any of what she said make sense to you?"

"Not a bit."

"Whatever it was certainly took the wind out of Crystelle's sails. What was the name she mentioned? Arnheiter?"

"I think it was Bern Arnheiter."

"I don't intend to pry into Ann Leigh's business. But plainly this involved the company, the threat of the suit. Under the circumstances, I think we should know what happened. I'll see if I can find out."

Joanna also was concerned for Ann Leigh. Clearly the afternoon had put a terrible strain on her.

"Ann Leigh isn't a worldly person," she said. "She may have stumbled onto a situation and not realized its ramifications. She could be in danger."

Walter nodded agreement. He laughed. "Did you see Middleton's face? As long as I've known him, that's the first time I've ever seen him speechless."

"I was watching Moon. I'm sure he was totally in the dark."

"I've been through some bizarre experiences as a lawyer. Today was one of the strangest."

Joanna did not answer. She was remembering Crystelle's expression. She wondered what information Ann Leigh could possibly possess that would disarm Crystelle instantly, and so thoroughly.

Chapter 27

Crystelle hurried across the fifth floor of the parking garage. She did not want to talk to anyone until she had time to regain her composure and make up a plausible story. But in her distress, she had trouble unlocking her car. Moon caught up with her just as the key turned. He grabbed her by the wrist and swung her around to face him.

"What was that all about?"

She tried to pull away. "Not now, Moon."

He leaned against the car, blocking her from the door. "Crystelle, you've got to deal with this. What'll I tell Middleton? He's fit to be tied."

"Tell him anything you want. I don't owe him a damned thing!"

"Yes, you do. When he took your case on contingency, he had a right to expect you to go through with it."

"I'll pay him off. Whatever it takes."

She attempted to jerk open the car door. Moon still blocked it.

"Even if you can't tell anyone else, surely you can tell me. What happened in there?"

Crystelle was bewildered. The almost surrealistic scene in

the conference room had left her feeling as if she were a child again, with her mother once more all-seeing, all-knowing, omnipotent.

How had Ann Leigh found out about Bern?

She pushed her way past Moon. "I don't know *what* happened," she said. "I've got to think."

She started the engine and backed out of the parking space, making Moon jump out of the way. She sped down the ramps, squealing the tires on the turns.

As she drove home her disorientation gradually began to fade. She remembered that Bern had mentioned calling Ann Leigh in his efforts to locate her. He had said that Ann Leigh "wouldn't give me shit."

How much had the idiot told her? What had made Ann Leigh remember his name? Who was her mysterious witness? Was she likely to go to the police? Or confide in someone who would?

By the time Crystelle reached home she was regaining her confidence.

She knew her mother well.

Ann Leigh would not go to the police unless driven to it. She was smart enough to know that once she did, all family secrets would be laid bare. And she would not want the precious image of Brod Spurlock tarnished.

But what if Ann Leigh confided in Joanna?

Crystelle thought that possibility through.

Joanna would not want the father of her sons branded a murderer.

And Joanna controlled Arnold Campbell completely. Even if Campbell suspected something, he would remain silent.

Middleton and Walter Trammel were bound by the rules of their client relationships. She did not trust either, but both knew where their bread was buttered.

Of those in the conference room who had heard and seen what happened, that left only Moon.

The more Crystelle thought about it, the more she came to see that he might be her unsolvable problem.

With his strong puritan streak, he had been troubled by simple adultery.

How could he possibly live with murder?

But she would have to tell him something. He would continue to hound her until she did.

She began to invent. For a while, nothing sounded right.

Eventually she created an explanation that might work: She had gone to Bern's house because he was threatening to tell a bunch of lies about her. He attacked her. In her panic, trying to get away, she had accidentally killed him.

It lacked brilliance.

But it might work. It would have to do.

She called Moon's leased house. There was no answer.

Through that evening, the night, and for the next two days and nights, she dialed his house without success. She drove by it several times.

His car was not in the drive. The house showed no signs of life.

She called his clubs, everywhere she thought he might have gone.

No one recalled having seen him.

She was growing frantic when he at last arrived at her house unannounced.

He came through the front door weaving. She thought he was drunk until she saw his eyes. They had a deranged, glazed look. He stopped in the door and looked at her.

"Crystelle, I know who Bern Arnheiter was," he said without a trace of emotion. "I went down to the *Star-Telegram* and read the clip files."

"Moon, sit down," she said. She reached for his elbow and tried to guide him into a chair.

He twisted away. "You were the woman in white, weren't you?" He paused, looking at her as if not really expecting an answer. "You killed him."

It was a flat statement. Plainly he knew far too much.

In that moment Crystelle abandoned her prepared story. It suddenly seemed absurd. She remained silent.

He grimaced, as if in pain. "Why, Crystelle? I've been

trying to figure this out for two days. I knew the minute I read the first clipping that you did it. If anyone had asked, I would never have thought you capable of it. But when I read those news stories, I realized that you are. What I don't know is why. There must be some explanation."

Crystelle felt her best chance might be the truth.

"Moon, I did it for us. You and me. He was about to wreck everything."

Moon shook his head so hard, he almost fell. "No! Don't try to bring me into it. Who was he? What could he possibly have done to you?"

"He was someone out of my past, from that crazy time I've told you about. He was blackmailing me, threatening to go to you and tell you a bunch of stuff, some of it true, most of it untrue. I knew you couldn't handle it."

Again Moon shook his head. "But murder! Who are you to condemn Brod? At least he was protecting his family."

"So was I. There's no difference. I was protecting you, me, our relationship."

Moon crossed the room and put his head against a doorjamb. He spoke with his eyes closed. "How could you possibly have done it, and gone right on, as if nothing had happened? We were together after that, many times, and you never gave me any hint anything was wrong. I don't see how you could manage that."

"I could because I love you, Moon. I didn't want to see you hurt."

He shoved away from the doorjamb with an unintelligible sound. "You must be the most evil person I've ever known. And to think I didn't see it! Who was this poor guy?"

"A nobody."

Moon put a hand to his forehead and rubbed his eyes. "You're right. I can't handle this."

Crystelle did not like the way he was acting. She felt a twinge of apprehension. "Moon, you're not about to do something really nutty, are you? Like go to the police?"

Again he shook his head. "No. I thought about it. I know I should. But then it'd all come out. Too many innocent people would be hurt. Josie. My daughters. Your mother. I can't do that to them."

Crystelle almost laughed. Saved by the three vapid daughters.

A messy murder case might knock them out of their bows at the debutante's ball.

"But I'm not going to have anything else to do with you," Moon went on. "I came here to tell you that. I'm relinquishing your accounts. They'll be in your name only. Do with them what you want. Don't try to call me, write, anything. It's over."

He turned to leave, but apparently another thought stopped him. "Back there for a while I thought I was in the worst hell possible. I didn't want to give you up. I didn't want to give up my family. What I didn't understand was that when I started playing around with you, I had already lost my self-respect, the most important thing of all."

Crystelle did not try to hide her derision. "Moon, I don't need any of your bargain-basement moralizing."

"Maybe that's trite. But it's true. I really think I've found myself now. I've thought it through, and I know what I have to do. I'll go ahead with my work. I'm good at it. No one can take that away from me. I'll see my daughters when I can, be as good an influence as I can be on them. If Josie wants to try it again sometime, maybe we will. But whatever happens, I'm never going to lose my self-respect again."

"Moon, you and Josie deserve each other," Crystelle said.

Moon studied her face, as if memorizing every feature for the last time. "I'll give you some more bargain-basement moralizing to chew on. You had everything, Crystelle. Beauty, brains, money. How in the world did you manage to fuck up your life and everyone else's so completely?" He turned and walked out the door.

That night Crystelle cried herself to sleep. But the next morning she awoke with a new resolve.

True, she had failed in all she had come back to Fort Worth to get—Moon, control of the company.

But she still possessed the three essentials Moon had mentioned—beauty, brains, and money.

With nothing to hold her in Fort Worth, she could now return to Europe.

There were other games to play.

Walter came into Joanna's office and closed the door behind him. He pulled a chair close to her desk.

"This has taken time because I wanted to be discreet. Bern Arnheiter was a former merchant marine, murdered on the far west side of Fort Worth. He was found in a rented house with a kitchen knife pushed through his ribs. The murder was never solved."

At first Joanna could not connect the information with what had happened in the conference room.

Then she understood. "Crystelle?"

"The police were told that a woman dressed in white was seen leaving the house on the night of the murder. The witness said she was beautiful. I didn't want to appear too interested, but as far as I could determine, Crystelle was never a suspect. At least her name isn't mentioned in police files."

"A merchant marine. Where was he from?"

"The police don't know much about him, other than his wartime service, and the fact that he served a prison term in California for armed robbery."

"Crystelle was in California for a time during the war." A vague memory stirred. "Her second husband—Doyle Galloway, the man she married after Moon—came by the house once while home on leave. He said Crystelle was running around on him while he was in flight training out there. He told me he hoped Brod could 'get her out of the gutter'—that was his phrase—but that he was through with her."

"It's plain Crystelle at least knows something about the murder. I thought she was going to faint when Ann Leigh mentioned Arnheiter's name."

"But how did Ann Leigh connect Crystelle with the murder? And she said she had another witness the police know nothing about. Who could that be?"

"Perhaps Ann Leigh's more worldly than you thought."

Joanna was thinking of something else. "She must have known, or suspected, that Crystelle was connected with the murder from the time it happened. What a burden that must have been on her!"

"She handled herself very well. And I gathered that Crystelle's revelations concerning Brod weren't complete news to her."

"Walter, she heard nothing from me. I haven't even dropped a hint about the material I found here."

"Middleton has been silent. I think we can assume that Crystelle's suit has been laid to rest."

"Shouldn't we find out for sure? Talk to him?"

"I think not. We shouldn't appear to be concerned."

"But Crystelle may be a murderer! And we may have essential information. What should we do about that?"

"Nothing. We're not directly involved. All we know for sure is that the man's name was mentioned. We aren't in possession of any facts pertaining to the case. And you might consider this: If Crystelle *were* charged with the crime, no doubt all would come out—her information about Brod, and what she was attempting to do here. At the moment, Ann Leigh seems to be the only one who can connect Crystelle with the crime, and she has made her decision."

Walter's reassurances helped to put Joanna's mind at ease. When nothing else was heard from Crystelle or Middleton through the next few weeks, she gradually assumed that the crisis was over.

This was confirmed a few weeks later when she heard that Crystelle had returned to Europe, and put her house up for sale.

During the months that followed, Joanna entered a period of deep contentment. Gradually she and Walter found their way into a comfortable relationship. They were more than friends, but less than lovers.

With the tension between them eased, Joanna no longer felt such overwhelming guilt around Peggy.

The company seemed to be running itself. Eight out of the first ten offsets drilled into the new pool were successful, and slowly the extent of the strike was defined. The reserves were even greater than Joanna had first hoped. Although troubles persisted at the old Houston refinery, and retail sales continued to decline, revenues from the new field put the company into the best financial condition in its history. Joanna found that she now had more time for the opera board and other fine-arts organizations. She enjoyed this work immensely, and began to accept more responsibilities in the community.

As the months went by, she found herself looking forward to the time when the boys would return to assume their roles in the company, to take some of the burden from her.

Only once was she reminded of Crystelle's attempt to take over Spurlock Oil.

One morning a plain white envelope arrived in the daily mail, addressed to "Mrs. Brod Spurlock." The postmark was New York. Inside were two clippings.

The first, a lengthy article from *The New York Times,* reported that Jerry Atchley, a convicted murderer, had been found strangled in his cell at a maximum-security facility. The article said Atchley had turned state's evidence concerning various crimes, and was scheduled to testify against the heads of Mafia-connected organizations.

Prison officials said they were completely mystified as to how Atchley's killer was able to enter and leave the locked cell undetected.

The other clipping, only three paragraphs in length, was from the New York *Daily News.* It reported that the body of Phyllis Lattimer, a known prostitute, had been found floating in the East River.

The envelope contained nothing else.

And there was no return address.

*   *   *

Kelly did not return to his freshman dorm in Harvard Yard until late Monday. Pinned to his bed was a note from his roommate, saying his mother had been trying to reach him since early Saturday. Kelly hurried down the hall to a phone booth and put the call through person-to-person.

"Kelly, I'm afraid I have bad news," his mother said. "Aunt Zetta died Friday night in her sleep. We had the funeral this afternoon. I'm sorry we couldn't reach you."

Both his mother and grandmother had written in recent months that Aunt Zetta "looked bad." Yet her death surprised him. She had always seemed so indestructible.

"I was in New York," Kelly said. "I didn't think. I should have left a number."

"I didn't expect you to come. There's no reason you should. We just had a small service at the funeral home. Most people who knew her well are gone now."

Kelly thought of the long-ago day at his father's burial when Aunt Zetta had raised a bony finger to point at a vault and said, "That's where they'll put me."

He shivered.

No doubt that was where they put her.

"It was sudden," Joanna continued. "We knew she wasn't in the best of health, but your grandmother had talked with her the night before. And Zetta said she was feeling fine. Apparently she died in her sleep without waking. Don't worry about not coming home. Zetta was the last person in the world to impose on anyone. How's school?"

"The term really hasn't started yet. I had a few days, so I went down and took in a few plays."

He felt a fleeting moment of guilt over the lie.

He had spent most of the weekend with Amy at the Algonquin.

"Weldon's home. He'll be working at the company through the summer, learning the ropes, but he'll go back to school in the fall."

"I know," Kelly said. "He wrote."

"Come to think of it, I do have more bad news. Remember Peggy Trammel? She died a week ago. She put up a long, hard battle. It was heartbreaking for Walter. Since you knew them, I sent flowers in both our names."

Kelly thought of the conversation he had overheard in his mother's office, years ago.

He wondered if his mother and Walter were still close and, if so, what would happen now.

"You're awfully quiet, even for you. Are you feeling all right?"

"Just a little tired."

"You eating okay?"

"Yes. Has Weldon started to work yet?"

"I'm not sure *work* is the right word. He's been wandering around the building for two weeks, asking questions."

Kelly laughed, envying Weldon.

"I'm sorry about Aunt Zetta," he said. "Tell Grandmother."

"I will. And you might drop a note to her. She had a flare-up of her heart a few months ago. She'd had more trouble with Crystelle, and I think that was the cause of it. Don't mention any of this in your note."

"I won't."

"Remember. Call anytime."

Kelly returned to his room with an unexpected sense of loss. He had always intended to talk sometime with Aunt Zetta, to learn more about the family's past. Her life had dated back to the days when his Great-grandfather Travis Spurlock owned saloons and whorehouses to entertain the cowboys passing through Fort Worth on the Chisholm Trail. In the house of her father, Aunt Zetta had met Teddy Roosevelt, famous Indian chiefs, senators, governors, congressmen. She must have known many family secrets.

And now they were gone.

Everyone on the floor was out to dinner. Kelly did not feel hungry. He sifted through the mail on his desk and found a letter from Weldon. As always, it was brief. Weldon tended to write in headlines:

Dear Brother,

Conditions here are unbelievable. We've got to hurry and finish school and keep this company from going down the drain. Believe me, we've got our work cut out for us.

Your brother,
Weldon

BOOK
THREE

KELLY AND WELDON

Chapter 28

Kelly had been drinking 180-proof grain alcohol on the rocks with Weldon all evening. He felt as if his mouth had been anesthetized. It was now well after midnight. Long-haired beatniks, booted cowboys, and barefoot waitresses in skimpy costumes milled around them in the downtown coffeehouse. Weldon's grim description of conditions at Spurlock Oil already had cast a pall over the exhilaration of Kelly's homecoming. He strained to hear Weldon above the din around them.

"I know I've griped about it for years. But prepare yourself, Little Brother. That place has to be seen to be believed. Nothing has changed since we were kids. Remember Old Man Campbell? He's still in charge of the staff. Mom sits at her desk in complete isolation. Every once in a while she'll crack her whip and everybody'll jump. There'll be a big stir for a few days. Then the place settles right back into the same old groove."

"What does Mom have you doing?"

Weldon made a face. "Ostensibly, I'm her understudy. I'm supposed to be familiarizing myself with operations. It's ridiculous. She keeps reaching into the bottom right-hand drawer of her desk and pulling out a book of instructions Dad left her before he died. Never mind that since Dad wrote those notes, we've had the Cold War, the Berlin Wall, Sputnik, and China has fallen to the Communists. Dad's still running that company from beyond the grave. Talk about spooky. It's like working in a mausoleum."

Kelly wondered what his own role would be in the company. Although he had been home from college two days, nothing had been mentioned, and this was the first time he and Weldon had been able to slip away and talk. Months ago Weldon had moved out of the house and into his own apartment. During the last few weeks he had been spending most of his time in Houston, studying operations there.

"What do the numbers look like?" Kelly asked.

"From what little I've been able to determine, terrible. Mom keeps her elbow on the specifics. But it's plain that big strike out in New Mexico several years ago is all that's kept the company afloat. The retail outlets are deadweight. The refinery is so outdated. We'd be better off buying on the open market. But I can't make anybody see that. Some of our service stations are right out of *Tobacco Road,* where you hand-pump gas up into a glass tank, and it runs out by gravity flow."

Kelly laughed. "You're putting me on."

"Like hell I am. Now the new interstate system is taking most of the traffic away from our stations. And no one in the company is paying the slightest bit of attention. If we want to stay in retail, we'll have to put up one hell of an outlay for new sites, new buildings. And we'd be going smack up against the majors. We'd lose our ass. We don't have the backup. We should get the hell out of retailing as quick as we can."

"Have you suggested that to Mom?"

"Just about every day. She says I just don't see the big picture. To her way of thinking, it would be going backward. You see, Dad put it all together, and we'd be taking it apart." Weldon finished his drink and slammed his glass on the table. "We're not running an oil company. We're maintaining a monument to Dad."

"What about the board?"

Weldon made a face. "An exercise in futility. They meet every three months or so and rubber-stamp what Mom and Campbell have already done. Usually the outside members don't even bother to attend. It's just Mom, Grandmother, Campbell, and now me. I suppose you'll be enshrined in a few months."

Abruptly Weldon left the table to get more drinks. As a coffeehouse, The Cellar had no license to sell liquor. But drinks were free to friends of the owner. Weldon had known the owner since grade school.

Kelly was growing more depressed as the evening wore on. He had been so eager to complete his long battle through college and graduate work to get home, to take his place in the company. And tonight Weldon had made it sound so bleak.

He watched Weldon at the counter, conning the man who controlled the 180-proof grain alcohol siphon. Kelly had seen Weldon so rarely during the last few years that he was still adjusting to the changes in him. Weldon had grown into a large man, with a barrel chest, the neck of a pro line-backer, and huge biceps. On first glance he appeared chubby, but in a couple of sessions of roughhousing during the last two days, Kelly had discovered that there was little flab on him. His face had broadened into an open, jovial expression that hardly matched his aggressive personality and quick wit.

Weldon returned to the table triumphant, put the drinks on the table, lowered himself into a chair, and resumed talking as if there had been no interruption. "Thing is, if we cut our losses in the refinery and retailing, we could use the revenue to get into something else."

"Like what?"

"Hell, look around you. New products, new opportunities are coming along every day. All you need is an idea. Remember Charles Tandy?"

Kelly nodded that he did. The Tandys owned Tandy Leather, and furnished raw materials to shoe factories all over the country.

"Charles Tandy was walking through his daddy's plant one day and saw piles of scrap leather waiting to be hauled off to be burned. He said, 'Wait a minute. We ought to be able to do something with that.' So he designed kits for making moccasins, belts, billfolds, all kinds of crap, and started Tandy Leathercrafts. Don't laugh. You know how many Boy Scouts need a merit badge in leathercraft? How many veterans there are in VA hospitals, needing something to do? Old people sitting around on their asses? Convicts in prisons? Total them all up, millions. Charles Tandy is in high cotton. Now he's thinking about doing the same thing for people who like to tinker with radios."

"Weldon, we don't know about anything like that," Kelly pointed out. "All the company expertise is in oil."

"Little Brother, you've just stated our biggest problem. Oil is the most volatile commodity on the market. When the East Texas field was discovered in the thirties, oil dropped to ten cents a barrel. It could happen again. A big new field in South America, anywhere in the world, and we'd be in deep shit. We've got to diversify, hedge our bets. Kerr-McGee is into uranium mining, heavy metals. I'm not sure that's the way to go, but we sure as hell should look around for something."

Kelly found himself resistant to Weldon's argument. He had always envisioned Spurlock Oil as a bright jewel among independent oil companies, envied even by the majors.

"I'm not sure we should move outside our area of expertise," he said.

"Hell, we can *learn* something else. And there are other things we should be doing. We should get the hell out of downtown. There's no parking space. That old building is deteriorating. Right now we could clear enough from it to put up a new place in one of the suburbs. That's where the action is. This town is expanding in every direction. Any investment on the edge of town would double, triple in five years."

Kelly laughed. "I can see why you have Mom upset."

"She ought to be upset. Money's being made all around us, and we're just sitting there on our dumb asses."

"Weldon, we're not exactly paupers. Some people would call us rich."

"Rich, shit! I'm talking *money*, Little Brother. So we own a piddling little oil company. In ten years, if we played it right, we could be feeding at the same trough with H. L. Hunt or Howard Hughes."

Weldon's intensity on the subject made Kelly vaguely uncomfortable. For a moment he did not know why.

Then he remembered Aunt Zetta once saying that Spurlock men always wanted to be bigshots.

"Weldon, there are things other than money," he said.

"Like what?"

"Being happy. Making a contribution to life around you. Feeling good about it."

Weldon looked at the ceiling and blew air up his nose. He leaned toward Kelly. "Listen, Little Brother. It's a mean old world out there. Nobody's worrying about *your* welfare. The big fish eat the little fish. That's the way the world works. Didn't they teach you *anything* up there in the effete East?"

Over in a corner of The Cellar a group began singing "Waltzing Matilda," the end-of-the-world theme from the popular movie, *On the Beach.* It was a sad, lonely dirge, and did nothing to lift Kelly's spirits.

"Weldon, I'm just not that greedy. I think I'll be happy with the oil company. Maybe even with the way it's being run."

"You'll see. It isn't being run. Mom's into everything else *but* the company. She's always on the phone, trying to convince some businessman the town will collapse if he doesn't contribute a bundle to the arts. She's chairman of this and chairman of that. Right now it's the Van Cliburn Quadrennial International Piano Competition." He stressed each word of the title. "It's all they can talk about. I'm sick of it."

"Maybe it's something worth doing."

"Shit. They've lost all perspective. They're calling that section north of the cattle barns the Acropolis of Fort Worth, for Christ's sake. It's downright embarrassing."

Kelly did not respond.

"Imagine showing some of your friends from Harvard around town and saying, 'Over there are the Stock Show cattle barns, and this is our Acropolis.' "

Kelly had to laugh.

"Mom's frenetic about it," Weldon went on. "She's always at some committee or board meeting, or talking about it on the phone. It's almost like she's running from something she doesn't want to face."

Kelly watched the group singing. They had their arms around each other and were really into it. He had a strong impulse to join them.

"She's got a boyfriend," Weldon said, raising his voice over the singing. "Did you know that?"

"No," Kelly lied.

"Maybe she's flesh and blood, after all. Walter Trammel, our lawyer. Tall, arrogant son of a bitch. He always looks at me like I'm something he found in his soup. His wife died of polio a few years ago. Must have been one of the last cases before the vaccine. You remember him?"

Kelly nodded.

"They're thick as thieves. They talk on the phone several times a day and go everywhere together. I don't know if they're sleeping together or what. It's weird. If they want to, why don't they go ahead and get married? There's nothing to stop them."

Kelly did not want to speculate, especially about his mother's sex life. He shrugged.

"Anyway, with all the committee meetings, solicitation campaigns, concerts, operas, receptions and shit, she's spending damned little time running the company. It's just drifting. I'm going crazy, knowing what needs to be done, but unable to do anything. I need you, Little Brother. It's time for a palace revolution. If we play our cards right, we can take over that damned company. Ease Mom out."

Kelly was stunned. He shook his head emphatically. "No, Weldon. I couldn't do anything like that."

Weldon held up his hands, palms outward. "Don't rush to judgment, Little Brother. Maybe you don't think so now. But wait till you get a bellyful of the crap they hand you. I can tell you right now, your Harvard magna cum laude, your MBA won't mean shit to them. They'll look at you and smile, and say, 'Well, Kelly, book theory's fine, but this is the way it's always been done here in the real world.' They'll be so condescending you'll want to puke. You'll see."

Kelly felt Weldon was forcing him into a situation he could not accept. He sought to make himself clear. "Weldon, I'm not like you. I don't want to make changes overnight."

"Nobly spoken, Little Brother. But just wait. In a month or two, you'll be just as fed up as I am. And while we're on the subject, I'll tell you one thing right now: If my situation doesn't change pretty damned quick, I'm leaving. I'll sue for my part of the company, and start my own business. Only one thing has stopped me. I've been waiting for you to get home, to see what we can do. But I'm not kidding. I don't intend to take the hind tit forever."

The "Waltzing Matilda" people filed up the steps toward the street, still singing. In a corner, a beatnik sat staring at the wall as if reading truths there that no one else could see.

All the elation Kelly had felt over his homecoming was completely gone.

He had prepared himself for years, carrying maximum academic hours through every term, driving himself relentlessly on through the summer months, yet keeping his marks high enough for honors.

And with his knowledge of the vast West Texas landscape, he had taken flight training, earning a pilot's license so he would be even more valuable to the company.

He had returned home expecting his accomplishments to be recognized, appreciated. He had expected to move swiftly into the middle of operations, working closely with Weldon and Joanna, putting into use the expertise he had accumulated.

Now, after his evening with Weldon, he felt only dread for the coming months.

Chapter 29

Kelly seemed restless. Joanna waited while he paced the office, examining the new Peter Hurd paintings. At last he settled down across from her desk. She smiled at him.

"This place make you feel like you're truly home again?"

He nodded. "Nothing seems to have changed."

Joanna was not yet accustomed to his height. He was at least an inch taller than Walter, and still painfully thin. And he was so serious. Joanna had not seen him laugh once since he had been home.

"Kelly, there's no reason you should start to work yet. Why don't you take some time off? No one would mind."

He gave her an abrupt shake of his head. "No. I'd like to get right to work."

"If that's what you want. I've thought it might be best for you to work with Mr. Campbell, while you learn the ropes. What do you think about that?"

"Fine, I guess. I have to start somewhere."

"This is a long-time dream of mine," she confided. "When Weldon first came home, he monitored procedures here in this office for several months. Now he's studying operations in the field. Once you become acquainted with the business side, and Weldon with the mechanical side, you two should make quite a team. I've looked forward to that for years."

Kelly did not respond. Joanna was growing concerned over his habitual reticence. She talked on.

"We've arranged an office for you down the hall, right next to Weldon's. Mr. Campbell will furnish you with whatever secretarial help you'll need. How does that sound?"

"Okay, I guess."

His lack of enthusiasm surprised her. She did not know what he had expected, but she remembered that college graduates often tended to overestimate their knowledge and to underestimate the need for experience.

"Kelly, I'm sure you remember that there are many facets to this company—drilling, production, refining, retailing. It's so involved that anyone needs time to get a good grasp on it."

He seemed so *glum,* Joanna was moved to reveal another dream, one she had not intended to mention so soon.

"Kelly, just between you and me, Mr. Campbell is no longer young. He's not in the best of health. I can't promise, but I'm sure that if you can become thoroughly acquainted with the business side rather quickly, there's a very good chance you might step right into that job within two or three years."

He gave her a humorless smile. "Mom, most of my MBA classmates are moving right into top management at sizable companies. I doubt I'll have any trouble."

So that *was* it. He had expected more.

Weldon had arrived home with the same attitude.

She decided not to press the issue. He would learn for himself.

"We'll see how it goes," she said. "I'll turn you over to Mr. Campbell now. I happen to know he has a conference late this morning, but maybe he can get you started in setting up your office. Then he can work with you this afternoon. I'll be tied up the rest of the day. The Cliburn contestants will start arriving tomorrow, and the number of last-minute details have become unbelievable."

"So I've heard," Kelly said.

Joanna gave him a sharp glance, trying to judge his depth of sarcasm. "I see you've been talking to Weldon. I thought you of all people would recognize the value of what we're doing. We'll have fifty or sixty of the best young pianists in the world on their way to Fort Worth. Don't sell your hometown short, Kelly."

Kelly's eyes widened in surprise. "That many?"

"We've had late cancellations, contestants who see they're not ready. The standards are high—in fact, too brutal, some think. From the start it will be as demanding as the Tchaikovsky, the Queen Elisabeth, the Leventritt, any other competition in the world."

"I haven't seen a word about it in the Boston or New York papers."

"You probably won't. I suspect they may be embarrassed for us, thinking we ignorant Texans will fall flat on our faces. Incidentally, I should have told you: one of the contestants will be staying with us. We'll put him or her in the west wing. I'm sorry we haven't had time to talk properly since you've been home. I promise, it'll be different, once the competition is over." She picked up the phone. "I'll call Mr. Campbell."

Clearly, Campbell had been anticipating the call. He arrived within seconds and shook hands with Kelly.

"Well, this isn't as if we were welcoming someone new to the staff. I remember when you used to come down almost every day after school. I'll show you to your office."

As they went out the door, Joanna picked up the artist's sketch for the cover of the next Annual Report and examined it.

The art was pleasing to the eye, but she was doubtful. Brod's reports had always conveyed a boldness she had never been able to achieve. Even though Spurlock Oil was a private company, Brod had believed a high-quality, detailed Annual Report was essential. He said bankers and others with a need to know were always impressed. Joanna had found this true, and had continued the practice.

She was penciling a notation, asking to see another, bolder sketch, when Bonnie buzzed.

"Beth Runnels on line two."

Joanna put the layout aside.

Beth was unusually brusque. "Honey, I know you're busy, and I hate to bother you. But I wonder if I could ask a favor."

"Of course," Joanna said.

"My cousin from Tulsa and one of her daughters are coming down for the Van Cliburn finals. I managed to get tickets. They'll be staying with me. I was going to send a car to meet them at the airport, but then I thought it would be nice if one of your boys could pick them up at Meacham, drive them here, and maybe escort the daughter to the finals. I promise you he won't be disappointed. Chandra is a lovely girl. Do you think one of your sons would be interested?"

Joanna laughed. "Beth, I honestly don't know. They don't confide in me. Kelly has been dating a former classmate. He denies it, but I think it's serious. He spends all his spare time with her. Weldon's in Houston, but he'll be back into the office before noon. I can ask him."

"I *would* appreciate it. You can tell him he won't regret doing me this little favor. You'll be here Tuesday, won't you?"

Joanna glanced at her desk calendar. On Tuesday, Beth and Gyorgy were hosts for a seated dinner, honoring the judges, before the evening competition.

"Of course we'll be there," she said. "I wouldn't miss it for the world."

"Let's see, I have you down for fair French, some Spanish. And Walter for excellent German, some French. That right?"

"Except you may have overrated my French."

"I've changed the place settings fifty times, trying to get it to work out. I only hope I can keep Gyorgy quiet around the judges. I'm sure he'll try to give them advice. You'll let me know about Weldon?"

"Either I or Weldon will call you before noon," she promised.

But it was after eleven before Weldon returned. He came
into her office, bringing the blueprints on proposed repairs
at the refinery. Without ceremony he dumped them on her
desk. She pushed them to one side. "How was Houston?"

"Hot and sticky, as ever."

He turned and was heading for the door. "Would you like
to go to the Van Cliburn finals a week from Saturday?" she
asked.

Weldon burst out laughing. "The pianner playing? Me?"

"You. Beth Runnels hopes you will be a gentleman and
escort her niece from Tulsa, who is coming down for the
finals. A lovely young lady, Beth says."

Weldon grimaced. "What's her name?"

"Chandra. Chandra Sykes. Beth has managed tickets."

Weldon stood with feet spread, hands on hips. "Sykes?
What does her daddy do?"

"It didn't occur to me to ask. She's Beth's niece. Beth was
your father's godmother. Isn't that enough of an introduction?"

"Sykes. Do they have money?"

Joanna hesitated. More and more, she was seeing a facet of
Weldon she did not like. In recent months, he sometimes
appeared to take delight in seeing how nasty he could be to
her.

"Weldon, I don't know whether they're rich or poor. But
since she and her mother are coming into Meacham instead
of Love, I assume they'll be traveling by private plane, and
that they're not exactly on welfare."

"Why me?" Weldon asked.

For a moment, Joanna wanted to get up from her desk and
slap him. "Because you are eligible, reasonably good-looking, the son of Beth's longtime friends, and a charming person, when you want to be. Beth doesn't know you also can be
disgustingly crass at times. And I want to tell you something:
This preoccupation you've developed about money doesn't
set well with anyone, including me."

"I don't like to be used."

"Weldon, if you have another engagement that evening,

I'll make excuses. But unless you do, I expect you to call Beth within the next few minutes and accept her invitation, and to be gracious about it."

Weldon gave her his slow, infuriating smile and did not respond. He turned and walked out of her office.

But a few minutes later as she walked down the hall, she heard him on the telephone, making arrangements with Beth Runnels.

He was perfectly charming.

"Our basic system was set up by your father," Campbell said. "When your grandfather was killed in that blowout in thirty-six, most of the company records were lost with him. They were all in his head, the terms of leases, drilling operations, overrides, everything. Your father had to reconstruct it all from old letters, courthouse filings, notes from your grandfather to the bookkeeper, to his partner, to himself. No clue was too small. We searched for every scrap. Your father did a masterful job. Most of our records on the older wells are still in your father's handwriting. I'll show you."

Kelly followed him downstairs to bookkeeping. As they walked along, clerks and secretaries stole furtive glances from their work. Kelly remembered the first time his mother had taken him into the office. This was not much different.

Campbell led Kelly into a walk-in vault and hunted through stacks of old yellow folders.

"Here. See? Your father's handwriting."

Kelly examined the neat, bold script, defining the legal location of a well, the depth and thickness of the pay formation, the results of early choke tests, and a complete breakdown on the ownership of royalties. Kelly had not seen enough of his father's handwriting to recognize it.

Campbell was awaiting a reaction. Kelly found himself resenting the personal intrusion. He gave Campbell an enigmatic nod and returned the folder.

"Of course, we've made a few changes since those days," Campbell went on. "Our system has evolved through trial

and error. Tested by time, you might say. I suspect it may
not bear much resemblance to what you've been taught at
college."

"We studied a wide variety of systems," Kelly said.

Campbell seemed diverted by his own thoughts. "A friend
of mine once opened a store to sell plumbing fixtures. He
thought he might save money by installing what he sold,
instead of hiring it done. He had no plumbing experience, so
he bought a book on it. But he said that when he crawled
under a house, he seldom found anything that looked like
what was in the book." Campbell laughed at his anecdote. "I
think that's what we have here with this accounting system.
It doesn't look like anything in a book."

Kelly seethed. Campbell's point, if not subtle, was plain:
As Weldon had predicted, Campbell was saying this was the
real world, where a Harvard magna cum laude and MBA did
not mean shit.

They continued their tour through the company, Campbell explaining many aspects of the operation Kelly already
knew.

Only the lab had changed considerably. Parker had died
at his desk of a heart attack years ago. Kelly's mother had
written him the news while he was still at Choate. He recognized none of the other personnel in the lab.

As they returned to the executive suites Campbell found
an effective way to dismiss Kelly for the remainder of the
day.

"A few years ago, I put together a little handbook for new
people in our department. It's rather simple. But maybe it
will give you an idea of how we operate, enough to start
asking questions."

Campbell rummaged in his desk and found a copy of the
handbook. Kelly took it down the hall to his bare office.

Written in cryptic style, the booklet effectively defined
the flow of information through the company. With the first
page Kelly recognized the system. It was not the best in the
world, but it was not the worst either. Immediately he saw
places where the system could be improved.

He had just finished reading the booklet, and was marking certain passages, when his phone rang.

"Walter and I are going out for dinner tonight," his mother said. "He suggested that if you're free, maybe you'd like to join us."

Kelly was tempted to ask if they still needed a chaperon. He fought the impulse. "I would, Mom, except that the Lathams have asked me over for a party at their house."

"In your honor?"

"Let's just say it's more in the way of an acknowledgment that I'm home."

"I see. Is Amy involved?"

"In a way. I'm taking her."

"I'd heard she was back home, teaching. It sounds like a devious plot to me. I think she's been after you a long time."

"Mom, we're just friends. She's only teaching at TCU while waiting to hear about her scholarship to the Sorbonne."

"I'm sure she'd forget every word of French she knows if you only asked the right question. And Kelly, you could do worse."

Kelly did not answer.

How could he explain his relationship with Amy Goodwin, even if he chose to do so, which he did not.

"Okay. Forget I said it," Joanna said. "But I know you're dating her. If you want tickets to the Cliburn through the next two weeks, let me know. I think I can arrange them."

"Thanks. I will. Tell Walter I appreciate the invitation, and convey my regrets," Kelly said.

He left the building that afternoon as depressed as he had ever been in his life. His first day on the start of his career, and already he was bored beyond belief.

He had seen nothing all day that remotely resembled a challenge.

"How'd it go?" Amy asked as they walked toward the car.

"Fine."

"You'd say that if the building fell down. Well, at least *I* have news."

Her eyes were alive with excitement.

"You heard?"

She nodded, laughing her pleasure. Kelly was glad for her, but disappointed for himself. She would be leaving, right at a time he needed her most. He stopped and kissed her. "Congratulations."

She leaned away from him to study his face. "You're really glad?"

"Of course. I know how much you want it."

"How are you so sure it was good news?"

"I've never doubted."

"To tell the truth, I haven't either. Not much! But it's the best possible news. Full scholarship. All I have to do is make the grades."

"A snap."

"It'll be a tight squeeze. My schedule at TCU overlaps by a week. But I've talked all day with people on both sides of the Atlantic. Everyone is making concessions for me. So maybe it will work out."

Kelly drove westward toward the setting sun. At seven-thirty, it was still shining as brightly as it had at midafternoon. He wondered idly if daylight saving was a plot to kill romance. Amy leaned her small body comfortably against him, with the wind gently ruffling her black, gamin-cut hair. She had kicked off her shoes and tucked her stockinged feet beneath her.

The residential streets skirted golf courses, expanses of greenery. He had put the top down on the convertible, but he left the air conditioner running. The cold air felt good in the heat of late afternoon.

The Lathams lived amid new homes behind the country club. Kelly drove along the curving street until he found the address.

The party was well under way. Ginny Latham met Kelly and Amy at the door and led them through the house to the back and a redwood terrace, dramatically poised over a small but rugged canyon. "The Wanderer" was playing from speakers tucked under the eaves. Several couples were dancing, the women in light summer dresses, the men in slacks and short-sleeved pullovers.

"Drum roll! Drum roll!" Ginny called.

Grinning, Mark Latham beat on an empty beer keg with the handle of a barbecue fork. Conversations were interrupted as people came across the terrace to greet Kelly and Amy.

He recognized almost everyone. Most of them were now a year or more out of college, older and heavier.

Mark brought drinks, and for a time Kelly stood talking with his former classmates, catching up on their careers, their wives, and, in some instances, their growing families. Someone took Amy away to dance. Slowly the sun sank beneath the western horizon and, almost in counterpoint, a full moon rose over the hills to the east. Soon Chinese lanterns lit the terrace. Guests milled back and forth from the house through sliding glass doors. In the distance were the runways at General Dynamics and Carswell Air Force Base. Occasionally conversation became impossible as B-58 Hustler bombers thundered overhead, fighting their way into the night sky.

Relaxed, mildly depressed, Kelly drank more than he intended. It was a superb party—quiet conversation, good barbecue, ample drinks, and close friends in the gentle warmth of the Texas night. His friends were full of talk about John Glenn and the space effort, the Kennedys, the Freedom Riders. Kelly gathered that most were "Kennedy liberals," pitted against their "Johnson conservative" parents. Kelly had been so busy through the last few years that he knew little of the political scene. Mostly he kept quiet throughout the evening and listened while his friends talked.

After downing an unwanted fourth drink, he was struck by a wave of giddiness. Suddenly he felt he needed fresh air, solitude. He wandered to a quiet corner of the patio. There he sat on a redwood bench in the shadows and watched the party.

The evening had added to his discontent. He felt so disconnected from the world around him. Already his contemporaries were well along in their lives. Most had homes, children. Their goals were clearly defined.

They seemed happy. But was this what he really wanted? A rambling ranch-style house, a host of like-minded friends? Weekend trips to the slopes in Colorado in season, Cozumel when they were not? Male camaraderie at the Fort Worth Club, quiet social evenings entertaining at home, or at the Rivercrest, Shady Oaks, or Colonial country clubs? A life built around symphony and opera, tennis and golf? A power boat at Eagle Mountain or Possum Kingdom and a plane or two in a hangar at Meacham? Volunteer work with fledgling arts organizations?

This was the life his friends had chosen. They had been away to college, mostly out of state. They had traveled widely and spoke familiarly of other cities, other countries.

Yet, they had come back to Texas to live. They talked excitedly of local events—the Cliburn competition, the new museums, opera, ballet.

He thought of his friends who were native Easterners. They took in stride the Boston and New York philharmonic orchestras, Carnegie Hall, and Broadway theaters, first-class museums. They considered the existing arts as their due, took them for granted, and made them a part of their lives.

If they wished, most of his Fort Worth friends could get their cultural fixes elsewhere. Some did.

But what drove them to return to Texas and attempt to build art institutions where none existed?

Were they following the example of the older generation?

Beth Runnels was perhaps a prototype, and for Kelly she posed a mystery. She could live in any of a half-dozen homes she owned, scattered over two continents. She moved among the upper echelons of any community. Why did she spend most of her time in Texas? With the demands made upon her by international corporations and organizations, why did she continue to devote so much effort to help mount creaky local operas, tenuous ballets?

Could he ever be content with this?

He thought not.

He wanted more.

Yet he had not even begun to define his goals, let alone achieve them.

"Here you are!" Amy said, coming up behind him. "I've been looking all over! You sick?"

"No. Just drunk."

She laughed and sat down beside him, folding effortlessly into his shoulder. "You *are* in a mood. I noticed it the first thing tonight. You've been faking all evening so as not to take the edge off my high." She poked him in the ribs. "Isn't that the truth?"

He did not answer. She knew him too well.

They had been sleeping together for five years, with countless weekend trysts in New York, Washington, Boston, elsewhere, and once they had spent most of a summer bumming around Europe. Even then her driving ambition had interfered: she was determined that someday she would be a high-placed administrator in the U.S. State Department.

She was willing to sacrifice everything, anything, to that goal.

Her ambition blocked all thoughts of permanence. Somewhere along the way their passion had peaked. In wordless recognition of the futility, they both had backed away. He now had other women, and he was sure she had other men. Their affair was over. But occasionally they still warmed their enduring love in the glowing embers.

"It really didn't go at all well today, did it?" Amy said. "Is it going to work out?"

"I don't know."

"Have you talked with Weldon about it?"

"Not really. He's spending most of his time these days in Houston."

"That's a good place for him."

"What do you mean?"

She shrugged. "He's more Houston than Fort Worth. Slam-bang. Deal-a-minute. Never look back."

"A typical Texan."

Amy giggled. "You *are* drunk."

They had laughed many times over constantly being introduced in the East as "not a typical Texan."

The party was winding down. Some of the guests were leaving.

Kelly and Amy hunted their hosts and said good night.

By the time they returned to her apartment, it was after two in the morning. They sat for a time in the car, exchanging kisses.

"You're welcome to come up," Amy said. "Bring your jammies?"

"I didn't want to seem presumptuous. I'll wear a pair of yours."

She put a hand on his arm. "Kelly, you don't have to feel obligated."

He laughed so explosively that the sound came out as a bark. "Obligated! Jesus! That'll be the day."

She persisted. "Sometimes I think we fall into bed out of habit."

He turned her to face him in the soft light from a distant streetlamp. "If I've ever, ever left you feeling I don't love you, I should be shot. I've always loved you. Surely you know that."

"Still, we'll have less than two weeks before I leave. I don't want you to feel that, just because I'm here, you have to spend all your time with me."

Kelly sighed. "Amy, the way I feel right now, you may be all that'll keep me sane through the next two weeks."

He helped her out of the car. They went up to her apartment and made love until the soft light of dawn showed through the blinds.

Kelly rose, dressed, and drove home to shower and shave in preparation for another day at the office.

Chapter 30

"I really regret missing the winner's concert," Amy said.

"I'll write you about it," Kelly promised. "But after the last two weeks, I'm sure it'll be anticlimactic."

They were standing in a wide corridor at Love Field in Dallas. Amy's flight had been called, and she had her boarding pass. Other passengers were hurrying past to gates farther down the terminal.

Kelly was exhausted, fueled only by a nervous energy that made his surroundings seem unreal. After last night's finals, they had gone straight to Amy's stripped apartment. There they had made love on bare sheets until time to leave for the airport.

"I'll be worried about you," he said. "Please write often."

"Kelly, I'm more concerned about you than I am about me. I know that eventually I'll get what I want. I'm not sure about you."

"I'll survive."

"I want you to do more than that. I want you to use all those wonderful talents and abilities you have. I'm not sure there's anything at Spurlock Oil that will use a fraction of them."

For a moment Kelly was almost overcome with the pain of her departure. She and the Van Cliburn competition had been his only salvation during the last two weeks. Throughout each day at the oil company he had been bored beyond belief. But his evenings had been filled with Amy and superb piano music.

Now it was over.

And there would be no relief from the boredom.

"Amy, I don't know what I'll be doing a year or two from now. Maybe . . ."

She quickly put a hand to his lips. "Kelly, let's not try to make plans. We've always made a point of never saying goodbye. Let's don't start now. This time, we'll just be a little farther apart, a little longer."

The velvet rope was lowered. Passengers began to board.

Kelly and Amy kissed until the loading bay was empty of other passengers.

And then she was gone, hurrying down the narrow passageway into the plane.

He walked to the windows in hopes of seeing her, but the plane was parked at the wrong angle. Slowly, it backed from the loading gate and taxied away. He still could not see Amy. He watched until the plane moved out of his vision.

Feeling alone and bereft, he walked back through the long corridors and out of the terminal to his car. He drove to the Dallas–Fort Worth Turnpike and started toward home with a growing reluctance.

Despite Amy's words, he was certain that their relationship was at last ended. She was too consumed with ambition, too confident of her own worth to be diverted from her goals. There was no place for him in what she wanted to do.

He was certain that someday she would succeed; eventually she would head a branch of the State Department.

He could understand her ambition; she would lead an exciting life.

For himself, he could see nothing ahead even remotely interesting.

The Van Cliburn competition had not improved his mood.

Through the last two weeks he had been surrounded by outstanding young pianists from all over the world. All were accomplishing so much with their lives. He recognized the discipline, the drive, the work behind their success. Many clearly were headed for a concert career.

The contrast with his own limited future at Spurlock Oil was inescapable.

In ten years, he might still be where Arnold Campbell was now, general manager, playing third fiddle to Joanna, Weldon.

He drove on home, hoping that after he caught up on his sleep, his prospects might look a shade brighter.

Less than an hour later Weldon shook him awake.

"Hey, Little Brother. Get up! Let's take Beth's people back to Meacham. Then we can go get a beer."

Kelly shoved him away. "I'll pass. I'm bushed."

"Come on. I need company. That Okie female would freeze the balls off a brass monkey. I'll bet she didn't say twenty words to me last night."

Kelly had caught only a fleeting glimpse of Weldon and his date at the finals. "You two didn't hit it off?"

"That's an understatement. All evening she acted like she had a cob up her ass or something."

"Why can't Beth take them to the airport?"

"She has other guests. And Gyorgy is off jabbering Hungarian with some other Hungarian."

"Weldon, I'd rather not."

"That makes two of us. But it's time for you and me to talk, Little Brother. And I've got to get back to Houston tonight."

Weldon's expression was serious. Kelly did not know if Joanna was home, but the house had ears, so he did not ask questions. He rolled out of bed and slipped on fresh slacks and a pullover.

"These women aren't exactly Jag or convertible types," Weldon said as they went down the stairs. "We'll take one of Mom's cars. She's off somewhere, probably with Trammel."

They drove the short distance to Beth's house. As they

were received into the foyer, Beth came from a roomful of people.

"It's so nice of you boys to do me this favor. You don't know how I appreciate it. Chandra and her mother will be down in a moment."

"It's our pleasure, Mrs. Gaspar," Weldon said.

"With all the excitement, I haven't been able to depend on Gyorgy for a single thing. Kelly, what did you think of the judges' decision?"

Kelly thought the winner, Ralph Votapek, played with more fire. But two of the Russians had shown rare technical perfection. "I probably would have called it the same way," he said.

"Well, I'm glad the Russians won the silver and bronze. But let's face it! There were some just as good. Did you see what *The Washington Post* said?"

"No, ma'am."

"Their critic said he had never seen *any* competition, anywhere in the world, run so smoothly and so efficiently. Bless him! Bless him! Your mother and I and half this town put three years of solid work into it."

"I know," Kelly said.

"Thank the Lord it's over. I'm exhausted. But you know what? Next week we'll go right back to planning the next one. Oh, here you are!"

Two women were descending the stairs. Beth's houseboy followed with the luggage. Mrs. Sykes was a step or two ahead, blocking Kelly's view. He did not see Chandra until she reached the bottom of the stairs.

He hoped his face did not show his surprise. In contrast to her mother's light complexion, Chandra was strikingly tawny. Her hair was lustrous black-on-black, worn straight and shoulder-length with square-cut bangs. Her eyes were dark and almond-shaped. She was tall and slim, and her face had high cheekbones and delicately sculptured features. On first impression, Kelly thought she was oriental. But he then realized that she possessed the exotic beauty sometimes found among American Indians.

Abruptly he became aware that he was staring. To his chagrin, he felt his face grow warm.

Weldon moved past him to direct the houseboy with the luggage.

"You haven't met Kelly, have you?" Beth said. She made the introductions. Chandra nodded to Kelly, but did not offer her hand. She did not smile or alter her expression. Kelly remembered Weldon's crude description and fought to keep a straight face.

He stood to one side and waited while Beth said good-bye. He held the door for the women and walked down the steps behind them. Chandra moved with the sure, slightly splay-footed grace of a professional dancer. He hurried on ahead to get the car door, but the houseboy beat him to it, leaving him feeling slightly foolish.

As they drove away toward the airport, an awkward silence fell. It was broken by Mrs. Sykes. "Before I forget, Weldon, I want to thank you for all you've done. We've had such a lovely time. I wouldn't have missed this trip for the world."

"It's been my pleasure, Mrs. Sykes," Weldon said.

"Kelly, did you enjoy the competition?" Chandra asked. Her voice was rich contralto, pleasing to the ear.

Kelly was tempted to tell her she should use it more.

"Tremendously," he said. "It was almost too much of a good thing. I wish it could be spread out over the four years, instead of crammed into two weeks. I feel half tone-deaf."

"Kelly sang four years with the Texas Boys Choir," Weldon said.

Kelly wanted to kick him, but the transmission hump was in the way.

"Then I must have heard you sing," Chandra said. "Did you sing in Tulsa in . . ." She counted back. "About fifty-four?"

"That was me," Kelly said. "Third from the left in the second row."

"All of you stood like little statues and sang your hearts out. Do you still sing?"

"Not even in the shower."

Another awkward silence followed. Kelly wished he had not been so flip.

"I'm confused about something," Mrs. Sykes said. "Doesn't Fort Worth have a commercial airport?"

Weldon and Kelly laughed.

"Not really, Mrs. Sykes," Kelly explained. "Dallas and Fort Worth have almost gone to war over it. Fort Worth built an international airport to serve both cities back in the early fifties. Dallas fought it tooth and nail, and the airlines wouldn't move. So it was abandoned. Now everyone in Fort Worth has to drive to Dallas to catch flights. And Dallas gets credit for our air traffic."

"This is all we've got," Weldon said, turning into Meacham Field.

Chandra directed Weldon to a twin-engine Convair parked on a back ramp. The pilot was waiting. Weldon got out of the car and helped with the stowing of baggage. Mrs. Sykes and Chandra waited until all was ready.

"If you young men are ever in Tulsa, please give us a call," Mrs. Sykes said.

Weldon thanked her for the invitation.

Kelly met Chandra's gaze. "Thank you, I will," he said.

Her expression did not change.

But he was certain she caught his emphasis.

Mrs. Sykes and Chandra boarded and the door closed. Weldon and Kelly stood by their mother's car while the plane taxied to the end of the runway, sat for a minute, then made its takeoff roll. Within seconds it was only a white speck in the northern sky.

"Damn but I want one of those things," Weldon said.

"My little Cessna's good enough for me," Kelly said.

They drove south toward the downtown skyline.

"What kind of Indian you think she is?" Weldon asked.

"Tulsa. That's mostly Osage, isn't it? Choctaw? Cherokee?"

"Maybe it wasn't a tribe. Maybe it was just a wandering Indian," Weldon said. "A fence-jumper."

He laughed at his own joke.

"You plan to date her anymore?"

"Nah. Stuck-up bitch. I've got something going in Houston."

Once past the stockyards on North Main, he turned right and crossed to University and headed south.

Kelly had no idea where they were headed. He did not ask.

Impatient, sometimes honking to clear slower traffic from his path, Weldon drove through the TCU campus to Bluebonnet Circle.

"Wait till it gets around that Mom's Cadillac was seen outside the Oui Lounge," he said.

After parking, Weldon opened the trunk of the car, pulled out a briefcase, and carried it with him into the lounge. Kelly followed.

Walking past the bar, Weldon went to a dimly lit table. When the waitress came, he ordered a pitcher of beer. He looked around the lounge, as if assessing the other patrons, and leaned toward Kelly with a conspiratorial air.

"Mom thinks I've been traveling around the state, studying the company. She doesn't know the half of it." He pulled a sheaf of papers from the briefcase and tossed them across the table. "How does this shit look to an honors MBA?"

Kelly turned through the papers in the dim light. He quickly found they contained the background data for the company's Annual Report of the previous year. He skipped through, noting only the totals and the general structure of the report.

"Everything seems to be here," he said.

Weldon tossed another batch of papers to him. "Now tell me how that report would look, if everything I've circled in red were factored out."

After examining only a few pages, Kelly saw his point. Circled were the money-losing activities. He flipped back to the first page and added the totals.

"Without these losers, profits of the company could be doubled," he said.

"At least! And nobody in that whole fucking place understands that! If you'd tell anybody in the company that you could double the profits in a year, they'd call you a liar."

"The other day I tried to show Campbell and Mom how we could streamline some paperwork," Kelly said. "They wouldn't even listen."

Weldon grinned. "I've thought of a way to make them listen. What you've got there in your hot little hands is a bundle of dynamite that'll jar that old company to its foundations. And Little Brother, that's exactly what you and me are going to do."

Kelly felt a moment of foreboding. "How?"

"When will figures for the Annual Report start coming in?"

"We're running totals on the first quarter now."

"What's the production schedule?"

Kelly hesitated, assessing what he had learned. "As I understand it, we assemble it quarter by quarter. When the close comes at the end of December, all is put into final shape for the printer. I think the annual meeting is in February."

"March," Weldon said. "You have access to the breakdowns?"

Again Kelly hesitated. "In a way."

Campbell kept a tight rein on the material. But as a stockholder, Kelly was accorded some clearance.

"Can you get all the figures?"

He would have to snoop into a few areas where he had not been granted access. "Maybe," he said.

"All right. Here's what we'll do. While Campbell and his crew put together the official report, you and I will assemble our own version, weeding out all this deadweight. You'll feed into our report all of Campbell's figures. I'll feed in the material I'm collecting in the field. Campbell's report will show how the company is operating. Ours will show how it *could* be operating, for a hell of a lot more profit."

"Mom still wouldn't listen," he predicted.

Weldon's grin widened. "The board could damned well make her listen."

"I thought you said she has the board in the palm of her hand."

"She had. Until now." Weldon glanced around the bar and leaned closer. "On the next go-round, you'll be appointed. And if we play our cards right, *we* can take control."

"How? We're only two of . . . what? Six?"

"Five. In the holy writ—that little black notebook in Mom's desk—Dad advises Mom to limit the board to five members. He believed that was the optimum number to fulfill state law, yet maintain firm family control. You'll be replacing Old Man Van Laningham. He must be eighty-five by now. Last I heard, pure oxygen was all that was keeping him among the living. Approval of his resignation will be the first item on the agenda. And Campbell's no spring chicken. He won't be around much longer. He's already talking of retirement."

"But that's still two against three."

"Don't count too quick. Granted, Campbell will knuckle under to Mom. He has gone to his knees for her so many times, it's pure habit. Grandmother will be the key. If we can convince her the company is losing money it should be making, I think she'd do something about it."

Kelly was dubious. "Weldon, as I understand it, Grandmother has never shown much interest in the company. She has allowed Mom full control."

Weldon nodded agreement. "That's why we'll have to work on her. You may not be old enough to remember, but I do. When Dad died, Grandmother didn't want Mom to take over the company. They had some hot arguments about it. If it hadn't been Dad's idea, I doubt Grandmother would have gone along with it. But this was the deal: Mom was to preserve the company until you and I were grown. You sure as hell look grown to me."

"Weldon, what is it you're trying to do? Even if we prove the refinery and the service stations are losing tons of money, Mom will just argue that they're a part of the company structure."

"We should get rid of them. Go back to being a highly profitable production company. Maybe we could set up a plan to help the present managers lease-purchase the retail outlets. Anything to get rid of them. We could sell the refinery. Or if there's no buyers, just close the damned thing."

Kelly shook his head. "Mom would never do that."

Weldon lowered his voice. "We can force her into it. You, me, and Grandmother."

Kelly could foresee the discord Weldon's plan would bring. "That would just about kill Mom."

"Oh, shit, Kelly. She'd get over it."

"No. I won't do that to her."

Weldon gave him a slow, appraising stare. "Don't say no too quick. Think it over. I've told you. If things at the company don't change pretty damned soon, I'll sue for my part and go off on my own."

Kelly examined the totals he had written on the scratch pad.

The possibilities *were* exciting: Spurlock Oil truly could be turned into a jewel of a private company, the envy of the industry. At the moment, it was a wasteful, plodding, disorganized mess.

But the emotional price would be enormous.

"Weldon, I can't do it to her," he said again.

Weldon hit the table with his fist. "Shit!" He sat looking at Kelly for a time before going on in a quieter tone. "Tell me, what do we owe her? She farmed both of us out when we were kids, me to the military academy, you to the choir. Kelly, I've never told anyone this. But I used to cry myself to sleep damned near every night. You know why? I only wanted a little attention from her, just enough to show she knew I was alive. And I never got it."

Kelly did not answer. He remembered the distance he had felt as a child.

Weldon stuffed the material back into the briefcase.

"Maybe I shouldn't expect you to buy it right off. All I'm asking is that you take what I've gathered, and study it."

He slid the briefcase across the table, rose, tossed a tip on the table, and walked out of the lounge.

They drove home without further discussion. Kelly went up to his room and collapsed. Before dropping off to sleep, he heard Weldon's car leave the drive.

More than an hour later he awoke from a fitful dream, deeply troubled.

It had been a nightmare, reminiscent of those he had endured as a child. He could not get back to sleep.

Fully awake, he pulled out Weldon's material, took it to his desk, and began studying it in detail.

On closer examination, he found the figures revealing in ways that perhaps not even Weldon realized. Sifting through the numbers, he found other expenditures that should be red-lined, dead losses that Weldon had missed.

Intrigued, he revised Weldon's estimates. The further he searched, the more he found.

At last he laid aside his pen and thought back to the years when he had spent long, happy hours at Spurlock Oil after school. He remembered being drilled by Don Parker on geological lore.

He still remembered all that Parker had taught him—the various tests to identify rocks, the complicated formulas to assess grades of oil and gas. He had assumed that someday he would be using that information while taking a vital role in the company's ever-exciting search for oil. His mother had bolstered that belief with her lectures.

He had worked hard fulfilling his end of the bargain. It had taken years to acquire the skills he had been told he would need.

Now each day he was performing the common work of a bookkeeper, while his former classmates were moving into key positions in industry, all across the country.

It was not fair. He had been at the top of his class throughout college and graduate school.

For years he had proved his worth to others.

Now perhaps he must do the same with his family.

Carefully, he totaled his revised figures.

With her obstinacy, his mother was costing the family a great deal of money that would never be recovered. It was being wasted, month after month, year after year.

If he and Weldon implemented their plan, and restructured the company from top to bottom, they would be doing her and the family an immense favor.

Surely in time she would see that.

He returned the material to the briefcase and dressed. After slipping downstairs through the silent house, he walked out to his car, started the engine, and quietly eased away.

Weldon's two-story town house was dark, but his Jaguar was in the drive. Kelly rang the bell and pounded on the door until it opened. He shoved the briefcase into Weldon's stomach as if it were a medicine ball.

"Count me in," he said.

He walked back to his car and burned rubber, leaving Weldon standing in the lighted doorway in his shorts, holding the briefcase, grinning in triumph.

Chapter 31

Hibiscus bloomed in profusion along the balcony facing the sea. Joanna awoke to their sweet perfume. She glanced at the clock on the tower in the village square. Just after seven. Beside her, Walter was still asleep. Easing out of bed, she slipped into a robe and walked out onto the balcony.

The bright morning sky was cloudless over the blue waters of the Caribbean. A cruise ship had entered the bay and bumboats were hurrying out to meet it. Below the hotel, in a tree she could not name, a bird of brilliant red plumage sang a peculiar three-note melody. She stood listening until Walter stirred behind her.

"I'm awake," he said. "Who could sleep? That bird is overdoing local color."

"He's protesting that the island has been turned over to tourists," she said. "Do you want to go down for breakfast, or have it sent up?"

"Up." He rose and went into the bath. He was never talkative in the mornings until after he showered.

She went to the phone and ordered papaya, scrambled eggs, toast, and coffee. Content with the real-life travel poster before her, she watched the ship anchor and waited until Walter emerged from the shower. When the cart arrived, they sat down to breakfast on the balcony.

"What'll it be today?" Walter asked. "Beach or shopping?"

"The beach." During the last two days she had explored most of the shops.

"Good. I need to bake the booze out of me."

They had spent the previous evening at a place called the Hideaway on the western edge of the island. During the evening Walter drank more than at any time since she had known him. Afterward, back at the hotel, they had made love.

Even after all the time since Peggy's death, they were still cautiously feeling their way into a physical relationship. Joanna for once had surrendered to passion without distracting thoughts or memories.

She supposed that Walter also was resolving his difficulties with the past. She did not know. They had never talked about it.

But her imagination played havoc amid his silences.

For a while Walter devoted his full attention to breakfast. But after finishing his coffee, he spread a map of the island and pointed.

"I may have a treat. For an outrageous bribe, I've been told of a cove no one knows. It's absolutely guaranteed we'll have the beach, the ocean to ourselves."

After dressing, they loaded their gear into the old Jeep Walter had rented the day after they arrived. Leaving the village behind, they drove eastward over a sandy road that was hardly more than a trail. Away from the sea, the landscape was rough and vegetation sparse, reminding Joanna of vast stretches of northern Mexico.

Walter was wearing tattered tan shorts, sandals, a short-sleeved bush shirt, and a woven-straw hat he had picked up in the village market. Joanna watched his lean, strong legs as he shifted gears to accommodate the constantly changing terrain. They talked little on the drive, enjoying the scenery, the remoteness.

Twice Walter stopped to study his map. Several miles farther he turned off toward the sea on the bare trace of a road. After a few minutes they descended abruptly into a cliff-locked cove.

It was picture perfect. The sand was white, the water pale green close to shore, deepening to emerald and cobalt blue farther seaward. Terns and gulls circled beneath the cliffs.

Walter hid the Jeep under the cliffs. They investigated the cove, then set up the beach umbrella. Walter unloaded the wine cooler and placed it in the shade.

When all was arranged, he settled into a backrest, stretched his long legs on the sand, and pushed his hat forward over his eyes.

Joanna lay on a beach towel beside him. For a time, the only sounds were of the surf, the gulls, and the terns.

"I believe I could become accustomed to this," Walter said. "Why don't we stay here another week? I don't have a single item on my calendar that can't wait. You could call Bonnie and tell her to run that outfit for a few days. Or turn it over to Brod and Kelly."

Joanna was not even tempted. "No. I have to be there."

Walter did not lift the hat from his eyes. "Why?"

"For dozens of reasons. We have a deep well nearing completion in Culberson County. It's been a worry from the start. The show has been marginal. I may have to make a difficult decision on whether to abandon it, or go deeper. And we have a bloc of leases expiring in Gaines County. I have to decide whether to allow the option to lapse, renew, or spud in quickly to hold the leases under the present contract. And in Runnels County . . ."

Walter raised a hand. "Please! A little of that could spoil my day."

He remained quiet for several minutes. After spreading suntan oil on her legs and arms, Joanna leaned against her backrest and watched the surf.

"You know, we could do this all the time," Walter said, still from beneath his hat. "When you come right down to it, I'm about half retired now. I could cut back even more, easily, take only an interesting case now and then. You could start turning the company over to the boys."

"No," Joanna said, more firmly than she intended. She softened her tone. "I can't."

Walter pushed back his hat and looked at her. "I seem to be missing something here. Weldon has been back almost two years. Kelly is supposed to be such a whiz. You could continue to supervise—"

"No," Joanna interrupted, not wanting to hear more. "It just wouldn't work."

Walter turned his head slightly and gazed toward the horizon. Moved by his disappointment, Joanna yielded to an explanation she never thought she would offer.

"Walter, I'm not sure I can ever give Weldon free rein with the company. I have a serious problem there, and I don't know what to do about it. As the oldest, he's the logical choice to be given control eventually. But there are reasons I just can't."

Walter waited, his silence pushing her to continue. She searched for words.

"Weldon has an ambition—a basic ruthlessness—I don't like. It scares me. He talks constantly about money. I've seen this in him since he was small, and he hasn't changed. He's impulsive, erratic in his thinking. He'll have one thing on his mind one moment, something else the next. He has all kinds of wild ideas. If I allowed him to have his way, he'd have the company in a turmoil within a week."

Walter still waited. Joanna felt required to go on, now that she had started.

"For instance, several months ago he came to me with a scheme for a joint venture on the north slope of Alaska, way inside the Arctic Circle. It would have required a tremendous outlay, far more than we're equipped to handle. I told him that, and he became furious. He insisted that we could borrow the money, hock our reserves and equipment, something we've never done. Another time he wanted to close the refinery, sell off all our service stations, and expand our production to two or three times its present capacity. He even brought that one up at a board meeting. I had to get short with him, right in front of Ann Leigh and Arnold Campbell."

Walter rubbed his stomach. "He offer any logical thinking?"

"Oh, he had assembled a few figures on costs and profit. He doesn't seem to understand the need for balance. You see, Brod organized the company so we never have all our eggs in one basket. Doesn't that make sense to you?"

"I don't know enough about it to offer an opinion. But I do know Brod's business abilities were beyond question."

"I hope eventually Kelly will be a steadying influence on Weldon. I'm sure Kelly will be a better CEO than Weldon, but he needs experience in dealing with people. Under pressure, he tends to turn into himself, and keep his own counsel when he should be talking."

Joanna watched as a sailboat came into view, two miles or more out to sea. Slowly it tacked away from shore.

"So I guess I'm really waiting for Kelly to mature," she summed up. "He'll be elected to the board at the next meeting, and that may help him to get a feel for the company. He has enormous talent. Campbell has been full of praise for him. He said Kelly quickly grasped the system, and has an almost uncanny memory for detail. He said that even veteran employees are now coming to Kelly for help in locating obscure files. Deep down, I feel he should be in charge, not Weldon, when the time comes. I don't know exactly how I'll manage that. But until I can, I must be there, running things."

Walter spoke hesitantly. "I haven't been around Weldon enough to get to know him. I think he resents me, my relationship with you. I suppose it's natural. But I've never had that trouble with Kelly."

"Weldon has never forgiven me for sending him away to military school and keeping Kelly at home. A situation came up—he was about to be expelled from public school—and I really had no alternative. But I think our troubles date back even further. He was old enough that he felt deprived during Brod's illness. I suppose in some ways I did fail him."

"I doubt that. You had a difficult situation, one you certainly didn't create. I'm sure you did your best under the circumstances."

"All the same, I think he's still filled with the same hostility he had as a teenager, toward me, other people. That may be what I sense in him, what you sense in him."

Walter did not respond.

"And I wish Kelly would be more independent. He still listens to Weldon too much. He keeps coming to me with ideas I know he got from Weldon."

"Maybe they think alike."

"It's more than that. When they were small they always had their heads together. They lived in their own secret world. I thought that ended when they were separated. But now I have the uncanny feeling they're still doing it. I know they've spent a lot of time together since Kelly came home."

"They hadn't seen much of each other for a long time. It could be that they're just getting reacquainted. That's to be expected."

"I hope that's it. Still, I wish Kelly would take charge of his own life more, pay less attention to Weldon. And I wish Weldon had more of Kelly's stability, his plodding ways."

Walter poured wine and sat for a while in a meditative silence, watching the surf.

"Joanna, this really concerns me," he said after a time. "I keep hearing hints of some kind of lingering guilt you feel about the boys, over how they were raised. That's rubbish. You did a remarkable job with them. But I think that now you should face the fact that it's over. You can't go on mothering them, trying to make up real or imagined shortcomings. Their personalities are set. They have the right to live their own lives, make their own mistakes. I'd like to see you devote more attention to yourself, your own life. You should be enjoying yourself more."

It was a long speech for Walter. Joanna recognized and appreciated the emotions behind it. During the last few months he had renewed his campaign urging her toward marriage. She had continued to resist.

She understood that if they had met as strangers, no doubt they would be married by now, taking delight in each other. But their relationship was so complicated, entwined with a wealth of vivid, intimate memories involving two other loves.

Joanna felt they both still needed time. The past was still so much a part of their lives.

"Walter, I love you," she said. "Lord knows I do. I couldn't have survived without you. But I can't just walk away from my responsibilities. Not quite yet. The boys just aren't ready. I'm working toward that goal, but it'll take time. I hope you'll be patient with me."

For an answer, Walter silently reached out and squeezed her hand.

He finished his wine and lay back, the hat once again shading his eyes.

Gradually his breathing altered as he dozed. Joanna remained awake, relishing the peace of the hidden cove, watching over Walter as he slept.

Every time he talked of marriage, she felt pulled in opposite directions until it seemed she would be torn apart.

She truly wanted a life with him. But she could not bring herself to tell him some of the other reasons behind her resistance.

The company had become the base of her existence, the end result of her accomplishments.

How could she tell him that she had found an identity with the company she could not give up?

In her battle through the years, she had gained recognition not only from within the industry, but also from congressmen, senators, and high officials in government. They often called, seeking her views. This sense of identity had led to other immense satisfactions. The Van Cliburn competition, just ended, was an excellent example. From a standing start the competition had been established on a par with long-standing contests in Moscow, London, Luxembourg,

New York, and she had been a driving force in that success. Her power base at the company made her an influence in the arts, politics, and community affairs.

The company was her whole life. It demanded so much of her time and attention that she felt marriage would be unfair to him.

Moreover, she also kept hidden from him an even darker secret:

She doubted she ever again would find contentment, limited to the role of wife.

Chapter 32

Sleeping each night in his childhood room, listening to the spooky silences of the house, Kelly soon understood why Weldon had moved out and into his own apartment. Joanna was gone most of the time. If she was not at the office, or out of town, she was attending one of her innumerable committee or board meetings, or at dinner somewhere with Walter.

Tired of pretending his enthusiasm to be home again, Kelly abruptly moved out of the house one weekend, into the first decent apartment he could find. It was Spartan, but it matched his mood.

When he told Joanna the following Monday that he had moved, she nodded acknowledgment but made no comment. Kelly assumed that he had been limiting her freedom with Walter, and she was glad to see him go.

He plunged into work on the clandestine Annual Report. Within days it became an obsession, filling the vacuum left by Amy, his schoolwork.

He compartmentalized his efforts. Throughout each day he labored over the bona fide Annual Report at Spurlock Oil, assembling numerical data from the field and reducing them to the simple summations required by the format.

At night he took the same material home and expanded it, using the sheer weight of detail to demonstrate the breadth of company losses.

Lingering late at Spurlock Oil, until everyone else but the janitors had gone, he systematically gutted the files, tracing costs, profits, and losses to their source. Every two or three days Weldon returned from Houston or West Texas with more ammunition.

Soon Kelly's apartment was filled with pilfered material. In the cramped quarters, he could not gain quick access to information when needed.

Seeking more space, as well as privacy, he rented a three-room suite in an insurance building off Bailey Avenue, leased desks and office equipment, and hired a secretary. Within days he had the material organized, and the flow of information under control.

He fell into a routine as he worked into the summer months. Each evening he labored well past midnight assembling work for the secretary when she came in at nine. After a few hours of sleep, he began another day at Spurlock Oil, gathering what he needed. In the evening, he returned to work on the clandestine report.

When Weldon saw the hideaway office, he was both impressed and dismayed. The wealth of material set off their first heated argument. "What are we doing with all this shit?" Weldon demanded. "We couldn't get half of it into a good-sized book, much less a sixteen-page annual report. Let's stick to the basics. The refinery losses. The bleed-off in retail sales. All this other stuff will only confuse them."

"Weldon, half the wasted money is tucked away in routine operating expenses. Refinery and retail account for only a little more than half of it. We've got to pull these hidden costs out and put them back where they belong. That's the only way we can show a true picture, give accurate totals."

"That's too complicated. They'll shitcan it without even trying to understand it. All we need to do is show how the refinery and retail outlets are losing money. Simple figures."

"But they'd be wrong," Kelly insisted. "If we limit what we put into it, our report will be just as false as Mom's."

"Kelly, not everybody's a fucking genius. Nobody would understand it."

Kelly had given the format considerable thought. Already he could envision the completed product. He tried to explain.

"We'll boil it down, break it into two parts. First, a brief summation, like the regular Annual Report. Sixteen pages. That'll show the totals you want. Then we can put the rest into a long supplement."

"We can't hand them a fucking encyclopedia! Who's going to read all this crap you've put together?"

"Weldon, who do we *want* to read it? Who are we trying to sell? Not Mom. We'd never convince her, not with another ton of facts. Not Campbell. He's as set in his ways as Mom. Hell, he's probably the guy who started hiding these expenses, years ago. And we're sure not trying to convince ourselves. We're doing this whole job for one person— Grandmother."

"She sure as shit won't understand it."

"Probably not. But all we've got to do is arouse her curiosity, enough that she'll go get professional help. Who will she take it to?"

Weldon thought about it. "The chairman of the board at her bank, probably. He has handled her trusts for years. Maybe her investments man. Probably both."

"Right. But she won't go to them unless she thinks there's a good reason. So we hit her with the big losses in our report. It's keyed to the summary, with all the backup figures. She doesn't have to understand the supplement. All we want her to do is say to herself, 'Could this be true? Could Joanna be that wrong?' The supplement will be written for her consultants. It'll have the language in it they'll understand."

Weldon was not completely convinced. "Okay. We'll try it your way, and see how it looks."

He labored on through late summer, into the fall. Gradually the report and supplement took shape. But as the figures jelled, Kelly's qualms grew.

The report—the boiled-down information—was devastating. In its simplicity, it indicted almost every business practice Joanna had been following.

When the totals for the third quarter finally came in, Kelly immediately recognized the impact they would have on both reports.

In Joanna's rosy analysis, they would appear to be pure profit. But after Kelly factored in the costs, his report would show staggering losses, the worst yet.

For the third straight day Campbell had phoned in sick. It fell to Kelly to take a breakdown of the quarterly figures to Joanna in her office.

He placed them on her desk without comment. She scanned the numbers carefully, smiling with satisfaction.

"Production is *way* up. And the refinery doesn't look bad. If we could find some way to boost retail sales, we'd be doing well on all fronts."

Kelly felt he should make one last effort.

"Mom, those are skewed figures. I know it's the way you've been doing it for years. But if you analyze the costs, the only department showing profit is production. And when you bring them all together, the losses are quite serious."

She laughed. "You've been talking to Weldon again."

Kelly could hardly contain his anger. "Mom, I was head of my class in graduate school. I don't need Weldon to tell me what I see with my own eyes."

She gave him her blank look. "What losses are you talking about?"

"Refinery costs carried as operations. Retail expenses buried here and there in production. The whole bookkeeping system is riddled with places where this is charged off to that, hiding where the money is actually going, just to make certain totals look better. It gives a false picture."

Joanna was now more than irritated. "Are you saying we have someone in the company making off with money?"

"No. I'm just saying this is bad bookkeeping, so bad you can't see where the problems are."

"Kelly, this system was set up by your father. During the war he handled multibillion-dollar budgets for the government. I said billion, not million. Are you claiming you're smarter, that less that a year out of college you have a better way?"

He made an effort to control his anger, and to explain. "This system may have worked back then, when the operation was simpler. Back then, the costs were right on target. But along in the early fifties, ways were found to hide these expenses there, those costs somewhere else. The practice grew. Now it's completely out of hand. Once you put everything back where it belongs, the totals show a different picture entirely."

"Are you saying we're not making these profits?"

"The profit totals are accurate. But if the hidden losses were faced, and eliminated, the profits would be doubled, at least."

Now she was angry. He knew from the way her eyes snapped.

"Kelly, why do you and Weldon have to criticize all the time? Why can't you simply learn the way things are done, and accept the fact that there are people around here with far more experience? It may interest you to know that we've had our system audited, year after year, without a single negative report. What do you think about that?"

"I think you wasted your money. They did a piss-poor job."

"Kelly, I'd fire any employee who talked to me that way."

"Fire me if you want. But remember I'm not an employee, or a half-assed auditor who tells you what you want to hear. I'm a stockholder who wants this company to be the best it can be."

"That auditing firm is one of the best in the state."

"If you'll read their reports, as I have, they only say your figures are accurate. Nowhere do they say you have a decent bookkeeping system."

"I don't want to hear any more about it. Maybe after you've been here a year or two, you'll begin to understand the way things work."

Kelly rose. "Mom, I promise you this: If I'm still here a year from now, things *are* going to work."

Often when Kelly met a woman who impressed him with her beauty and charm, he would discover that within a few weeks he could not even remember her face. But with Chandra Sykes the pattern seemed to be reversed. As time passed he had only to close his eyes to see her elegant, aristocratic features, her calm, analytical gaze, and to hear her soft, melodious voice.

One evening he caught up on his work on the clandestine report. It was almost complete. Only a few more additions were needed from the refinery in Houston.

On impulse, Kelly picked up the phone and placed a person-to-person call to the Sykes residence in Tulsa. The operator left the circuit open. Kelly heard the brief conversation with Mrs. Sykes.

"Who did you say is calling?"

"Mr. Spurlock in Fort Worth."

"Which Mr. Spurlock? Could you tell me, please?"

"Mr. Kelly Spurlock."

"She's not here right now. Please tell Mr. Spurlock he may be able to reach her at her sorority house in Norman."

She supplied the number.

Kelly was puzzled. Weldon had said she was a college graduate. Nothing had been said about her still being enrolled at the University of Oklahoma.

When Chandra came on the line, her voice was cool and distant. Kelly quickly decided not to risk small talk.

"I thought I should call and tell you. Lily Pons will be singing *Lucia de Lammermoor* here week after next. If you could possibly come down Monday the twenty-sixth, I will wrangle tickets."

"Tell me, why should I come to Fort Worth to hear Lily

Pons, when I could go to New York or somewhere and hear her with a much more professional cast?"

Kelly thought he heard a teasing tone in her voice. But he was not sure.

"For one thing, Fort Worth's cleaner."

She laughed. He was encouraged enough to go on.

"Second, Fort Worth is closer. Just a hop, skip, and jump over the Arbuckles. Third, I will personally see to it that you dine most sumptuously."

"Sounds tempting."

"I've saved the pièce de résistance. Maestro Kruger always likes to offer surprises. This time it's a young Mexican tenor, singing his first major role in this country. His name is Placido Domingo. Everyone who has heard him says he's going places."

"That *is* tempting. A friend of mine heard him in Mexico. But I'm sorry. I really can't. I have several other commitments."

"I'm sorry too," Kelly said. "Perhaps some other time."

"Perhaps. Thank you for the invitation."

She hung up.

To hell with her, Kelly thought.

In the days that followed he tried to dismiss her from his mind, but failed. He kept seeing that delicately shaped face and almond eyes, framed by lustrous black hair. He kept hearing her haunting voice.

He felt frustrated. She had given him no encouragement. She did not seem the slightest bit interested in him.

Weldon's assessment of her might have been crude, but unfortunately it seemed to be right on target.

Campbell's illness persisted on into the winter. As Campbell's assistant, Kelly found his responsibilities increasing daily. In effect, he stepped into Campbell's shoes as general manager. Among his many duties was directing the compilation of the official Annual Report.

The fact was not lost on him that he was now in charge of the very material he was pilfering. None of the department heads or accountants working with him entertained the slightest suspicion that their numbers were being put to double use.

At times his reluctance to go through with the clandestine project became almost unmanageable.

He was fully aware what the effects would be on his mother. In his weaker moments, he was kept going only by his conviction that he was working for the good of the company, and that eventually she would understand.

In January all the numbers were assembled. At Spurlock Oil, the Annual Report went off to the printers. Kelly worked the clandestine report into its final shape.

Weldon flew in from Midland, looked over the result, and exploded.

"It's too fucking complicated! Maybe you understand it, but it'll be Greek to everyone else. The supplement is too long. Who's going to plow through all this crap to trace the losses back to their source?"

"It's keyed," Kelly said. "Anything you want to know about the report, you can look up in the supplement."

"The report is too confusing. It looks like a bunch of bullshit. Nobody's going to wade through it. You've got to make it more simple."

They argued through most of a night in their secluded offices. The next morning, Weldon flew to Houston.

That evening Kelly was working on the problem, trying to simplify the report, when he was struck by inspiration.

He wondered why he had not seen the solution before. He called Weldon.

"I've got it," he said. "We'll print in red ink all of the expenses that should be eliminated. It'll make the report and supplement a blueprint for restructuring the company."

Weldon was dubious. "Can you do that?"

"It'll take a hell of a lot of work. But it'll knock their eyes out. Nobody, not even Mom, could miss the point."

"We're running out of time," Weldon pointed out. "You can't fuck around with it."

"I know," Kelly said. "I'll get right on it."

Through the next five days he worked almost around the clock, ferreting out the numbers to be printed in red.

At last the clandestine report and supplement were sent off to the printer.

When the proofs arrived, he called Weldon. They met at their hideaway suite. Weldon sat down at a desk and turned through the report. Most of the pages were almost solid red ink. He was grinning.

"Wait'll Grandma sees this," he said. "I think you've done it, Little Brother."

Kelly was indeed pleased with the results. Joanna had selected the artwork and type for the bona fide report, and Kelly thought it lacked flair. For the clandestine report and supplement, he had chosen bolder typefaces, a more striking design.

Weldon read all the way through the pages. When he finished, he reached into his briefcase and pulled out a bottle of bourbon to celebrate.

"We're ready," he said. "Hot damn! I can't wait to toss this onto that conference table, right in front of Mom. I can promise you one thing, Little Brother: All hell is about to break loose at Spurlock Oil."

Chapter 33

"The first item on today's agenda is the resignation of Mr. Van Laningham," Joanna said, glancing to make certain Bonnie was recording her words in shorthand. "You all have a copy of his letter, tendering his resignation for reasons of health. Do I hear a motion?"

"I move that Mr. Van Laningham's resignation be accepted," Weldon said, grinning at Kelly.

With some irritation, Joanna saw a look of private humor pass between them. She made a mental note to warn them she expected professional conduct at future board meetings.

"Mr. Van Laningham was unable to be with us today," Joanna went on. "I have drafted a letter to him from the board, expressing our gratitude for his many years of service. Bonnie, will you please read the letter?"

While Bonnie droned away, Joanna indeed sensed that something was wrong. Kelly kept shifting in his seat and would not meet her eye. Weldon definitely was sharing some private joke with him.

"Do I hear a motion?" Joanna said when Bonnie had finished.

The letter also was approved. Joanna was relieved that

Van Laningham was finally off the board. She had not seen him in two years.

"Since this leaves a vacancy on the board, the chair will now entertain nominations."

"Joanna, please allow me," Ann Leigh said. "I proudly nominate my grandson, Kelly Spurlock, to fill the vacant membership on the board."

"Second," Weldon said.

"Do I hear any other nominations?"

She waited through a respectable silence. "No further nominations being received, we will now vote on election of Kelly Spurlock to the board of Spurlock Oil. All in favor say aye."

Campbell, Ann Leigh, and Weldon smiled at Kelly as they responded.

"Opposed nay. Election carried."

The board rose and welcomed Kelly to its ranks. Ann Leigh circled the table to kiss her grandson.

Again Joanna felt a twinge of apprehension. Kelly seemed more embarrassed than happy with the attention.

"We now will take up the other items on today's agenda," she went on. "We have a bloc of leases expiring in Scurry County. Although we have yet to drill in that area, I recommend strongly that we renew."

She cited seismographic reports and other data suggesting that the bloc merited exploration. Her recommendation was routinely approved.

She moved on through the short agenda, mostly routine. When she finished with the last item, she signaled for Bonnie to distribute the Annual Report.

She paused while the board members glanced through the pages.

"Due to Mr. Campbell's illness, most of the report was assembled by our newest member," Joanna said, mostly for Ann Leigh's benefit. "In consideration of his inexperience, I sent the final draft to an accounting firm for a professional opinion. I'm happy to report they were unable to find a single mistake, and that they said Kelly's summations were superb."

She smiled at Kelly, conveying her pride. Again he looked away. She hesitated, seeking clues to his odd behavior. Seeing none, she went on with her presentation.

"I'm gratified to point out that profits were up considerably throughout last year. About fourteen percent. With several new producers going on line, this year should be even better."

She plowed on through the report, commenting on the most significant figures. The members of the board followed her analysis, turning the pages on cue.

Joanna glanced at her watch as she finished her presentation. She was scheduled to attend an Arts Council meeting within the hour, and the timing was close.

"Does anyone wish to discuss the report?"

Weldon glanced at Kelly and leaned forward in his chair. "As a conscientious member of the board, I believe it behooves me to mention the astronomical losses in the operation of our refinery, and the rapidly dwindling revenues from our retail outlets. I have certain recommendations to lay before the board, calling for a complete restructuring of the company to stop these losses, and to double our profits."

It was almost a repetition of what he had pulled during the last board meeting. Furious, Joanna signaled for Bonnie to stop taking notes.

"Weldon, there's no need to bring that up again."

"But there is, Mom," Weldon said. "We have new data to be considered. So this is new business, not old."

Kelly spoke for the first time in his new role as a member of the board. "Mom, I think you should listen to Weldon."

Joanna stared at him. She had known he was impressed with Weldon's ideas. But she hardly expected him to back Weldon on this in a board meeting.

Kelly met her stare without flinching. "I also strongly believe the company needs drastic restructuring to cut expenses that are bleeding it white. Mom, I've tried twice to talk to you about this. I told you it was serious. You wouldn't listen."

Ann Leigh and Campbell sat frozen, mystified by the turn of events. Beyond her anger, Joanna was embarrassed that the growing rift with her sons had been made so obvious.

"This is neither the time nor place to discuss this," she said.

"I don't know of a better time or place," Weldon said. He reached into a bulky briefcase and placed a stack of printed material on the table. "Just to give you an idea of what we're talking about, Kelly and I have put together an analysis of the company's excessive operating costs. For simplification, we've adopted the format of the regular Annual Report. As you'll see, our study parallels it all the way through. But unnecessary expenditures—costs that could be eliminated— are indicated in red. You'll also see that with restructuring, the profits of this company through the last year could have been more than doubled."

He handed each board member a booklet slightly larger than the Annual Report.

Joanna picked it up with trembling hands. It was professionally done. The cover was bold and authoritative, precisely the effect she had sought for years to achieve. She opened the cover and glanced through the first few pages.

The text was filled with red ink.

"Weldon, you're out of order," she scolded. "Nothing like this should be presented to the board until it has been reviewed by qualified financial consultants."

"Mom, none of my professors ever called me an idiot. And let's not forget that the newest member of our board would be greeted with open arms by any financial consulting group in the state. He spent hundreds of hours on this. What he has done would cost a bundle from any consulting firm. You're getting it free. I helped. He and I did the work in our off-hours, and paid for the printing out of our own pockets."

Unbidden, Bonnie had resumed recording the meeting. Joanna was too distraught to stop her.

She was slowly realizing the depth of the conspiracy between her sons. Clearly they had been plotting this for months.

"We also published a supplement, keyed to the totals in the report," Weldon said. "The supplement gives you the complete background on each figure, explaining exactly how it was derived."

He distributed another booklet to the board. It was in the same style as the bogus report, but much thicker.

Joanna thumbed through the supplement. Nothing in it made immediate sense.

"At the back of the report, on page sixteen, we offer a summary of our conclusions, and our recommendation for a plan of restructuring," Weldon went on. "As you will note from the figures, if all the excessive expenditures are eliminated, net profits indeed would be doubled."

"Weldon, I can't make heads or tails of this," Ann Leigh complained. "If all this red ink is unnecessary expenses, why are we spending that money?"

"That's our point, Grandmother," Kelly said. "We *shouldn't* be spending it. Basically, we recommend closing the refinery, and selling the retail outlets. Most of those expenses you see in red ink are hidden away, written off to operations or production. Weldon and I have dug them out. It's money we're losing every day, week in, week out."

"I don't know what to think," Ann Leigh said. "Mr. Campbell, do you have anything to say about all this?"

Campbell's lengthy illness had left him pale. He had grown even more pallid throughout the meeting.

"Mrs. Spurlock, I would have to study it at length," he said. "I'm as surprised as you. Our bookkeeping system was established years ago by your son Brod. Perhaps we've improvised here and there, through the years, but we've never been called into question."

Joanna felt the interruption had gone on long enough. She shoved the booklets away from her.

"Weldon, I see nothing here that is new," she said. "This proposal is the same one you made last spring. It was rejected. What you boys don't understand is that your father set this company up in a certain way. You don't just come along and destroy proven operating procedures overnight."

"Mom, conditions have changed since Dad died," Kelly said. "And the company hasn't changed with them."

"Kelly, you've just gotten a little too big for your britches," she shot back.

He gave her a blank stare and did not answer.

Ann Leigh had been reading the red-ink report and ignoring the exchange. She looked up.

"Joanna, if the boys are even halfway right about this, maybe we should look into it."

Her words, completely unexpected, raised a familiar warning flag. Joanna remembered that Ann Leigh had been strongly opposed when she had assumed the presidency of the company after Brod died. In all the years since, Ann Leigh had talked often of how she felt the company really belonged to the boys. It had occurred to Joanna that Ann Leigh, the majority stockholder, seemed increasingly eager to turn the company over to them.

Joanna felt cornered. She wanted to end the meeting, get away, reassess her stand, decide what to do. She picked up the bogus report and flipped through the columns of figures and long paragraphs of explanation.

"Weldon, I'm scheduled to be at another meeting in twenty minutes. We can't possibly absorb all this now."

"Of course not," Weldon said. "I propose we call a recess for at least two or three days, maybe a week, and give everyone time to study it. Then we can discuss it."

"I think that's a fine idea," Ann Leigh said.

Joanna was momentarily relieved to escape further argument. "Very well. Would a week from today be satisfactory with everyone?"

She monitored the silent nods around the table.

"Then we stand recessed until next Monday."

Gathering her stack of papers, she started for the door. Kelly, already on his feet, turned to say something to her.

But she did not want to talk with him or anyone. She strode past him without a glance.

That evening, after a difficult meeting of the Arts Council, she spent more than two hours studying the bogus report. Although she painstakingly followed the keys from report to supplement, she could find no substantiation for the outrageous statements made in the summation.

The red-ink totals seemed fictitious. Opening her own Annual Report, she attempted to correlate the figures. Nothing seemed to match. In her Annual Report, everything was neat and tidy. The red-ink report had losses everywhere.

On her urging, Walter came over to examine Kelly's work. Walter went slowly through it, constantly checking the figures against Joanna's routine Annual Report.

While he worked, she had time to think, and her anger grew. She could see that the boys had violated every trust she had placed in them. They had acted as thieves in the night, robbing the company of facts and figures for their own purpose.

At last Walter put the reports aside. He scribbled on a pad, adding and subtracting figures.

"Understand, this is far out of my field," he said. "But it seems a highly professional piece of work. There's no way I can check all the numbers. But those I have been able to trace match those in your own Annual Report."

"They've been stealing material from the report all along," she told him. "Kelly was in charge of it, so he had full access. As soon as he received the figures, they traced them back to the origins in the field, to show how they were derived."

Joanna thought of all the safeguards she had imposed against unauthorized access to confidential company material.

Unwittingly, she had turned the foxes into the henhouse.

"I badly misjudged their maturity," she said. "I must get them off the board. How in the world will I do that?"

Walter ducked the question. "Joanna, I'm only an attorney, not a parent. This is plainly a family affair."

With a week to prepare, Joanna carefully planned her counterattack. She was determined not be put on the defensive. And she certainly would not condone the dismemberment of the company.

When the board again met the following Monday, she did not waste time with preliminaries. She gave each of her sons her most withering glare.

"First, I want to say that I consider what you two have done contemptible beyond words. You have violated my confidence in you, trespassed in areas where you had no business being, all behind my back. I'm ashamed of you. Kelly, what you've done is unforgivable. In Mr. Campbell's absence, you were in charge of the Annual Report. You took that information and put it to unauthorized use. What do you have to say for yourself?"

Kelly spoke calmly. "Mom, I had two choices. I could go on doing the work of a junior accountant, ignoring the bad business practices around me, or I could team up with Weldon, and demonstrate once and for all how this company should be operating."

"So you chose to oppose me."

"I'm not opposing you. It's for the good of the company. You'll benefit from this, along with everyone else."

"I see. You're so smart you know more than your father, Mr. Campbell, everyone."

"I only see that Dad's plan is outdated. It became invalid when the interstate system left our service stations in the backwater, when automated refineries came along, reducing costs for our competitors. Can't you see that?"

Joanna felt on the verge of losing all self-control. "Kelly, I'll not sit and hear you criticize your father."

"If Dad were alive today, he'd be the first to accept our restructuring plan."

"I've studied your so-called report," Joanna said. "I've given it a great deal of thought. I see nothing in it that merits further discussion."

"Joanna, I don't think we should dismiss the boys' proposal so lightly," Ann Leigh said.

Joanna thought she saw Weldon and Kelly exchange a knowing glance. For a moment, she wondered if Ann Leigh was a part of the conspiracy.

"I'll admit I couldn't make heads or tails of it," Ann Leigh went on. "But all that red ink convinced me something *might* be wrong. That summation says we're realizing less than half the profits we should be making. That upset me. So I took it to the man who handles my trusts at the bank. And I must say, he was impressed. He just kept going on, saying what a thorough study it was. He said if those figures are accurate, the company should consider restructuring."

"The figures are accurate," Weldon said.

"Mom, we're only asking that you look into it further," Kelly said. "If you don't trust our work, hire an outside firm."

Joanna turned to Campbell, who had remained silent throughout the discussion. "Mr. Campbell, what are your feelings on it?"

He glanced at Ann Leigh. "I disagree with some of the terminology. I wouldn't call those expenses hidden. I'll admit that handling some of them that way was a matter of convenience, a practice that grew with time. But we always knew where they were. As far as the restructuring is concerned, that's for the board to decide. It's more a matter of business philosophy than operational procedure."

"Boys, I won't be bullied. The refinery, the retail outlets are essential to the company. I won't be a party to selling or dismembering them."

"Or even consider it?" Weldon asked.

"I've already considered it. And if the board insists on opposing me, I'll resign before I'll see it happen."

"Oh, Joanna!" Ann Leigh said.

Joanna felt close to tears. "I mean what I say!"

Weldon leaned forward over the table. Even in her anger, Joanna was impressed with his deliberate demeanor, his total self-control.

"May I remind everyone that we're here as board mem-

bers, not as a family. And as board members, we have strong
evidence of an ailing company that badly needs fixing. Kelly
and I don't claim to be infallible. In acknowledgment of that,
I formally move that we hire an outside firm to examine our
analysis and proposal."

"I second the motion," Kelly said.

Joanna felt numb. "Boys, I'm warning you."

Weldon looked at her calmly. "I believe we have a motion
before the board. Is the chair going to act?"

Joanna saw no way out of a vote. "All of you heard the
motion. Ann Leigh?"

"Joanna, I'm sorry. But I really think we should do this."

"I vote yes," Weldon said.

"I vote no," Campbell said. "The company has operated
profitably all the years I've been here. I see no reason for
change."

Kelly was as pale as Campbell. "Mom, nobody wants you
to leave. This is for the good of the company. Please understand that."

She ignored his appeal. "Kelly, how do you vote?"

"For."

"Then you hereby have my resignation," she told them.
"You can do whatever you see fit. I wash my hands of it."

"Joanna, don't be that way," Ann Leigh said. "Please reconsider."

Joanna rose and walked out of the room, out of the building.

She did not start crying until she was on the West Freeway, en route home.

"Are we still in a meeting?" Bonnie asked.

"Good question," Weldon said. "We haven't been adjourned. We still have a quorum. We should decide what to
do about this situation. I say we're still functioning as a
board. Anyone have any problem with that?"

Kelly was too emotionally spent to answer. He could not
forget the look on his mother's face as she left the room.

"I want to say something at this point," Ann Leigh said.

She glanced at Bonnie. "I don't believe this needs to be a part of the record." She looked at Weldon and Kelly. "What you boys have recommended may be right. I don't know yet. But surely there was a better way to go about it. You've hurt your mother terribly."

"Grandmother, she's blind on the subject," Kelly said. "You saw that here today. Even faced with the facts in plain print, she wouldn't consider them. It's been that way ever since we've been home."

"Maybe so. But she has worked night and day for years so the company would be here when you boys got back. And this is the thanks she gets. I want you boys to apologize for what you've done to her."

"I'm not apologizing for anything," Weldon said. "She should have recognized how hard Kelly and I worked on this, even if she's incapable of understanding its value. As far as I'm concerned, she owes *us* an apology."

Kelly felt that as yet none of the board members had absorbed the fact that Joanna had resigned.

"What about the company?" he asked. "There'll be decisions to be made. And at the moment we have no president and chief executive officer."

"Joanna will be back," Ann Leigh said. "I'll talk to her. She's just upset right now."

Kelly had seen her anger. He knew the depths of her obstinacy. "She won't be back," he said.

"I don't think so either," Weldon said. "At least not for a while. Kelly's right. Company operations won't come to a screeching halt just because the board has had a tiff."

"I believe we should wait a while before we do anything," Ann Leigh insisted.

"Grandmother, we have a dozen rigs in operation," Kelly said. "There will be crises that can't be postponed. Maybe we should name someone temporarily."

"I can understand that," Ann Leigh said. "Mr. Campbell, I know you've been ill . . ."

Campbell held up a hand, palm outward. "Mrs. Spurlock,

under the circumstances, and in view of my condition, I don't think I should be considered."

"All right. Understand, I wish Joanna hadn't left. But she has. If we do anything at all, maybe we should name Weldon temporary president and temporary board chairman. He's oldest. He's been here longer."

"I second the motion," Kelly said.

Campbell nodded assent, making Weldon's appointment unanimous.

With dramatic slowness, Weldon rose and walked to the end of the table and took his mother's chair.

It was a gesture so decisive, so significant, that it seemed to give pause to everyone in the room.

Kelly knew that if he had been named, he would have conducted the remainder of the meeting from where he was sitting. He also knew it was this instinctive flair for drama that gave Weldon his knack for handling people.

Weldon glanced at Bonnie. "At this point, I think we should define our circumstances for the record. In a sense, we constitute a new board. Please take this statement."

As Weldon dictated a summation of events, named the board members present, and described the actions just taken, Kelly ceased listening, plagued by a fresh rash of doubt.

Weldon's performance was entirely too studied to be spontaneous. Kelly's growing impression that the board was playing into Weldon's hands troubled him deeply.

He wondered if he himself had been manipulated by Weldon all along, and conned into assembling the bogus report. Weldon might even have foreseen from the start that their mother would resign before she would knuckle under.

It was a disturbing thought.

Weldon reached the end of his statement and paused.

"In case anyone has forgotten, the original purpose of this meeting today was to make a decision on whether to go forward with the restructuring plan."

"Weldon, after all that's happened, I think it's entirely too early to vote on that," Ann Leigh said.

"Grandmother, we're losing thousands of dollars every day," Weldon said.

"That may be. But I won't be railroaded on this. I believe we should give it a great deal more thought before we do anything."

"Kelly and I couldn't agree more," Weldon said. "As I said earlier, while we have every confidence in our plan, we feel we should seek the opinion of people more qualified. I've made informal inquiries with three financial consulting firms. None comes cheap. But they're the best in the game. We could hire one to come in and study our operations from top to bottom, and to advise us on the feasibility of our plan. The delay would be brief—only a few weeks—and the expense tax deductible."

He distributed a typewritten list of cost estimates.

Kelly recognized the firms. They were indeed the best in the business. He wondered when Weldon had found the time to talk with them.

"The New York outfit is probably best on finances," Weldon went on. "But the Austin firm has had far more experience in the oil game. They might find something the other people would miss. Since the estimates are not far apart, I recommend we go with the Austin company."

"Well, maybe this *is* a good idea," Ann Leigh said. "It would have to be done eventually anyway."

"Kelly?"

"Fine with me," he said.

"Mr. Campbell?"

Again Campbell silently nodded assent.

"Then the board unanimously agrees to retain Peregrine Financial Consultants of Austin to examine Spurlock operations, and to make recommendations on the proposed restructuring plan."

He paused while Bonnie's pen scratched, then glanced around the table. "I believe that's everything. Anyone have anything else?"

Kelly was still remembering the expression on his mother's face when she stalked out of the meeting.

"I move that the board send flowers to the absent chairman," he said. "Along with a letter urging her to reconsider her announced intention to resign."

"I second the motion," Ann Leigh said.

Weldon hesitated only briefly. "I doubt it'll affect her decision. But I agree it'd be a nice gesture."

The motion carried.

"Do I hear for adjournment?"

"I so move," Kelly said.

"All in favor? Motion carried." Weldon gave Kelly a big grin. "I think we can call this a fair day's work, and a new start for the company. We stand adjourned."

Chapter 34

Kelly was totally unprepared for the attention newspapers and television devoted to the Spurlock board meeting. Apparently the story of two young, hotshot sons ousting their mother from the presidency of a multimillion-dollar oil company proved irresistible. Texas newspapers gave it page-one attention. *The New York Times* devoted half a column to it on the business pages. Kelly received several phone calls at his apartment from news writers. He declined to talk to them.

Obviously someone had not been so discreet. Much of the information in the newspapers clearly came from within the board room. Too many details could have come from nowhere else.

Kelly was certain that Joanna would not have talked with reporters. Nor would Ann Leigh, Bonnie, or Campbell.

That left Weldon.

In *The New York Times,* an unnamed "well-informed source" was quoted as saying the two Spurlock brothers wanted "to take the company in a new direction," and that the plan was "fiercely opposed" by their mother.

When Kelly entered the Spurlock offices the following

day, he sensed a new atmosphere. Employees spoke to him, but they seemed cautious, guarded.

He walked down the hall past the executive suites to the president's office. In the reception area, Bonnie was cleaning out her desk. She would not look at him. Kelly walked on into his mother's office. Weldon was ensconced behind the desk, leaning back in the chair, talking on the phone.

From the conversation, Kelly gathered he was talking with a news writer. Newspapers were spread across the desk.

"Hell no, I won't tell you our secret plan," Weldon said. "If I told you, then it wouldn't be secret, would it?"

He laughed, winked at Kelly, and listened for a time.

"All right, I'll give you something you can use," he said. "Please quote me accurately. I'm sorry my mother reacted as she did. Understand, it was only a business disagreement, nothing personal. My brother and I hope she'll reconsider, and return to the presidency. If she doesn't, she's still a stockholder, a member of the board, and a strong voice in the company. But the rest of the board has given my brother and me support to move forward with our project. Got that?"

Again he listened for an interval. "That's all I have to say about it," he said. "Thank you for calling."

He hung up the phone. "Fourth one this morning."

Kelly gestured to the newspapers. "Weldon, I feel shitty enough without all this. Why did you talk to them?"

"Hell, they would have got the story anyway. They might as well get it right. What's wrong? You having second thoughts?"

"Not about the plan. But I'm worried about Mom. I tried to call her. She won't come to the phone. I called Walter. He said she won't talk to him, either."

Weldon lit a cigar. "She'll get over it."

Kelly kept remembering the expression on her face when she left the conference room. She would not "get over it" soon, if ever.

"Is Bonnie quitting?" he asked.

Weldon shrugged. "I don't know. She was throwing things into boxes when I came in this morning. She hasn't said a word to me, and I haven't had time to worry about it."

The phone buzzed. As Weldon picked it up, Kelly walked out to Bonnie's desk. She was cleaning out the middle drawer of her desk.

"Bonnie, you don't have to leave," he said. "Nothing has changed. Weldon and I want you to stay."

She turned to face him, her dark eyes blazing. "What do you mean, nothing has changed? Everything has changed. I don't want to spend a single day in the same building with you two ungrateful little turds."

Despite his concern, Kelly had to suppress a smile. Never before had he heard Bonnie use such language. "Bonnie, your loyalty is misguided. Mom may change her mind. She may be back."

"No, she won't. You two have broken her heart."

Bonnie began to cry.

"It isn't like that at all," Kelly said. "Weldon and I didn't want to oppose her. But it was the only way. I'm sure she'll see that eventually."

Bonnie reached for a tissue and dabbed her eyes. "I don't suppose you've noticed the pride she's taken in running this company all these years. I should have whipped you and Weldon good when I had a chance. You may not remember, but I used to baby-sit you when you were real small."

"I remember," Kelly said.

"Your mother took over this company when there was no one else. It was a man's world here then, and they bucked her at every turn. But she hung in there and won their respect. I don't suppose you know anything about that, do you?"

"Some," Kelly said.

"She didn't want to put her life into this oil company. But she did. For you! And this is the thanks she gets. Now you two little squirts come along and tell her she's been doing a shitty job all along. How do you think that makes her feel?"

Kelly knew he did not owe Bonnie an explanation. But he

remembered the times she had served as his surrogate mother.

"Bonnie, please understand. The family—Weldon, Mother, myself—has an obligation to employees, consumers, everyone who depends on Spurlock Oil. Sure, we've been turning a profit. But these are good times. And that profit is eroding every day. What's going to happen when hard times hit? We should be keeping the company healthy so it can weather any storm."

"I'm not saying you're wrong about the company. But you didn't have to hurt her like that. She would have turned the company over to you before long anyway."

"No, I don't think so. Weldon and I would've been thirty-five or forty before Mom ever saw us as grown."

"As far as I'm concerned you still have a lot of growing up to do."

Kelly felt he should make a gesture. "Bonnie, if you really want to leave, we'll make special arrangements. I don't know what provisions the company has for early retirement, but I know that for years you put in many hours above and beyond what anyone could have expected. No one could complain if we add some kind of bonus. I promise we'll do right by you. But I hope you'll reconsider and stay."

Bonnie looked around her office, as if memorizing every detail. "No, I don't think I will. I have grandchildren I want to enjoy before it's too late. I've seen Weldon in operation enough to know that the changes around here have only started. I don't want to see any more of them."

Joanna had left word downstairs that she was not to be disturbed under any circumstances. But Walter merely brushed past. No one had the temerity to stop him.

When he knocked on her door, Joanna was lying on the daybed in rumpled pajamas. She kept him waiting while she washed her face, slipped into a robe, and combed the worst tangles from her hair. In the mirror she saw that her eyes were bloodshot, but she could do nothing about that. She went back to the daybed before giving him permission to enter. He came straight to her and held her hands for a time before saying anything.

"Everyone's been concerned about you. Kelly called me twice. Ann Leigh wants to talk to you. There are a lot of messages downstairs."

"I don't want to talk to anyone yet. Have you seen the papers?"

He nodded.

"It's so humiliating! I wonder what Ann Leigh thinks. She always hated public attention so. Now here's some she helped create."

"Calla Lily said you haven't eaten. Joanna, you must eat."

"I don't want anything."

"Nonsense. I'll bring you up a tray. You'll feel better with something inside you."

While he was gone, she showered and changed into a housedress. Although she really had not wanted food, the aroma of the tray he brought was enticing. She drank the orange juice and coffee, and nibbled some of the eggs and toast.

Walter waited until she had finished. He put the tray aside.

"Now. I think we should talk. I said from the first I would stay out of this. But it's taking too much of a toll on you. I'm going to stick my nose in."

"Walter, I really don't think you should. This doesn't have a thing to do with you and me."

He answered obliquely, a habit she sometimes found annoying. "I saw the flowers the board sent. I didn't read the letter attached to them. But I know the contents. They want you back."

"No! Whatever else, I won't go back."

"Let's look at this objectively. Your ego has been hurt because you were opposed, defeated, in a business decision. That's all. It happens to business executives every day. You shouldn't take it so personally."

She had to fight back her temper. "Walter! Don't try to play amateur psychologist with me!"

He raised a hand defensively. "Please, hear me out. You've

been the Boss Lady down there for twelve years. This is the first time you've ever been challenged by your board. You should take it in stride. It's part of the game."

"But Walter, what they're doing is wrong. It'll ruin the company. I know it will."

Again Walter help up a hand. "Just for the sake of argument, let's consider that you might be wrong. The rest of the board certainly thinks you are. But Kelly says they're willing to explore it, talk about it."

"Do you think I'm wrong?"

"I don't know. But I must admit Kelly's analysis made a lot of sense. I think there's a possibility that you're wrong."

"Even if I am, they rode right over me!"

"Let's consider something else. Your ego isn't the only one involved. Think what it took for the boys—especially Kelly —to oppose you."

"Kelly's the worst of the two. I've never been so disappointed in anyone. Walter, I've thought a lot about this during the last three days. Weldon is impulsive. There's a cruel streak to him. I've always known that. You can never put any trust in what he might do, or not do. Ann Leigh is flighty. She can be led. But Kelly! I never thought he would do this to me!"

"He's hurt as much are you are. He adores you. He always has. I used to see it in his eyes back when the three of us went to concerts together."

"Then why did he do it?"

"Let's examine the situation from his perspective. Ever since he was knee-high, you've held him up as the whiz kid. He responded, did all you expected of him, and more. But when he came home from college, you stuck him away like some hothouse plant. He's dying to use his brains, his talent, all he's learned. He also wants to prove himself to *you.*"

"Did he tell you all this?"

"No. But I've seen it in him."

"Well, that isn't true. I told him from the first I had confidence in him. I confided to him that within two or three years, he probably would have Campbell's title."

Walter smiled. "Joanna, in two or three years, many of his classmates will be heads of companies larger than Spurlock Oil."

"He's part owner. In time, he'll own almost half of it."

"All the more reason he should be groomed, tested with responsibilities now. He has the capabilities. That analysis he did would have been a major undertaking for a firm with a large staff to do the crut work."

"Still, he's inexperienced on practical matters."

"He knows that. After you left, the board agreed to hire a consulting firm to examine Kelly's work. Kelly was in favor of it."

She could not curb her curiosity. "What else did they do?"

"Kelly isn't much of a talker, but he stressed that Weldon's appointment is only temporary. Some of the newspapers had it wrong. I gathered from what he said that the remainder of the board meeting was amicable, and that all hope you will return."

"Walter, it looks like they're pushing Kelly's plan through. I won't go back and preside over the dismantling of the company. I won't!"

"Then there's this: Ann Leigh said that if you won't come back as president, then she'll resign as chairman of the board in your favor. She said she has already talked to Kelly and Weldon, and they've agreed."

"That's always been more or less an honorary position."

"It doesn't have to be. Kelly and Weldon need a voice of experience. No one knows more about day-to-day operations than you. They know that. The way I see it, this could turn into an ideal situation, with Kelly and Weldon doing the detailed work, you directing the overall operation."

"You don't know Weldon. He won't take direction from anyone. And now I'm not so sure about Kelly."

"Still, you would be a leveling influence on them. And chairman of the board could be considered a promotion." He pointed to the newspapers at the foot of the daybed. "It might put those stories to rest."

Despite her resistance at the moment to anything concerning Spurlock Oil, Joanna was tempted. What Walter said was true: As chairman of the board, she could turn the position into one of power. Ann Leigh would continue to listen to her, as would Campbell. Maybe even Kelly. No matter what Weldon wanted to do, she might still control company policy.

It would not be easy. She was sure that if she accepted, many battles lay ahead.

"You would be free to devote more time to the arts," Walter went on. "I've always suspected you find that work more enjoyable. You would have more time for yourself, something you've long needed. And you could continue being the Boss Lady."

"That's the second time you've called me that," Joanna said. "I don't think I like that. It makes me sound so cold."

"Some people have the impression you are—even people who are around you a lot. You keep your emotions so guarded. But, of course, I know different. I remember the way you responded to Peggy. I've never seen such compassion in anyone for a comparative stranger."

"The Boss Lady," Joanna said again, testing the words on her tongue. "Walter, I don't like that at all."

Walter laughed. "Really, it's one of your more endearing traits—your supreme self-confidence, your vitality, your command of every situation."

"No one ever told me that."

"The reason you're taking this so hard is because you're not used to being crossed. I've always known that about you. From the first you've insisted that our relationship conform to your terms. I've gone along. Maybe I shouldn't have. But it was too nice an arrangement to protest. Now, with all this, the situation has changed. It's foolish for us to rattle around in two houses, maintaining two households. Joanna, let's get married."

Joanna did not answer immediately.

Her life had changed too drastically in only a few days.

She needed more time to become accustomed to it.

Chapter 35

Peregrine Financial Consultants completed their study in just over two months and their report was delivered three weeks later. Almost every phase of Kelly's plan received high praise. Quibbling was reserved to a few minor points where Kelly himself had larded his suggestions with qualifying phrases.

The board again met briefly in special session. Although there were no surprises, it seemed to Kelly that every member was fully aware of the significance of the board's actions. From the first, Joanna was cool to everyone, but offered no strong opposition.

The session moved so rapidly that Weldon's new private secretary had difficulty keeping pace.

Ann Leigh tendered her resignation as chairman and Joanna was elected to fill the post.

Weldon's appointment as president and CEO of the company was made permanent.

Citing his failing health, Campbell resigned from the company, but retained his seat on the board.

Kelly was named vice-president and general manager.

The report of Peregrine Financial Consultants was approved, and the question of restructuring was placed before the board.

"Ann Leigh, I suppose you haven't changed your mind," Joanna said before the vote.

Kelly had feared that his grandmother might waver, but she gripped her purse and held firm.

"Joanna, I've asked everyone I can think of for advice. They all say the same thing. Weldon and Kelly's plan will double our net profits, and put us in a much stronger position. There's no way I can vote against it."

"Then I'll say no more about it," Joanna said. "But I think that someday we'll regret this."

With Joanna and Campbell opposing, the restructuring was approved.

The only question left was when the restructuring would be put into operation.

"We're losing money every day," Weldon said. "Now that the plan has been approved, I say the quicker we put it to work, the better."

No one offered argument.

The session was adjourned.

Kelly attempted to intercept his mother.

Again she walked out of the conference room without looking at him.

Since the restructuring required action on two fronts, Kelly and Weldon split the work. Weldon began negotiations to sell the retail outlets. Kelly agreed to dispose of the refinery.

He flew his Cessna to Houston early on a morning in late June. The flight was pleasant until he was well past Austin. An inversion had hung over the coastal area for several days and the air around Houston was hazy yellow and heavily laden with chemical odors. The day was hot and humid. As Kelly landed, the sun was only a dark red disk, hardly visible above the man-made atmosphere.

After renting a car, he checked in at the Shamrock. He

then drove to the refinery east of town, across the Ship Channel, in an area crowded with petroleum plants.

He had phoned Superintendent Ramsey Peck that he would be visiting, but he had given him no inkling of the reason.

When Kelly arrived at the plant, the superintendent was seated in his office, built into the corner of a warehouse and workshed. He rose, shook hands, and motioned Kelly into a chair. He was a huge man, several inches over six feet, with a large paunch and massive jowls.

Kelly did not waste time. "Mr. Peck, there's no way to soften what I'm about to tell you. The board of Spurlock Oil has decided to close this refinery. All personnel will be taken care of—reassigned, given early retirement, paid off, whatever. Details will be worked out on an individual-case basis."

Peck sat and stared at Kelly as his ruddy face acquired a gray sheen.

"The board decided? But why? Our processing was up last quarter."

Somewhere outside the office a jackhammer started up. Peck did not appear to notice.

"It's simple economics," Kelly said, raising his voice over the noise. "The land beneath this plant is worth more than the machinery. You more than anyone should know how expensive it is to maintain and operate."

"But I don't understand this. We've already cut back to the bone. Mrs. Spurlock insisted last year we trim the work force by ten percent. We've done everything she asked."

"Mr. Peck, I'm not here to debate. The decision has been made. You and I will carry it out. Today you can shut down the plant and inform the personnel. If you'll have all the workers assembled here at ten tomorrow morning, I'll address them, reassure them that they'll be taken care of."

Peck had not yet grasped the full significance of the closing. He shook his head.

"They can't all be here at the same time, Mr. Spurlock. A crew has to be watching the plant twenty-four hours a day."

"Not if it's shut down, Mr. Peck. You can close the valves

on incoming oil immediately. Go ahead and process what's in the system. The residue can be trucked away. While you do that, I'll be downtown, selling what's in the tank farm. If you need me, I'll be at the Shamrock through the remainder of the day."

Kelly had skipped breakfast. He drove to a restaurant for an early lunch. By the time he returned to the hotel, newspaper reporters and television cameramen were waiting in the lobby.

He was surprised that they had already learned about the closing of the plant. He had never dreamed that they would be interested. The Spurlock refinery was small by comparison, and not of major significance in the oil game or, he was sure, to the Houston economy. But they wanted a statement. He could only assume that everyone in the industry was wondering what the maverick Spurlock brothers would do next.

He made quick arrangements with the hotel management to conduct an impromptu news conference in an anteroom off the lobby.

Into the glare of television lights, he once again defined the closing as a matter of economics.

"My brother Weldon and I feel that Spurlock Oil should concentrate on what it does best, finding and producing oil," he told them. "We intend to concentrate our energies in that direction."

In answer to questions, he explained that most employees would be given new duties.

"We maintain and operate an extensive pipeline facility. Their talents are needed. Some may elect to retire. It's too early to know the exact figures on how many will remain in Houston."

The news conference was accorded front-page treatment in the late afternoon editions. The evening television news carried clips of him speaking.

Before Kelly left the hotel the next morning, Weldon was on the phone. "What the hell is this? You go down there to sell an old, worn-out teakettle, and the next thing I know you're a fucking movie star."

"They caught me by surprise," Kelly admitted.

"I suppose we should have expected it. Anything to do with oil is big news in Houston. Everyone I talked to down there said you looked like a tall, lanky Paul Newman. How's it going?"

"Okay. I'm going out to the plant now to talk to the workers. This afternoon I'm meeting with two guys from Bartlesville who may be interested in salvaging some of the equipment. I've already had feelers from three groups inquiring about the land. I'm setting up those talks tomorrow."

"That town doesn't exactly sit around on its ass, Little Brother. Try and close a deal before the publicity cools."

"According to the morning paper, the mood isn't good at the refinery," Kelly told him.

"Then fuck 'em. We don't owe them a paycheck for the rest of their lives."

"I'll know more when I talk to them," Kelly said.

"You're not the only one making news. Mom and Walter are finally getting married."

Kelly was not surprised. But he had not expected to hear secondhand. "She call you?"

"No. I haven't heard a peep out of her. For some reason, she told Grandmother. I suppose because of Dad. Grandmother called and told me. She said she was sure you'd want to know."

"When's the wedding?"

Kelly hoped he could send a gift, some gesture toward reconciliation.

"Nobody knows. She told Grandmother they were planning a quiet ceremony. 'No fuss,' was her term. They're going off on a long honeymoon in the Pacific. Tahiti or some damned place."

The news left Kelly dejected.

Earlier, Walter had said he was sure that eventually her anger would fade.

But now Kelly wondered.

She had not bothered to tell him about one of the most important events in her life.

He spent almost a month salvaging portions of the refinery. The remainder he sold for scrap. Gradually the land was cleared.

But the real estate negotiations dragged on through the summer and into early fall.

One evening he returned to his hotel room exhausted and bored. On a whim, he picked up the phone and called Chandra's number in Oklahoma. From the first she seemed a bit more friendly.

"I saw your name in the news a while back," she said. "Mother sent a clipping from the Tulsa *Trib.* It was quite a long piece."

He had not yet grown accustomed to the attention. "I hardly thought it'd be news that far away."

"Any item with the word *oil* in it gets printed in Tulsa. The story made what you're doing sound interesting."

"At times," he said. "At others, it isn't"

Through the last four weeks he had been working alone amid strangers. In his disconnected mood, he felt like talking, and she seemed receptive. He told her of the difficulties he had encountered at the refinery.

"For years we've had these employees in Houston, jammed together with a million other people, battling crowded freeways, contending with the heat, humidity, and pollution. Now we come along and offer them a job taking care of a pumping station out in West Texas, with only jackrabbits for company. And you know what? They refuse to go. We hadn't expected that."

She laughed. "Is the job still open? I love jackrabbits."

"Apparently few people do. You should hear the reasons our employees give for not moving. They've always lived in Houston. Their children don't want to change schools. Their house here is paid for. Their wife needs to be near her doctor. It's given me a new perspective on what some people consider important. They choose comfort over responsibility, independence, challenge. I would've thought it'd be the other way around."

They talked for a while of the vast differences in the atmospheres of Houston and San Antonio, Fort Worth and Dallas, Tulsa and Oklahoma City.

When Kelly at last glanced at this watch, he was amazed to discover that it was after one o'clock in the morning, and they had talked more than three hours.

He apologized for keeping her awake.

"I don't mind," she said. "I'm a night owl."

It was the first self-revealing remark she had made.

"Me too. I've always done my best work at night."

"I'm glad you called," she said. "I've enjoyed it."

The long conversation gave Kelly a warm glow through the following day. He kept hearing her haunting voice, seeing her delicately chiseled face.

Two nights later he called her again and they talked for more than an hour.

The late-night calls became a delightful routine.

In October, as the first step in expanding exploration and production, Kelly opened an office in Midland, four hundred and fifty miles to the west. Negotiations over the land in Houston continued to strike repeated snags.

For weeks, Kelly flew his Cessna back and forth between West Texas and the Gulf. Throughout his traveling, he constantly found himself looking forward to returning to his hotel room each evening for his late-night talks with Chandra.

Slowly, he learned more about her. She loved dancing, but hated nightclubs. She was not exactly a vegetarian, but she seldom ate meat. She liked movies, but disliked walk-in theaters. She preferred drive-ins. She loved concerts and ballets, but disliked crowds. For her, any seated performance was a trade-off of desire and dislike.

Gradually they discovered they had much in common.

She had earned a degree in anthropology and was now pursuing related studies in archaeology, while serving as proctor in the sorority. She had studied ballet seriously six years, giving it up only when she felt that the demands interfered with her development in other fields.

Sensing her deep reserve, Kelly never asked probing questions. Instead, he carefully filed away every revelation, no matter how slight.

In bed in his darkened hotel room, with her in bed at her sorority house, if was like conversing with a disembodied voice. The dreamlike aura of their conversations led both to intimacies they otherwise might never have shared.

It was an unorthodox courtship. But it was effective.

On a day in late November, Kelly had just sat down to lunch with two oilmen at a hotel in Midland. His guests were speculators who held leases to a large tract south of Hobbs, adjoining a promising bloc held by Spurlock Oil. Kelly was hoping to work out an exploration arrangement with them.

As Kelly and his guests examined the menu, the door to the kitchen banged open and a Mexican in a cook's apron ran into the dining room, yelling, "El Presidente has been shot!"

For a moment Kelly thought he was talking about the president of Mexico. Then the man yelled, "Kennedy! Kennedy!" and began crying. Waiters gathered around the man and returned him to the kitchen.

Kelly and his guests rose and went into the lobby, where a crowd quickly gathered around a television set. The announcer kept repeating the same message: Gunshots had been heard in Dealey Plaza in Dallas, and President Kennedy had been taken to Parkland Hospital.

As if mesmerized by the television screen, the crowd stood silent through long minutes until the announcement came that President Kennedy was dead.

The display of emotion around Kelly fascinated him even as he was swept up in it. A line formed at each of the public phones in the lobby. Within minutes all flights to Dallas were overbooked as Dallasites competed to get home to their wives and families. Kelly's luncheon guests wandered away, too stunned to think of food or simple amenities. Some of the men paced the crowded lobby, talking inanely with anyone who would listen.

Kelly returned to his room and watched television through the incredible afternoon. Bulletin followed bulletin in dizzying fashion: Lyndon Johnson had taken the oath of office aboard Air Force One at Love Field and the nation had a new President. A policeman was shot. Lee Harvey Oswald was arrested, and held as the assassin.

That night Kelly again called Chandra. They talked for hours as they watched the same network repeat, over and over, the already familiar scenes: the Kennedys at breakfast at Hotel Texas in Fort Worth; their arrival at Love Field in Dallas; Kennedy walking past the Secret Service men to shake hands at the barriers; the crowds cheering as the presidential caravan moved through downtown Dallas; the photograph of Johnson taking the oath aboard the plane, Jacqueline Kennedy by his side, her skirt still stained by her husband's blood.

The scenes, astonishing news only hours before, already smacked of history.

On the following day—Saturday—the recriminations began. Dallas, the pundits said repeatedly, was "a city of hate." Texas was described as a netherworld where violence was a way of life.

Kelly received a call from Weldon.

"You hear what those shitheads are saying on television? I never thought I'd ever feel sorry for Dallas. But I'll swear, they're going to drive me to it."

Then on Sunday, Jack Ruby shot and killed Oswald in the basement of the Dallas police station—a scene captured on television.

Kelly sat in his hotel room, alone and emotionally depleted.

It seemed as if the world had been touched by a strange new form of insanity.

He called Weldon. "Listen, I'm taking the week off," he said. "Everybody's wandering around like zombies out here. It'll be impossible to get any work done."

"You coming home?"

"No. I think I'll just get away for a while."

"Where to?"

"I don't know. I'll keep in touch."

But he did know.

He made a night flight to Oklahoma City under a bright, starry sky and landed just after dawn. He rented a car and drove to the University of Oklahoma at Norman.

Chandra did not seem surprised to learn that he was on campus. "I have classes this morning," she said. "But I'll be free at one."

"What would you like to do?"

"Nothing. Just goon around. Who feels like doing anything?"

That afternoon, guided by what he now knew of her, he drove her away from the campus, away from the sprawling suburbs of Oklahoma City.

They dawdled along lonely rural roads, stopped to talk to grazing cattle and horses, and watched cottontails and jackrabbits at play in remote fields and pastures. It was silly, and fun. They watched birds. They sat silently in the car and thrilled to the brilliant hues of a sunset over the Canadian River breaks.

Magically, the insanity of the last few days slowly was restored to perspective.

Once again Kelly was thrilled by Chandra's quiet, natural beauty, her unaffected manner. She seemed to have none of the artificial poses he had encountered in so many women.

That night they strolled around the campus. Kelly recalled that his father had earned a degree here, back during the Depression. He wondered if his father had walked these same paths with some young woman, sat and talked at the same fountains.

That first day and evening became the pattern for the week.

In the mornings, Kelly walked the campus while Chandra was in class. He explored the older engineering and science buildings where his father had attended classes, the library, the student union. He was amused that students apparently assumed he was a young professor and gave him deferential nods.

In the afternoons, he and Chandra went for long drives, talking, absorbing the peace and loveliness of country roads.

Occasionally they kissed, but Kelly did not push further.

Between them the knowledge grew, unspoken, that they were two reticent, deeply reserved people who nevertheless had managed to find each other.

They were aware of, and awed by, the potential permanence of their relationship.

Chapter 36

Weldon looked up from his desk. "Well, the wandering boy returns." He put a finger to his lips, left his desk, closed the door to his office, and walked to his locked files in the corner. Kelly sank into a chair and waited.

"Reason I wanted to see you, I'd like for you to put those magna cum laude mental calipers on this, and tell me if it looks feasible. What do you know about Wilcox Petroleum?"

"Not much," Kelly said.

Wilcox was one of the largest outfits operating in West Texas. It was competing with Spurlock Oil on almost every front. It's people were exceptionally secretive in a traditionally wary industry.

Yet Kelly kept running into them everywhere. Despite his efforts, they had sewed up the exploration area south of Hobbs he had been attempting to lease.

Weldon pulled a large folder from the files and tossed it into Kelly's lap.

"Look at this stuff and tell me what kind of tender offer we should make to buy them out."

Kelly searched his face to make certain he was serious. Wilcox was two or three times the size of Spurlock Oil.

"How could we possibly do that?"

Weldon laughed. "It's all in there, Little Brother. Sometimes us little fishes got to eat the big fishes if we're going to grow. Just think about it: Wilcox has everything we need—pipelines, leases, equipment. Their operation almost exactly parallels our own. In one fell swoop, we could accomplish what would take us years of normal growth."

"Where would we get that kind of money?"

"Easy. Once it's a done deal, we'll have all those lovely assets." He pointed to the folder. "I've drafted a plan. Look at it and see if you can punch any holes in it."

Kelly took the folder to his apartment and began reading. From the first he was intrigued with Weldon's elaborate plan. It was bold, clever, and imaginative. Struggling through Weldon's scrawled notes, he was pleasantly amazed at the scope of Weldon's financial wizardry. He spent most of the night calculating, examining the possibilities.

The next morning he took the plan back to Weldon. "It's tempting," he said. "And it'd work. But it's too risky."

"Why?"

"No margin. Suppose we run into a steady string of dry holes? It could happen. You presume a stable market. The price of oil could drop. We easily could fall into a situation where we couldn't service those huge loans."

"Hell, Little Brother. Just crossing the street is a risk. What I'm asking is, can it be done?"

Kelly nodded. "Sure. It's feasible. But it scares me. I know it'd scare Grandmother, Mom, Campbell. You'd never get it past the board."

Weldon broke out a fresh cigar and lit it. "I just might. All we have to do is con Grandmother. Mom's due back week after next. I'd like to ram it through while she's gone, but Grandmother would balk at that. So we'll play it by the rules. Stick around a few days and we'll work up a presentation. Then we'll see."

Kelly took Weldon's rough notes and set to work. He wrote a preliminary draft of the project, couching the text in the most positive terms he could invent.

Still, the venture sounded risky.

For days he fenced with lending institutions, determining what money was available, at what price, and on what terms. The search was difficult, for he had to take care to avoid any hint of the nature of the project.

Fortunately the numbers were more encouraging than Kelly anticipated. He went back to the beginning of his text and strengthened his prose. But Weldon was not satisfied.

"This sounds like we're trying to bankroll a crap game," he said. "Let's concentrate more on the assets."

Going beyond Weldon's information, Kelly searched for everything in print concerning Wilcox Petroleum. Inventing reasons, he talked with former Wilcox executives, gleaning every scrap of knowledge they retained. Slowly the extent of Wilcox holdings became more evident as details were added.

Weldon read the new version with enthusiasm.

"If this doesn't do it, nothing will. I want you to come with me when I talk to Grandmother."

Weldon made an appointment and they drove out the following afternoon. Ann Leigh led them into the parlor, where they were served coffee and cake.

Ann Leigh's old house was full of childhood memories for Kelly. Often when his father was even more ill than usual, Kelly and Weldon were sent over to their grandmother's house for the day. Kelly remembered their games in the halls upstairs, in the trees out back. Almost nothing had changed. The house was still deathly quiet, in a calm, noiseless neighborhood.

Weldon was barely able to subdue his impatience with the coffee and cake. He sat nodding agreement while their grandmother described her intermittent chest pains, her last trip to the doctor. Weldon allowed her to exhaust the subject before moving on to the reason for their visit.

"Grandmother, have you seen the new quarterly statement?"

"Oh, my yes! It's just as you boys said it would be. The profits just flat doubled! It makes me sick to think of all the money we lost all those years, not even knowing. I'm so proud of you, what you've done."

Weldon gave Kelly a knowing glance.

"There's more where that came from, Grandmother. Kelly and I have a plan to put some of that money to work, double profits again."

She smiled. "Oh, my! Already?"

"The idea came to me, and Kelly researched it. Thing is, we have to move quick on it, or the opportunity will be gone. You know what a troublesome competitor Wilcox Petroleum has been."

Ann Leigh nodded. "They have been for a long time, before you boys were born. Your grandfather and Bryant Wilcox hated each other. I think they even had a fistfight one time. If I remember right, Bryant's been dead for years. One of his sons was running it."

"The son's dead too," Weldon said. "None of the family is in it now. The company went public back about fifty-two or -three. Kelly and I want to buy it, take it under the Spurlock umbrella."

Ann Leigh turned to Kelly. "Could we do that?"

"It would be quite an undertaking," Kelly admitted. "But we've found that the Wilcox assets are worth more than the cost of the stock. We would be buying at a bargain-basement price."

"The banks would see that," Weldon pointed out. "We would have no trouble with the financing."

"It sounds like something that would require a great deal of study. Why does it have to be done so quickly?"

Kelly remained silent, allowing Weldon to do the lying.

"We've heard, just by accident, that the Wilcox board is aware their stock is underpriced. They're about to issue new stock, increase their debts, reposition the company. When that happens, the opportunity will be gone."

"Joanna won't be back until next week. It doesn't have to be done before then, does it?"

"No," Weldon said. "But we want to call a board meeting as soon as she returns. We've brought you an outline of our plan. It's self-explanatory. Basically, we'll obtain loans to buy the stock, pledging Wilcox assets as collateral. We would use Wilcox income to pay off the loans. So really, we won't be out any money at all."

"That sounds positively illegal. Can it be done?"

Weldon looked at Kelly, tossing him the ball.

"There would be some maneuvering. But if all goes well, Spurlock Oil wouldn't be out a cent."

Ann Leigh picked up the folder. "We've never had to borrow money, not since I've been on the board. I wouldn't like to do that."

Kelly and Weldon had known this would be her principal objection.

Weldon spoke quickly. "Grandmother, that's the best way to do things these days, use other people's money. That leaves you free to do whatever you want with your own."

"Still, it's borrowing." She turned through the proposal. "If you boys don't mind, I'd like to see what Mr. Wilkins down at the bank thinks about this."

"Sure," Weldon said. "As long as you stress to him that it's confidential."

On the way back downtown Kelly and Weldon again argued over whether they should have allowed her to take the plan to Wilkins. Kelly felt the banker would be too conservative, and advise against the plan. Weldon thought he would see the assets, the probability of making a large loan, and recommend it.

The argued until they were back at Spurlock Oil.

Weldon paused before stepping out of the car. "What do you think? Will she go for it?"

"I don't know. She probably won't decide until after she talks to Wilkins."

"The whole plan rides on her," Weldon said. "Campbell will be against it. So will Mom. That leaves Grandmother as the swing vote."

Kelly did not answer.

He did not want to reveal that he also had lingering qualms.

* * *

Kelly had not seen his mother since her marriage. After a long honeymoon cruise in the South Pacific, she and Walter had spent several months in the Mediterranean. For the first two minutes of the board meeting he could not determine what was different about her. She had acquired a deep tan, and she was a bit slimmer, yet there was a further change he could not define.

"I understand we are here to act on a plan Weldon and Kelly have drafted for the acquisition of Wilcox Petroleum," she said. "Obviously, I haven't had much time to study it. So I'll ask Weldon and Kelly to explain it, and to answer any questions you might have."

She leaned back in her chair as Weldon started his presentation, and it came to Kelly what he had noticed: She carried herself with a deeper serenity.

Normally she would have been alert to every reaction, staying on top of the meeting. Now she sat back and listened, as if what Weldon said was only of passing interest. It almost seemed as if her mind was elsewhere.

She had spoken to him before the meeting, and he had told her how happy he was for her, how much he thought of Walter. She had thanked him with more of a detachment than a coolness.

Kelly sat listening as Weldon went through the now familiar proposal, feeling that perhaps he was the only one in the room fully aware of all the risks in the project.

Weldon assumed he would vote yes.

In truth, he was still on the fence.

"Does anyone have any questions about the details?" Weldon asked.

They did. Campbell asked about interest rates, tax advantages, loan payments vis-à-vis the general revenue, and other aspects of the plan. Ann Leigh wanted the specifics on the exact source of the money to make payments on the loan. Kelly helped Weldon with the answers.

Joanna sat listening, offering no comment.

At last the questions ended.

"I suppose it's time for discussion," Joanna said. "Mr. Campbell, how do you feel about the idea?"

Campbell was reluctant to take the lead. He glanced at Ann Leigh, who had given him no clue.

"Frankly, I think it's too much of a gamble," he said. "There are too many intangibles. A shift in tax structure, a bad run of luck in production, a dip in the price of oil, any unexpected expenses could place the project in jeopardy."

"Weldon?"

"Mom, it was my idea. I've thought it through a thousand times. I'm for it."

"Kelly?"

He wondered why she was asking opinions in that precise order. She probably had known that Campbell would be against it. Had she sensed his own indecision? Was she trying to kill the project early, without putting Ann Leigh on the spot?

Kelly hesitated. He thought of the tremendous risks, all frighteningly real. Campbell was right. Under a series of adverse circumstances, the heavy commitments easily could drive the company into bankruptcy.

Yet Weldon's vision was awesome—a well-integrated company, sprawling across West Texas, drilling wells, pumping oil and feeding it into a wondrous array of pipelines to the Gulf ports and refineries.

The acquisition would make Spurlock Oil one of the largest among independents.

He also thought ahead to more headlines and news stories about "the maverick Spurlock brothers."

He liked the sound of the phrase. It smacked of Batman and Robin, the Lone Ranger and Tonto.

He felt a moment of elation, of overwhelming confidence. Even if the deal went sour, Weldon probably would come up with some solution to save the company.

"I see the risks," he said. "But I also see the potential. I'm for."

"Ann Leigh?"

"Joanna, I wanted to talk to you about this. We've never

borrowed money before, and I never dreamed we ever would. Not millions! I had about decided against it before I went down and talked to Mr. Wilkins. He agrees with what Mr. Campbell said. It's just too risky. So I vote no."

Joanna sat for a moment, looking at the board.

"It seems we have a tie vote," she said. "Two for, two against. Anyone want to switch?"

She gave Kelly a long, searching stare.

He assumed she was giving him an easy way out; he could change his vote, go with the majority, and leave Weldon dangling on his own.

He returned her stare and did not answer.

"You boys!" she said. "You think you're so damned smart. You come in here with this elaborate plan and you talk risks, risks, risks."

She paused. Kelly felt as if he was about to endure another of the long lectures he and Weldon once received, sitting on the leather couch in the library.

"Let me tell you about risks," she said. "Your grandfather Clay once put his family home in escrow so he could hock it to drill a well he believed in." She glanced at Ann Leigh. "Did you know that?"

Ann Leigh's mouth opened in surprise. "No."

"The loan paper is in the company files." She turned back to Kelly and Weldon. "Your grandfather gambled just about everything he owned to get in on the booms at Ranger, Burk, Desdemona, Mexia. Your father put the company on the block time after time, to lay a pipeline to the Gulf, to build a refinery, to go into retail, to hang on to those New Mexico leases that we're enjoying now. And I can tell you something about risk. Try going in with a company the size of Humble on a deep test, striking a pool, and scrambling to match them barrel for barrel on production."

She tossed her copy of the presentation to the middle of the table.

"Don't think you've invented the oil business with this. You are sadly lacking in experience, knowledge. Brass will only get you so far. You've left out some of your strongest points. For one thing, acquisition of Wilcox would give us facilities to develop our leases along the northwest edge of the Horseshoe Atoll, something we've badly needed for a long time."

Kelly was bewildered, and appalled. The advantages of Wilcox pipelines, pump stations, and tanks along the atoll had not even occurred to him. He knew only vaguely that the atoll was a horseshoe-shaped, submerged limestone formation stretching more than a hundred miles across West Texas. Containing pockets of oil, it was believed to be the remnants of an atoll in an ancient sea.

"Another thing. With Wilcox gas wells in the Panhandle added to our own, we could raise our volume guarantee and win higher rates from the utility companies. There are several other advantages you failed to mention."

She pointed to the proposal. "But that's a good piece of work. I've had my own experts look it over, and they agree that with a little diligence, risks should be minimal. You've created the plan. Maybe you have enough sense to carry it out. I hope so."

She paused. Kelly was still confused, trying to absorb the unexpected direction of the lecture. Weldon, Campbell, and Ann Leigh also sat spellbound.

"I vote for," Joanna said. "So the proposal carries." She glanced at Ann Leigh. "Mother, you wanted to put the boys in charge of the company. We might as well let them play with it, as I knew they would." She looked at Weldon. "I'll send you a memo about the points you left out, the steps you should take. I believe that concludes our business for today. We stand adjourned. If you'll excuse me, I have to run."

She rose and walked out of the conference room.

Weldon was the first to recover.

"Now I know how Lazarus felt." He reached for a stack of folders. "Come on, Little Brother. We've got to go talk to a securities man."

When the tender offer appeared on financial pages across the nation, the results were exactly what Kelly anticipated.

Business writers wrote eloquently of "the big gamble" by the "maverick Spurlock brothers." They pointed out that Wilcox was not only a much larger company, but was usually considered far more aggressive. The writers expressed doubts that Spurlock Oil possessed the resources to effect a takeover. Directors and other officials at Wilcox Petroleum agreed, terming the attempt "ridiculous" and "preposterous."

But in a string of interviews, Weldon treated the takeover as an accomplished fact. As the financial battle raged, it received extensive coverage.

Kelly retreated to Midland. For a time he managed to avoid the spotlight.

But within weeks it became clear the Spurlock bid would be successful. Even the most entrenched of Wilcox officials began to concede defeat.

Preliminary talks began for the merger. As the author of the plan, Kelly opened the negotiations.

For a time, he lived in two worlds. Throughout each week he endured a constant succession of meetings, slowly meshing Spurlock facilities and projects with those of Wilcox Petroleum.

Late at night, and on weekends, he continued his unorthodox courtship.

The cross-country flights from Midland to Oklahoma City and back never became tiresome, for the scenes below were seldom the same. He flew over the golden hues of fall, the scattered whiteness of winter, the rich greenery of spring.

Occasionally he and Chandra attended sorority or fraternity dances, or seated performances on campus and in Oklahoma City.

But mostly they preferred to be alone.

Wandering about the countryside in his leased car, they explored small towns that had changed little since the turn of the century. Strolling almost deserted streets, they investigated the merchandise of old hardware stores, the rusted, ancient machinery of blacksmith shops. They hiked in state parks, and sipped coffee in rustic cafés. They toured a cotton gin as it processed the last bales of harvest. They sat by the side of the road and watched farmers drill winter wheat, and plow fields for spring planting.

At night on country roads they transfixed raccoons in the glare of their headlights, and laughed at possums waddling off into bushes. By day they photographed hills covered with wildflowers, and stopped to watch spiders spin their webs.

On one unforgettable, magic evening, they sat quietly in a field, surrounded by hundreds of birds singing a symphony to a gorgeous sunset.

Often they talked the entire night through, cautiously granting each other access to their most personal thoughts.

Kelly described his growing up without a father, the distance he had always felt between himself and his mother, the close bond he had developed with his brother, despite the fact that they had been reared apart throughout their adolescence.

With some chagrin, he described the secret fears he once had harbored of ceilings and signs and runway cars. Chandra laughed and held him close. He told of the rigid discipline of the Texas Boys Choir, and gave it full credit for turning his life around.

And late one night Chandra touched on a subject never before mentioned between them.

"My father was a full-blood Creek. He grew up around whites, so I have no ties at all to my Indian heritage. It honestly never occurred to me that my interest in anthropology and archaeology might stem from a search for my roots. In my senior year it was pointed out to me by a smart-aleck boy. He said it as a joke, but I knew the truth of it the minute he said it."

She told of growing up in Tulsa. "My father made the oil booms at Cushing, Drumright, and Healdton in the twenties and thirties. He was twenty-three years older than Mother. It must have been a strange marriage. But I really think they were happy. He died when I was eighteen—my freshman year."

Kelly planned his marriage proposal carefully. He waited

until one night when they were parked in front of the sorority house, in the exact spot where they had talked so many hours. From the distance came the voices of students singing in the tavern a block away.

He was certain the proposal would be no more than a formality. He was completely unprepared for her answer.

"Kelly, I do love you. I do want you. I believe we're right for each other. But I don't think it would work."

He was stunned. "For the Lord's sake, why not?"

"This may make you angry. But please hear me out. The reason is your family. They mean so much to you, and I know I just wouldn't fit in. And I certainly don't want to be the cause of ill feelings between you and your family."

"Chandra! That's ridiculous! I'm asking you to marry *me*, not my family."

"Still, you need your family. They are so much a part of you. I can understand that. But I see too many possibilities for serious conflict."

"Name one. Just one."

"All right. You say you feel a close bond with your brother. I can accept that. I'm sorry, but since you asked, I must tell you this. I thought Weldon was the most conceited, overbearing person I've ever met. Never in my life have I ever taken such an immediate dislike to anyone. Forgive me. I'm only being honest."

Kelly was so heartsick, he could not respond.

"And that first day I met you, when you took Mother and me to the airport, I thought you were just like him. Because of Weldon, I almost missed knowing you. You seemed cold and arrogant that day. But I was intrigued that you sang four years with the boy choir. Somehow that didn't fit my first impression of you. Then you called that night from Houston and spoke with such insight and compassion about your employees down there. I decided I might have been wrong about you. And I was."

"Maybe you're also wrong about Weldon."

"No. I'm sure Weldon didn't waste one minute worrying about his employees."

Kelly remained silent.

"There's something else. We've told each other our most intimate feelings. But there's something very important you've never discussed. I've been waiting, but you've never mentioned it."

Kelly suspected he knew. He wanted to be certain. "What's that?"

"Your estrangement from your mother. I know more about it from newspapers and gossip columns than I've heard from you. Don't talk about it if you don't want. But please see my position. With your partnership, there'd be no escape for me from Weldon. And I would have to contend with your situation with your mother. Kelly, I can't marry into a family where there seems to be such dark, secret undercurrents."

For a moment Kelly was whisked back to his childhood, and adult discussions he had overheard.

"There's no secret," he said. "And the newspapers have exaggerated the situation. She's angry with us, but I wouldn't call it an estrangement. Mom's a very strong-willed person. When Weldon and I opposed her, we were thinking of the company. But for some reason, she took it as a personal affront. I feel bad about it. But Weldon and I were right, and she was wrong. We've proved that. In time, I think it will all blow over."

"And if it doesn't?"

"Then I'll go on feeling bad. I've made several attempts at reconciliation. I don't know what more I can do. She seems to be softening some. She backed our last project, and saved it in the board meeting."

Chandra paused. "Kelly, I'll always love you. Getting to know you has been very important to me. But I value my tranquility too much. You've been in the middle of an uproar since we met. And I see tumultuous times ahead for you, as long as you stay so closely attached to Weldon, the company, and your family. I can see that I would become the center of the friction, and I don't want to be a part of so much unpleasantness. So my answer is no. I'm sorry, Kelly. But I can't marry you."

She burst into tears, bolted from the car, and ran into the sorority house.

Kelly remained at the curb for several minutes, so emotionally devastated, he did not trust himself to drive on the narrow, crowded streets.

But after a time, he started the car and drove back to his motel.

The next morning he turned in the leased car and flew his Cessna back to West Texas.

During the next few weeks he plunged into work with a vengeance, knowing he must not surrender to his despondency. By sheer willpower, he managed to put aside his disappointment for hours at a time.

He attempted to convince himself that there were other women, that eventually he would find someone he could love just as much as Chandra.

But at last came a lonely night in Amarillo. Thinking of Chandra, their closeness, the wonderful days and nights they had spent together, the potentialities of their relationship, he grew increasingly angry with her.

And with himself.

Almost from habit, he dialed her phone at the sorority house. When she answered, he did not even bother to identify himself.

"You say you love me," he said. "I think that's enough basis for me not to give up. Will you agree to see me again?"

Chandra burst into tears. For a time she could not stop crying.

Kelly waited until she could speak.

"After you left, I cried for two weeks," she said. "I've called myself every kind of fool. I guess I just didn't know how much I love you. If your proposal is still open, I accept. Understand, I still believe every word I said that night. But I'm now prepared to take the bad along with the good."

* * *

Joanna was elected to head the Arts Council only weeks after she returned from her honeymoon. She thought she saw Walter's hand in her selection. But she was not sure.

It was a demanding job. As her term approached, she turned the library into an office and hired two secretaries to help handle the extensive correspondence and telephoning.

The council was responsible for raising money for all of the city's performing arts—seven organizations in all. The museums were supporting members. In addition to raising funds, she was expected to coordinate all arts activities, so that two performances would never occur on the same night and limit ticket sales on each.

She spent much of her day on the telephone, talking with the directors of various foundations, the most influential leaders in business, convincing everyone that financial support of the arts was an important part of their responsibility to the community.

Seldom a day went by that she did not have committee meetings or planning sessions on the terrace, in the library, or in the living room.

It was, indeed, a job for a Boss Lady.

Walter stayed loftily above all the activity. After their marriage, Joanna had redesigned the upper floor, creating a large master bedroom in the west wing. Walter spent much of his time there, reading, watching television.

Opening letters at her desk one morning in May, she encountered a note written in a neat, familiar hand:

Mom,
    In June I am marrying a most lovely young lady. Her mother is planning a church wedding, which imposes the traditional obligations. I know you are still angry with me. But for the sake of my bride, if nothing else, I hope my family will participate.

                                                    Love,
                                                    Kelly

Joanna read the note twice, her irritation growing.

At least he could have included the name of the bride.

She picked up the phone, called Walter, and read him the note.

"Doesn't he say who to?"

"No. And I haven't the foggiest. I feel so stupid. I don't even know who he has been dating. Do you suppose you could find out from someone?"

Walter hesitated. "Joanna, why don't you just call Kelly and ask him?"

"Because this note is a ploy. He didn't mention her name on purpose, so I would have to call him."

Walter laughed. "Why don't you just admit he has gotten the best of you for once?"

She attempted to reach Kelly in Midland, but the receptionist at the Spurlock office there said he was out in the field. Joanna took the name of his hotel, intending to call him that evening.

But the phone rang a few minutes later and it was Beth Runnels, bubbling over with excitement.

"Honey, Ella just called with the news! Isn't it wonderful? Chandra's a lovely, lovely girl. Forgive my pride if I say Kelly couldn't possibly have done better. And of course I know Chandra couldn't have either. Kelly's a real prize. It's surely a marriage made in heaven if there ever was one. I hope you're as happy about it as I am."

Joanna bluffed her way through the conversation, saying that of course she was delighted.

But her brain was in a whirl.

She remembered that Beth's cousin had brought her daughter down for the finals of the Van Cliburn competition. But it was Weldon who dated the daughter. She was sure of it. She remembered that Kelly attended the finals with Amy Goodwin.

"And those little scamps!" Beth went on. "Ella said she had no inkling of it. She didn't even know they'd been dating! Did you?"

"No. Really, I didn't."

"Ella said she told Chandra, 'Why, honey, you two hardly know each other,' and Chandra said yes, Momma, they did. She said Kelly had been flying up almost every weekend since late last fall. Isn't it too romantic for words? Have you heard from Kelly?"

"He dropped me a note. I've been trying to reach him."

"Joanna, I know you two have been fussing. That won't affect this, will it?"

Joanna did not hesitate. "Of course not."

"Good, he's a fine boy. That's what counts. He's so full of energy and ambition. You may disagree with him, but sometimes I think all we can do with younger people is stand back and watch. Gyorgy and I'll be going up to the wedding, of course. I know everyone will want to go, so we'll probably take the big plane, the whatchamacallit. If you and Walter want to go with us, just let me know."

"Thank you," Joanna said. "I'll keep it in mind."

"You can be sure Ella will be turning that town upside down, getting ready for the wedding. You'll find her a wonderful person to work with. She knows everybody. Ella was really the apple of her daddy's eye. There were a few noses out of joint when she married John Sykes. No one in the family could understand it, his being so much older and all. But he was a remarkable man, and he made Ella happy, so it has all turned out marvelously well. Would you like to have Ella's phone number?"

Joanna took down the information.

As soon as she was off the phone with Beth, she called Walter.

"Beth Runnels just let the cat out of the bag. It's Chandra Sykes. Her family is from Tulsa. John Sykes. Chandra's mother is Beth's cousin, Ella Sykes."

"I've heard of them. Oil people. He had a ranch near Sapulpa. Polled Herefords. I think he died four or five years ago."

"Beth referred to him in the past tense. Weldon escorted Chandra to the Cliburn finals. I didn't see them in the crowd. Did you? Do you remember what she looks like?"

"No. I didn't see them."

"Beth told me so many times what a lovely girl she is, I'm beginning to get suspicious. Beth indicated it will be a huge wedding."

"What do you plan to do about it?"

"Do I have a choice? Kelly has me boxed in. Of course I'll go through with it. But I resent his putting me in the position of finding all this out secondhand. He could have told me."

Late that evening she reached Kelly at his hotel.

"I got your note," she said. "And Beth Runnels called. I've more or less committed myself to participate in your wedding. I wanted you to know that."

His voice sounded husky. She wondered if he was coming down with a cold.

"Mom, I'll be forever grateful. For Chandra's sake, I hope we can put our disagreements behind us."

Joanna steeled herself, remembering the humiliation of seeing her name in the newspapers.

"Kelly, I'm still very angry with you. What you did was unforgivable. But certain proprieties must be observed, and I'll honor them."

"I'm sorry it has to be this way. But if you had listened to us in the beginning, respected our opinions, everything would have been fine."

"You and Weldon got what you wanted. And you didn't care who you hurt getting it."

"Mom, I have only one favor to ask. Chandra has nothing to do with this. Please don't let your anger toward me carry over to her."

"I can't promise anything," Joanna said. "But I'll try."

She hung up without saying good night.

From his chair, Walter had been monitoring her end of the call. He looked up from his magazine. "You two are too damned much alike," he said.

Joanna's first glimpse of Chandra came at a reception for the attendants. Just as Joanna and Walter arrived, Kelly saw them at the door. He put an arm around his bride-to-be and guided her toward them.

Chandra's pronounced Indian features were such a complete surprise that Joanna concentrated on keeping her face devoid of expression. Chandra was wearing a simple tunic dress that enhanced her tall, lithe build. She moved with the grace Joanna recognized as the result of ballet training.

"Mother, Walter, I would like you to meet Chandra," Kelly said.

As Joanna exchanged simple amenities, she had difficulty taking her eyes from her prospective daughter-in-law. At first she seemed painfully shy. Her beauty was rather breathtaking. But she revealed little of her personality.

Kelly and Chandra walked Joanna and Walter through the crowd, making introductions. Then Kelly and Chandra moved away, circulating through the throng.

Joanna and Walter did not linger, since the reception was principally for the younger generation.

"I think Kelly has a real winner there," Walter said on the way back to the hotel.

"I can't quite figure her out," Joanna said. "I don't know if I like her or not."

"There'll be plenty of time to decide that," Walter said.

The rehearsal dinner, with Joanna and Walter as hosts, was a complete success, without a bobble anywhere that Joanna could see. She knew that Kelly was immensely pleased; she could see it in his eyes.

The wedding itself filled the church to overflowing. A full chorus, the huge organ, and ranks of attendants lent the ceremony a celestial aura. Weldon served as best man, and one of Chandra's cousins was matron of honor. Gyorgy gave the bride away. Joanna assumed his selection was a gesture to Beth.

A full orchestra played at the wedding reception. After the bride and groom cut the cake, Gyorgy read a poem composed for the occasion. It concerned love flying thousands of miles on gossamer wings.

As the bride and groom prepared to leave, Joanna walked

up to them. Kelly had turned aside for the moment, joking with Weldon and two fraternity brothers who had flown in from the East.

Joanna made a point of speaking directly to Chandra. "I hope you two will be very, very happy."

Chandra looked up with an odd combination of shyness and steel. "I'm sure we will be, Mrs. Trammell. Kelly's happiness is the most important thing in my life. I will fight to see that he has it."

And then the newlyweds were gone.

"What do you suppose she meant by that?" Joanna asked Walter in the car.

"I don't know. She did seem to be conveying more than she said."

Walter was silent for a time.

"I'll tell you, though," he added. "Her father had the reputation of being a real heller. If push came to shove, I think I'd want that young lady on my side."

Chapter 37

When Kelly awoke, Chandra brought him coffee and lay down beside him. "Well, where are you off to tomorrow?"

He was still groggy. For a moment he could not remember. He had spent the last three days in Houston, merging Spurlock and Wilcox pipelines into an integrated system. His head was still full of facts and figures.

Then it came to him.

"Amarillo. I'll have to leave early. I have a meeting at ten with natural gas distributors. We're cutting a new contract."

Chandra rolled over to face him. "Kelly, is this all we have to look forward to the rest of our lives? Me sitting here waiting, day after day, week after week? You coming in once every week or two so tired you can hardly talk?"

"This is only temporary," he promised. "As soon as we iron out the final kinks in the merger, all will get back to normal."

"That's what you promised me six months ago. Can't you see that *this* is normal? You've been dashing from here to there ever since I met you. I see no end to it."

Kelly could not offer a valid argument. If anything, the pace had grown even more hectic since they returned from their honeymoon, almost a year ago. Many of the Wilcox executives had resigned, leaving a vacuum in management. Kelly spent most of every week in the field, and sometimes the weekends as well.

For a time the building of their new house had kept Chandra occupied. But now that it was finished, she was at loose ends. She was not well acquainted in Fort Worth, and Beth had been living at her home at Palm Springs in recent months.

"Why doesn't Weldon do some of the fieldwork? Why does it always have to be you?"

It was an old issue. "He's the president," Kelly explained again. "He should be in the office."

"He's also the big wheeler-dealer. You're the quiet-spoken brains of the outfit. Yet you go out and cut the deals. It seems to me you two have your roles backward."

"I'm the detail man. Weldon has the big ideas. I put them into practice."

"You're smarter."

Kelly did not argue. Weldon was difficult to explain.

He could not get across to her that Weldon had a mind so inventive, it was almost scary. One of the business magazines had termed the Wilcox merger "pure legerdemain." And it was. Weldon used assets in a Zen-like manner, making cash appear to be in two places at the same time.

Chandra was quiet for a moment. "Kelly, I've never asked you, because I sensed it was too personal. But since I'm so involved, I think I deserve to know. What is this strange bond between you and Weldon? You two are so different. But he seems to need you. And for some reason, you seem to think you need him."

With the question, images of the rambling, silent house of his childhood came to mind. Kelly remembered eavesdropping on adult talk of an unhealthy interdependence.

"I'm not sure. Maybe it was because, for a crucial time, all we had was each other. Mom was always so—distant—wrapped up in Dad's illness. Weldon and I stuck together for mutual comfort. People thought he dominated me, but he didn't."

She studied his face. "No?"

"Not really. In some ways I was tougher, and he knew it."

Chandra laughed. "I thought Weldon invented the word."

Kelly shook his head. "He's tough on the surface. But deep down he's vulnerable. I always knew the tough-guy image was just a pose. Chandra, I've never told this to anyone. But I want you to understand. I used to hear him crying a lot in his room."

"Because his mother ignored him?"

"That. Other disappointments. You see, Weldon and I reacted differently to the lack of attention. I was always eager to please, working for approval. Weldon swaggered around and acted as if he didn't care. But he did, even more than I. He tried to earn approval by being the toughest guy around."

"And he's still earning approval, as the biggest wheeler-dealer around. Is that it?"

Kelly hesitated. "I never thought of it that way. Maybe so."

"And you're still the good little boy, doing whatever's expected of you."

Kelly did not answer. But he wondered if, in his analysis of Weldon, he might have discovered a crucial truth about himself.

Chandra sighed. "Not that I like it. But in a way I can see the necessity for all the hard work right now. You and Weldon are building something for the future. But Kelly, I want you to be thinking about this: It can't go on forever. Our marriage will deteriorate. You're changing. I'm losing that wonderful man who flew a thousand miles every weekend to share jackrabbits and sunsets with me."

"I'm still flying almost as far to share a bed with you."

"That's not the same and you know it."

Kelly slipped his arm beneath her head. "Chandra, if all goes well, we should have the company running smoothly by spring. All we need right now is a good man in Midland.

When we find him, we can turn most of the fieldwork over to him. Then I'll be back in the office here, nine to five."

"Weldon won't be able to tolerate that."

He looked at her in surprise. "I don't know what you mean."

"Just wait and see."

A few months later Chandra learned that she was pregnant. Despite her convincing charade, Kelly knew she did not consider it the best of news. She often had said she did not want children until their lives became better-ordered.

For a time there was hope this might be accomplished. Kelly's predictions proved accurate. Gradually the chaos of the merger faded into a smoothly functioning system. Kelly found a man qualified to run the Midland office and began to shift his work load. Soon he was spending most of his time in the Fort Worth office.

But one afternoon Weldon called Kelly into his office and handed him a single sheet of paper.

"Take a look at this! Isn't it enough to make you puke?"

Kelly scanned the brief page. It was a schedule of Spurlock payments to the Internal Revenue Service.

"If we're not bleeding in one place, we're bleeding in another. You have any idea how we can save some of that money?"

"Not offhand."

Every tax loophole had been utilized to the fullest. Still the tax outlay was growing. Spurlock Oil had become a victim of its own success. Instead of the dry holes Kelly had feared, the increased activity had yielded a string of solid producers. With the Johnson administration's escalation of the war in Vietnam, the market was far better than originally projected. Moreover, price restrictions on natural gas had been raised, and the deep gas wells in the Panhandle, acquired from Wilcox, had become real treasure troves.

"Congress keeps bitchin' about the depletion allowance. But if it wasn't for that, we wouldn't be making it."

That was not exactly true. The twenty-seven percent allowance gave oil producers an incentive to risk the rising costs of exploration. But it did not account for total profits.

"I may have a solution," Weldon said. He picked up an object on his desk and tossed it to Kelly. "Know what this is?"

"A roller bearing?"

"That, my friend, is a *frictionless* roller bearing, the marvel of the nineteenth century. They'll hold your turning crankshaft in your engine until the rest of your car falls apart. They keep your wheels turning around and around without flying off. Sealed into an electric motor, they'll last just about forever."

Kelly put the bearing back on the desk. Weldon picked it up and bounced it in his hand.

"This little jewel was made by a third-generation company up in Pennsylvania. Granddaddy made journal boxes for the railroads. Pop made bearings for tanks, planes, cars, electric motors. Now, for some reason, the third generation has fallen upon hard times. The company has lost money the last five years. Beautiful big losses for the last three."

Kelly saw the direction of Weldon's rambling. A tax trade-off.

"No, Weldon. We don't know a thing about making ball bearings."

"We don't," Weldon agreed. "But when you come right down to it, what the hell do we know about drilling for oil? You know a little bit of geology you picked up around here as a kid. I know the theory of the mechanics, the hydrology involved. But could you or I go out and drill a well? Hell no. We hire it done. These people in Pennsylvania know how to make bearings. They just don't know how to make a profit doing it."

"What makes you think we would?"

"We doubled, tripled, quadrupled the profits around here, didn't we? The way to make money today is to manage money. And Little Brother, that's what we do best."

"Weldon, a factory's a lot different."

"What's there to learn? Crap goes in one end, crap comes

out the other. The rest is figuring costs. This outfit's for sale. I haven't approached them. But I've had some shills go in, nose around, ask a lot of questions. That place is loaded with assets. They have the reputation, the market. All those lovely tax losses would be like money in the bank. I think we can get that factory for a song."

Despite his reluctance, Kelly was intrigued. It did indeed sound like the perfect tax solution.

"What would be the outlay?"

"Not much. But that's your department. My flunkies have written a report."

He rose from his desk and unlocked his safe. He withdrew a bulky package and handed it to Kelly.

"Look it over and see if you can find where that outfit's losing money. If you catch a glimmer—just a glimmer—we'll go in and buy it. Word is that everyone else is afraid of it. I think we can turn it around."

Kelly took the report home and spent several nights in his den, analyzing it, recasting the figures.

He caught several glimmers.

When he took the report back into Weldon's office, Weldon was standing by the window, putter in hand, knocking a golf ball up a little ramp, into a cup. Each time he did, the ball rolled back down a small chute and landed in position to be hit again. Weldon was giving the game his full concentration. At last he missed and tossed the putter aside. He returned to his desk, opened a folder, and glanced through Kelly's figures.

"To begin with, their labor costs are way too high," Kelly explained. "There's obviously a lot of union featherbedding. But their main trouble seems to be that they're making too many products. Every time they shift from one size bearing to another, they have to stop and retool. I strongly suspect the true costs aren't factored in and added to the price of the product."

Weldon turned the pages, reading the figures.

"The featherbedding has been mentioned. That's strong union country. Molly Maguires and all that shit. But we'd be new owners. They'd have to renegotiate with us. I think we can lick them. But no one said anything about this retooling. You sure about this?"

"It's all there, in their own figures. Only the extent is in question. They probably don't know themselves. But I think that's where they're losing a lot of money."

Weldon grinned. "Little Brother, let's buy the fucking thing. Just you and me. We can set up our own company, Spurlock Industries. We could keep it separate from the oil company."

"Wouldn't we lose the tax advantages?"

"Not if we play it right. I've been looking into it. Here's the loophole: Spurlock Industries would own our chunk of Spurlock Oil. The tax advantages would accrue to our stock. We should come out smelling like a rose."

Kelly laughed.

More legerdemain.

"So far, those people haven't received a single offer. We can probably get it cheap. Then you can run up there, put the factory on track, find someone to run it for us."

Kelly raised his hands in a defensive gesture. "Weldon, I can't go off with Chandra about to have a baby. She needs me at home."

"Hire a nurse. Six nurses. A full-time doctor. Shit, Little Brother, if we don't acquire that factory by the end of the year, it'll cost us millions."

Kelly did not have a ready argument to that. Weldon's tax ploy would make a lot of money. Only the idea itself seemed awry.

"We're oil people," he said. "I'm not sure I want to own a factory."

"Look around you. Diversification has become the name of the game. There's no end to it. We can set up Spurlock Industries, and add as many companies as we want. As long as we charge off interest and buy the tax losses, it'll be like owning a press with a license to print money." Weldon laughed, relishing the thought. "Just think of all the run-down companies out there, like Spurlock Oil, waiting for us to come along and put them back on their feet. There must be hundreds!"

Kelly did not answer. While Weldon's theory was sound, it was also scary.

Already the growth rate of Spurlock Oil was judged phenomenal.

Now Weldon was wanting to start a whole new ball game.

But the prospect *was* exciting. Without the Spurlock board, and the restrictions of the family, they would be free to do anything they wished to do.

The possibilities were unlimited.

And once again it would be the Spurlock brothers against the world.

Their partnership would be everything Kelly once had dreamed it would be.

The factory clung to the side of a steep hill above a rounded ravine common to that region of Pennsylvania. Old and drab, the main building stretched for three hundred yards. Most of the administrative offices were contained in a smaller addition, erected during the early past of World War II. Below the plant, rail spurs ran the length of terraces beside the river. A narrow steel bridge dating from the twenties connected factory and the town on the opposite bank. The structures along Main Street were old and grimy, but a cluster of new businesses flourished along the highway west of town. There Kelly found adequate space in a motel to set up his offices. His connecting rooms quickly became headquarters for the acquisition.

As Weldon had said, the factory dated back through three generations of McCaffertys. The grandfather had died in the late twenties. His son, Nicholas McCafferty, chairman of the company, was now in his early seventies. He claimed to have retired, although Kelly found him constantly on the scene. His son Hugh was president and chief executive officer.

Acquisition of the company was progressing, but slowly.

Each day Kelly drove his rented car across the bridge to the factory, where he spent the day accumulating material and studying the operation. At dusk he carried his gatherings back to the motel, where through the long evenings he studied the information. Usually he ordered meals sent up to his room. More often, he forgot.

Aside from the factory, he paid little attention to his surroundings. Not until the end of his second week did he begin to notice that he was the object of much curiosity in the community. Wherever he went, gazes lingered on him. During his fact-finding tours about the plant, his questions were answered politely, but faces remained guarded. He was "one of those Texans who bought the factory." No one knew exactly what to expect.

He soon came to understand that, in a sense, he and Weldon had purchased a town, for its residents depended on the factory for a livelihood. Now everyone was waiting to see what would happen to both factory and town.

Kelly felt burdened by the responsibility. Spurlock Industries' decisions would affect hundreds of employees, their families, the entire valley.

He began to work with care.

By the end of the third week he had amassed a long list of drastic steps that would be required to lift the company out of its ocean of red ink. The changes were far more sweeping than those he had envisioned originally.

He phoned Weldon to discuss his revised opinions.

Weldon listened in silence until he was through.

"Well, Little Brother, there's nothing else to do. Don't even bother talking about it with them. Just stick it to them."

"We'll have trouble with the unions," Kelly warned.

"Hand them an ultimatum. Either we reduce the work force, or close the factory. They can take their pick."

Reluctantly, Kelly summoned the McCaffertys into a meeting the following day. Nicholas McCafferty insisted that three other company officers also be present, on the grounds that they were not only longtime managers but also stockholders.

Facing the five men at a conference table, Kelly could see no way to soften what he had to say.

"Basically, you are making too many products. When you add man-hours and miscellaneous costs, you are losing money on each specialty item. Our first step must be to terminate these products as soon as current orders are filled."

He handed out the list of models to be abandoned. Hugh McCafferty was the first to react. "Good Lord, man! This is half our production!"

"It's the half that has put this company in trouble," Kelly told him. "If special orders are accepted in the future, the per-item price must reflect the additional expense."

"I don't think you understand," the younger McCafferty said. "We have to accept these small orders to land the big ones. If we didn't do the short runs, they'd go elsewhere."

"That may have been true once," Kelly said. "It isn't now. I found only three correlations between short runs and profitable accounts."

The elder McCafferty was still mulling over the list. "Mr. Spurlock, we've done business with most of these people for decades."

"At a considerable loss," Kelly pointed out. "Your cost projections are fine, Mr. McCafferty, as far as they go. But they don't factor in the intangibles—insurance, social security, pensions, deterioration of machinery, heating, the handling from factory to dock, dozens of other actual expenses. I have completed a rundown."

He distributed copies.

The old man was still the fastest thinker. While the other executives were studying the figures, his mind was leaping ahead.

"Half the production," he said. "That means we'll have to cut half the work force."

"Slightly more than half," Kelly said. "The items we're eliminating are the most labor-intensive."

The elder McCafferty's face paled. Kelly feared for a moment he was having a heart attack.

"There's no way we can keep these men on the payroll?"

"Not unless we find enough additional orders immediately. I see no prospect of doing that."

The old man slowly shook his head. "I never thought I would live to see this."

The meeting ended on that glum note.

As Kelly left the plant, Hugh McCafferty followed him into the parking lot. "Mr. Spurlock, I know you've been working terribly hard, hardly leaving that motel. How about a change of pace, a relaxing dinner? The company has membership at a country club over in Pittsburgh. The food is above the ordinary."

Kelly was not in the mood and there was work to be done. But clearly McCafferty wanted to talk. "I appreciate your thoughtfulness," he said.

Kelly had learned much about the man during the last three weeks. Now in his late forties, he had flown more than a hundred missions off a carrier during the Korean War. Shot down by enemy fire, he spent two years as a POW. The man had a quiet friendliness about him that Kelly found engaging. Despite the obviously strain of losing the family business, he was cooperating in every way to effect an amiable transfer of ownership.

They left the factory and drove through the town, bleak with the false cheer of Christmas holly tossing in the cold wind at each intersection. The store windows were already dark and the town appeared deserted. McCafferty drove on to Pittsburgh under a gray, lowering sky that threatened snow. Kelly watched the rolling scenery while, from behind the wheel, McCafferty kept up a running, knowledgeable commentary on the history of the region.

McCafferty waited until after the leisurely dinner before introducing what was on his mind. Over brandy, he brought up the plight of the plant.

"Mr. Spurlock, you've been examining our books with a fresh perspective. I'm wondering if you can tell me. Where'd we go wrong?"

Kelly did not need to be evasive. "I really don't know."

"Was all of this inevitable?"

"No. At some point—I don't know where—a hard look should have been taken at the aging machinery, the unprofitable favors done for customers, the featherbedding. With sufficient outlay, and close attention, it could have been turned around."

"You understand, it isn't that Dad's soft. I remember him from the Depression. He was hard as nails."

"The situation probably built so slowly that no one involved could have noticed," Kelly said by way of comfort.

McCafferty seemed not to have heard. "This may kill Dad."

Kelly assumed they had arrived at the core of the reason for the dinner. He spoke cautiously. "Hugh, under the circumstances, I believe we've been generous in our consideration of your father's feelings."

"You have," McCafferty conceded. "But you see, he's so humiliated by all this. He identified totally with the plant. He feels personally responsible for everything that has happened. He thinks he has let the entire community down. I'm now convinced you'll put the company back on its feet. I was wondering if there wasn't some way that Dad could be a part of it, in some minor capacity, if only with a meaningless title."

Kelly recognized the suggestion as a request. He felt he should make the matter clear.

"Hugh, I'm sorry, but I can see no way we could do that. In rebuilding the company, we need to make a clean break. Your father still holds personal relationships with the unions, the customers, suppliers, people throughout the plant. His presence would be a detriment to everything my brother and I are trying to do. The people we're dealing with would try to go around us, by going to your father. A title would confuse them. It just wouldn't work."

McCafferty toyed with his brandy for a time in silence.

"Well, I certainly appreciate your frankness. I suppose I'm still disoriented, or I would've figured that out for myself.

But I know, as well as I know anything, that my father will be dead within a year. He simply will not survive this."

"I'm sorry," Kelly said again. "I'll talk to my brother about it. We might be able to think of something. But I really can't offer much hope."

"I'd be grateful for anything you can do."

"What about yourself?" Kelly asked. "As I understand it, the sale will leave you with considerable capital. Have you made any plans for going into business for yourself?"

McCafferty shrugged. "Oh, I'll survive. I really haven't thought ahead. All of this requires a big adjustment in my thinking too."

On the drive back, he continued to talk. "You see, I was the crown prince around here. My father ruled this valley for twenty years before I was born, and my grandfather before that. I grew up with it. When I came back from Korea, I was paraded right up Main Street. You'd have thought I fought the war single-handed. Now I'm no longer the crown prince. Believe me, that'll take some getting used to."

McCafferty drove Kelly back to his motel. As Kelly returned to his suite the phone was ringing. He picked it up.

"Where the hell have you been?" Weldon shouted. "I've been ringing this damned phone for an hour."

"Talks," Kelly said.

"You about got that mess wrapped up?"

"Weldon, it'll take a few more days."

"You find anyone to run it yet?"

"No. There are some other things to do first."

Weldon exploded. "God damn it, Kelly, I sent you up there to find somebody to run that plant, not to settle down and run it yourself. I need you back here."

Kelly waited until he had his temper under control. "Weldon, you didn't send me *anywhere*. I *came* here because this job needed to be done."

"Well, what the fuck are you doing? You've been up there three weeks."

"This can't be rushed. Tonight I had a long talk with Hugh

McCafferty. He was asking if we couldn't keep his father on with some kind of a title. I explained the situation. But I wish there were some way we could do it. Hugh says this will kill the old man within a year. I'm afraid he's right."

"He should have thought of that before he went broke. Tell them not only no, but hell no. We can't allow a McCafferty within a mile of that place. If that's all you're doing up there, holding people's hands, get your ass back down here. I've got us a hot new prospect. What do you know about lumber?"

"Probably as much as you do."

"Funny, funny. There's a lumber mill up in Oregon that learned how to fly high back during the war. They've been trying to come down ever since. They haven't made it. Sounds like our kind of people."

"Weldon, the lumber company can wait. I'm about to become a father. It's almost Christmas. I'm going home to spend the holidays with Chandra, and wait for the baby."

"Listen, if we don't buy this mill now, somebody'll come along and beat us to it. Everyone's getting into this conglomerate act. There are too many buzzards, and not enough carcasses."

"Wait'll I get back. Then we'll talk about it."

Kelly broke the connection, waited for the dial tone, and called home. Chandra answered almost immediately.

"You okay?" he asked.

"I have my good days, my bad days," she said. "This has been a moderately good day."

"Been back to the doctor?"

"No. I thought I'd wait until you get home."

Kelly dreaded telling her. "Chandra, I'll have to stay here another three or four days. Then I'll be home."

The line remained silent.

"I'll be home for Christmas," he promised. "And I've served notice on Weldon that I'm staying home until after the baby arrives. But I may have to go out to Oregon sometime after the first of the year. Weldon says we have a new prospect."

Again the line remained silent for a time. "Why can't Weldon go to Oregon?"

"Because I'm the one who handles the numbers."

"You mean because you're the one who does the work while Weldon sits behind his desk and plays the big executive."

"Weldon finds and closes the deals," Kelly said. "No one does it better."

"What if the baby doesn't conform to Weldon's schedule? Can Weldon make a deal on that?"

Kelly did not answer.

Chandra sighed. "Kelly, you told me how painful it was for you, growing up without a father. His absence was understandable. That was wartime, and men were expected to give their lives to it. But you're killing yourself to satisfy Weldon's greed. Nothing else. Kelly, will your son grow up barely remembering his father?"

Kelly did not have a ready answer. She was so sure it would be a boy. "This won't be forever," he promised.

"Dead is forever. When I call that motel at two or three in the morning, you answer on the first ring. You're still up and working. When I call at seven in the morning, you've already left for the plant. Even if I didn't know you, it'd be plain how little sleep you're getting. Are you eating? I'll bet you're skin and bones."

Kelly avoided a reply. That morning he had noticed his belt felt loose, even at the tightest notch.

"Does the Oregon trip mean you'll be away another month? While I cope with a new baby?"

"Chandra, at this point I don't know. I only heard about it tonight. I've no idea what's involved."

Again the line was silent a moment. "Kelly, I want out," she said quietly.

Irrationally, his first thought was that she meant out of the marriage. But before he could react, she went on.

"This life we're leading is stupid. We don't need the money. Both of our families are comfortably well off. We could be enjoying each other, raising children, instead of squandering our lives on Weldon's colossal ego. Please, Kelly. Don't go to Oregon. Tell Weldon we want out. You could go into business for yourself. Retire and live on the income from your stock. Anything but this."

Kelly thought of the way the fledgling conglomerate was structured.

"It wouldn't be that easy."

Chandra groaned. "I wish I knew why Weldon has such strange power over you."

"Weldon doesn't have any power over me."

"Yes, he does. You're ten times the man Weldon could ever hope to be, yet you let him dominate you unmercifully."

Kelly remembered an earlier time, another conversation, when that charge had been made.

"It may seem at times that he does. But he doesn't."

"Then why do you do his work like this? I want to know."

"Chandra, it's my work too. I'm a full partner. We're earning our place among the competition."

"See? You even sound like him. I can hear him saying it: 'Money is how you keep score.' How trite can you get?"

"It's not just the money. We're doing some good. And there's satisfaction in that."

"Doing good? How? Buying worn-out old factories for a song?"

"By saving the plant, jobs."

He spent the better part of an hour describing the town, the people, their economic dependence on the plant.

"We'll save about half the jobs now," he concluded. "And there's a chance the plant can come back, be bigger, stronger than ever, even more important to the community than it was."

"That may help those people in Pennsylvania, but it gives me little comfort. I hope I don't have to try to explain to your son some day, when he wonders why his father sacrificed his life rebuilding run-down old factories."

Chapter 38

In the second weekend of January, after two false alarms, Chandra gave birth to a seven-and-a-half-pound boy. Kelly and Chandra had agreed on the name John, for her late father. Although Weldon pitched several temper tantrums, Kelly remained in Fort Worth until his son was born. But after Ella Sykes came down from Tulsa to be with her daughter and grandson, Kelly felt he was free to leave for the Pacific Northwest.

He flew his Cessna to Portland and drove up the magnificent Columbia River gorge to the lumber company, perched on the side of a mountain in the Cascades.

He was met by the owner, an elderly gentleman by the name of Angus MacKenzie, who took him into an office in the main building.

"What do you know about lumbering, Mr. Spurlock?" MacKenzie asked.

"Absolutely nothing," Kelly admitted. "I'm only here to look at the cash flow, to see where your mill got into trouble."

MacKenzie glared out at the world from behind a set of fiercely bushy eyebrows. He had a lean Scots face and wild mane of white hair, partially covered by a corduroy cap. He wore khaki trousers, matching shirt, and a mackinaw jacket. His office was lined with raw spruce. Kelly savored the pleasant odor.

"I thought maybe you was from one of those lumber companies back in Texas. You have them there, don't you?"

"In East Texas," Kelly told him. "I'm from several hundred miles west of there. I've never been inside a lumber mill."

"Good God! Don't know a thing about lumber? Why you buying my company?"

Kelly saw no reason not to tell him. "For the tax losses. You see, we have a profitable oil company. If we can absorb losses from the companies we buy, it's like money in the bank."

MacKenzie gritted his teeth. "Jesus God! I've put sixty years of hard work into this place. Now the only reason it's worth anything is because it's losing money!"

Kelly remained silent. He had the whole story in his briefcase. It was a classic case of the hazards of partnership. MacKenzie and his brother started the company as young men and ran it successfully for more than a half century. Then the brother died and his half of the company fell into a family squabble and long litigation. In buying out his in-laws at an exorbitant price, MacKenzie got into trouble and never recovered. His wife was dead, and his only son had been killed in a logging accident in the forties.

"Those big outfits tried to buy me out," MacKenzie said. "But I've seen what they've done to other places. I held out as long as I could. When your brother called, I was at the end of my rope, or I wouldn't have sold then. Want to go look at what you bought?"

Kelly nodded.

MacKenzie led him to a pond where huge logs were floating, waiting to be processed.

"They're trucked in, dumped in the water to preserve them," MacKenzie explained. "They'd rot, lying on the ground. There's one going onto the bullchain now. That's the start of the milling."

Kelly and the old man walked up a steep ramp to where they could see the log entering the mill. It was sprayed constantly by high-pressure streams of water. Dirt and bark went flying.

"They're washed so dirt won't dull the saws," MacKenzie shouted above the noise. Huge mechanical arms came down, gripped the log, and moved it into position. "Now the nigger's taking it into the gang saws. They'll rip it into cants."

As Kelly watched, the log was sliced like an unusually wide loaf of bread. The mechanical arms rolled the slices onto conveyers. A worker stood manipulating levers. Some slices went one way, some another.

"Now they'll go into the trimmers," MacKenzie shouted. "Watch your step."

They walked down into another part of the mill, where huge saws were carving the slices of log into rough planks.

Describing each step of the process, MacKenzie led Kelly on through the lumber mill. He watched a dizzying array of planks whipping through the planing mill, emerging to be graded, cut into lengths, and stacked. They walked through the huge kiln sheds where the finished lumber was dried and cured.

At last they returned to MacKenzie's office.

"Have any idea what you've just seen?" MacKenzie asked.

"It was an education," Kelly said. "But I'm really just here to look at your books."

"You've just seen the last mill in the Pacific Northwest still putting out a quality product. I don't ship green lumber. I don't cut corners in the kiln. Any employee of mine who fudges in sorting or grading is fired on the spot. By God when a dealer buys from MacKenzie, he knows what he's getting."

"I can appreciate that," Kelly said. "But you've been losing money."

"I've been paying out too much money to the goddamn banks. That's all that's wrong. I couldn't seem to turn the corner."

"That's why I want to look at the books," Kelly said. "Maybe we can find some way to cut costs."

"Friend of mine sold out, and the new outfit sent in time and motion engineers with their stopwatches. You're not one of those stopwatch fellows, are you?"

"No," Kelly said. "I'm trained to manage organizations, handle money. That's what my brother and I do. We buy companies, see how we can run them more efficiently."

"You went to college to learn that?"

"Yes."

MacKenzie looked out the window to where a truck was arriving, piled with logs.

"You learn anything in those books about knots?"

"About what?"

"Knots." He gestured to the window, the mill. "That's what this is all about, Mr. Spurlock. Knots. These new conglomerates won't tolerate knots, and accommodate them to the product. They want to grind everything into pulp, stamp it into composition board. They do the same with people. Everyone has to conform to a sameness. How can you put a price on all the lives that have gone into a place like this, made it what it is? You're buying people too. Don't you know that? It's a new kind of slavery, that's what it is. A new serfdom. Grinding people into composition. By God I hate to see it."

Kelly did not know how to respond. He remained silent.

"Most of those men out there have been with me twenty, thirty years," MacKenzie went on. "You'll find a lot of hard knots among them. They're nonconformists. No conglomerate will ever grind them up."

"Mr. MacKenzie, at this moment I don't know what we will do with your company. I'll have to study the situation, and talk with my brother."

"Do what you want," MacKenzie said. "The place is yours. You bought it."

Kelly spent three days examining the company's records. Then he began a study of the industry itself, calling suppliers, dealers, customers. After a week, he felt he had gained insight into MacKenzie's problem. He talked it over with Weldon.

"MacKenzie's in the wrong market," he explained. "He makes outstanding lumber, and sells it to construction companies, home builders. But that market is moving more and more into economy wood. Green, quick-dried, lower grades. MacKenzie can't compete in price and turn a profit. That's his bind."

"So what do we do?"

"Sell to cabinetmakers, window-and-sash plants, furniture houses. I've surveyed that market. They pay for quality. I think it'd work."

"Shit, Kelly, we can't mess around with this forever. Let's put somebody in charge, cut costs, hang on to it two or three years, bleed off the losses, then sell it to one of the conglomerates. That's what I figured we'd do."

"This would make it worth more."

"Who'd we get to run it?"

"How about MacKenzie? Weldon, this place seems well managed. He has a good work force. I can't find much fat anywhere. He's just selling his product too cheap."

Weldon snorted. "He's about a hundred years old, isn't he?"

"Seventy-five. But he's fit. I'd hate to tangle with him."

"How long would that take, setting up this new market?"

"Two, three weeks."

Weldon paused in indecision. "I don't know. I need you back here to look into another deal. Maybe we'd best go the other way, hire a professional manager."

Kelly thought of MacKenzie's knots. Gradually Weldon's way would grind up, destroy what MacKenzie had taken a lifetime to build. More quality would be gone from the world. He felt he should make an effort to save it.

"Weldon, you seem to believe I can analyze companies on paper. What makes you think I can't in the field? MacKenzie has assembled a good work force. They're loyal to him, been with him for years. Believe me, if we break up what he has here, the company will be worth less money."

The argument seemed to hold appeal. "All right. Go ahead and set it up. But get back here pronto. Unless you get the lead out, we may lose out on another deal."

Kelly took his plan to MacKenzie the following day. The old man quickly agreed to stay on to run the company, but he was dubious about aiming for a different market.

"We tried that once, back in the forties," he said. "We didn't make a dent."

"Their sources of supply have changed," Kelly explained. "They used to depend on hardwoods. Now those forests are mostly gone."

"Where'd you learn that? In college?"

Kelly laughed. "No. But they taught us how to explore markets."

During the next two weeks Kelly worked with MacKenzie on plans to convert the mill to shorter lengths, better finished products. They hired a specialty salesman, who guaranteed that he could open up the new market. At last Kelly felt his job was done.

On Kelly's final evening in Oregon, MacKenzie reached into his desk, pulled out a bottle of fine Scotch whisky, and poured two sturdy drinks.

"Here's to the college boy," he said. "God, how I misjudged you, young fellow."

Kelly raised his glass in acknowledgment of what he supposed was a compliment. They finished the drink. MacKenzie poured two more.

"But I'm curious, Mr. Spurlock. You could see I made a mess of running this place in the last few years. Why'd you decide to ask me to stay on?"

Again Kelly raised his glass.

"Let's just say I found a knot I doubted could be ground up."

The baby lay on his back in a blue bassinet. As Joanna leaned over him, his eyes focused on her and his arms began to work like tiny pistons.

Joanna examined his features. His eyes and hair showed

traces of Indian heritage, but in his face Joanna saw close resemblance to Kelly as a baby—the same calm expression of pleased anticipation.

"May I hold him?" she asked.

"Of course."

Chandra gestured Joanna to a rocking chair, picked up the infant with his blanket, and handed the bundle to her.

Holding her first grandson seemed the most natural act Joanna had performed in years. Rocking gently, she was transported back to the unforgettable pleasure of holding her own babies.

It was the first time she had been in Kelly's house. She had long put off a visit, not wishing to imply by her presence that she had forgiven what he had done. But she knew he was out of town. She had seen items in the newspapers reporting the growing list of acquisitions by Spurlock Industries—a roller-bearing factory in Pennsylvania, a lumber company in Oregon, a toy factory in Iowa, a farm machinery plant in Wisconsin. Walter had convinced her that her lingering anger with Kelly should not extend to Chandra and the baby.

"Weldon was a colicky baby," she heard herself saying from the depths of memory. "He cried all the time and drove us frantic. We never discovered the reason. Eventually he seemed to grow out of it."

Chandra was seated in a facing chair. "John doesn't cry much, thank the Lord. I don't think I could stand it if he did."

Silence now reigned throughout the house. Joanna had heard servants below, earlier, but now all was quiet.

"Kelly shouldn't be leaving you alone like this," she said. "It's too much of a responsibility, rearing children alone."

Chandra did not respond. By her silence, Joanna assumed it was a delicate subject.

"I remember once when Brod was away, during the war. Kelly came down with a racking cough and high fever— almost a hundred and six. Most of the doctors were away in military service at the time. That was before penicillin and the wonder drugs, so you never knew what might happen.

Brod was in secret work—directing fuel supplies for the invasions, as it turned out. It was days before I could reach him. By then, the crisis was over. But I'll never forget how helpless I felt."

"Kelly calls every night," Chandra said. "I know that if an emergency came up, he would be home in a matter of hours."

Joanna did not pursue the subject further. Already she had said more than she intended.

But it seemed to be weighing heavily on Chandra's mind.

"Kelly keeps saying his traveling is temporary. I'm beginning to wonder. It just goes on and on."

"I wish they'd forget all that and be content with the oil company," Joanna said. "I always knew they'd be adventurous. But I never dreamed it'd be so extensive."

"It's Weldon's doing. I think Kelly is just going along with him. Sometimes I feel Kelly is really unhappy, and wants to get out of it, but doesn't know how. It's like he's chained to Weldon."

Joanna heard bitterness in Chandra's voice. The conversation had turned far more serious than she wished. Chandra seemed to be fishing for information. Joanna did not want to appear overly secretive to her daughter-in-law, who had a right to know.

"The boys have always been close," she said. "I've never really understood it. They've plotted and schemed together since they were in rompers. In many ways, they complemented each other. Weldon would take Kelly out of his natural introversion, give him some get-up-and-go. And Kelly was a steadying influence on Weldon. Sometimes I think it's like the two sides of the same coin."

"Then you don't think there will ever be an end to it?"

Joanna recognized it as an important question. She answered carefully.

"Chandra, I really don't know. Weldon always seemed to dominate Kelly, drag him into things. But I've always seen evidence that Kelly is a stronger person. I wish I could find a better answer, but I can't."

The baby sounded a mild complaint in Joanna's arms. His tiny fists moved, and he left no doubt what he wanted.

Chandra rose. "If we can swap chairs . . ."

Chandra took the baby, unbuttoned a strap of her jumper, opened her blouse, and he began to feed. Her movements were so disarmingly unaffected that Joanna was completely charmed.

Framed in soft light from the windows, Chandra and son offered an intimate scene worthy of an artist. The baby fed voraciously, eyes half closed in contentment.

Slowly the baby became satiated and drifted off to sleep.

Joanna gestured that she would leave.

Chandra gently returned the baby to the bassinet and walked back downstairs with Joanna. "I'm glad you came. Kelly will probably call this evening. Is there anything you would like me to tell him?"

"Only that I said John is a beautiful baby."

"Please come anytime," Chandra said at the front door.

"Thank you, I will," Joanna said. On impulse she added, "And you and John come visit us when you can."

She left the house, knowing full well that this first visit was the start of a hopelessly addictive habit.

As Spurlock Industries continued to expand through the next few years, Kelly and Weldon perfected their operational style. Usually Weldon made the initial contact, stressing his Texas accent and good-ol'-boy demeanor throughout preliminary negotiations.

"All that sounds real good," he would tell the owners. "My brother Kelly will be there in a few days to iron out details."

After Weldon's country-bumpkin approach, Kelly's arrival came as a sobering surprise. He now traveled in a Learjet, accompanied by two accountants. Cool and taciturn, Kelly concentrated on driving a hard bargain. Yet he implied he might be making unauthorized concessions.

"I'll have to get this approved by my brother," he warned repeatedly.

By the time Weldon returned at the end of the talks, the

sellers were eager to deal again with "the friendly one" who held the power of approval. And until the closing session, Weldon lived up to their expectations. Jovial, a backslapper, a font of racy and off-color jokes, he lulled the sellers into a relaxed mood.

Only late in the game would the sellers learn that Weldon was indeed the "tough" one.

It was the good-cop, bad-cop routine with a difference. This time the good cop looked like the bad cop, and the bad cop like the good cop. Weldon and Kelly usually closed the deal before the sellers sorted out the players.

In the early seventies a national news magazine published a cover story on "the maverick Spurlock brothers of Texas" and "the financial empire they are building."

Kelly was disturbed by the article. It was full of facts and figures that could only have come from Weldon.

On the cover, the artist successfully captured Weldon's self-confident, go-to-hell grin. He was portrayed full-faced, conveying his ebullient good spirits. Kelly was shown behind him, in quarter profile, looking over Weldon's shoulder with an unsmiling, wary, analytical gaze.

The text said that Weldon was "a hale fellow well met," and that he seemed never to encounter a stranger. Various unnamed "associates" were reported as saying that Kelly was "secretive, cold, and aloof, difficult to get to know."

And to Kelly's chagrin, once again the story was reprinted of how the sons "kicked their mother upstairs" to board chairman, and assumed control of the oil company, "which laid the base for the building of their empire."

"Insiders" were quoted as saying animosity still prevailed between mother and sons.

The claim held enough of a kernel of truth that it could not be effectively denied.

The story gave Spurlock Industries an added boost. During the next few months offers poured in. Acquisitions came even faster.

As the pace continued to quicken, Kelly experienced times of supreme happiness, and of agonizing dissatisfaction.

As long as he remained immersed in work, everything appeared to be as it should be.

Again it was the Spurlock brothers against the world, just as he had dreamed as a boy. He reveled in the hard negotiations with powerful men, the clear-cut victories.

It seemed what he was born to do.

But in his quieter moments he was nagged by the knowledge that Chandra was immensely unhappy, and that life was passing. On each visit home he often was disoriented momentarily by the changes in his son. It seemed that one day John was a baby, the next a toddler, then a superactive boy dashing full-tilt about the house.

He no longer offered Chandra the hope that eventually the demands upon him would ease.

He no longer believed the promise himself.

Other sources of unhappiness grew. Unlike Weldon, he could not become hardened to the disruptions the acquisitions brought to people's lives. As he restructured companies, hired new management, solved labor problems, and trimmed costs, he often had occasion to remember Angus MacKenzie and his "knots" who refused to be ground into composition.

From owners to the lowest employee, he continually came across these knots. Hugh McCafferty wrote that his father had died within four months after Spurlock Industries acquired his roller-bearing factory. In Atlanta, faced with trimming the work force by thirty percent, the manager of a shoe factory hanged himself in the executive washroom. In acquisition after acquisition, Kelly saw fear in the faces of workers as they stared at him, fully aware that he held awesome power over their jobs, their lives.

Weldon reveled in this power.

Kelly was deeply perturbed by it. Numbers he once regarded as exquisitely neat and precise on paper had now assumed faces and form. No longer could he forget the impact of the thousands of pink slips he had dispensed, dating back to the closure of the refinery in Houston.

Kelly was further concerned that in their preoccupation

with Spurlock Industries, the oil company was receiving short shrift. With a new staff of managers, the oil company was yielding an excellent profit. But not much attention was being paid to long-range goals.

Joanna's memos pointed this out regularly.

"The company is making a profit, but only at the expense of new exploration and its reserves," she wrote. "Anyone can pump oil out of the ground, which is basically what we're doing. We should be finding new sources, building our reserves, so expansion can be done rapidly if the need arises. This takes time and effort. But we should be doing it."

Afterward, Kelly was sure that not even Joanna dreamed her point would be driven home in such dramatic fashion. In the fall of 1973 the Arab embargo shook the petroleum industry to its foundations.

Almost overnight the price of oil shot from three dollars a barrel to ten and more. As cars lined up at gas pumps across the nation, pressure was put on the oil industry to make up the shortfall.

Kelly and Weldon put Spurlock Industries on hold while they sought ways to increase the production of oil. Until he saw the figures, Kelly had not realized how far they had allowed their oil reserves to dwindle.

With every oil company drilling at peak capacity, and with doctors, dentists, lawyers and other investors entering the oil game in droves, rigs were in short supply. Spurlock Oil's production rate was at its lowest level in years. Clearly they had been caught napping. Something had to be done immediately.

Weldon drafted an elaborate plan for expansion and called the Spurlock Oil Company board into emergency session.

They met on a rainy day in early October. Kelly had just concluded a hectic series of closures in different cities, and felt disoriented from his abrupt return to Fort Worth. As they filed into the boardroom and took their places, it seemed to Kelly as if he were in a time warp, thrust far into his own future. His mother, Campbell, and Ann Leigh seemed years older. Weldon had gained weight, lost more hair, and appeared positively middle-aged.

Joanna opened the meeting and called on Weldon to explain his plan.

Weldon had prepared graphs and charts. He distributed them to the board.

"This will require a considerable outlay," he warned. "Drilling costs have gone out of sight, and they're still climbing. We'll have to compete for leases. Options that brought ten dollars an acre two months ago are going now for hundreds, even thousands."

He explained that independent drilling contractors were now booked far ahead. He proposed buying new rigs with a complex system of financing, using funds from current production.

Kelly was exhausted from his trips. He attempted to follow Weldon's logic, but failed to see it. Nothing in the search for oil was guaranteed. A series of dry holes could wreck Weldon's plan and create a monstrous shortfall.

Weldon completed his presentation.

"Discussion?" Joanna said. "Kelly?"

He wondered why she called upon him first. Perhaps she knew he was not prepared.

"Mom, I just got back from Augusta late last night. I haven't had a chance to study it."

She gave him her familiar blank look.

"Mr. Campbell?"

"I see risks," Campbell said. "I'd like to know more about the prospects on those leases. I'll have to study it."

"Ann Leigh?"

"Perhaps I'm an old fogey, but it bothers me to borrow that much money. It took us forever to pay off what we borrowed for the Wilcox merger."

"We retired those notes well ahead of time," Weldon pointed out.

"That's true," Ann Leigh admitted. "And I really feel we should be getting in on this boom. These opportunities don't come along often. Joanna, what do you think?"

"I hate to say I told you so. But remember, I told you so. I think we've lost out on this boom. All that has been demonstrated in the last few weeks is that the price of oil is highly volatile. It could come down just as fast as it went up. Faster. If that happened, we would be stuck with the outlay, trying to pay off loans without adequate revenue."

"The experts are saying oil may go to forty dollars a barrel," Weldon said. "Maybe higher."

Joanna smiled. "The experts told Johnstown that even if that old dam did break, the level of the river would rise only eighteen inches. Experts said the *Titanic* was unsinkable. Experts told the people on Martinique that even if Mount Pelée did blow, the town of St. Pierre was safe. Thirty thousand people died. It doesn't always pay to listen to the experts."

"I'm confused," Ann Leigh said. "I don't know what to think."

"Mom, this may be high noon of the oil business," Weldon insisted. "We can't afford to sit around and lose out on it."

"Maybe so, Weldon. But if the price should drop, with the outlay you're proposing, it could be a very long *afternoon*."

"We'd have the rigs, the wells. We'd still be producing."

"At a loss on every barrel, with these drilling costs. Weldon, a lot of people could get caught out in this one."

"What would you do?" Kelly asked.

"I think we should reposition ourselves to increase production as much as we can, using what facilities and leases we have on hand. We might pick up a rig or two, or some really promising leases. But I'm dead set against any sizable outlay."

"Joanna, everyone else is making a lot of money in this," Ann Leigh said. "Clay always said he made his money by plunging every cent into the booms. I hate to tie the boys' hands. They've done wonders so far."

Joanna did not answer.

With growing apprehension, Kelly saw that he would be the swing vote. Joanna and Campbell would be against. Weldon and Ann Leigh would vote for.

"Weldon, do you want to delay a vote?" Joanna asked.

"No," Weldon said. "We've got to move on this."

"All right. All those in favor."

Weldon and Ann Leigh raised their hands. Neither noticed that Kelly did not join them.

"Against?"

Campbell raised a hand. After a moment of hesitation, Kelly raised his own.

Weldon stared at him openmouthed. But Joanna did not seem surprised.

"We seem to have a tie vote," she said. "The chair votes against. Weldon, I suggest you draft a new proposal, more along the lines I suggested. I'll send you a memo. I believe that concludes our business for today."

Kelly rose and walked straight back to his office. As he expected, Weldon followed close on his heels. Weldon entered the office behind him and slammed the door.

"What the fuck was that all about? Why the goddamn hell did you do that?"

Kelly did not feel like talking about it. "Weldon, the numbers didn't look good. I think Mom's right on this one."

"Why the shit didn't you tell me?"

"You didn't ask."

"I guess you know you've blown it. We'll lose out on the only oil boom in our lifetime."

"This isn't a boom," Kelly pointed out. "It's a temporary shortage because of a fluctuation in supply."

"Whatever. Since you're so goddamn smart, let's see *your* plan. Forget the trip to Pocatello and work on it. Let's see if *you* can salvage anything out of this goddamn mess."

Weldon stormed out, again slamming the door. Kelly sank into the chair behind his desk, already thinking ahead to drafting a new plan, spending a few precious weeks at home.

Chapter 39

In the beginning, it was Walter's idea. Returning from a symphony performance in Dallas, traveling along the old Turnpike, now a freeway, they both were lost in their own thoughts. They had ridden for miles in silence before Walter spoke.

"Why don't we have a good, old-fashioned family Christmas?" he asked. "With Weldon and Kelly home, we could have everyone over for Christmas dinner."

Startled, Joanna responded from reflex. "Oh, Walter, that would never work."

"Why not?"

"There are too many undercurrents. For one thing, Chandra can't stand Weldon. And you can't either. Don't deny it."

Walter laughed. "I could endure him for one day."

Joanna thought about it. The idea *was* tempting. But drawbacks abounded.

"Walter, the split on the board is getting worse, not better. Weldon is furious with Kelly for going against him. Now they're fighting about this new production plan. And Walter,

I still haven't forgiven the boys for what they did to me. I've tried. But it won't rest. Just when I think it's behind me, it crops up again, like in that magazine story."

Walter drove several more miles.

"I also was thinking of Ann Leigh," he said. "This may be her last Christmas."

With a pang of remorse, Joanna saw the truth in his observation. Ann Leigh had been taken to the hospital twice in the last five weeks with heart palpitations. She often complained of dizzy spells. The doctors said her heart was deteriorating.

"I'm also thinking of little John," Walter went on. "He's old enough to remember a Christmas spent with his great-grandmother."

And grandmother, Joanna thought.

The seed was planted. Through the next several days the idea grew. Joanna could not put it out of her mind. Perhaps she owed it to her family. And she also felt she owed it to Walter. Peggy had said that Walter always wanted a family. Now in a way, he had one.

Joanna called Chandra to see if the invitation would interfere with any of her plans. Chandra's response was immediate.

"I'll have to discuss it with Kelly. But I feel sure he would love to have dinner with you."

Ann Leigh was enthusiastic. Weldon acted as if he could not care less, but Joanna felt that he, too, was touched by the idea. He said he would come.

Joanna began preparations. She erected a Christmas tree, lights, decorations, the works. With Calla Lily she planned a sumptuous dinner of turkey and dressing, cranberries, yams, gravy, and a variety of cakes and pies.

She wanted the day to be absolutely perfect.

"Maybe we're not exactly Norman Rockwell," she told Walter. "But I do hope we can spend this Christmas together as a family."

* * *

"Clay drove us out to Breckenridge once during the boom there," Ann Leigh said. "I'll never forget it. Brod and Loren were about John's age. Crystelle was still a baby."

The family sat around the log fire, listening. Walter had served drinks, and adroitly enticed Ann Leigh into her memories. Joanna watched the reactions of her family. Weldon, Kelly, and Chandra were totally engrossed. Despite their differences, they were all third-generation oil people. John, seated on the carpet at Ann Leigh's feet, was also following the story. Perhaps some day he would be fourth-generation.

"We climbed the stairs to the top of the courthouse," Ann Leigh went on. "From there you could see a thousand oil derricks. At least they said it was a thousand. I didn't count them. But it certainly looked like a thousand. Some were still drilling, some pumping. It was like being in the middle of a big bed of red ants. Trucks and equipment were going every which way. It was a sight to see."

She paused, remembering.

"There were no paved roads then, you know. And not many bridges, either. The dust was terrible, and it clung to your clothing, skin, and hair. Sometimes we had to wait for an hour or more while the men moved big boilers and other heavy equipment across creeks and washouts. Sometimes they had trucks. But more often they used mules, harnessed into spans of four, six, or eight animals. Clay said sometimes they used oxen for the really heavy equipment, but I didn't see that."

Ann Leigh's account seemed at end.

"Did you see any other boom towns?" Chandra asked.

"I saw Ranger and Burkburnett, but not until after the peaks of the booms. I'm told that Breckenridge was tame by comparison. It was wild enough for me."

"My father was at Healdton, Three Sands, some of the other booms in Oklahoma," Chandra said.

"Clay went up to Oklahoma and drilled one time when he was a young man. He always laughed about it. He said he and his partner drilled through four pay formations without a show of oil, and there were gushers all around them."

"I didn't know that," Kelly said.

"It was a long time ago. Before I met him, even," Ann Leigh said.

Joanna thought of Beth's story of Ann Leigh and Clay's dramatic departure from a dance, leaving Ann Leigh's first husband beaten to a pulp on the floor. Perhaps nudged by the memory, Ann Leigh fell silent.

Joanna moved into the awkward pause.

"Let's have the tree," she said. "John, come on. You can deliver the presents. Your great-grandmother will play Santa Claus."

Quickly she organized the ceremony. She moved Ann Leigh into a straight chair beside the tree. Kneeling, Joanna handed each present to Ann Leigh, who called out the name on the tag. John delivered the present to the recipient. Everyone waited until each gift was opened before going on to the next.

As soon as the ceremony was over, Joanna hurried into the kitchen to check on the dinner. All was progressing on schedule.

The men went into the library to watch a football game on television. John played in the hall with a toy he had received. Joanna left Ann Leigh and Chandra to their own devices and supervised the setting of the table.

At last dinner was ready. The family gathered, and Joanna directed the seating. Walter returned thanks. The wine was poured, and dinner began.

Joanna remained in high spirits. The day was progressing perfectly, just the way she had planned.

Kelly rose from the dinner table and followed Walter and Weldon back into the living room.

Weldon was still preoccupied with the football game they had watched. "They'll have to build a pass defense if they ever want to beat the Aggies."

Walter made a reply that Kelly did not hear. He knew he was a rarity: a Texas male who did not care for football.

For some reason Kelly could not define, Weldon had been irritating him all day. It was not the cigars, or the occasional backslap. He was used to that. And Weldon had been on his best behavior around Chandra. Kelly knew he should be grateful.

But Kelly felt himself locked into a sadness he could not shake. He had gone upstairs to use the bathroom, and found that everything on the second floor was different. His boyhood room had vanished in drastic remodeling. The old master bedroom was no more. Weldon's room had been combined with another.

Kelly had trouble finding the bathroom in his own childhood home.

He watched his son, playing in the hall with a toy, just as he himself used to do. He remembered the fears he once had entertained, and the nightmares. As John sat on the floor, turning a wheel of the toy experimentally, Kelly wondered if his son was ever troubled by such a vivid imagination, by such thoughts.

He did not know. Away from home for weeks at a time, he hardly knew his son. But from what he could discover, they were much alike. John also seemed to be turned inward, a thinker, a worrier. Kelly thought of what a tragedy it would be if his son followed in his footsteps, growing up into a world forever fearful, constantly threatening.

With the help of the boy choir, he had found himself.

John might not.

Chandra moved across the dining room, helping Joanna set the house in order after dinner. He noticed for the first time that her hips were fuller, more mature, more alluring. Gone was her ballerina slimness. She looked at him and her eyes lingered, conveying a hunger for his presence. He also wished they were home, lounging in bed, talking, instead of here.

Walter was speaking to him. Preoccupied, Kelly had to ask him to repeat.

"I asked if you will be home through the rest of the holidays. I thought we might get together again."

"Yes," Kelly said. "I'll be home at least through the first of the year."

"Little Brother, you forget," Weldon said. "You have an important trip to Chicago next week."

Kelly had made his decision. "I'm not going."

Weldon jerked around in his chair. His voice rose. "Like hell! What are you talking about? Kelly, you damned well better be up there by Tuesday. I've got it set up."

Kelly thought of his insight a moment ago into the lives of Chandra, John, himself.

"Weldon, you or someone else can go," he said. "I'm staying home for a while."

Weldon's face assumed a red tinge. "Like shit! You're the one who did the figuring on that deal. No one else can talk with those people about it!"

The women had stopped moving in the dining room. Chandra came to the doorway, concern on her face. John sat motionless in the hall, listening. Kelly heard his own voice as if it came from someone else.

"Weldon, I'm tired," he said. "I don't want to do it anymore. I want out."

"What the shit are you talking about?"

"I mean exactly what I say. I want out of Spurlock Industries. I don't want any more to do with it."

Weldon rose, his fists closing in his old Jimmy Cagney stance. "You can't do that! There's no way in the world we can break up Industries. It's all locked together."

"There's a way," Kelly said. "It could be separated."

Weldon looked around the room at the impromptu audience. "What's behind this? Do you have Walter working on some kind of legal skullduggery?"

"No," Kelly said.

Weldon took a step toward Joanna, standing in the doorway to the dining room. "Are you in on it?"

"No," Joanna said.

Weldon dropped back into his chair and leaned toward Kelly, hands on knees. "Kelly, Little Brother, don't be crazy! You'll fall flat on your face without me!"

Kelly spoke from a newfound certainty.

"No, Weldon. It'll be you who'll fall flat without *me*."

"Bullshit. I'm the one who held it all together from the first. What about that first company we bought? Up in Ohio? You were going to bring that old man back into it and ruin everything. I stopped it."

"Pennsylvania," Kelly said. "And that old man died before the ink was dry on the contracts. We killed him."

"That lumber camp. The shoe factory. The union in Illinois. You always were ready to give in. You know numbers, Little Brother. But you're just not tough enough. I have to do the work."

"Then do it," Kelly said. "I'm through."

"Like fuck you are! Kelly, I'll sue your ass. You and me are locked in an ironclad partnership. It can't be broken."

Walter raised a hand. "Weldon, I'll thank you to watch your language in my house."

Weldon turned on him. "*Your* house! That's a laugh. Butt out, Walter. This is family. It doesn't concern you."

Joanna came flying out of the dining room. "Weldon, you apologize this instant! This *is* Walter's house. This *is* his family."

"Joanna, it's all right," Walter said.

"Apologize!" Joanna said.

"That's the way I talk," Weldon said. "I don't apologize for it."

"Then get out of my house! Walter's house!"

"Joanna, it's all right," Walter said again.

"Get!"

Weldon rose and started for the door. He stopped and looked back at Kelly. "Call me tomorrow. You're upset. I don't know why. But we've got to talk about this."

"There's nothing to talk about," Kelly told him. "I'm through with Industries. I've thought it all out. I'll send you a plan for dividing our holdings. I think you'll like it. You'll get most of the money."

Weldon stood and looked at him for a long moment. "You sure you won't reconsider?"

"No."

"Then to hell with you." Weldon looked at Joanna. "I still think this is your doing."

"No, Weldon. It isn't. I'm glad to see it, but I had nothing to do with it."

"This isn't the first time you've sent me away. You never really gave a damn about me."

Joanna began crying. "Yes, Weldon, I did. I cared, very much. I don't know what happened. I don't know why you're the way you are, and I'm the way I am."

Weldon glanced at the house, the people in it.

"Merry Christmas, everyone."

He turned and walked out the door.

A silence fell, broken only by Joanna's quiet weeping. Walter rose and held her close for a moment. Ann Leigh and Chandra came and took her into the library to lie down. John resumed playing.

"Can you really break up Industries?" Walter asked.

Kelly nodded. "A way has occurred to me during the last few days. It's so simple, I don't know why I didn't think of it before."

Chandra came into the room and signaled to Kelly that she thought they should leave. He nodded, rose, and gathered their Christmas presents.

Joanna had regained her composure. She came down the hall to see them out the front door.

"Chandra, Kelly, I'm sorry our Christmas celebration was ruined."

Chandra looked up at her, smiling. "Joanna, I truly think this may be the best Christmas of my life."

"We have before us the resignation of the president and chief executive officer of Spurlock Oil," Joanna said. "Do I hear a motion?"

"I move that Weldon's resignation be accepted," Ann
Leigh said.

"Second," Kelly said.

Campbell nodded, making the action unanimous.

Joanna glanced at Kelly, concerned. He seemed terribly
drawn and exhausted. The dissolution of Spurlock Industries
had been a long and bitter battle. But eventually Weldon
had accepted the plan. Kelly had won the oil company stock,
most of the real estate, and a few shares in Texas banks.
Weldon had taken all of the companies Spurlock Industries
had acquired, and most of the available cash. As Kelly had
foreseen, Weldon got the best of the deal. But Kelly had
been satisfied. He had emerged with all of the stock in Spurlock Oil.

"We are left with a vacancy to be filled," Joanna said. "Do I
hear a motion?"

"I nominate Kelly," Ann Leigh said. "I believe he has
earned it."

"Second," Campbell said.

"Then it's carried," Joanna said. "Congratulations."

Kelly held up a hand. "Wait a minute. I'll accept the presidency under one condition. I think Mom should be the
CEO, as well as board chairman. We need her experience,
especially throughout the confusion of this oil embargo. We
need her clout with the other oil companies, the government, the respect she has gained. So I hereby nominate my
mother as chief executive officer of Spurlock Oil."

"Second," Ann Leigh said.

Campbell nodded.

Joanna was deeply moved. She recognized Kelly's gesture
not only as a reward, but also as acknowledgment of emotions between them long unspoken.

"With such a gracious nomination, I can only accept," she
said. She turned to the stenographer. "Please make me several copies of that. The next time a news magazine mentions
me as being kicked upstairs, or downstairs, I'll send them a
copy."

* * *

It was Ann Leigh's last board meeting. Two weeks later she was rushed to a hospital, and died a few minutes after arrival.

Joanna managed to reach Crystelle in Spain. She declined to come home for the funeral.

Ann Leigh's will left all of her estate to a foundation, to be administered by Joanna, for the benefit of the arts and other community projects.

She was buried next to the empty grave of her husband, under a tombstone bearing both of their names.

The irony did not escape Joanna.

Clay Spurlock had been absent from her bed through most of her life. Now he was missing from her grave.

Late in the spring Kelly received a call from the executor of Ann Leigh's estate.

"Kelly, last week I came across some material your grandmother stuck away," Nick Willoby said. "I don't know what to do with it. Conceivably, it might concern the company. But I'm reluctant to show it to your mother. I'd like for you to step over here, read it, and tell me what you think."

Kelly walked the three blocks to the bank under a warm afternoon sun. Willoby took him into a small room near the main vault and brought Kelly a large safety-deposit box filled with papers.

"I'll leave you alone with it," he said. "Take your time. You won't be disturbed."

At first Kelly could make little sense of the stack of diverse papers. Some of it read like a bad detective novel. Other sheets obviously were photographic copies of New York police files.

But as Kelly read further, the confusion gradually cleared. He understood that Ann Leigh had hired an investigator to follow Aunt Crystelle around the country.

When he came to the name of Grover Sterling, he began reading more carefully.

He remembered the name, the rumors.

Then he came to the description of a murder on the West Side of Fort Worth.

According to the investigator, Aunt Crystelle had gone into the "house in question" early in the evening, and emerged after midnight. The investigator claimed he had crouched in the bushes beneath a window and listened to the conversation of a man and woman through a stethoscope pressed against the windowpane.

He included what he could remember of the conversation.

The investigator said the body of a man was found in the house the following day, a kitchen knife plunged through his chest, into the heart.

Newspaper clippings concerning the murder were sprinkled through the report. The name of the victim, Bern Arnheiter, meant nothing to Kelly. After finishing the material, he sat for a time absorbing all of its implications.

He understood Willoby's quandary: Ann Leigh had squirreled away evidence in a murder case.

And the prime suspect was still alive.

Questions abounded. Why had Ann Leigh put an investigator on Aunt Crystelle's trail? Why had Aunt Crystelle gone to great lengths to obtain, illegally, copies of police files on the murder of Grover Sterling? Why had Ann Leigh kept this volatile material all these years?

Willoby returned. "Through?"

Kelly nodded.

"You see why I can't just destroy it. I first thought of showing it to your mother. But considering the contents, I was reluctant to do so."

"She may be aware of it," Kelly said. "But maybe not. I think your first instincts were right. I'll call her."

She arrived within minutes. Again Willoby explained the discovery, his quandary.

"I'll leave you two alone to discuss it," he said.

Joanna's face showed no emotion as she read through the first portion of the material. Kelly grew ever more certain that it held few surprises for her. Occasionally she slowed in reading, as if ascertaining certain details.

She carefully read the portion concerning the West Side murder.

When she finished, her eyes were filled with tears. She brought out a handkerchief. "What a terrible burden this must have been for Ann Leigh."

"You knew about all this, didn't you?"

She shook her head. "Walter and I guessed. But we didn't know. Not for sure."

Kelly felt the return of his old frustrations. "Mom, I'm thirty-three years old. Don't you think you owe me an explanation?"

She did not answer immediately. Kelly felt she was searching for any possible way to keep from telling him. Apparently she found none.

"Do you remember an evening, back when you were about five, and I took you and Weldon out to a movie?"

Kelly thought back without success. He shook his head no.

"Your father insisted I take you boys out for the evening, and leave him alone in the house. I didn't want to go, but he insisted . . ."

Kelly sat and listened, mesmerized, while she told a long story of murder, blackmail, and family hatreds enduring through three generations before his own.

The story took him back to his childhood, replete with interrupted conversations, adult innuendos, and the overwhelming sense of a deep mystery beyond his years.

Joanna described her first days at the company, her discovery of incriminating evidence. She told of Walter's help and support. She recounted the board meetings when Crystelle presented her ultimatum, and Ann Leigh's soft-spoken threat that had so effectively stunned Crystelle into silence and inaction.

"We were certain your grandmother knew something about this man's murder," she concluded. "But we didn't know exactly what."

"Why haven't you told me all this before? Didn't you think I had a right to know?"

Again Joanna wiped her eyes with the handkerchief.

"Kelly, how in the world could I tell you I suspected that your father might be guilty of murder?"

He could sympathize with her thinking. But the answer still fell short.

"Mom, don't you realize that Weldon and I heard all those rumors when we were kids? And later? We had to live with them, without the luxury of a single defense. Surely you could have given us some facts."

She was still crying. Kelly waited.

"Ann Leigh had a theory that there was a genetic strain in Spurlocks that made them do these things. How could I tell you that you might have it?"

Kelly remembered his eavesdropping on a long-ago conversation when his grandmother had voiced that belief.

He laughed. "I can guarantee you, I've never had the slightest inclination in that direction. And I'm sure I never will."

"What about your son?"

Kelly did not answer. The question gave him the first inkling of the terrible burden his mother had carried through the years.

He realized it was one he also might carry to his grave.

Joanna sighed. "Really, I think it's rubbish. But I don't know. If you think back over the years, a case might be made for Ann Leigh's theory."

Kelly disagreed. "I can understand what Dad did. I think any man in the same circumstances might have done the same thing. He had a wife and two sons, and he knew he wouldn't be around forever to protect them."

"I know. I've thought it through a thousand times."

The pile of papers still lay between them.

"What'll we do with this stuff?" he asked.

Joanna put a hand on the papers before answering. "Ann Leigh's solution was probably right. We'd best hang on to this. Crystelle is Crystelle. She'll continue to be a potential threat to us, to the company, as long as she remains alive. These papers are insurance."

She left, hurrying back to the company for an appointment.

Kelly found Willoby and asked him to return the papers to the vault, and to arrange new signatory cards.

He walked out of the bank. The downtown canyons were filled with late afternoon shadows and pedestrians spilling out of the offices. As he kept pace with them, Kelly thought back over the day's events, back over his life.

He was gratified that many questions had been answered, so many old mysteries solved.

And he remembered something else about that long-ago conversation he had eavesdropped upon:

Aunt Zetta had said that Texans were unusually ambitious because they were builders, creators. She had defended the Spurlocks as merely being more Texan than most.

Savoring the thought, Kelly did not return to his office. Instead, he walked to his car and drove home, leaving it to the janitors to turn out the lights.